HER MONSTROUS BEASTS

E. P. Bali's
House of Romantasy

Her Monstrous Beasts is a work of fiction. Names, characters, places, incidents and locations are the product of the author's imagination or are used fictitiously. Any resemblance to actual events, locations or persons, living or dead is entirely coincidental.

This first edition published in 2025 by
Blue Moon Rising Pty Ltd
www.epbali.com
ISBN ebook: 978-1-923159-27-3
Paperback: 978-1-923159-36-5
Hardback: 978-1-923159-37-2
Exclusive Edition: 978-1-923159-38-9

No Generative AI was used in the creation of this book

Cover Design by David Gardias
Xander Illustration by Rami fon Verg
Chapter Artwork by Wisp Tale
Formatting by E.P. Bali

A Note on the Content

I care about the mental health of my readers.
This book contains some themes you might want to know about
before you read.
They are listed at www.ektaabali.com/themes

This one is for all of you who've stuck with this series thus far. We got here together, and now we'll watch the end of it together. I love you all xo

Her Monstrous Beasts

5

L.P. Bali

Prologue

Savage

Halfeather House
Just over a year ago

"There, you are bound. Now go and find my daughter."

We watch Mace Naga leave Halfeather House. Well, Xander and Scythe watch him and his servants while I raise my new, marked finger to my mouth and stretch my tongue out, ready to lick it.

Quick as any serpent, Xander slaps my hand away from my tongue. "That's disgusting," he snarls, smoke streaming from his nose. "Do you want serpent juice in your mouth?"

I gape at him. Why didn't I think of that? "What do you think it tastes like?"

"Leave it," Scythe growls. "The marking will come off when we get the job done."

"Right," I say, clenching my hands into fists and glaring at the smoking carcass of Halfeather House. Our regina. The one who rejected and ran away from us. The one who tried to kill me! We have to deal with her, and fast.

One of Scythe's new recruits, Beak, is kneeling on the ground between some cages we managed to save, fiddling with the keys. The old cockatoo had a whole coop of birdies hidden in one of the rooms. Plenty of skinny chickens are now plucking around the grass, looking for food. I rub my own empty tummy.

"There's no sign of our new brother," Scythe says, looking at the sky. "I've never seen a signature like it. An order that has power over shadows and eyes that can kill."

Xander swears under his breath, probably upset he's not the only mythical shifter in the pack now.

"They have a fucking basilisk," he says with a lot of disgust. "Newly healed by our regina, no less. I don't even think she knows."

"A big snake," I explain to myself. I thought killing with my bare hands was cool. Imagine killing with your eyes! I wonder if I can make him show me how it works.

"*Mace* has a fucking Basilisk," Scythe corrects. "And no, it's clear she had no idea. Their one and only kryptonite is supposed to be the call of a rooster. "

"We need a cock-a-doodle-doo pet?" I say excitedly. I've always wanted one. Quickly scanning the birds bobbing around us, I locate the biggest. He's black with red frills like a real gentleman, and there's a clip on his foot with the tag. For some bizarre reason, he's already making eye contact with me and even takes a step forwards like he wants to say something important.

I attempt to speak his language, crouching low. "Bok bok bok!" The rooster cocks his head and lets out a sound like a question. "I knew it!" I cry, simultaneously leaping and tackling him to the ground. He gives a mighty squawk of complaint and I bring him close to my chest and smooth his feathers down. "He's got a great voice!" I say, locking his wings tight and standing up to show him to my brothers. "And I think he likes me."

"What does his tag say?" Xander asks, reaching for the thing and yanking it off. The bird cries out again, but dragon healing magic seals the bleeding wound the tag left.

Xander reads, "Property of Halfeather House. His name is Eugene."

"Yew- jean!" I sound out. "Well, he's *our* property now. Will you swear him in, Scythe?"

My brother looks at Eugene, who shrinks into me like he's scared. I rock him like a baby to show him we won't eat him...yet.

"Shift," Scythe commands, the word pulsing through the air like a big drum.

Eugene lets out a cluck before shifting in my arms.

PART ONE

Chapter 1

Aurelia

My rage only grows as I fly away from my mates. It expands like a gathering storm, as the image of the four other parts of my soul flashes through my mind: eyes blank but faces furious as they pursued to kill me. As they'd been *commanded to*.

My blood is alight with fire in the cold of the night, my massive wings keeping a mighty pace as my snout points towards Animus Academy. There is only one thing keeping the draconic madness of vengeance at bay.

Just one.

And that is the vision of Xander, looking up at me from the ground, his eyes very much alive with a midnight darkness upon his neck. A skull with five beams of dark light curling around it.

His mating mark has returned, but different from before.

There was no light emanating from it like a normal mating mark. It was black as a void. I just know it has some meaning I can only grasp at.

Why did the ancient magic he'd broken decide to bind us back together? Does the Wild Mother think he deserves it? Do *I* even think Xander deserves this?

The heat pounding through my veins sends my mind scattering.

Get back home. Get back to the nest. Think. What do we fucking do?

I can barely feel the weight of Minnie, Marduk and Yeti on the hard scales of my back. I know they clutch each other tightly as we speed over the earth, one of my shields surrounding them like an egg of protection against the wind that would likely shred their skin.

My mind races, my heart pounds, and my lungs fill with hot need. To burn the world down.

How dare she? *How. Dare. She.*

My mates. My family. The ones *I* love? Taken by one: Katerina Crocodylus.

Is this how my mates felt when I was taken from them? Is this some divine retribution for my own crimes? I couldn't give a fuck about the *meaning* behind it.

When the Academy's towers finally spear up from the horizon, the school appears to me like it never has before.

Perhaps it's my new dragon-eyes, but the place glitters with warm light that whispers, *Welcome, my lady.*

This is a language I may have felt brushing against me before, in the quiet moments as the academy settled down to sleep, but now its communication is clear.

Golden lights blink in a diamond pattern above the building that is the animus dorms. It reminds me of the lights airports use to guide planes at night. Guards in the four towers around the school haven't aimed their long-range darting rifles at me yet, and it's Marduk who reminds me, his deep voice shouting above the wind, "I'm calling the guard dogs, Lady Boneweaver!"

As the Caspian tiger shouts into his phone, I feel a strange twinge in my heart at that address. My title. Something that brands me as *other*. As the last.

A telepathic request knocks on my mental shields. It's one of the wolf guards. I oblige him.

"You're not gonna torch us, are you, Lady Boneweaver?" comes the gruff voice.

"No," I growl in reply.

"Then you're clear for entry. The usual spot."

My brows furrow at the cadence of this conversation. It's not the normal way the guards speak to the students. I brush it out of my mind as I near the protective dome around the school. Its power ripples through the air like a heat wave, but I don't feel its threat upon my dragonhide like I normally do upon my eagle feathers. Two of the guards raise their hands in greeting as they make eye contact with me, and I ignore them as the dome dissolves in submission.

I stretch out my wings, angling them snoutward so I lose speed and glide towards the lights on the roof of the animus dorms. Landing heavily on the left side of my body, I grunt, carefully easing my weight back onto my sore right hind leg.

The Devi pack hastily levitate themselves off my back, Minnie's teeth chattering in the cold. Smoke streams from my nostrils, hot and charred, as they head towards the door that leads to the staircase. I stand there, staring at them, my chest heaving.

Yeti's arm snakes around Minnie's waist, and my gaze sweeps north-eastward, where my mates are. My heart squeezes. Nausea roils in my belly.

Minnie whispers my name, and I grimace against the pain of it, closing my eyes and calling forth my human form. I shrink, my hard scales disappearing, and I'm aware of the night's chill. Wings disappear into shoulder blades, the flagstones of the roof becoming hard under my soft human soles. While I might know the world outside is cold, my skin itself is on fire. I breathe heavily as I stalk towards the staircase. The three tigers part for me, their faces grim.

It's Minnie whose fingers brush my bare elbow. "Lia, we can't do anything rash."

I round on her, white smoke turning to black as it charges out of my nose. "You don't know what I'm capable of," I hiss. "No one does."

My friend's dark eyes glitter under the stars as she returns my ire. "*I've* always known."

I turn away, snorting like the dragoness I am, to pace upon the flagstones, my shoulders hunched, murderous thoughts racing through my mind. Bloody images. High-pitched screams. The crunch of bones breaking under my fangs. The taste of human flesh on my tongue.

Minnie stalks behind me, her normally sweet voice low and harsh. "I've seen you break your arms for your friends. I've seen you surrender yourself to your enemy for those you love. I've seen you re-grow a limb out of sheer determination."

I lower my head as I reach the edge of the roof and turn around, predatory and intent as I stop before my tigress. My human voice is dragon-rough. "And that's the least of me."

Minnie's eyes fill with angry tears as she nods. "Yes. We'll get them back, Lia. I know it."

I snarl into the air, smoke dissipating in a cloud around me. "I need them back. I need to feel that crocodile's hide in my mouth. I need to drink her blood."

It's Marduk who says carefully, "My lady, this will be...challenging."

I turn to hiss at him, baring my teeth. "I'm familiar with *challenging*, Marduk. Nothing in my life has ever come easy." My huff is sardonic. "Not even my mates came to me easily."

"How the hell did she even achieve this?" Minnie says, exasperated, staring at the sky. "I've never seen any magic like it. And what was that powder the hyena matriarch was sprinkling around?"

"I didn't even think it was possible," Yeti says darkly. "To change reginas so easily. Surely it can't hold?"

I turn towards the front of the school, looking out at the Hunting Games field. "Bone," I say softly. "What you smelled on the wind was my bone, Minnie."

Minnie chokes in horror.

"I fear they had the correct ingredient," Marduk sighs. "There's no more powerful a substance they could've gotten their hands on."

She'd used my own bone against me. Foul, terrible creature.

A growl rumbles through my being. I don't know how long The Collector had planned for this, but my bet was on a long time. She'd always had a jealous eye on Scythe. Had always run her eyes down my mates like they were meat to be consumed. "There has to be a way out. All spells can be broken." I've studied serpent magic since infancy. Even blood covenants can be broken as Savage reminded us all with the amputation of his finger. "I'm not as familiar with hyena witchcraft." The admission cools me a little. "But we know some who are."

Marduk's eyes are alight in the dark, like shiny marbles of

mystery. "I shall call our Dabu pack friends, my lady. They will be keen to help." He gets out his phone and strides into the stairwell, his feet silent on the stone.

"Come inside, Lia," Minnie says gently. "Are you hungry?"

I clench my teeth. How could I be hungry for human food after everything that's happened? Minnie must see my struggle, and she shakes herself. "Let's at least get off the roof, please?"

My eyes cast themselves back out into the dark of night once again, reluctant to leave the open air. As if we might see our loved ones driving up the road to the academy. As if Savage would be leaning out the window with the wind in his hair, waving at me. I tear my eyes away. Stupid. *Stupid.*

They're not going to come back to me.

I'm going to have to tear them from her clutches. The entire world is about to find out what happens when you fuck with the Boneweaver pack.

Chapter 2

Xander

No Light, No Light – Florence and the Machine

S he'd been ready for us.

The Collector stands, shoulders tense, a darting rifle resting on one shoulder. It's currently aimed at Savage, who's mindlessly fighting ten on one with two darts already in each thigh. If I were a nice and helpful person, I would tell them to bring out the bear-strength darts. But my helpful days are over.

Instead, I swipe a joint right from the fingers of a nearby guard. He protests for a single second before my glare cuts him short. I choose a patch of grass against the wheel of the Jeep closest to me, stretching out my legs and crossing them at the ankles, Savage's mad growls the backing track to my music.

There is something distracting me from the bedlam. Something that burns like dark fire on the side of my neck. A mark of a new kind.

After Lia flew away with the Devi pack, Katerina Crocodylus commanded us back to her. Without a clear goal to occupy our minds, it took all of five seconds for *it* to begin.

My brothers have descended into their beasts. Deeply. No doubt the only way their minds can cope with the violation that's just occurred.

The *swapping* of our regina.

Nothing could be worse than my own crimes, but this is a new sort of low for The Collector. She'd done her research and came ready with the equipment, and the hyena queen in tow.

The old witch, for her part, is perched at the edge of the passenger seat of the first vehicle, both hands resting on her cane with an expression of shrewd amusement as she watches Savage, with his jowls around one of the guard's shoulders, get shot again, this time in his neck.

Whatever spell the old witch used to bind us to The Collector is powerful, but my brothers are the strongest beasts I know.

Lyle is out of action in one of the elephant-grade vehicles, shot in both knees and shoulders, then suffocated until he passed out. She'd known his rabid lion might be a problem and came ready with obsidian bullets. She doesn't know that Lia is the only one who can tame the feline. What is she going to do when he wakes up?

Scythe stands stock still next to Katerina. His shark teeth are out, black eyes swallowing the whites, but he is eerily still. Great-white-shark-still as he was commanded by our new master.

I surmise that it's some type of aquatic freeze on his psyche. He's *gone cold*, as we call it, and while he can be violent in this state, it's calculated. Right now, he seems to await instruction from his new regina.

My stomach twists at the thought, a sudden roaring echoing in my head. The witch's spell has affected me too, but its hold is weak. I feel the need to obey the crocodile, but with a little effort, I've found that I don't *have* to. I just have to maintain the ruse of obedience.

I raise my hand to my new mark, and all I know is the sick feeling of watching Aurelia in her blue dragon form fly away from me, confusion, rage and fear shattering her sapphire eyes. She's probably thinking she's all alone. That she's been abandoned once again. I hope Minnie will stop her from coming after us claws first, but it's a blessing they got her out of here at all.

Tonight, Lia will sleep alone. She will fret. She might cry—

The thought of her crying makes my fists clench. She's been through enough and has never been broken by it. But...she doesn't have any of us now. In the history of royal fuckups, this is perhaps our worst. Second only to the devastation at the Lily Institute.

I never saw it coming.

Savage finally falls with a thud, drawing my attention back to the chaos. Satisfied, The Collector turns around and jerks her chin at me. "I want him in obsidian. I don't trust him as far as I can throw him."

I barely suppress a growl at the thought of losing my powers, but I feel the urge to oblige her, and I give in to it. "As you say, regina."

Actual vomit surges up my throat. Usurper, charlatan, swamp-fucker, would all be more appropriate titles for her. The only thing this creature deserves is the same fate as my own father: being ripped apart, piece by piece.

Katerina raises her brows but says nothing, turning away to Scythe and stroking a finger down the square of his jaw.

As the kangaroo shifter guards cautiously approach me with the heavy black chains, I stick my arms out and stare across the estate grounds at what remains of my father. His corpse lies in the grass, the heat still steaming in curls from his lifeless, wingless, heartless body.

The one good thing about tonight is that my mother got the vengeance she deserved. I can hear her shuffling around in my sister's room on the top floor of Drakos estate, her injuries still bleeding. I know Selena has been watching this scene with bated breath. I know the hatchlings are bundled up in blankets, set far away from the windows where their grandmother guards over them.

I let them wind the chains around my wrists, and it's then that I note the familiar, unusual scent. Connor avoids my eyes as he helps secure the chains in place. He wears a silver collar around his neck now, having signed his contract with The Collector a few months ago. I pretend not to notice when he clangs around a solid black padlock.

He makes a fuss of fixing the lock in place before stepping away and handing the key to Katerina.

But the magic that is supposed to snuff out my magic does not activate. Connor hasn't locked it properly.

Trying not to smirk, I snuff out my own eyes. The golden orbs of light that give me vision wink out, and my world is plunged into the unforgiving dark. My ears take over, picking up every forsaken sound in my vicinity.

"So beautiful," The Collector coos at what I'm guessing is Scythe's cold face. "And all mine." I can hear the manic glee in her voice and the curve of her smirk. A wave of hate barrels through me. She turns to her guards, snakeskin heels wrenched out of the pristine turf as she saunters towards the convoy of vehicles. "Let's move out."

I heave myself to my feet as Savage is dragged, his breathing even and heavy in sedation, into his own vehicle. Naturally, I choose the one The Collector is climbing into, while the hyena matriarch groans to standing, the joints in her old knees popping and cracking.

She huffs in my direction. "The Wild Goddess has never loved you, has she, boy?" she croaks. "What did you do? Stab her in the back in a past life?" Cackling at her own joke, she turns to take her seat.

"That wasn't me," I mutter. "All I ever did was curse her name."

"That'll do it," she pipes. "A woman scorned is..."

"A woman *out for revenge*," The Collector snickers.

I say nothing as I climb into the back seat of their Jeep and turn my head eastward, in the direction of my regina.

Chapter 3

Aurelia

I prowl in my room, from end to end, all night. A pair of Savage's track pants and Lyle's T-shirt cover my body and I don't want to shower because that'll wash their scents off me. One of Scythe's business shirts is clutched to my chest so that every time I inhale, I get a lungful of their combined scents.

It's the only thing that calms my rage and the blind urge to charge into the night, towards The Collector's property and wrench my soul-pieces back. My new leg aches dully at first, but as the first rays of dawn pierce the window, I blink in frustration against the lightning bolts charging down my thigh.

The need to rest is powerful, but the emotions roiling through me like a summer storm are more so. My eyelids grow heavy, the pit in my stomach yawns open, and I shake out my hands to try to rid them of their new tremor.

My eagle form comes so easily to me in times like this. My feathers feel like armour as they cover my skin, my beak like a spear, instead of useless soft, human lips. My legs are a lot shorter, the talons so much more powerful than feet. If I cocoon myself tight enough, perch myself just so on the window ledge, I might be able to catch some sleep.

* * *

I awaken with a start, shaking my head out of the deep reverie with an annoyed chitter. The high sun beats on my face, and I reflexively crane my neck to check on my mates—

Of course, I am alone.

Spreading my wings out in anger, I quickly scan the academy grounds for anything unusual before sweeping to the floor. The empty room, the cold bed, the lack of any mumbling from Savage or any grunting from Xander. The absence of any deep voices or the colossal powers of my mates...

I had gotten used to how much space they take. How much their presences, alone or combined, brushed up against me in gentle reassurance. I hop my way to the door, nudge it open with my beak, and stalk out with narrowed eyes.

"Going somewhere?"

The eagle-shriek from my throat is sudden as I turn around in alarm.

Sabrina's fingers, busy crocheting with blue wool, never cease their movement as she stares at me from beneath the hood of her black jumper. "You're more tired than you realise if you missed that I was here."

With a long-suffering groan, I shift into human form, falling back onto my ass and stretching out my sore leg. The backs of my eyes burn as the fatigue clutches at my muscles with brutal fingers.

"I don't want to sleep, Sabrina."

"Yeah? And I don't want to be awake, but here we are."

I cast her a dark look.

"And you can't even say anything to that because at least *your* mates are alive."

I squeeze my eyes shut and hang my head back against the raw burn of pain.

"Sorry, I shouldn't have said that," Sabrina mutters.

"It's fine."

"None of this is fine. But it's going to look a whole lot worse if you don't sleep."

"They put you here because they know I can't say no to you, didn't they?"

"Yup. Me and these two."

An excited squeak makes my eyes fly open to see a blue fluffy bullet shooting towards my face before Henry smacks himself into my cheek, squeaking and chittering and rubbing all sides of himself against me.

"Oh, thank fuck." I cuddle the excited nimpin against my face, rubbing my thumb over the top of his head. Eugene clucks out of the shadows beside Sabrina's couch, and I grimace weakly at him. "Come here."

He hurries over and settles himself against my new leg, looking up at me through his bedazzled goggles.

"What are we gonna do?" I whisper to them.

"We're gonna eat, then sleep," Sabrina murmurs, bringing out a brown paper bag. "I'm going to microwave this juicy chickie burger someone left us. If you don't want to shower to get rid of that blood on you, at least wash the dust off your face and then get into your pack bed."

I open my mouth to protest, but she points a finger at me. "They're *alive*, Aurelia Boneweaver. And you're gonna get them back, but with a full stomach and your full brains on board. I won't have you sleep deprived in some sort of Boneweaver psychosis. Don't—" She cuts her hand through the air. "I've heard the guards gossiping about how you went *cold* at Drakos House. We're not going psycho *today*. If you're going to go apeshit crazy, I want you to be sane when you do it. Got it?"

"Fuck you, Sabrina," I mutter, rolling onto hands and knees.

"And fuck the world," my leopard friend drawls. "But thank the Wild Goddess for microwaves."

Sabrina, to my great dismay, returns from the microwave to supervise the washing of my face and holds the bed sheets open as I climb in like an elderly lady, creaking and sore. She hands me the burger, and I force it and a glass of apple juice down with a sour expression. She, Eugene and Henry proceed to climb into bed with me and I don't have the energy to protest.

"My assassin twins are guarding the staircase," she says, pulling up her hoodie around her nose, likely to block out the scent of my mates. "Beak keeps asking for you, but Marduk said to leave you alone because you may be in the mood to tear someone apart."

I frown as I curl my limbs up towards my chest, feeling Henry taking up his usual position at my crown, burrowing himself into my hair as he enjoys. Before I can reply, I'm asleep again.

* * *

When I wake up for the second time, it's not Sabrina in bed with me, but Stacey, playing a cooking game on her phone, muttering under her breath.

"Oh, are we up?" she asks, leaning over to peer at me with her almond-shaped eyes.

I roll over and rub my face, kicking the sheets back. "I feel less tired," I mutter, pushing myself up and scanning the room. Stacey's backpack lies against the door, and her two nimpins chirp at me in greeting. "But I need to get up now."

"Yeah, Minnie said you'd say that!" Stacey leaps out of bed, her blonde plaits swinging wildly. "And you smell a bit funky, by the way. It's better if you shower and *then* go to the meeting."

"What meeting?" I say sharply, downing the glass of the water on my bedside table and testing my leg. It's found its strength, but I'm going to have to watch it today and I send healing down to it to smooth away any excessive inflammation. If I need to fight, I need to be in my best physical condition.

"Yeah, something's gone down," Stacey says, picking up Eugene and striding into the attached bathroom. I hurry after her, goosebumps erupting all over my naked skin as Henry levitates alongside me. "Beak'll tell you."

Ten minutes later, I'm showered, with my teeth aggressively cleaned and my hair brushed, dressed in leggings and a tank top, stepping out of the hidden staircase to the lower part of the animus dorms. Sure enough, the pale, dark-haired twins are on guard, daring anyone to look their way, which no one does because they're cold, hard beasts. They escort Stacey, Eugene, Henry and me to the Rec room on the ground floor.

When I arrive, Marduk, Minnie and Beak are standing around a table, talking softly. Minnie has her pink sparkly folder in hand.

Beak's face brightens. "Aurelia."

Stacey and the twins leave us, quietly shutting the door with a definitive clunk. "What's going on?" I ask suspiciously.

The smile slides off Beak's tanned face as his expression becomes serious. "There are a few things you need to know." He pulls out a seat at the table.

Carefully, I sit down, placing Eugene on the table before glancing at Minnie and her mate. Minnie is the only one who gives me a reassuring nod. Henry buries himself in my hair once again, and his old reassurance settles my heart. Just a little.

There's a knock at the door before it opens to reveal Yeti, leading in a middle-aged man in a suit with long brown hair. He smells like a jaguar and I recognise him, but I don't know where from.

Strangely, he stops on the opposite side of the table and bows to me before sitting down. "Lady Boneweaver, my name is Rufus. I help Mr Kharkorous with the administration side of his enterprises." He gives me a soft smile. "You might have seen me at the Jewel of the Jungle."

"Of course," I say quickly. That particular night had been a whirlwind, and there had been many new faces. "How...can I help you?"

Something about his demeanour turns grave as he opens the business folder. "A few months ago, Mr Kharkorous made some adjustments to the ownership of his multiple corporate entities...in the case of his death or return to sea."

My stomach drops. Like, completely out of my body. This was when Scythe had intended to *return to sea* in a permanent way. Of course, it would make sense that he'd prepped for the business side of things.

"Scythe is not at sea," I hiss. "Nor is he dead."

Rufus' head snaps up. "Of course, my lady. However, he was quite explicit with me about the succession of his estate. Both he and Xander Drakos were the existing directors of his enterprises, but he listed an additional name."

Ignoring the fact that Savage is not listed as director, my heart leaps into my throat as Rufus levels me a look. "That name is yours."

I stare at Rufus. The jaguar clasps his hands over his papers and lowers his eyes respectfully. "As neither director is available, Kharkorous Enterprises is left to you."

My throat is suddenly dry. Scythe has given me his empire.

The room swims a little. The floor trembles. The wooden table vibrates. Minnie reaches over and squeezes my hand. Beak says in a low voice from next to me, "You're not alone in this, Lia." Slowly, the room quietens, my power settling down as I slither back into a sense of calm.

"Your first salary has been transferred into your account. Each morning, I will call you to provide a brief of the current events and action points for the day. Some will be more pressing than others." So this is who Scythe spoke to every morning. Rufus slides a piece of paper towards me, but the letters are a little blurry. "I'm afraid there is a matter of importance that cannot be delayed. I need a signature on this."

"What's it for?" I croak.

"An execution order."

My mind is suddenly sharp, and I sit up, the black words on the paper suddenly focusing. "Whoever for?"

"A young beast caught sifting for information. He was a spy for an opposing crime lord. Not a very good spy, obviously."

"And...this is normal for Scythe to sign?"

"It is due process, my lady."

"And there's *formal* written documentation for it?"

Rufus seems surprised by my questions but does not miss a beat. "Mr Kharkorous prefers it this way, but these papers are burned, and the files deleted at the end of each week by Mr Drakos himself."

I'm stumped by this level of organisation. "What is the name of this beast?"

Rufus leans forwards and squints at the paper. I scan it quickly. *Simon Clawson.* My brows shoot up.

"A Clawson?"

"He used a pseudonym, of course, but we picked up on it quickly and proceeded to observe him as he moved around our warehouses."

It's Yeti who adds, "It's common practice for the crime lords to plant spies in each other's organisations. We weed them out, but they keep coming. We send ours; they send theirs, and on it goes."

"So, we have spies at the Clawson House?" I ask carefully. Minnie goes still.

"I imagine we do," Yeti says, glancing at Beak.

"Who?"

"Only Scythe would know that," Beak says. "Only he knew I was a plant at Halfeather House."

I quieten at this information, reading the formal lines of the paperwork. So clinical. So businesslike. "Hold off on this." I slide the paper back across the table. "I'm not signing it."

Rufus doesn't reach for it. "My lady—"

"My own execution was scheduled not all that long ago, or has everyone forgotten about that? I won't sign this."

Yeti shakes his head. "Every beast in the state will know about Scythe's absence within days, Lia. You're going to have a giant target on your back, and they're all going to try their luck. Showing mercy will make you look weak."

"I've always had a target on my back," I say evenly. "And life is hardly a mercy. He's my cousin once removed, did you know? Cassius Clawson was my mother's mate."

The table goes quiet, and I stare defiantly at them all, one at a time, until I get to Rufus. "I did not misspeak, Mr Rufus."

He nods solemnly and takes back his paper. "As you say, Lady Boneweaver."

"That will be all for today. I'll expect your phone call tomorrow morning."

Rufus hides whatever reaction he may have had, standing and bowing over his folder before Yeti leads him out. I sag in my seat, squeezing the bridge of my nose as the urge to burst out of this room tries to overwhelm me. What the fuck just happened?

Beak reminds me of his presence by clearing his throat. Sighing, I open my eyes. "I would like to ask everybody except Beak to leave the room, please."

Minnie smiles kindly at me and rubs my shoulder in support as she gets up and leads her mates out. When they've all left, I turn to the American eagle. Beak has always been a handsome male with his dark blond spiky hair and big biceps. From the first moment I'd met him, I'd swooned over his frat boy charm. That had all faded since I met my mates of course, but he'd always been sincere with me.

"How much do you know?" I ask flatly.

"Scythe had a question for me a little while back," Beak admits, sitting back in his chair. "Would I take a new regina, if I had the chance?" My fists tighten in my lap. "I was honest, and said I'd not considered it. Then he asked if it were *you*, would that change anything?" He looks back at me, dead in the eye. "And I said it would be a good way to spend the rest of my Goddess-forsaken life."

I want to punch the seriousness off his face. When Scythe had revealed to me, down in the carpark of the Lily Institute, that he'd been thinking of leaving and swapping himself for Beak, I'd been so angry I'd shattered glass. "As I said before, my mates are not dead. Mates are not *musical chairs* to be swapped and inserted in and out!"

"No, but your mates are not here," Beak says, a hint of steel in his voice. "They are not here to protect their regina. To serve her." There is a glint in his eye that I've never seen before. A fierce devotion that shone for a regina he once had and a great pain that nearly takes my breath away. "But I'm here. Without a regina. I want to help you. Let me."

"They're coming back," I say quietly.

Beak takes a deep breath, putting his hands up in surrender. "And when they do, I'll step back into the sidelines like I always have. But I've worked for Scythe, Lia. I know how things run. Same as Yeti."

I pinch the bridge of my nose again, turning the enraged thoughts around. If I'm going to get through this, if I'm up against the nastiest beasts of this world, I need all the help I can get. Beak is a good eagle. I lower my hand. "We need to talk about boundaries, then," I say firmly. "You follow my orders. You don't try...You don't try anything."

"I wouldn't dare," he says softly.

"Alright." I nod. "Then we have work to do."

When I walk out of the Rec room, Minnie, Stacey, and Sabrina are huddled together. When they see us, they rush at me. "Do you realise what this means?" Minnie asks, nearly jumping out of her pink shorts.

"What?"

"You're a mob boss, Lia!" I stare into the middle distance above Minnie's head. "I think the Boneweaver Bitch is a good title," she cries. "Or maybe the Boneweaver Don."

"Boneweaver Baddie," Stacey sighs wistfully. "The slogan options are endless."

I know my friends are trying to make light of a *very* bad situation. But the way Marduk is looking at me now has me on edge. "What is it?" I ask him.

"I want to suggest," he says slowly, tilting his head to the side in a way I can tell Minnie finds endearing. "That my good shark-friend felt this decision was a good one. Felt that you would be capable. That he has faith in his regina." He has no reason to be saying things that make the backs of my eyes burn and my hands tremble. "I have never known a more decisive beast, Lady Boneweaver," Marduk continues ruthlessly. "Nor a more calculated one."

"Is that supposed to make her feel better?" Yeti asks contemplatively.

Marduk's voice is incredulous. "Yes."

Chapter 4

Ghoul

"**P**ass the chippies, Addy." I sit down in the office chair of the surveillance room, gesturing to the good General Black Adder. He silently passes me the bag of potato chips—chicken flavoured, of course. I take the bag and pull one of my gloves off with my teeth, dropping the fine black leather into my lap before delving into the bag. "What part are we up to?"

Ten screens are mounted before us in the surveillance room in the basement of the new Naga mansion. Usually, the screens show various external hidden security cameras and audio feeds, but the one in the very centre now shows a permanent re-run of what's now being fondly called *The Battle of Drakos Estate*.

"The Boneweaver girl is spitting blue fire." Adder gestures to my regina, breathing a stream of electric blue flames out of her giant muzzle.

"Have we figured out why it's that colour?" I ask, leaning forwards, as if I'm confused by this.

Adder sighs. "No, but my thermal senses confirm that it's hotter than regular dragon fire." I feel my own power gathering behind my eyes in response to that. Adder's head snaps towards me as his thermal organ picks up an anomaly. "Don't do that shit here, Ghoul."

I lean back in my chair with a smirk. "Don't worry, you're not on my hit list. Or are you?" I cackle.

The radio on the table goes off, Charlotte Naga's commanding shriek coming through. "Prepare for entry. ETA two minutes. All teams at the ready."

Adder sighs. "It's finally time."

Both of us get up, and I toss my empty packet onto the table, brush crumbs on my pants and put my gloves back on. We traipse up the long steps into the light of the ground floor and round the house until we get out to the hidden corridor built into the laundry room. Outside, serpents are bustling around with last-minute preparations, and it's at the front entrance that Adder and I go our separate ways. He and the other generals head out with their chosen teams to hide in their allocated positions around the house and grounds.

I've never really had a team. Just a few diehard fans who circulate around me, sniffing at the fumes of death I leave behind.

Charlotte Naga awaits with one of them, Natalia, a young captain with dark hair. She's exchanged her commissioned uniform for a maid's dress today. In her hands, she holds a tray, nodding at Charlotte's repeated instructions. The Naga princess sees me and stiffens, her perfectly made-up face smoothing out into a mask almost as cold as my own bone-mask. "General, everyone is getting into place."

Cobras are naturally bossy. They can't help themselves, and I can practically see Charlotte's hood snapping out in the form of her blonde Marilyn curls. I've never actually seen her shifted form, but I'm sure it's as cold and cunning as her human one.

"Want a smoke for the nerves?" I ask lightly, reaching into my pocket and flicking out my black case of hand-rolls.

She wrinkles her nose, but it's pert and delicate. A lot of males like her face, but in the long years I've known her, that face has only ever disgusted me, for more reasons than one. "Put those away before they see it."

"I'll be a good little boy," I coo at her. "Don't you worry about it." I turn to Natalia, and the captain straightens unconsciously. One of the hands holding her tray should have a curling black B tattooed on it, but she covers it with makeup every time she's not in uniform. Didn't even flinch when I jokingly suggested they tattoo themselves in homage to me. The next day, a bunch of them all walked in to proudly show me their forearms.

Natalia bows over her tray of pink lemonade, little mint leaves poking out from the top. "Good girl," I say in approval. "Smiles on, voices sweet." She nods eagerly, keen to please me. Charlotte, on the other hand, presses her lips together. I suppose she is yet to forgive me for old Uncle Ben.

Who was lucky I didn't kill him more brutally than I did.

The sound of an engine grows louder, and I detect a limo.

"Get out of here," Charlotte hisses at me. I hiss back as Mace strides out of his office, straightening his suit. I nod at him before heading towards the dining room. It's opulent, with Charlotte and the housekeeper giving their best show of wealth. The money Mace made on the sale of his daughter not once, but twice via Xander and then The Collector, on full view here. Golden chandeliers, a long dining table with place settings for twenty. Crystal goblets, silverware, and best of all: a new golden Naga crest adorning the mantel above the fireplace.

Gathering my shadows about me, I sink into the corner of the dining room where I'll get a full view of everything. After some fuss and bother, our esteemed guests are greeted then guided in, one by one, flutes of green iced tea in their hands.

Ablo Obon arrives first in his limousine, the black feline king regal in his sweeping patterned robes. The queen of the avians is up next, Irma Goldwing, with a scrunched-up nose and severe black business dress. Queen Lunissa breezes out of her car with her usual faint smile and multicoloured gauze skirts.

So, everyone except the dragon and marine orders are represented. Xander's mother didn't reply to our invitation, of course, as she remains in her treasure haze over Drakos Estate. The usual marine candidate is, of course, *tied up* at the moment, thanks to Katerina's lusty greed. They are seated at Mace's dining table, served canapés and a light lunch before Mace sets his napkin aside.

"Your big announcement," Ablo says, clasping his fists at the table. "Surely you have wooed us enough, Mace."

The serpent king smiles thinly at them all. "My big announcement," he says gravely, "is that—"

Irma, the slightest of the group, is the first to succumb, her entire body going stiff, her eyes going wide as she comes to a realisation. As if she feels my fangs sinking deep. Her own healing will try to fight the venom, so we dosed her the hardest and she'll have to be dosed regularly from now on. The wolf queen's mouth opens in shock before she too goes still as stone. Petrified within her human body. Ablo jumps up from the table before stumbling backwards in horror.

"Is that," Mace repeats, "I am taking over."

"What have you done?" Ablo clutches his chest and gasps.

I throw my shadows away. Emerging from the corner of the room into full view, I give the feline regent a little wave. He goes ashen. "Basilisk venom paralyses the victim upon penetration, eventually killing them," Mace drones as if giving a eulogy. "However, when consumed in micro-doses, it puts the victim in a suggestible state. As such, when consumed in larger doses, it can put a beast in a catatonic state. You can still hear, see, and feel everything...but you cannot move except to breathe and blink. In a few moments, you also won't be able to make your own thoughts. Effectively..." Mace takes a deep, satisfying breath. "You are now mine."

"The others will not accept this." Ablo fights my venom, but his speech is strained. "They will rise against you. The tigers—"

"Naturally," Mace says. "Tiberius Clawson will take care of the tigers. As for the rest—this is why we will make a statement." Charlotte returns to the room with a camera and tripod. "One by one, the big houses fall," Mace continues his sermon. "And the world will remember those beasts fell by *my* hand. A superior species."

Whose hand? Because it couldn't possibly be *my venom* that did it? "*The* superior species," I agree.

Mace does not turn away from the scene. "You know what to do next, General."

I bow low and change honorific for dramatic effect. "With pleasure, Your *Majesty*."

Chapter 5

Aurelia

There must be something about shifting into a dragon that gives a girl the audacity of a cis-gendered white man.

An old version of me might have exploded into a thousand pieces or shut herself in a cavern under the school. It's funny because I know those options are still there. They're just not appealing anymore.

Back in my pack's suite, I pace up and down the length of the sitting room where my best friend dramatically recounts the morning's events. "And *then*," Minnie pipes, holding a whiteboard marker between her fingers like it's a cigarette. "She goes, 'I did not *misspeak*, Mr Rufus.'"

"I did not misspeak!" Stacey shrieks, holding her own face in both hands. "Holy shit!" Eugene gives a cock-a-doodle-doo of agreement.

"Anyway," Minnie says, tapping her marker against the full-size whiteboard Marduk levitated before the dining table ten minutes ago. "We need an action plan for the rescue." In the middle, she's written: OPERATION CROCO-DOWNFALL. "Step one is to see how we go about breaking the spell on this regina-swap thing The Collector has managed. We've contacted our hyena witch friends for a consult," Minnie says, putting a large tick against her first point. "Where are we on that, love?"

Marduk clears his throat and straightens from his dining room chair. "The Dabu clan will be here in an hour."

"Great," I say, nodding my thanks at the tiger. "Anything that can be made, can be un-made, right?"

But as it turns out, the making of spells is more complicated than I thought. When Hyacinth Dabu and her two mates arrive, grim-faced and sombre, we explain exactly what happened down to the sprinkling of my powdered bone. At that part, the room starts shaking again, the pain in my leg shooting down anew. I rub my thigh, channelling my power down into it instead of around.

Hyacinth sighs as she regards me, her brown face the picture of concern. "The matriarch of our order is both manipulative and precise. I've always known she was powerful, but this is something no one has ever seen."

My stomach turns. "So what? New spells are invented all the time. We have the formula. In it must be the solution."

But Hyacinth gives me a knowing look. "This isn't serpent magic, Lia. There is no writing in venom; there's no code. Hyena magic has always been...mysterious. Full of myths and legends and old wives' tales."

"And bone powder," I mutter in disgust.

"But," Hyacinth says, meeting my eye, "there has always been one foolproof way to undo a spell."

I stand from my chair, smoke streaming from my nose, understanding her immediately. Hyacinth regards me with sincerity. "Would you stand with me?" I ask directly. "Or are you loyal to your matriarch?"

"What's going on?" Stacey whispers to Sabrina.

Hyacinth stares at me. "It will be more difficult than you think. Many have tried before you."

Power gathers within me, rallying to be used. Rallying for blood. I take a deep breath, looking out of the window. Scythe trusted me with his empire. He has faith in my decisions. I know this world just as he does. Know the risks. Understand where the power lies. Where it has lain for so very long.

"Until now," I say carefully to the room, "my strategy has been a defensive one. I keep reacting to the blows sent my way. But defence is the strategy of prey." I turn back to Hyacinth, full meaning in my gaze. She seems to understand because she rises to her feet, her mates with her. "I will do this the old way. I'm sure she'll appreciate that."

Hyacinth grins. "I have a blood quill."

"Perfect."

She retrieves a black quill and dry inkwell from her backpack and hands them to me. I sit down at the dining table and set the inkwell to the side. Minnie rushes forward, unclipping a clean piece of paper from her folder. Raising my left hand, I shift my incisors into cobra fangs and prick my left index finger. The venom, mixed with the blood, seeps out of my finger, and I squeeze it into the inkwell. Combined with the anticoagulant effect of my own venom, the blood flows freely and makes it easier to write with it like ink.

Serpent kings and queens have been writing letters in their own blood and venom for centuries. I'm just joining in on the action. I dip my quill into the mixture and begin working.

Ten minutes later, I'm done. I set it down and look at my handiwork before carefully folding the letter and placing it in an envelope Minnie hands me. Without another word, I nod at Beak, and he pushes off the wall he was leaning against, following me down the stairs to the dormitories below. Yeti also follows.

Stacey and Minnie whisper in the sitting room behind me. Marduk seems to be explaining things to them. "She is making her move," he says.

I head down the corridor, stopping outside one of the rooms. "Is this one of them?"

"Three of the seniors occupy this room," Beak confirms.

Yeti has a strangely amused glint in his eye. The bloodthirsty bastard. He knocks on the door above my head. Somebody within groans. There's a dragging sound before the door opens to reveal a skinny, dishevelled male no older than nineteen. "Oh...shit, uh—"

Beak shoves his way into the room, pushing him aside. The room has two sets of bunk beds on either side and two desks between them, but it's cluttered with things they've scavenged across the years, trinkets and trash in every corner. It smells of male sweat and rubbish. "We've come for a visit, Stuart," Beak says, scanning the room for other people and finding none.

"Th-There's no one else here," the hyena stammers in a nasally voice. "They're in the dining hall."

"Great," I say, "you need to get dressed and pack a bag."

"What, why?" he asks, clutching his blanket around his shoulders like it's going to save him.

I hold out the note. "You're going to take this to your queen. You're going to leave now and not stop until this is in her hands. Do you understand me?"

He hesitates, mouth gaping like a fish. "W-Where's Mr Kharkorous? Mr Fengari?"

A rage takes over me. There comes a sound like a terrible lion's roar in my head. My hand whips around his throat as I seize him, squeezing. A draft of my power lashes around his body as I snarl into his face. The floorboards vibrate under our feet. "They are not here," I say in a low, dangerous voice. "I am. And I *said*, do you understand me, Stuart?"

He lets out a terrified, choked squeak, and I release him. He staggers backwards, loudly drawing in air but vigorously nodding. "Yes, Lady Boneweaver! I'll do it right away!"

I storm out of the room, power pulsing through my veins. It feels like it's pooling in my head, my hands, my feet. It feels like it's going to bring the entire building down. My body burns as I speed down the corridor. My leg aches by the time I reach the stairwell, so I shift into my eagle form. But as I snap my wings out and lower myself to the ground floor, I realise something with surprise.

This form is not quite right.

I burst out of the front door, Bastien the gargoyle's whoops of glee almost drowned out by the roar in my head. A roar that started when I saw Xander injured by other dragons during the fight at Drakos Estate. *They are not here. I am.*

For the second time in my life, I shift into my dragon form. Rage and fury incarnate, I grow colossal. My mouth becomes a muzzle with sharp teeth that I bare to the sky. Human shouts sound about me, and screams of terror, but all this fuels the need I have to declare myself. I launch into the sky on powerful thighs, sweeping my wings out and down. I cut through the air, my snout aimed at the animus dorm, the stricken faces of the animus students glued to their window as I pass over them, aimed right for the roof.

I land heavily, the structure groaning under me. Or is it sighing with relief? My roar charges into the sky, the deep sound vibrating through my body, my bones, the only thing to placate this maddened fury. My blood becomes fire, and power spirals into my lungs, rotating with power like a gathering cyclone. One inhale. One exhale, and my vision is obscured with retina-blinding blue so hot it heats up the stone beneath me.

My anima declares itself to the world. And we will not be defied. Not until our mates are back within our nest. Not until our enemies lie in bloody, torn pieces upon the grass. Below, the humans gather; guards in all black and students with bare skin stare up at me. The animas of my pack and the hatchlings stand with them, panting, faces flushed.

A redheaded woman stands among them, a shawl tight around her shoulders. She raises a hand, her palm outwards like a blessing. She wears a small smile, and her eyes are twinkling.

I hear her words inside my head, soft as flickering candlelight. *"The academy has a new guardian now. That's all I ever was. There is a power here that must be protected, and if you so choose, you can tap into it."* I can only stare down at her. *"If you need me, I'll be at the Agnis family property. Goodbye, Aurelia."*

Chapter 6

Xander

It takes them all night to drive to The Collector's property deep in the outback. They have to stop three times to re-dose Lyle and Savage. A low growl would make the convoy stop, and the roos wouldn't even risk opening the metal doors of the trucks, but poked their rifles through small holes in the side and shot each thrice.

"So civilised," Katerina said, reaching over and patting me hard on the cheek. "Say, 'Yes, regina.'"

I repeat the words, even as they try to choke me. I keep listening to the sky for the sound of dragon wings, wondering if Aurelia has made it back to the Academy by now. Wondering what her next move will be. There has to be some way I can contact her. Some opportunity I can take to send her a message that I have my own mind. That we are okay for now.

We arrive at the property close to dawn. Katerina's house is encased in scaffolding to repair the damage I caused when I tore the place apart to find Lia. Connor gets out first as part of the feline team to help levitate Lyle and Sav inside. Aurelia's feline friend inhales sharply as I clamber out of the Jeep. I land on the gravel with my chains clattering, dutifully falling in behind Katerina and the hyena matriarch.

I risk a little power usage. *"Pass me your phone at the first opportunity,"* I mentally project to Connor.

"Take them all to my room," the crocodile instructs. "I never want them out of my sight.

My stomach turns at the implication of this as Scythe and I are led inside the property. I can't see if her stone crocodile statue has been set right after I moved it, but I'm not entirely sure who else would have been able to move it without a truck or crane. It doesn't matter now, however, as the scent of women's perfumes mingle in the air along with various types of animas.

We're marched through a series of echoing corridors and tiled floors until we get to an even colder room, the AC on full blast. "I have three cages set up and ready," Katerina sighs as if she considers her own work arousing. Her scent casts a pall over me as she tugs me forwards by the chains and leads me towards the left of the room, where the scent of metal is strongest. "And one last touch—" Cold metal circles my neck before clipping into place. The rustle of keys clicks the lock into place before she prods me hard in the bicep, indicating I need to move forward.

With my jaw clenched, I drag my feet into what I assume is one of the cells, and she swings the door shut and locks it. I don't move anywhere. I remain fixed at the bars, listening to my shark-brother's steady, slow breathing. Savage and Lyle are levitated into the room, their breathing wet and slow from sedation, as they are locked into their cells one by one. Connor enters, then leaves, his gait the slowest of them all.

I sense no pregnancy in him, nor any signs of heat. Scythe had mentioned to me that Connor was here on a scientific study contract. In exchange for research, he would get money to help his poorly grandfather, who had been the one person in his family to stand by him when it was discovered he was a male with a female spirit.

The room becomes awfully quiet, and my stomach turns as I hear Katerina rubbing her hands along Scythe's body. She hums with pleasure. "Come and lie on the bed, Scythe."

I suck in a breath as my brother moves onto the bed.

Katerina hums again. "As your regina, I command you to kiss me."

Blood pounds in my head as I hear the rustle of cloth. My power lashes out, draconic telekinesis holding Scythe away from Katerina.

"Kiss me!" she commands angrily.

Scythe moves against my power, and I hold him still. I won't allow this. Not now, not ever. Not after everything he's been through. Not just hours after he'd slain his first enemy, my own Uncle. My shark-brother strains to complete the command, but I hold him like steel around flesh.

Katerina makes a displeased sound. "Fetch me a glass of water."

I loosen my hold and allow Scythe to complete this command and get off the bed. His business shoes click across the tiles until he gets to an echoey area that must be the ensuite. When he returns, Katerina takes the glass and gulps it down before setting it on a wooden bedside table. "Take your clothes off," she commands.

Fuck this vile creature.

Scythe moves, cloth moving against skin as he takes off his business shirt and drops it to the ground.

"Take your pants off," Katerina commands.

I clench my teeth as I hold Scythe's hands still. He pushes against me, forcing his will against mine. I sense his hands vibrating against our opposing forces, but I hold on to him with everything I have. Sweat trickles down my spine and I clench my teeth against the rage. Katerina huffs, and I let out a relieved exhale

"Turn the fuck around, dragon. Your eyes make me feel sick."

Silently, I turn and face the wall my cell shares with Savage and Lyle's.

"Scythe, lie next to me and go to sleep. I'll deal with you later. You, dragon. Sit down and sleep."

Sighing through my nose, I take up a position against the wall as Katerina's clothes come off and she heads into the bathroom. What a fucking pervert. I slide to the floor and come to rest on my ass, ignoring the command to sleep. Scythe can never be left alone with Katerina. None of my brothers can. I will sit and keep vigil every night, if I fucking have to.

* * *

Around midday the next day, Katerina gets out of bed to check on my wolf and lion brothers, darting them for good measure. She's going to run out of darts if she's not careful. I'm sure she has the biggest supply in the state, but how long is she expecting to keep this up? I don't feel as exhausted as I should, having had to stay wide awake all night and I think part of it is adrenaline still courses through my system from the fight at Drakos Estate.

"Dragon." The volume of Katerina's voice increases as she stands before my cell and unlocks it. "Get up, we're heading out." Scythe's breathing is coming from the door.

"I need to use the bathroom. Scythe will need it as well," I tell her.

"Don't tell me what Scythe needs." She mutters under her breath about the spell not working as planned as she walks away. "Be quick about it."

As I head to the ensuite, wondering if this is how Lia felt when I held her captive in my room. I had never intended it, but when the time came and my father gave me the golden collar, it had felt right in a twisted way. The part of me I kept locked away had wanted to keep her close. Had wanted her scent to remain by my side, and had wanted to keep my eye on her.

It had started as hate. And then I'd spent more time with her. Every moment of my day and night, actually. I began to see past the screen of my blind hatred. It had taken my forced physical blindness to really see the perfect parts that made her special. The delicate sound of her breath, the reliable thump of her heart, the sad sigh between her lips.

The way her skin—

The sudden mental image of my father dragging Aurelia's shark's body up the aisle before my wedding ceremony flashes across my mind's eye and I retch into the sink. My returned mark burns even more when I splash water on it, the droplets sizzling into steam as they hit my skin. I find the edges of the sink with my hands, and I'm unaware that I'm gripping so hard until I hear a fine crack. I have half a mind to tear the thing out of the wall and swing it at the reptile behind me, but a strange cooing stops me short.

When I return to the bedroom, the crocodile is running a brush through Scythe's hair as he sits still and cold on the bed. "Are you going to do mine next?" I ask in a dead voice.

I feel her eyes on me. "Yours isn't pretty."

Mine is much longer than Scythe's, but silver hair is a whole different thing. In the cages behind her, Savage growls and rolls over. Lyle twitches, stretching his paws out as he wakes up, his breathing ragged as the confusion hits him. This is going to be fucking interesting.

Katerina stands, apparently satisfied with her work. She turns towards my beastly brothers and commands, "You two stay," then she turns to me. "Both of you walk in front of me where I can see you. We're heading to breakfast."

Savage's black wolf form gets to his feet as we leave, and it's not until the door closes behind Katerina that a mighty, angry roar rattles the walls. The crocodile halts us with a sharp command, and I'm forced to stop as she storms back into her room and barks, "No noise. No growling. No barking. No roaring."

The room behind me goes quiet save for heavy breathing. Katerina makes an approving noise and exits the room. "Continue on," she says, shoving at my back like I'm an idiot.

Silently, Scythe and I walk down the corridor, and I follow my nose to the food. To my surprise, we end up outside, a little way from the entrance, under a marquee built for shade from the harsh outback sun. Food is laid out on a long table where the hyena matriarch is seated, sipping, from the smell of it, an espresso.

A little way from the table, someone is crying; another is whimpering, and I smell human blood and the tang of steel. There are humans in cages here.

The Collector bids us to sit down, and I feel the witch's eyes on me. Scythe is instructed to eat his lemon-marinated salmon. I'm starving, but I haven't been instructed to pull forwards that plate of bacon I can smell. "Look at him," Katerina says. "Do you really think the spell is covering his dragon animus?"

"At least partially. It would be wise to test it."

It would have been *wise* to leave us the fuck alone.

"Better get to it then," Katerina says. "Xander."

"Yes, regina?" I say obediently, turning towards the sound of her voice.

"There are some humans from the wildlife protection league who tried to break in and steal some of my breedable females. That can't stand, can it?"

My blood heats, my heart pounds, and I say, "No, it can't."

"Will you protect your regina?"

"Always." I'm going to vomit acid onto this dirt.

"Follow the guard." She gives a signal, then chains clank, a lock clangs open, and a quiet female whimper turns into a sob. The prisoner sounds young. She's not a child, but a young woman. Probably around Aurelia's age. "Kill her."

Without my powers, she's forcing me to do this with my human hands. A vision of Aurelia flashes through my mind's eye. Specifically, her screaming on the floor of my cavern, glass shattered around her, half of her right leg still missing. My blood wants to explode through my eye sockets.

I decide that Katerina Crocodylus can't die. She needs to suffer for this. If I am to stay here and look after my brothers, she must be convinced I'm under the curse and there can be no hesitation in my movements.

Somehow, I convince my legs to stride right up to the young lady. I can't tell her I'm sorry. I can't stop her murder. Once again, I find myself helpless to powers more malevolent than me. She doesn't fight as I approach her. Doesn't do anything except pant and whimper, the scent of her tears filling my nose. I snap her neck efficiently, then carefully lay her on the ground.

I'm just thankful it's me and not Savage or Lyle. Savage would be ruined by this.

The hyena matriarch sniffs, and I can't tell if it's from disgust or contempt. "He cries blood," she says. "What a joke."

I put my hands behind my back to hide the fact that I need to clench them into fists. Darkness follows me like my own personal Grim Reaper. I thought I was becoming a better male. I thought my time doing bad things had come to an end. How stupid I'd been to even entertain the thought.

"Well, the rest need to go too," Katerina says. "Take your earphones out."

I stop breathing. Of course she wants to go for the throat. This spell allows her to take full advantage, and she isn't going to waste the opportunity. With the obsidian chains around me I can't shift, but my Berserker genes will still take over. Swallowing the lump in my throat, I nod. "Yes, regina."

Let her take out this bloodlust on me. By the time she gets to my brothers, she'll be satiated and will hopefully leave them alone. I take out my earphones and put them in my pocket. The doors to the cells screech open. There's no red haze that takes me because I can't fucking see. But it's still 'red' in my ears, and in my head. In my blood-soaked, blackened soul. It's a sort of song. Ugly. Malicious.

The entire time I'm chasing and killing these humans, I'm fully aware, unable to control the way my body wants to maim, to destroy. The screaming soaks into me like wine, and it fuels me to tear and break and snap. Human screams come and go. Blood mists the air. I can't help but revel in it. So much.

I need *more*. I can't escape it.

Then, far away, I hear the sound of something new. My head snaps southward. Scythe's head—and further away, Savage and Lyle's heads too—snap in the same direction.

The sound is pure violence. Pure agony.

It's the rage of my regina.

I shake my head as the sound reverberates through my skull. It focuses me enough to allow me to think. To go still. Settling down on my haunches, I close my eyes and listen to the one who tugs at my soul.

A regina rampage is a thing of myth. It is usually driven by the death or danger of children. Very occasionally, however, the capture or death of a regina's pack drives its central mate into a frenzy of bloodlust.

My skin erupts in goosebumps, and my mouth curves into a smile.

Chapter 7

Ghoul

I'm overseeing the editing of the new videos when the serpent king slithers into the room. Everyone stands and bows.

"At ease. Ghoul, I need you to visit the Crocodylus property immediately. The hyena matriarch has received a venom-writ missive and assumed it was me. It wasn't. We need to determine which of our people has the audacity to be sending such a thing."

"A missive? Like a letter?"

"Correct."

Katerina had alluded to her plan to secure Scythe and his brothers. Gloated, in fact. I never would have believed it unless I'd seen the footage at Drakos Estate for myself. Everyone is unsettled by the hyena's witchery, but the underworld lords are more excited that she's removed Scythe from the chessboard. One less formidable enemy. One less hurdle.

The Clawsons sent her flowers. Mace sent chocolates.

"I'll head out right away, Your Majesty." I bow again and take my leave, heading upstairs into the night.

Dematerialising into shadows is my favourite thing. There are few things more delightful than becoming nothing...and becoming everything. During the day, it's not as fun because I'm confined by the lack of shadows. But the night is *all* shadow.

I am darkness. I am the thing that goes bump in the night. The bogeyman, as Savage likes to call me. Silently, I can travel across the world, watching the humans and animalia who are up to no good. Who do their work at night. But the thing that catches my eye the most are the little pretties. The sparkly lights that shoot out of houses every so often. As a teenager, I liked to count them, name their colours and rank them for their beauty: The souls that leave this world and come to mine.

Not all those who die meet me in the shadows. Most are directed elsewhere and we pass each other by like sailing boats in the dark. Sometimes I wave, but some of them are led to the shadow realm. These, I like to watch. They soar through the ether, and the shadows reach out like grabbing hands, snatching them up.

Tainted people. Monsters like Xander. Like Titus. Like me. Those who've blackened their spirit so badly the light can't even stand them. A lot of them wander in between for a while, lost and hungry, often angry. I don't know what happens to them once the shadows have devoured them and I can't see their souls anymore, but I can only hope it's the worst. We have only ourselves to blame for that.

There are no souls for the shadows tonight, however, as I soar over the vacant land and The Collector's barbed-wire fence. Her servants don't see me until I re-materialise on her white-tiled doorstep. The two roos at the door jump three feet in fright.

"Settle down, boys; it's only the big bad basilisk," I jeer. "Croco-dearest is expecting me."

The two males resettle their automatic rifles on their backs and open the door. One of them leads me to a sitting room where the statuesque form of Xander stands obediently with his hands behind his back, ever the humble servant. The Collector and the hyena queen sip herbal tea at a small table. The hyena has a secret dash of bourbon in hers.

"You have a pet dragon," I say, bowing low.

The crocodile offers me her hand, and I take the thing and smack my lips in the air over it. "That and more." She grins with all her teeth. "They are quite obedient. Xander passed all my tests."

Straightening, I eye Xander over the table. She's taken his powers so everyone can see his scarred, empty eye sockets. He smells of human blood and charred fury. But only I can see the black mark on his neck. Seeing it in person, I understand now that it's a stunning thing of higher work. And I think he and I are the only two people on the planet who know what it means.

I turn my attention to the unopened envelope sitting before the hyena. "What, scared of a little paper, old lady?"

"I'll give *you* something to be scared of, little boy," she gruffs. I smile with my fangs. "It has the smell of serpent magic all over it," The Collector says impatiently. "Tell us if it's dangerous."

"Oh, I'm sure it's dangerous," I say lightly. "That's why we should open it straight away."

"Is it going to detonate or something?" The Collector snaps. "We should do it outside."

"Doubt it." I shrug. "Go on, your witchiness."

The hyena matriarch eyes me in a nasty sort of way before she slides her finger under the seam of the opening. Nothing happens when she opens it, nor when she slides the letter out. But as she unfolds it—

"Argh!" Her shriek nearly pierces my eardrums as she drops the paper like it's burned her. Sure enough, the paper steams and hisses on the tile floor, and the hyena queen is glaring at her now reddened hand in rage.

"Oh look," I say brightly. "It looks like there's blood on your hands, Your Highness." I bend down to pick up the steaming note. It doesn't hurt me, of course; its job is done.

There is no scent on the paper itself as I open it up, but I would know the scent of my regina's venom in any life. There, written in a mixture of venom and blood, is a complex sigil so ancient, it pre-dates the arrival of animalia into this world.

My pretty little snakelet did this? But of course she did. She'd been trained since before she could write. Mace Naga took his serpentine magics seriously, and she'd read the writing in the cata-combs under the Naga household competently. Scythe had gotten shot by the venom bullet because she'd missed a piece, but she wasn't going to be caught off guard this time. Mace is going to be *pissed* when I tell him.

"What does it say?" The Collector asks carefully. She doesn't want to appear weak or fearful, though I know she's being very cautious.

"So interesting," I say painfully slowly. "I can't be sure."

"Stop playing, boy," the hyena queen snaps.

I bare my fangs at her. "This venom is Aurelia Boneweaver's." I let that sink in. Xander doesn't so much as flinch. But the animas—their pupils dilate, and their brows lift in surprise. "She has sent you an ancient symbol serpents send to their enemies," I continue, professionally. "She has marked you for death."

Now it may be a trick of the light...or the shadows, but a brief smile twitches the lips of the hyena matriarch. Maybe people lose control of their face in old age, I don't know.

The Collector scoffs, and the moment passes. "What a stupid girl."

And a feeling that I've never known, a feeling I've been waiting for, glowing like the moon, expansive like growing shadows, begins to spread through my chest. Not stupid. Brave. Bloodthirsty.

The hyena queen shares my sentiment. "You should not underestimate her," she warns, wrapping her hand in a handkerchief. "She means to try something."

"Of course she does," The Collector scoffs. "But she has so many eyes on her she can't get away with anything at all. Mace, for one"—she nods at me—"won't be far off with his own plans, and we'll all be set."

There's an urgent knock at the door, and Connor walks in. I know him from my studies of the students while I was play-acting as a guard at the academy. He has a cotton ball taped to his arm where his blood looks like it has been taken multiple times for The Collector's experiments. I sense more samples have been taken from him, at the very least his bone marrow and multiple rounds of egg harvesting. But if he's in human form right now, that means he's in between collection cycles.

"What is it?" The Collector snaps.

"So sorry, my lady, but Mr Pardalia is, uh...well, he set up a protest on your...in your...."

"Set up a what?" Katerina's heels clack away across the tile towards her bedroom. Without being asked, I follow her and

Connor down a series of corridors. My brows knit together at the lionesses' strange tone. The moment The Collector steps foot into her room, she lets out a feral screech. "Back in your cages! Back, you asshole!"

And then it hits me...and my nose. I peer into the room to confirm.

Lyle has shat on Katerina's bed.

Savage is watching from the corner, and there's a naughty gleam in his eye.

"I can see your smirk," Connor hisses, side-eyeing me a good distance from the doorway. "Might want to hide that."

"I don't need to hide anything, Connor." I grin wider.

Katerina has procured a dinosaur-strength cattle prod from under her bed, and she zaps Lyle with a furious cry. The lion obediently whips around and walks back into his cell, plonking himself down on the floor and peering at her as if he's done nothing wrong.

"If you put it in the sun," I say very helpfully, "it might help take the stains out."

Chapter 8

Aurelia

I sit on top of the academy for a long time. No amount of coaxing could get me down from my perch, where I stare out, narrow-eyed, growling low in my chest, the taste of embers in my mouth.

My breath is a pant at first. Threatening, heated. But it's important to me that I stay in control. To recognise my power and not let it take me over into the wild madness that feels so tempting. So I settle my breath into slow waves of deliberate control, sending my overflowing power out to fortify my protections around the school. Next, I seek out my mates, closing my eyes and feeling for them through the air. Calling out to them. Nothing returns. Not even a snicker from Ghoul. I can feel their existence. They live. They breathe. But I am blocked from them.

It's after dark that we get a visitor. From my perch, I see the marking on the car. A lone car. A lone tiger. *"Minnie,"* I call into my friend's mind. *"Send Marduk to see which tiger dares enter my domain."*

A few minutes later, I hear Bastien calling a greeting to the Caspian tiger as he stalks out of the animus dorms and heads out to speak to the guards at the gate. Only then do I descend from my perch onto the grass below to sit and wait for Marduk to return. Minnie and Yeti come out to wait with me, my friend perching cross-legged on my left claw and leaning back into my shin like it's an armchair. We watch as her mate returns with a strange, grim expression and a black piece of paper in one hand. "It's addressed to you, Lady Boneweaver."

Accepting that my current form is not conducive to holding paper, I shift back into my human shape, and Minnie hands me the dressing gown she was using as a blanket.

Once I'm covered, I take the letter from Marduk, and sensing no malignant powers on it, I tear it open. It's written in white ink, the scrawl large and dominating the surface of the paper.

"Tacky," Minnie mutters as she reads from my side.

I request an audience with Lady Aurelia Boneweaver tomorrow night at 6 p.m. at Clawson House to discuss matters regarding her protection.

Lord Tiberius Clawson

The words on the paper ignite my blood, and I feel the urge to shift into hard scales again. Passing the letter to Minnie, I blink hard in my rage. Did he send such a letter to my mother's mate before he killed him? Did he use such kind words when instructing his felines to tear down the Lily Institute and kill hundreds of vulnerable animalia inside?

Minnie breathes hard through her nose and grants me a blessing by speaking first. "He wants to see you in person. Lia, I don't think you should do it."

I meet Marduk's eyes, cunning and assessing. There is an eternal wound there. Just as Minnie is scarred by Titus' rejection, so are her mates, powerful as they are. "They mean you no good, Lady Boneweaver," he says. "Nothing good can come out of this. But..."

My smile is dark. "But we may learn something." He nods. Learn something that might end them. "The tiger that delivered the letter?"

"He is detained," Marduk says.

I turn to Beak. "Put him in a locked room for the night. Take any electronics from him."

Yeti follows after the eagle. "I'm coming too."

Minnie takes her remaining mate's hand for comfort, and it lightens my heart to see it. But my leg also aches, and I'm cramping from sitting on the roof for so long. "I need a shower," I mutter, hobbling back inside. "We really need a lift. This building is very ableist."

"Say no more, my lady!" I flinch at the sharp voice of Bastien the gargoyle and glance up at him, sitting above the entrance to the dorm. He beams down at me through his monocle, and spindly arms wheel excitedly as he points inside. "Lo and behold!"

Both glass doors swing open of their own accord. Frowning, I head inside and stop short. Before, the left of the tiny foyer of the dorm had only held stairs. Now, nestled into the wall before the first step is a single-person lift.

"Wait, why didn't you do that for her before, Bastien?" demands Minnie.

The creature shrugs. "She wasn't the lady of the house before. It'll only open for her."

Still frowning, I press the button for *up* and the metal doors whir open. A soft golden light reveals a black lacquered fancy elevator interior with gleaming gold buttons.

"Now you don't have to storm dramatically up and down the stairs," Minnie says. "And your leg won't hurt so much."

I get inside and press the topmost floor.

"Beat you to the top!" Minnie says.

As the doors close before me, Minnie's pink Converse pop off the floor as she levitates herself to race. I don't know how I feel about special rules being made for me, but if the school really is mine to command, I could use it to our advantage.

To my surprise, the topmost floor is the rooftop. I stick my head back inside the lift and go one level down, and it opens directly into my pack dorm from a spot that used to be the bare wall. Minnie, flushed-faced and panting, clears the topmost stair and lands in a heap. "You win," she says in a muffled voice. "The corridor is longer than I estimated." I stand there for a moment as she pants. "I think I need to see my mates," she admits, her eyes glancing down at the black envelope still in my hand. "Will you be alright?"

"Of course," I say quietly. "I'm sorry."

"Don't start. Otherwise, we'll be saying sorry to each other every five minutes."

We say our goodbyes, and I finally head into the shower, where I don't even touch the hot water tap. I'm too riled up. Too ready to blow fire onto the world. Tomorrow night is too far away, how am I supposed to sleep tonight?

When I exit the bathroom into the dark of the bedroom, red gleaming eyes stare at me through coiling shadows from the corner of the room. "Don't go, it's a trap," Ghoul says.

He'd been secretly listening! Hidden in the shadows around the dorm, perhaps. "I know all about traps, Ghoul," I say irritably, toweling my hair dry. "I don't want to see you right now."

"I don't care, my sweet little venom."

"Come to gloat?" I try not to look at him, glaring out the window instead. Whenever he has his shadows up like this, I can't see his mating mark. It doesn't matter, though, the pull I feel towards him is inexplicable. My feet take a few halting steps towards him.

He hums as if amused. "The way I see it? You have no idea *what* you're doing."

I find myself standing before him, furiously pointing out the window. "Get the fuck away from me, General." I'm pretty sure that's how he gets around—flying through the windows. It's not like he's ever walked through doorways whenever he's snuck into the academy.

His shadows recede, revealing the dark figure underneath. Instead of his usual bone mask, tonight his face is painted with the white skull pattern. "Forgetful little thing, aren't you?" That voice gets deeper. Huskier. "We made a deal." I go still, my eyes narrowing in suspicion. Fangs glint. "You promised me your venom at any time of my choosing. That was in exchange for passing a little message to your friends, remember?"

Throwing my towel onto the bed with a feral sort of aggression, I turn away to leave. "Come back another time, you bastard."

I feel his heat behind me, radiating like something toxic. Poisonous. A muscled arm snakes around my waist, tugging me close to a tower of muscle at my back. He smells like leather and something spicy as he lowers his mouth to my ear. "I do enjoy it when you're like this."

Unbidden, I turn to see his face and find those lips mere inches from mine, the fangs poking out. His scent is intoxicating, filling my head, my torso, and surging all the way *down*. His hand, gloved in firm black leather, comes up to hold my jaw. "I think I'd murder someone to get your venom in my mouth, snakelet."

The memory comes back to me, at Drakos Estate, when he'd milked me for my venom for their so-called research. Not long after, they'd injected me with hormones to make me go into heat.

Some of that time is a haze. Being in heat is like that. It can be like coming out of a dream. You're a different person, and afterwards, your memory can be hazy. I remember that I'd been insatiable. I remember that Xander had carried me to his room and had called Ghoul.

They'd...helped me. Ghoul had drunk my venom, but then Xander had left, and Ghoul remained...

"We never fucked at Drakos Estate, did we?" I ask curiously. "I would remember that." His body is a stone pillar at my back, and I remember the sensation of being close to him.

He chuckles, his thumb finding my lower lip and brushing against it. Suddenly agitated that my memory is foggy, I turn and shove him. It does little to actually move him, but I get to put distance between us before I do something stupid. Ghoul bares his fangs at me. "You bounced in my lap, fucking my fingers until you were so exhausted you fell asleep, snakelet. *I*, however, have not fucked you yet. You'd remember that."

Wild Mother, I *do* remember some of what he describes. I'd been dizzy from all the panting and...*bouncing,* as he calls it. I cross my arms and regard him. He regards me back, those red lasers harsh, those shadows lazily dancing around his shoulders. Slowly, he stalks backwards and sits in Scythe's armchair. A finger beckons. "Sit on me, pretty poison."

I don't move a fucking inch.

Fast as serpents, two bands of shadows strike out. My arm whips up to reflexively cover my face, but they band around my hips, firm yet velvet soft. I'm yanked off my feet and fly forwards, right towards Ghoul. I'm forced to raise my feet, and he catches me. I'm breathless as he chuckles, arranging my thighs on either side of his. Pressed against him, I glare down into his eyes.

"I would never strike you, let alone your face," he says matter-of-factly. "I might hurt your little fangs, but then how else would I get my sweet venom? Open up." He strokes my cheek with a finger, and his lids lower across his eyes, turning the red beams into tiny half-moons. I bare my own fangs in annoyance. "There she is. Now, think about biting me as hard as you can."

He's lucky I make good on my deals, otherwise I *would* be tearing up his neck right about now. I feel the venom surging out of my fangs and lower my mouth over his.

Ghoul parts his lips on a practically reverent breath. His tongue snakes out, licking at one of my fangs hard enough to draw his own blood. I snarl softly, that serpent part of me rearing her ferocious head. Hands tighten around my hips, and he surges forward, covering my mouth with his. I rear backwards, annoyance sounding from my throat, but he holds me firm as he drinks from me. I shove at his chest with my palms, and he moans into my mouth, wrapping his arms around my waist and locking me in place.

He swallows once, then twice. And I can't help it then. My hips grind against his. My hands slide up his chest, his neck, and cup the edge of his painted face.

His shadows slide around my shoulders, brushing at my hair and neck, touching my mating mark. My skin tingles, the regina in me needing so much more.

"*You hate that you love this,*" he says into my head. "*You hate that I love it so much.*"

"*Fuck you.*"

"*That's it, baby. Give me all of your rage.*"

He holds me tight, and he's fucking correct. I hate how, in the arms of this basilisk, this general of my father's court, it's the first time I've felt grounded in two days. As the venom in my glands nears empty, I feel light. The place between my legs is heated. I burn for my mates, and it makes me squirm.

Finally, I'm empty, and he pulls away, his arms sliding down my thighs and onto the armrests on the chair. He sits like a king, watching me with no small amount of pleasure sitting there, panting, horny out of my mind. But I'm not in heat, so I can control myself. I climb off him.

"I enjoy our little visits," Ghoul says, wiping the side of his mouth with a thumb. "The Clawsons are up to no good, snakelet. Don't go tomorrow."

"I'm not taking your advice."

He shrugs. "Yeah? And what happened the last time I warned you not to do something?"

With that, the monster disappears into the dark.

Chapter 9

Aurelia

The next morning, I wake up with that feeling of emptiness yawning just a bit wider. My power claws under my skin, keen to get going. But there is much to do before we leave for Clawson House tonight.

We meet at Raquel's hospital room. We've all been feeling their absence, and I want them to feel included while we plan. Our wolf anim lies quietly breathing, and I watch their lashes twitch.

"*Raquel,*" I call into their mind. "*You're safe now. Come back to us.*"

Guilt oozes in my chest as I'm met with silence. The doctors are saying that we just need to wait. That it's only a matter of time, and Raquel's mind just needs to rest from the trauma of being split from their body for so long. It only makes me more antsy. It was my fault to start with, and I need to be smarter in my attempts to fix things.

"We've been to Clawson House before," Minnie says evenly. "And…"

"And I've been in their prison," Sabrina finishes from her spot in the corner, Blair and Blade hovering protectively over her hooded form.

"She's not going back there," Blair says firmly before looking down at Sabrina and saying more softly, "And you don't have to talk about it if you don't want to."

Blade nods and clutches the bag of cakes she likes. It makes me smile to see them protective of her. She deserves that.

My hand fists the edge of Raquel's sheet where it hangs over the bed. "No one's doing anything they don't want to," I say in a low voice. "But we need some clarity on what's inside the property."

Marduk unrolls the poster onto the rolling table. "I have the blueprints, Lady Boneweaver."

"How you source these things, I'll never understand," Minnie says under her breath. It's true. Marduk had somehow been able to find the blueprints to Naga House as well, which should have been impossible. The twins, Stacey, Eugene, Henry, Yeti, and Minnie crowd around the table, looking over the house. Beak shows me a bird's-eye view using maps on his phone, pointing out important landmarks on the way so I'll know exactly where to land.

"And you'll be able to cover all of us?" Yeti asks.

I nod, ignoring the creeping feeling suddenly winding its way through my stomach. This reminds me of the time my mates and I had planned to sneak into Naga House to retrieve my mother. I'd used a bubble shield to cover all of us to get in all the way until we'd reached the underground portion of the house. Then we'd come across Uncle Ben.

I squeeze Raquel's hand. It's thankfully warm. "As long as I can see you," I tell the Devi pack, "you'll be covered. After that, you're alone."

Marduk nods, a new light in his dark eyes.

* * *

We gather at the top of the animus dorms as night falls.

I'm not sure if shifting into a dragon is something I'll get used to. I don't have Xander to ask, but it's a strange thing. There's no other form that feels like smoke and fire and yet has weapon-like scales and aeroplane-sized wings. It feels like power and does little to sate my growing bloodlust.

"Are you okay?" Minnie whispers where she's levitating next to my head. "You've been so quiet today."

"*I want to kill people, Min,*" I reply into her mind. Something worse than simply killing, but I won't mention it now. "*I have to hold all of that inside, and it's...*"

She nods, stroking my brow. "Driving you nuts."

"*Something like that.*"

I have a feeling that if Ghoul had not taken my venom yesterday, I'd be in a real state tonight. He had no intention of 'helping' me in that way; it was for his own personal benefit, of course, but he'd unknowingly done me and my overactive Boneweaver power a favour while my mates are not here. The tigers climb on at the front, and Beak takes up the back position, cuddling onto Marduk.

I can't help it, really. It roars out of me—the fire, the sound of pure animal rage. Minnie's shrieks are drowned out, and I envelop them in a protective bubble before I jump up into the air. There's no more hiding. Not anymore.

I don't soar up as fast as I want to, not with one of my legs hurting so much when I leap. But the wings and the force provided by my other limbs are enough to have us levelling out in the night sky above the clouds.

An eagle's cry registers, and I realise Beak has shifted and is gripping onto my scales with his claws. He can't keep up with dragon wings, of course, so I slow down just enough and he's able to fly up my body to my neck where he clutches on. I think he just wants to see the view, the feeling of flying at this velocity and altitude.

"*It's something else, isn't it?*" I tell him. "*Seeing the clouds like a blanket beneath you and nothing but stars above.*" He calls his agreement.

We get to Clawson House an hour later, nestled in a wealthy estate of affluent felines. The cream and gold rendered brick house is king of the hill, enclosed in a fancy golden fence. The house used to be Ablo Obon's family house until he sold it and moved to a different suburb. No one actually knows whether he was blackmailed into moving, or if Tiberius offered him a huge sum for the pretty property. I'm betting it was the former. We already know he likes to fight dirty.

I switch my shield around the Devi pack to an invisibility one before I touch down as lightly as I can. Beak gets to the ground first and shifts, catching the bag Marduk tosses to him and getting out his clothes. I can't see them, but I feel Minnie, Marduk, and Yeti levitate themselves off my back. From now on, we're to act as if they don't exist.

I shift into human form, and Beak rushes over with my clothes, his hands all over my bra and knickers. I snatch them from his hands and quickly shove them on before my professional attire. Sabrina helped me pick them out, of course, and my friends all demanded we go for what they're calling 'mob boss chic.'

It's nothing less than a power suit. A navy-blue blazer trimmed with white, and matching suit pants with golden buttons. Beak starts wielding my hairbrush, and I narrow my eyes at him. He backs away with his hands in the air. Carefully brushing my long tresses out, I slick them back into a high pony, smoothing down the sides.

My anima wants to wear anything other than this. It wants to be naked and in scales and fangs. "How do I look?" I ask, distractedly tugging at the blazer.

When Beak doesn't reply, I frown up at him through the dark. He's smiling softly. "You look different from the day I first met you."

I stare at him. How could I forget the day I'd met my mates? How could I forget the day my life had changed forever? And he's right; I'd been a different person then.

That Aurelia didn't know what had happened to her mother. Had never broken a bone. Had never shifted into a wolf, a shark, or a dragon. That Aurelia had run when she'd been told to. And she'd never had her mates taken from her.

I turn my face towards Clawson House. "That Aurelia is gone now." Because someone darker has taken her place. A beast who craves flesh between her teeth.

Minnie sniffs somewhere to my far right, and I nod in her direction. With a deep breath, I set my shoulders and begin walking up the hill to the gate. We are let inside quickly and efficiently. Beak speaks for me in the way that I've seen the beasts of mob bosses do, and when the giant, intimidating guard tigers look me over, I level them an unsmiling look, letting my power fan out unhindered.

Unapologetic. I know they feel it by the sudden defensive set of their shoulders.

One thing about felines is that their telekinesis puts them at a huge advantage over other orders. With a single thought, one of them can flip you backwards and send you flying out the door. Couple that with male arrogance and you've got a bunch of assholes on your hands. There needs to be clear communication that I outrank these guys in power. It's the only thing felines respect—the Clawsons, most of all.

Minnie, Marduk, and Yeti are careful to follow close by as we are led inside the opulent house, the golden downlights washing the grand entrance hall in deceivingly warm light. The place smells like feral male tiger, and from what I know about this place, Tiberius encourages his beasts to wander around as feral, and in some cases, as rabid as they like. Titus had arrived at the academy completely rabid, after all.

We are led into a formal meeting room just off the main hallway, the high ceilings giving the impression of lofty importance. There's an alcohol cabinet off to one side, and a rectangular table in the middle takes up most of the space. It can seat four on each side, and as Beak pulls out a middle seat for me, the guards leave to summon their *noble* leader.

They haven't tried to murder or maim me yet, so it's looking promising, but there is the faint scent of marking urine in the air, so I'm not completely impressed. That's definitely from Titus, I'd put money on it. I imagine him lifting a leg over the table, and my mood improves somewhat. Beak stands at my right elbow, and I feel Minnie and Marduk station themselves behind us. Yeti is on his own now.

They make us wait, of course. Ten minutes go by, then fifteen, and I try to stop my bristling as a girl in red lingerie, complete with garters, brings us tea in plain white teacups. Just as I'm contemplating asking for Beak to put me out of my misery and pour me a whisky, the door opens and Tiberius walks in, Titus hunched and stalking at his back.

I give them both a droll, bored look that would likely get another anima struck. They're both intimidating males, hulking slabs of muscle, midnight dark beards and combed hair over tanned skin. Titus' heavy black brows are drawn over his dark eyes, and he looks exactly like he did the last time I saw him at the Jewel of the Jungle when Xander had a meeting there. And I had been naked.

This seems to be fresh in Titus' memory as he sits down, placing a laptop on the table. His new steel jaw can't smile—the exposed metal teeth make their own permanent awful smile—but his eyes can still leer at me well enough. "Nice to see you with clothes on, Lia," he says in that new, rigid, metallic voice.

Beak shifts at his overfamiliarity. *"Not a word, Beaky,"* I tell the eagle in his mind. To Titus, I say, "You were running the last time we met, were you not? I'm so glad you made it home safely after Xander almost killed everyone."

"Ah, yes. Xander Drakos," Titus says. "Wasting away in one of Katerina's tiny cages. He's probably getting fucked up the ass by one of the beasties she has in there. What I'd pay to see that on video. In fact..." He gets out his phone and makes a show of typing out a text.

"Quite obsessed with that, aren't you?" I shoot back, sitting back in my chair.

Titus opens his mouth, but his father waves an impatient hand as he sits. "That's enough." His voice has a hint of alpha-command that rakes along my skin, and his gaze is ever so *hard* on mine.

"Says the brother-killer," I respond flatly.

Tiberius Clawson, as hardened a mob boss as Scythe, has a face of stone. "Let me be frank with you, girl," he says. "You are exposed. Without mates. With many enemies. There is a giant target on your back, and there is nothing you can do to stop the dark powers of the world from doing what they want with you." I remember The Collector's threats. I know what she would have done to me. Tiberius claps his hands. "We will provide you and your animas with protection. We will ensure the multiple dangers that are after you are kept at bay."

My brows rise. "In exchange for what?"

Titus snaps his metal jaw, dark eyes glinting. "You. I gave up an inadequate regina. But I'll have you as a mate. It's a win-win." *Sow dissent, break us apart.* My stomach sinks at the words that will slash at my sweet, best friend. Titus leans back in his chair. "Minnie used to talk about you all the time." He puts on a high-pitched voice. "'Lia is kind. Lia is the *best* person I know. The *bravest*.'"

My heart clenches. "I am loyal to my friends, Titus. I would never betray Minnie's trust." My face twists in disgust. "Something you could never hope to understand in this life. You or your kin-slaying father."

Tiberius snarls. "You are out of your depth, little girl. You don't know the powers you're playing with. *Death and worse* are knocking at your door."

I huff through my nose. "You forget one crucial thing, Clawson."

"And what is that?"

I lean forwards in my seat. "Those powers. That serpent who raised me taught me a thing or two before he cast me out. I don't need you."

Tiberius sighs and gestures to Titus. "We thought it might come to this."

The brute becomes excited, his movements quick and eager as he opens the laptop before him, presses a few buttons, and swings it around so I can see the screen.

Ice trickles down my spine as I register a grid of camera feeds. I recognise the location immediately. "At least Xander was good for a couple of things when he switched sides," Titus remarks. "Got us a live feed from inside Animus Academy. But look here—" He clicks on one of the smaller feeds, enlarging it so I get a night vision view of what looks like one of the caverns under the premises. Two males—lion students I recognise—are standing by large pipes, looking at their phones, the screens lighting up their faces. Titus gets out his own phone and dials. We watch the taller lion answer.

"Do it," Titus barks before hanging up.

The animus on the camera feed sticks his phone in his pocket before getting out a screwdriver.

"What are you doing?" I snap.

"Tampering with the academy water supply," Titus says smugly.

The lion drops his screwdriver and holds his hand out to the other, who gives him a bottle of something he proceeds to squirt into the plumbing.

"Old fashioned toxin," Tiberius says. "Just like you, we learned from the best."

They mean my father. Poison has always been the serpent's weapon of choice. I shake my head in disbelief. "The school is dragon-made. It won't allow you to—"

"It won't be able to purify the water in time," Tiberius says. "Not with how much we're dumping into its system. Oh! Look, dinner service is running."

Titus cuts the camera to one in the dining hall where students are lining up at the buffet and several of them are in line for the cordial that Theresa is filling at the tap. Stacey is at the head of the line, with Gertie and Henry on her shoulders and Eugene tucked under one arm. She takes a cup of cordial and drinks. I suck in a breath. Nothing happens. Stacey walks towards our usual table and sits down. "Any minute now," Titus drawls.

And it does take a mere minute for other students to collect their jugs and drink from their glasses. I can only watch as Stacey goes rigid in her seat, reaching for her throat. She sways, the ever-watchful males from the surrounding tables frowning. Stacey collapses to the floor at the same time as another student behind her. Minnie makes a choked sound from behind me.

I leap to my feet at the same time Titus does. But he's snarling in Minnie's direction. "Piggy!"

Chapter 10

Aurelia

"**M**INNIE!" I scream into her head, exploding out of my seat and sprinting for the door.

"Let's go!" Minnie shouts, and I feel my friend's telekinetic power surrounding me and hurling the both of us out of Clawson House. Beak and Marduk shout out behind me, but there's no time. I tear off my jacket and shift with powerful force. My phoenix form beats her powerful wings, carrying me into the sky as I gather my power behind me like a rumbling storm. Small but strong hands grab my ankles just as I release my power and, like a lightning bolt, shoot us through the ether.

The sonic boom resounds through the air in our wake as my world turns dark, my feathers plastered against my skin as I scream through the air at the speed of sound towards Animus Academy. Seconds later, the dragon magic of the property puffs at my skin, and I screech to a halt before I overshoot. Minnie sobs loudly as I release the shield around her and she decompresses.

"*THE WATER IS POISONED!*" I broadcast into the school, nosediving towards the dining hall. As we reach seven feet, Minnie lets go and levitates herself to the ground, allowing me to shift into cheetah form and land lightly on four paws. I sprint into the dining hall after Minnie, ready to locate the poisoned bodies.

We are met with chaos.

My ears fill with shouting. Some students have shifted and are howling or screeching. Tables have been knocked over, and there is food and cordial spilled everywhere. I shift back into human form. Guards run towards me from the outside. "It's the water!" I shout. "Bring the healers, quickly!" Someone shoves an orange jumpsuit at me. It's tossed to the ground just as quickly as I survey the number of people lying unconscious on the floor.

There's about twenty, some already with an avian shifter over them. Theresa has a hand over two students. Minnie passes me my phone. I must have dropped it when I shifted, and she used her power to bring it with us. On it is a text message from "Unknown."

Welcome to our world. You are just one whore in it.

Heated blood surges through my veins.

Minnie rushes towards our table, where Sabrina is sobbing next to Stacey. A magpie from third year is sweating over her, hands over her stomach as she concentrates. I hobble over to them and shove the girl aside. "Tend to someone else."

The girl mutters an expletive but does as I ask. My power surges into Stacey as Minnie strokes our lionesses' ombre hair. My healing power registers her blood and the poison, and it takes concentration to block out the chaos around me. Poisoning is the most difficult thing for avian healing powers to deal with. There's no one *thing*— no wound to knit together or bacteria to eliminate.

Instead, I have to surge through her blood, isolating the bad stuff from the good and neutralising it. It would have reached her heart and brain if not for the quick work of the avian I'd just shoved aside. This is going to take hours. It would help if we knew exactly what it was, but all I know is that Tiberius said—

I snarl in awareness and immediately shift my left finger into a sharp claw and prick my right index finger. Shoving up Stacey's shirt, I write serpentine symbols in my own blood. My father taught me the attacking types, but he'd taught me the defensive ones too. And if there is one thing serpent magic has an affinity for, it's blood and poison.

Once I'm satisfied, I get off my knees and search the dining hall. Hope, a nurse often in charge of the medical centre, is here in scrubs. I hobble over, sharply calling her name. She looks at me with widened eyes. "There's a toxin in the water, likely serpentine. If you have anyone fluent in serpent magic, you'll need them to do some blood magic on the patients. That'll halt it long enough to get them to medical for proper assessment." I cringe when two nurses start CPR on the patient they're hovering over. "Give me room," I say, holding out my bleeding finger.

Two hours later, the dining hall is cleared and everyone who could be saved is at the medical centre with most of the medical team. Three students couldn't be revived, and I watch a young nurse, with tears in her eyes, trying to close the eyes of a second-year wolf. We broke his ribs during CPR, and my blood is smeared all over his abdomen. There are still IV lines in him.

Marduk, Yeti, and Beak are on their way back in a stolen car. They won't be here for hours according to Minnie. As I stand and watch what remains of the day, it hits me with all the force of a sledgehammer.

I did this.

Horror winds its way up my spine, followed by something else. Something that charges through my blood with the fire of a raging volcano. My lungs fill with smoke. But my power comes up against someone else's. I turn to find Minnie, her back turned, staring at another deceased student as Theresa covers his face with a sheet. Minnie also feels accountable for the actions of her once-mate.

I shake my head. Maybe Tiberius is right. Maybe I *am* in over my head. Maybe I'm not cruel enough, or cunning enough to survive in a world of monsters.

But I *am* something else. I am powerful enough.

Something critical cracks inside of me. Power spills in my belly, and it fills my bones. I take a deep breath and exhale black smoke, rolling my shoulders as my vision changes. Minnie's power shifts in the air, like a current of wind gathering into a cyclone. Her breathing is heavy, not strained, but like a bellows under the weight of her power. When she turns around, Minnie's eyes shine with a deathly light I've never seen before. Goosebumps erupt all over me at that look of utter rage.

She steps towards me, our eyes locked in an unspoken, sacred promise. "Take me back," she hisses through clenched teeth. "Take me to Clawson House, Lia."

The two of us, both reginas of broken packs, of broken hearts, of justice gone too long unserved, stride back into the night.

Chapter 11

Aurelia

innie and I don't speak as we head outside. We don't have to. We've always understood each other on a deep level. She is the sister of my soul and I of hers.

And now, we are sisters of blood.

The guards, feeling our powers, step back, and when I shift into my phoenix form, blue sparks shoot out of me from the force. Minnie hisses as one of them catches her, but she blots it out with a quick hand and nods at me, rising into the air, her arms out like an angel.

If she is the angel of death then I am her valiant steed.

Mighty illuminated red-feathered wings sweep through the darkness as I feel Minnie's hands grasp my ankles again. Surrounding her with a shield, I gather my power. But this time, Minnie gathers hers too, like powerful wings of her own. A fierce cry erupts from both our mouths as we rocket across the land.

This time, I come to a supersonic halt just before we come up the hill to the property. It gives us time to survey the house and grounds. It gives us time to mark our prey. The guards shout as they see us, likely confused as to why they're seeing a phoenix grace the sky. They're gobsmacked as they see me up close, mouths hanging open as they come to see us. But this time, when we stride onto Clawson land, we are both visible, both our powers lashing outward in tendrils like the edge of a tornado.

As the tigers raise their guns, Minnie cuts through the air with her hand and they both fall to the ground, unconscious. We round on the house, and my tigress screams up its length. All her rage, all her fury out in full force. The windows shatter. Every last one becomes nothing but glittering dust. There are screams from the inside as the confusion begins, but Minnie doesn't stop. I shift into human form, and she holds out her hand to me.

A dark smile touches my lips as I take it. I feel her heartbeat in her hand. It becomes a drum, the beat of which sings out to my own heart. Then I too reach out a hand, and we begin our destruction.

The house gives a low, agonised groan, and more screams sound from inside as it trembles on its foundations. Dust falls from the roof. The earth quivers. We start at the top, shifting the ceramic tiles and making them crumble, followed by the roof beams, snapping under our will.

People run out of the house, and after a surprised shout, they make a beeline for us. I let Minnie carry on as my shark teeth come out and I feel their electrical impulses. I squeeze their hearts rapidly, and they fall to the ground, clutching their chests until they pass out. Sometimes telekinesis hits my shield and I smirk up at a high window, knocking that tiger out too.

Minnie's grip is tight around my hand as she makes the second level shake. White dust falls onto the bodies lying in the front yard. I let my power roll like an ocean wave through the house, catching each and every person left cowering inside and knocking them unconscious. I bring them outside, roughly dumping them on the lawn with the rest. The only people I can't reach are those in the cells underground, but they'll be safe for the moment.

There is only one person who fights me, and I allow it.

Titus stalks out of the house, brushing crumbling drywall off one massive shoulder. His steel jaw and teeth shine under the flickering lights of the house. "Piggy." His voice is jeering. "Stop this."

"Use my name," Minnie hisses, her hand sweeping downwards, the palm now facing directly towards him. Titus takes a threatening step forward, but Minnie's power halts him. The hulking tiger raises his own hand, but then his eyes widen, the whites showing all the way around.

Frozen in place by Minnie's violent power, Titus seems to vibrate. His body goes stiff, and his eyes widen in horror as each second passes. Those mechanical jowls part in shock as the night seems to press on him.

"Use. My. Name." Minnie grits out as her ex-mate's nose begins to bleed, then the corners of his eyes, but he refuses to relent. Minnie lets go with an angry scream. Titus stumbles back and falls flat on his ass, staring at his once-regina in a sort of confused disbelief. Scrambling backwards, he finds his feet and *runs* for his life.

"That's right!" she cries. "Run, you soulless bastard!"

We turn our gazes back to the crumbling mansion. There are shouts behind us now, from the other big houses down the hill, and in the distance, a car screeches into the street. An alarm is going off somewhere, but under our combined powers, the electricity of the house winks out and all suddenly becomes dark.

More screaming tires tell us that multiple cars have come to a stop behind us. A dull roar sounds in my head just before a colossal telekinetic wall slams into my protective shields. I dig my bare feet into the Clawson turf and grit my teeth as Tiberius Clawson comes flying over his front gates wearing an expression of utter fury. He must've gone somewhere after our meeting, a few of his guard beasts in tow.

And now they've returned, raging at the sight of their crumbling property.

Minnie sweeps her arms up and out before slamming them forwards in a telekinetic blast. Tiberius is thrown back in midair, but recovers, righting himself. Three tigers are throwing open the gates, and I focus on them as Minnie shouts something at Tiberius. These tigers are some of his best, no doubt, and one of them takes advantage of my quick glance at my friend, and I'm caught by a force that sends me flying backwards. I catch myself just in time, baring my shark's teeth.

They flinch at the sight of me. They flinch again as I hold their hearts under my power and squeeze until they burst. All three collapse at the same time, and Tiberius gapes at his beasts. That's when Minnie strikes. She drives a spear of her power right at his big old head, and it catches him, forcing his skull to snap backward. But

Tiberius is a nasty, strong beast, and he recovers quickly, roaring as he punches the air with power that makes Minnie skid backward. She's pouring sweat, breathing heavily now.

I realise she's not going to be able to do this alone. Something flickers at the edge of Tiberius. I blink hard as the image of a male, slightly taller than Tiberius, steps out from behind him. He's transparent, barely there, but I would recognise him even though I've only met him once, a very long time ago. He's impossibly tall, broad-shouldered, and has the same dark-haired features shared by all the Clawsons. The ghost of Cassius Clawson smiles at me.

I know sharks have the power to see ghosts and spirits, and I'd wondered if I would ever get to see one. Something in me is bonded anew as my mother's second mate casts his gaze around the property, a light shining in his eyes before he nods at his brother.

"He was always weak around his feet."

I blink at the deep voice, both near and distant at the same time, but Cassius doesn't take his eyes off his brother's sweating form. Without hesitation, I concentrate my power into a precise form, thin and straight. Throwing my hand diagonally across my body, I slice it through the air in a cut that ends by my side. Tiberius screams as he topples over.

Minnie roars, and I whip my head to see her tearing into tigress form and bounding over to the fallen beast. She's on him in seconds, tearing into his throat with violent canines. Blood spills as Minnie shakes Tiberius by the neck.

"I'm proud of you, child," Cassius says, looking up from them. His dark eyes are sad and shiny. "In another life, I would have heard you call me dad."

I blink my tears away, hardly believing it. That here and now, I meet my mother's second mate. "I'm sorry," is all I can choke out.

He gives me a handsome, wry smile, and suddenly, I can't believe my mother chose my father over this magnificent creature. "Don't be," he says. "I'm going to my regina now." A second later, he's nothing but a whisper on the night's breeze.

There's a strangled sound from the driveway, and I turn. Marduk and Yeti are staring at their regina with shocked awe. Marduk's face is glowing, and Yeti is rapidly blinking. Beak is next to them, a deep frown between his brows as he surveys the carnage. I see what he's looking at. It sort of looks bad, I suppose. "You came back?" is all I say.

Minnie snarls over Tiberius, looking at the newcomers with big, adrenaline-soaked eyes. Upon seeing her mates, she shifts back. "Oh, hi." Minnie pants heavily, picking out a piece of flesh from her mouth and pushing her pink locks back like she's just had an intense workout and not at all like she just brought down an entire mansion and is now covered in blood.

To be fair, what *does* one say after you've laid waste to your enemies?

"We felt it," Marduk says faintly.

"Your rage," Yeti finishes

Beak steps towards me, and I pull him aside to give the Devi pack some space. "Are you alright?" he asks.

"Yeah," I say casually. But really, my head feels like it's under a pillow, and I feel numb.

"We need to get out of here," Beak says urgently. "The human police will cause some problems. Can you—"

"We'll dragon it, yes," I say quickly.

We're in the sky two minutes later, once Marduk stops kissing Minnie's cheeks and realises blue and red lights are travelling down the street.

I'm wary of any pursuers as I fly. That feral part of me I always keep at bay opened right up with the fighting, and my blood is still hot from it. The council sends hunters after events like this, but with Tiberius being an underworld crime lord, they might leave it for the other crime lords to deal with. The falcons could come after us. Or they could pursue us on foot. Neither happens, however, and the skies are quiet and cool by the time I land on the hard stone of the animus dorm.

As I shift back into human form, my eyes are burning and my leg aches with old pain. But as I survey the dark skies, the dark grounds of my home, there are a number of things on my mind.

Minnie is in Yeti's arms, covered with a thick jacket, her eyes tightly closed as if she doesn't want to look at anything. I don't think I want to tell her I'm proud of her. They're not the right words.

Words aren't even enough now. She requires a medal of some kind, and I'll have to think about that at a later date.

But it's Sabrina who bursts out of the door, Blair and Blade behind her, who makes me stumble for the first time tonight. She lays eyes on Minnie and me, her hood thrown back, eyes wild and glistening. Her face crumples like tired paper, and she rushes at us with a sob. "You *said*—" My friend's voice crunches like old leaves as she draws us together. "You *said*—" Fingers dig into my arms, desperate for me to understand. "You said you'd do it, and you did."

"Kill them all," Minnie says thickly. This is the first emotion any of us have seen from Sabrina for months.

"And we did." I brush wet hair off her face. "Minnie and I took care of it."

"Thank you," Sabrina sobs. "Thank you."

It takes a while to calm our leopard friend down. In the end, Blair has to carry her back to the pack dorms. Minnie and I watch her in quiet, satisfied solidarity.

"There will be consequences," Marduk warns. To his credit, he doesn't accuse us of anything. Doesn't berate us as silly girls doing something reckless or insane. I think it's because he's just as nuts, but I appreciate it all the same.

"That's why I'm putting us in lockdown early," I say. "Beak, notify the guards. Same protocol as the heat lockdown. Take any tiger guards off the roster for a week. Wolves will be best, and I want the birds patrolling the northern highway. We'll probably be safe tonight, but tomorrow, I'll take the night watch myself." Beak nods, a slight smile on his lips as he leaves. I turn to Marduk and Yeti. "Did I miss anything?" I'm trying to take my new job as guardian seriously. I'm not even entirely sure what Celeste meant by it.

"Is your psychic shield around the school still active?" Yeti asks.

"Always is." My father is always a threat, and for all we know, Titus will go straight to him.

"Then there's nothing more we can do."

A sudden weariness creeps up my legs, and I feel the need to sit down. That feeling travels upwards, trying to drag me to the depths of hell. I expended a lot of power tonight. Minnie is in much the same position and will likely sleep for ages now, but at least she has her mates to help her feed and replenish her power.

I bid everyone a quick goodnight, and we depart. Minnie is hurried to the pack dorms, and Beak strides off to instruct our guards. I wander into the silence of my pack's suite, my ears still ringing, my skin still tingling from the flight. My excess of power had been a problem before I'd left for Drakos House, and I'd needed my mates to take my spillover. At Drakos Estate, it hadn't been a problem because I was recovering from Xander's mate severing. Then re-growing my leg had taken all of me. It still takes a lot out of me to deal with the newness of it, and of course, the ongoing pain. For the first time in a long time, I feel depleted.

I rummage for microwave meals in the freezer and find one, setting it up to heat while I sit at the dining table. Alone. "I wish you were here," I whisper into the night.

Chapter 12

Xander

A call comes after midnight on Katerina's personal phone. She wakes with a grumble, huffing up at Scythe, who stands still beside her bed. I won't let him so much as sit on it, no matter how much it makes my ears bleed to hear her screaming.

After my display with the animal activists, she trusts me a little more, taking off my shackles as long as I'm in my cell beside her bed. She says it's so she knows whether my eyes are open or closed in the dark, and it gives me great satisfaction to know that she finds my empty eyes creepy at night.

"What?" she snaps into her phone.

My ears perk up. She often gets calls in the middle of the night, but it's always about 'product' or 'stock', and it's never made her react like this. I keep my eyes closed to avoid attention but listen keenly to the voice on the other side of the phone.

"Clawson House is in ruins," a male voice says. "Two of them were there. The tigress I don't know, but the Boneweaver girl was by her side."

My heart stops beating. Aurelia and Minnie were at Clawson House. Whatever the fuck for?

"Let me get this straight," Katerina says, pointing violently at the air. "Tiberius is dead, Aurelia Boneweaver did it, and this all happened just now."

"The tigress took his throat," clarifies the male. "I don't know where Titus is. They killed a few others, but *his* body is nowhere to be found, so we assume he is alive."

I almost choke on my own spit and have to crack my eyes open to see this once-in-a-lifetime scene. Katerina leaps out of bed, hurls herself out the bedroom door, and doesn't see my light. I stare at the open doorway in shocked disbelief, and some new, insane feeling that might very well be pride.

What the actual fuck, Lia?

Slumping against the wall, I toy with my earring, trying to think of the possibilities. It's because of this that I'm still awake when I feel it. Something I've only felt once before, in Halfeather's dungeon, so long ago.

A regina's call.

This time, I know what to expect, and my astral form practically leaps out of my body. I stride through the bars of my cell to check on my brothers. Lyle and Savage are still in beast form, snoring in their cells, with no sign of their astral forms. Scythe remains stock still in his corner.

Looks like I'm seeing Lia alone. Eagerly, I shoot up towards the ceiling and right through the solid brick. Flying in human form is so strange, but I'm lifted by pure magic into the night and over the land at roughly the same speed as my dragon form.

Halfeather's dungeon was only a few suburbs away from where Lia used to live behind Charlotte Naga's house, but Animus Academy is hours away from The Collector's property in the outback. It takes a while to get there, but by the time I'm sinking down through the roof of the animus dorm and into the living room, I'm riled up, heart pounding and ready for...I can't even describe what.

"I can't believe you did that," I drawl, striding into the bedroom.

Lia whips her hand out from inside her shorts, where she'd been playing with herself, and sits bolt upright in outrage. There is a sheen of dust and sweat on her skin as well as fine specks of blood. Her dark hair is loose and tousled in a halo around her.

"I didn't think it was working!"

"It was just far is all."

"Are you— Are they—" She looks behind me, which hurts a little, looking for her mates.

"They can't come," I say. "I checked the cell next to me before I left..." I trail off as I realise this was the wrong thing to say because she leaps out of bed and storms—hobbles, to my dismay—up to me with pure rage in her eyes.

"Did you just fucking say *cell,* Xander Drakos?"

I see it in stark definition. The rage that carried her to Clawson House and tore it down. "I've always known there was dragon fire in you," I say softly, meeting her rage with pure, solemn awareness.

Her eyes drop to my neck, where my new, black mark shines with all the light of midnight. Those sapphires are engulfed by her pupils and I watch in fascination. She casts her gaze away, glancing at the room behind her. "Ghoul didn't come either," she sneers.

"He's likely unable to step away considering the chaos right now."

"Right." She sounds disappointed.

A growl awakens in my chest. "Are you— You can't *like* him, Aurelia."

Her eyes narrow, dark lashes framing her rage. "What a strange thing for *you* to say, Xander."

I take the hit, like I'll take every hit from her from now on. "Point taken."

Her power surges around her in an aura of red and black— something I've never seen from her before—eyes glistening, posture feral. She is wild in a way that I once would have sneered at because I didn't know what it meant. Now I understand that it's her full force coming out. She's showing who she really is underneath all the shields. She's showing everyone what real power looks like.

It gives me goosebumps.

It's then that I notice a tremble at the edges of her being. With some alarm, I see that she's depleted her power. "Have you eaten?"

She scowls at me, her rage only growing. "I hate you." Whipping around, she paces the room, her sore leg giving her an uneven gait. "Tell me about these cells my mates are in. Are they being fed? Is she hurting them?" A regina in full force. Slightly unhinged, but in full control. No one else could be regina of my brothers. "Wipe that fucking smile off your face." Her eyes are murderous on me, staring unblinking at my form. Her nostrils flare, unconsciously looking for my scent.

"If you're going to kill me, I'll wholeheartedly let you," I say. "But can it wait a week or so? We need to plan—"

"Fuck your plans. Fuck everything!" she hisses, stepping up to me threateningly.

Yes, baby, *yes*.

Even being the second-worst-mate in existence, I know what my regina needs. I step around her rigid body and lean down to whisper in her ear. "Let me fuck your fury out of you."

Aurelia shivers, her bare shoulders trembling. But she wants to be angry. Whirling around, she smacks me across the cheek with the full force of her body. Before now, she's been too tired, in too much pain to be furious at me. At the world. But with her dragon at the forefront, with fire threatening to split her veins, she has finally given herself permission.

So I don't move. Don't so much as flinch. I take it with my eyes closed, savouring my regina's furore. "Good girl," I whisper. "Now do it again."

She stands on her tiptoes. "Don't tell me what to do," she whisper-yells right into my face.

Once, I might have pulled away. Now, I press closer, touching my forehead to hers. "One of the things I always thought I hated about you was your need to fight for those you love. For your friends. For Savage, Lyle, and Scythe. A part of me wished someone would have fought for me when—"

She shoves at my chest with a choked noise, storming away for all of three steps before she storms right back, poking me hard in the sternum. "Let's get one thing very fucking clear, *Xander Drakos*. There is no one in *any* world who can take my mates from me. There is nowhere you can hide. Nowhere *they* can hide *you*. I will destroy everything and everyone in my path until you are all back in my nest. *Including*"—she bares her teeth at me—"your cursed ass. Is that understood?"

My hand flies to my heart as something crumples in me. I didn't realise how much I needed to hear that. How much my soul needed to hear my regina declare herself for me. It's my dragon that comes forward, his voice nothing but gravel and smoke as he steals the words from my mouth. "Yes, my queen. You are ever merciful."

Her eyes simmer as she glares at me with pure, feral grace. "Call me regina!" she cries, her voice near shrill.

I can hardly believe it—my luck, the gift she's just given me. I have to wrangle my excited dragon back so the human in me gets to drop to his knees and whisper, "Yes, regina."

The movement seems to placate her as she grabs my chin in a painful grip and demands, "Now kiss me."

I surge upwards, crashing my mouth into hers. She claims my bottom lip with her teeth, biting hard enough to draw blood. I groan, catching her around the waist and pulling her down onto me. It doesn't fucking matter that I'm in astral form, apparently; when a Boneweaver regina wants to fuck her non-corporeal dragon-mate, she will. Her legs come around me as she drags her fingernails up my arms and rips my shirt open. Astral buttons go flying to either side before she wrenches the material off me.

Aurelia almost tears her tank top when removing it, and I can't help but drag my teeth down the column of her neck. She cries out, grinding against me. "Fuck, I can taste you," I say as her scent, her sweat, fills my nose and mouth. She is sweet and salty, fiery and smoky all in one. Like golden vanilla lit on fire.

In response, she buries her hands in the hair at my scalp, tangling the long strands between her fingers, and wrenching my head backwards. She hovers her mouth over mine, and it's torture not to be able to kiss her. Her breath is smoke, and it streams over our faces. I bunch the top of her shorts in my fists.

"I could blast fire onto your face, Xander," she snarls softly.

"And I would love every fucking second of it." Fabric screams as I tear her shorts in two, and she scrambles out of them and undoes the zip of my trousers. She tugs them off in commanding, hurried movements, her naked body, blazing with heat, touched by moonlight and waiting for my tongue.

There is no underwear gracing her body, nothing between us as she settles onto me and shoves her tongue into my mouth, biting and sucking like she wants to tunnel into me. She tugs on my hair, and I find her clit with soft fingers, already wet for me. She makes a sound of discontent and grabs my hand, pressing me harder into her, showing me how she wants me to be. How she needs me to devour her.

It's all the permission I need to grab her around the waist and wrench us to standing, before tossing her onto the bed. She bounces on the mattress, her face terrifying and beautiful. But I lunge for her, commanding her wrists and holding them above her head, angling my cock against her entrance.

"Fucker," she spits.

I lick up the centre of her breasts, stroking up her neck until I get to her ear. She struggles against me. "Remember your safe word, regina?" I rumble.

"Fairy bread," she pants. I would do anything to shove my cock in her aggressively like she wants, but we've only fucked twice so far and my cock is still the biggest in the continent. So instead, I rub myself against her vulva, coating it in her slick. "Just put it in, you asshole."

The light from my eyes illuminates her face as I gaze upon her, angling my hips down again. "Impatient regina." My voice is rough from the exertion of holding myself back. She arches her spine as I tease her entrance, trying to get me inside by locking her ankles around my hips.

I release her wrists so I can graze my palm down her breast and toy with one dark, perfect nipple. She wants more stimulation, needs more of me, and I can't help but need more of her. My cock twitches as I urge it inside of her, feeling her tense and flex around me. I don't have the cock ring with her name on it right now, but it's her moan that makes my balls grow heavy with need. "Gods, you are perfect," I groan against her neck.

"Gods, you're a jerk," she pants, squirming as I fill her completely. "Fuck, Xander."

Her insides are flooding, dripping hot onto my cock and driving me to insanity. It takes everything I have, but I wrench my cock out. "On your fucking knees."

She makes a strangled sound out of outrage as I rear back, and it's not quick enough, so I grab her good leg and flip her over. She scrambles onto her knees, throwing her long hair over one shoulder as she tries to strike me again, but I grab her hips and wrench her against my cock. Grabbing a fistful of her hair, I give her what she wants and shove my cock into her, faster this time.

She screams in satisfaction, fisting the sheets of the bed. I tug her head back and thrust into her, hard, one hand cupping her neck to open her mouth into mine. I fuck Aurelia as she kisses me, her tongue furious and demanding. And when she breaks for air, I fuck her harder, sending my power into her, sending her strength for what she needs to do. She takes all of me, screaming into the ceiling, her eyes clenched shut, sweat glistening on her skin.

My regina only gets wetter, tensing around me like she needs even more. I let go of her hair and reach for her dripping pussy, coating my thumb until it's soaking. I rear back just enough to position my thumb at her sweet asshole, teasing the entrance with each thrust. Aurelia lets out a strangled, "More," and I am but a servant, so I give it to her, burying my thumb into her heat, working that tight circle of muscle.

She comes with a shaking vibration, her body twitching around my cock so hard that I come instantly. My cum roars towards her cervix, and I have to remove my thumb, gripping her stuttering hips as I slam my release into my regina. Her power reaches out towards mine, a golden band that twines around my own darker storm. Light and dark, they dance and spin, and I crack my first grin in what feels like years as Aurelia's power caresses my own. I send all of me into her, filling her reserve, and she sucks it all in, accepting it hungrily.

When she is sated, Aurelia collapses onto the bed, and I follow her, keeping myself inside her as long as possible. I don't want this to end. I don't want to leave her here all alone. My heart breaks at the thought of it. I need to clean her. To feed her. To hold her safe in our bed and hear everything she did today in minute detail. To rub balm onto her sore leg and send my healing into it. Her hair is a tangled mess, and there is no one to brush it.

"Go," she whispers into the fingers she has pressed against her lips. "Go and tell them I love them. Tell them I'll tear the world apart for them."

It takes every ounce of my dark will to take my cock out of my regina and leave her in the pack bed. In this moment, I hate the world. I hate what I am even more than I did before. I was a broken, cursed beast before today. But now, I feel like a whole other part of me has died.

Chapter 13

Ghoul

This is perhaps one of the few reasons Lady Katerina Crocodylus would exit her compound and leave her most prized collections behind. She does bring Xander with her, still untrusting of the silent dragon, and when she enters Naga House, he stalks in front of her, before slipping off to the side like a bodyguard.

I make a show of craning my neck to make sure his headphones are in place. Those glowing eyes don't show what direction he's looking in, but I know he'd be sneering if he had the choice. "The silver collar almost matches his eyes," I say in greeting.

"General," The Collector coos, in leather pants and a black halter neck tonight. She reminds me of Catwoman with her red lipstick.

I never liked Catwoman.

"All you need are little black ears," I say, putting my gloved index fingers beside my head, pointing upwards. "Then you're ready to burgle yet another regina's pack from her."

Her dark eyes simmer as she regards me. "Jealous, love? I wish Mace would let me have your basilisk ass. You would look so lovely on a chain."

I bare my drawn fangs in a smile. "As much as I enjoy chains, my lady, I tend to kill my lovers. So...perhaps it would be a good pairing after all."

Her lids lower, unimpressed, but she doesn't get a chance to reply as Charlotte Naga, escorted by Generals Adder, Brown and Taipan, bustles from the dining room. "You're here. Lovely. Come through, Lady Crocodylus."

Titus already sits in the dining room, with a bourbon and empty plate beside him. He was in a right state when he turned up, near hysterical, and now he glowers at us as we join him at the table. Mace stands on the far side, near two wingback armchairs. In them are the wolf and avian queens, their wrists bound in tourmaline shackles.

"You really did it," Katerina says, stopping short to stare at the captives. "I'm impressed, Mace."

"Of course he did it," Titus says through his metal jaw. "They were all a bunch of fucking idiots, and the human politicians will love this."

"Your own achievement is profound," Mace says in a way that gives away nothing about his real feelings. Everyone here is a mate-betrayer. By anyone's measure, the worst people on the planet are in this room. But everyone turns to Xander, who also schools his fine, dragon features. I wonder what he sees with his magical eyeballs.

"I've done my part well," The Collector says, taking a seat at the table. "We've eliminated our main enemies. What's your next move?"

"The next fucking move is to avenge my father," Titus snarls, thumping his meaty fist on the table. "I want that Boneweaver girl dead."

"I do not want the *last* Boneweaver on the planet *dead*," Mace says evenly. Katerina nods in agreement.

"Then something needs to be done about her," Titus snaps. "She's out of control, and this is the first of it, you mark my words." He quiets, scowling into space. "You didn't see her eyes. They were *mad*. Get her out of the fucking country. Hell, get her off of the fucking planet, if that's what it takes."

"She'll be depleted after this attack," Mace says, glancing at me. "I will take care of it."

My shadows tug at me. They've always had a little mind of their own, and now they caress my own mating mark, my cheek, drawing up to my eyes where they are always at their thickest, protecting the rest of the world from me.

The urge to kill everyone is something I always have to fight back. A little laser beam here and there, and the world would be totally different. That level of power is something the others have always been wary of. But Mace would never let me around his family unless he was sure I wouldn't get tempted. The various marks on my body itch. Mace's venom. My own. Aurelia's.

"If I might suggest..." Katerina drawls, running a red fingernail across the lacquered mahogany. "The girl has proven strong. Even what Flores and I did didn't break her. But I think we've come close with the loss of her mates. She is wild in her movements. If she continues on a rampage, she will act without precision. I think we can get even closer with just one more little push." The Collector sits back. "I still want my money's worth from that girl. It's a lot of zeros for no eggs, Mace."

Her concern is for her business only. She doesn't care about Aurelia's welfare, only that she got her chance at breeding whatever it was she kept in the dark under her property. That, even *I* haven't figured out yet. "It better not be a sloth you're trying to stud," I say. "Or some exotic pigeon from Peruvia."

The Collector gives me a look that suggests she wants to gouge my eyes out and toast them like marshmallows over a campfire. "I need to be heading back."

"You won't stay?" Charlotte says with surprise. "It's almost dawn."

"I want to get back," Katerina repeats. It gives me great delight to see her fretting like this. To see her *paranoid.*

"To your pack," I confirm. "Or swamp? What *is* a group of crocodiles called again?"

"A group of crocs is called a death trap," Titus growls, proving he's useless once again.

"And the metal-head knows some words," I say in a surprised voice as The Collector gets up from the table, muttering under her breath.

"I'll be in touch," she announces.

Mace strides over, examining Xander standing stoic and

listening by the door. "Your father would not have taken you back if it were not for me," he murmurs, low and arrogant. "I suggested it may be one of the few things to break the company of Scythe Kharkorous, and I was right." He smirks, reaching up to pat the dragon on the cheek. "You did the job better than anyone else could." Xander gives no reaction. Not so much as a lip twitch or an eye flicker. I'm impressed. Mace turns to Katerina. "Watch the evening news tonight. You won't want to miss my announcement."

Ah, yes. Phase two is about to begin.

Chapter 14

Aurelia

Beak meets me on the animus roof the next night, settling his giant claws onto the wall and fluffing out his wings. The academy is in complete lockdown, to the chagrin of many of the students. But word has gotten around, whether from illicit phones or via the wolves, of what happened at Clawson House and everyone settles down quickly. The eagles, falcons, and a few cockatoos—whichever avians Beak trusts—have been patrolling the main roads all day, as asked.

"Anything to report?" I ask, crossing my arms as I survey the night sky. There is a chill in the world that makes me want to rub my arms, but I can tell it's the absence of my mates that has me feeling cold.

I can still feel the aftereffects of Xander's *significant* presence inside me last night. With his healing funnelling through me, my leg has not ached at all today. The sight of his towering astral form sauntering through my door ignited me in a way bloodlust had not. He had not been the first ghostly person I *wanted* to see. I'd wanted to hear Savage's singing voice or Scythe's glinting eyes, or Lyle's imposing stride. But when I saw him, something in me realised he was the one I'd *needed* to see the most. That black mark...those glowing eyes...the arrogant posture.

He understands what it means to be alone. He understood that, in that moment, I needed fire and brimstone. Scythe has always said that Xander and I are more alike than I think. We are mirrors, and it triggers both of us to see our reflections.

Presently, Beak shifts into human form to be able to speak. He keeps his front respectfully angled towards the grounds, so I don't have to see all of him. "Nothing of note all day." Those sharp eyes are dilated as they take in every inch of me under the sliver of the moon.

It's dark tonight. A night for predators.

Something in him knows that about me now. Perhaps they'd always sensed it, but males have an awful habit of using what they see with their eyes over their good sense. Now that he's seen what I can do, what I wilfully have done, he's...enamoured.

"Keep away from me," I warn, stretching out my shoulders and tugging off my stretchy mini dress. "I'm not in the mood for talking tonight. I'll rest once every three hours. Who is my partner?"

"Me, my lady."

I nod, and shift into dragon form. Beak explodes into his eagle form reflexively, getting out of the way by diving down. I spear upwards and through the blue dome, leaving beak to use the avian guards' exit in one of the watchtowers. He'd told me the best way to patrol the academy was for two fliers to do that, one flying clockwise, and the other anticlockwise. I'll be flying a lot higher than him with my bigger size, but this way, we won't get lazy-eyed by the unchanging landscape.

My nighttime vision as a dragon is superior to anything else. I can see heat signatures in tiny specs below, so anyone in a moving car would flag my attention right away. It takes me over an hour to settle into the patrol. I'm hypervigilant and locked in from the get-go, and the agitation from the awareness of my possible oncoming enemies never fades.

With the lockdown, I can't talk to my friends except by phone, and Minnie was in no mood to talk today. Yeti graciously told Sabrina and Stacey about what had happened while I brooded in my room. I don't even get the comfort of Henry or Eugene for the next three days while I wait for the consequences of what Minnie and I had done.

The council had been all too keen to request my execution

before. They had been all too keen to take Savage to Blackwater Prison. I'm sure my father will use this as a way to spin the story to make me look mad and in need of putting away or something worse, and they would surely come to the academy to confront me.

Rufus and Marduk rang me this morning and asked if I wanted to go into hiding somewhere else. Their voices had been cautious, as if already knowing the answer.

"I've done the passive thing," I'd said. "I've tried hiding. I've tried waiting. I even gave myself to them. Enough of that."

My phone had rung again after Marduk, the number unknown. I didn't pick it up. Instead, I rang Hyacinth Dabu and asked her some more questions, then I consulted some of the serpent textbooks Beak had brought me from the library.

I've made observations. I've had…thoughts.

There are no Council of Beasts trucks blasting down the road for the rest of the night. It's not until the 5 p.m. news the next night that my spoon halts five centimetres in the air above my microwave-ready meal. Beak sits straighter on the armchair next to me.

Minnie's name flashes across my phone, and I pick up. "Turn on the news," she says.

"Already watching it."

My father is on the screen, his gaunt face covered in makeup to give his ashen complexion colour back. Darkness hovers around him, coiling like a cobra ready to strike.

Has struck. Because the headline reads:

NEWLY APPOINTED COUNCIL OF BEASTS AUDITOR HRH MACE NAGA SAYS CORRUPTION MUST BE STOPPED AND CHANGES MUST BE MADE.

My father smiles, and it gives me the feeling of being yanked under water. "We've discovered several concerning things regarding the running of the council. I'll be conducting a full investigation. Until then, I've been given full license to ensure everything continues to run smoothly. The safety of the human population has never been a priority. The event a few nights ago proves that this is out of hand. Things need to change. We're going to do it together."

He shakes hands with the human state premier, a woman with long brown hair, who smiles widely while everyone claps. Flashes from multiple cameras light up their faces and white teeth.

"He's been given full authority," Minnie says in disbelief. "Who authorised that?"

"He did," I say simply, sitting back on the couch as venom suddenly burns in my gums. "He's always wanted this. Always planned it. This was his long game." I laugh, and even to me, it sounds cold. "He actually fucking did it with our help, Min. He's got the council members in a hole somewhere, using what we did as his excuse." And he'd twisted our carnage to his advantage. We'd *accelerated* his plans.

"I'll find out what I can." Marduk's voice is faint on the line as he no doubt stares at the TV like we all do. "But I'll need to leave."

"They could be dead, for all we know," I say. "Some of them, at least." My mind wanders to my fifth mate.

Chapter 15

Aurelia

"**M**aybe we made a mistake that night, Lia," Minnie says, her eyes red-rimmed. "Maybe I shouldn't have killed Tiberius."

The lockdown is over, and we're sitting with Raquel in their hospital room again. Henry and Eugene are perched on the wolf anim's legs, gazing at their face. This is not the first time that Minnie has said these words to me. "It's normal to doubt yourself after killing someone, Min," I say gently. "But you did the right thing."

She's not sure of herself. But I am. Especially after seeing the state of the medical wing with the number of poisoning patients who are still here, including Stacey. The place is still in chaos, and short staffing is such a problem that I've been charting Raquel's observations for them while we're here. We'd helped shower Stacey this morning and put her safely back into bed to rest so the nurses could attend to the sicker patients.

Tiberius was not only responsible for them, but for the Lily Institute's destruction *and* Cassius Clawson's death, and by the look Sabrina is giving me, she thinks the exact same: The Clawsons needed to be put down. "You'll get over it, Min," Sabrina says darkly. "Blair and Blade say you get used to killing beasts after a while." Wisdom from assassins doesn't help Minnie in her fretting.

"I've never been more sure of something," I say. My best friend looks at me like she's not sure I'm well. "I understand you think I might be biased," I say evenly. "But my father's new political position has only proven me right. He means..." I don't want to scare my friends. I don't need them more fearful than they are. But they don't know Mace Naga behind closed doors. They don't know the level of his ambition and the lengths he'll go to. The lengths he's been planning since even before he became the leader of the serpent court. I take a deep breath. "I'm just going to say that the signs are all pointing things out to me. We need to take action."

"Like what, Lia?" Minnie breathes.

"I need my mates back," I say firmly. "That's first."

Eugene clucks in agreement, and I hand him a blueberry. Henry has understood that I've needed my space lately. That Stacey, Raquel and Sabrina have all needed him more than me. No doubt the violence pounding through my veins at every moment has set his psychic metres on alarm. But he turns to me now, those huge, liquid black eyes glistening. I hold out my hand, and he chirps in greeting, levitating himself to settle onto my palm. I raise him to my face, and he licks me on the nose.

"You're doing a good job," I whisper to him. "You're such a good nimpin." He closes his eyes and sways a little, enjoying my voice. My hand trembles. Hastily, I lower him to the mattress. Henry tries to find the source of my anger in my eyes. I'm afraid that if he looks too long, he'll find it. "Such a small creature shouldn't carry such large burdens. Leave that to the big, nasty beasts."

"Leave that to the big boss bitch," Sabrina drawls. "The head of Kharkorous Enterprises." Why does my heart twang every time she says that? *Because it means he's not here to look after things. It means his shark eyes aren't going to appear around that corner and pierce my soul.*

In Henry's eyes, I see trust. I see the same in Sabrina's. Even Minnie, despite her current torment about the Clawsons, trusts me implicitly. I realise it with all the force of a cricket bat to the head. I know Raquel would trust me too. That's why they came for me the night Savage asked them to help contact me at Drakos Estate.

Eventually, me and my thoughts leave my friends for the library. Eugene alone tails me like a faithful shadow as I head for the section on serpents. The academy must have hidden books away at some point, only to reveal them later. Everything we could find, I've taken back to our dorms, and we've exhausted the school's supply. But I hunger for more. So I get out my phone and call someone I've been avoiding speaking to.

"Aurelia?" The soft voice is gentle in my ear, but there is a new power that Selena Drakos carries with her now.

"I'm sorry I didn't call sooner," I say. "I...didn't know—"

"I understand," she says, a door closing in the background. "Are you alright? Have you heard anything? I've been scouring the news and social media, but everything is quiet, and with Mother's treasure haze, we have to keep a low profile. She won't let me leave."

I'd since learned that a treasure haze originated from hard-won or hard-spent objects from a time where dragons lived in mounds of their own gold and jewels. Eventually, it transitioned to parents and children, and then, between mates. Lady Drakos had nearly died in the fight to kill Flores, and she'd won Drakos Estate. It will be impossible to approach those lands without incurring her wrath.

"The lady of the castle is okay?" I ask.

"She's obsessive about feeding the hatchlings and cleaning them. They think it's funny and pretend to go into treasure hazes over silly things like chocolate and their plushies. We're all good here; we just have to wait this out."

Reassured by this, I move onto business. "You heard about Clawson House?"

I give her a quick recap and expect to get berated for it, but she seems to understand my heightened state because all she says is, "I wish I was there to help you."

"I'm going to get them back, Selena," I say.

She says the one thing that could give me heart right now. "I know you are."

"Are you able to access your underground library?" I ask. "I'm researching a few things." We speak for a while after that, and Selena tells me she's going to scan some pages and email them to me, since Lady Drakos is only letting food delivery drivers in and out of the house right now.

That night during my patrol, I return to the top of the animus dorm for my three-hourly break to find five missed calls from Rufus, my new advisor. Swearing under my breath, I return his call. He picks up on the first ring. "Lady Boneweaver, you need to see this video that's currently circulating all over social media. I have done my best to take down any reposts, but it's gone viral and spreading fast—"

I look down at my screen to see the video he's sent me and almost drop my phone in the process. Under the strobe lights of a nightclub, Katerina Crocodylus wears a sexy outfit that is more lingerie than dress, lounging on a red loveseat in a roped-off area. On her hand is that nefarious silver bangle she wears with the chains. But connected to them this time are four all too familiar figures.

The other pieces of my soul are chained to her, their heads bowed, their naked skin bare for everyone to see, coloured lights bouncing off them like there's something to celebrate. Only Scythe is clothed, his signature black shirt crisp, those silver strands ever perfect. The Collector laughs over her shoulder, replying to something unintelligible. "The Boneweaver girl can come and see them if she wants. See if they want her back." Everyone around her laughs.

All I see is red.

I explode into dragon form and roar into the night. The building shakes beneath me. Somewhere, glass breaks. There are screams from inside. Tearing into the sky, I'm nothing but a terror of muscle and sinew in the dark.

Chapter 16

Aurelia

Pushing my dragon's body to its full acceleration makes my blood roar with satisfaction. I charge through the air like a battering ram, following the four golden threads and one dark, tattered thread from my phoenix sight that all point in one direction.

My mates. The pieces of my soul are still tethered to me. Nothing could sever that except wilful breaking. As it is, Xander's mark is still there, only dark and frayed like an ancient flag.

The land blurs beneath me, and I'm glad for my second, clear eyelid snapping into place on autopilot because that wind could cut a bitch. It's not long before the bright lights of the city twinkle before me. There's no draconic welcome here like at Animus Academy, only unassuming points of light. But this city has never seen a dragon like me.

I come upon it invisible and silent, letting my threads pull me in the right direction. It takes only a minute to realise where this confrontation will take place. The Jewel of the Jungle. They had been at some other club in the video, and this move feels purposeful. Katerina knew I would come.

Suddenly, my senses are painfully sharp, and every sound and smell hits me. Everyone knows I was at Clawson House, and for all I know, this entire event has been to lure me out of Animus Academy. Well, trap, I see you and I raise you one. Boneweavers don't do traps, we fucking smash through them.

I begin my spiralling descent, circling the place and marking it with dragon eyes. There are as many cars parked here as there were the day of my debut. Every forsaken criminal beast of the city must be here to see *the show*. Heat fills my lungs, and as I exhale black smoke, I narrow my eyes at the surroundings of the Jewel. There is nowhere for a dragon to land. Oh well.

I pick out a group of expensive-looking cars—Mercs, two custom-painted Lambos, and a sleek limousine. Only when I'm twenty feet from the ground, do I reveal myself, throwing off the invisibility shield and extending my feet. Male shouts sound from the Jewel's entrance, but they're quickly swamped by the CRASH of metal collapsing under my heavy dragon legs.

It sends a twinge up my new leg, but I let out a roar of annoyance and that seems to make everything better. There's a metallic shriek as I climb off the now-tangled mess of metal, my claws scratching against the steel, but my eyes are on the multiple beasts sprinting towards me, their mouths dropping open.

"*Keep back,*" I spit into their minds, throwing out a band of telekinesis to shove them all backward. It's really annoying that I didn't think about bringing clothes. The last time I'd entered the Jewel, it had been on a leash, also naked. At that time, being naked had been a power move of Xander's. Now, I'm going to have to make this a power move of my own.

Huffing in warning at the males gaping at me, I shift into my human form. The first time I shifted down from my dragon form, I'd felt vulnerable, a little less powerful assuming my human skin. Right now, I forget about all that and sink into my dragon's brain further as I shrink. My tough hide disappears, but I lower my head into a predator's posture, focusing my attention on the enemies at the perimeter. A cool wind brushes over my flaming hot skin, but I don't cover my body with my hands and instead sink into a stalk right past my audience. My power floods the carpark so I can feel for anyone coming up behind me, at the same time giving warning to every beast in the vicinity:

The strongest regina in the city has arrived, and she's in the mood to kill.

I let my power flood into my new leg, making sure I don't show any sort of hobble or weakness there. The scars on my stomach might show, and eagles might be able to tell my legs are different, but it doesn't matter.

Making my way towards the entrance, I let the leers of the males bounce off me. I'm not in the mood to entertain this fuckery tonight. With my heart pounding the beat of a war drum, I clear the carpark and follow the path up to the guarded entrance. The beasts follow behind me, two of them running up ahead with great urgency. Every step heats my blood. Every breath I exhale is black smoke.

There are four guards at the entrance, none of whom are hyenas or tigers. There is one croc, to my surprise, a bear, and two serpents. "Looking good for a little—"

The serpent has no time to react as I throw out a whip of telekinesis and lash it around his throat, constricting it so hard he starts flailing in silence. I don't give up until he's crumpled on the ground like old clothes. Without a second glance, I continue inside.

And it feels different this time. The Jewel of the Jungle always had this sense of latent danger. A place where the wrong look, the wrong word between parties could end in a massacre. Indeed, both times I'd been here *had* ended in bloodshed.

That scent of lifesblood never goes away. It's just mixed with alcohol, ferality, and sex. My power builds around me like unfurling wings, and I let it brush against the walls, the ceiling, the floor. I send my awareness out to the entire space and the creatures that lie within it, letting my steady heart beat set the tempo of my stalk.

An anima in gold lingerie halts when she feels my power, her tray of drinks trembling before she slowly turns around in the way of prey, swivelling on a stiletto in a smooth, predictable motion. Finally seeing me, she inclines her head and steps back to indicate she's not a threat. I don't acknowledge her because my prey lies elsewhere in this watering hole. Gentle light touches my face as I step onto the main floor. The bar lies on the far right, lined with beasts, and it's packed like a theatre in here.

The low couches and tables are grouped into claimed order sections. Everyone keeps to their own company here unless there is a specific reason to interact. My blood sizzles as I stalk down the main aisle, immediately catching the combined scent of my mates. My heart nearly stops when I see them. A shriek resounds in my head.

The crocodile has come out of the water, presenting herself as if on show for the world to see. Her claimed area is against the wall, where she sits like a queen on a low-back chair. Nothing I've been through, nothing I've endured, barring the death of my mother, has been worse than this.

She has...undone them. Like a child tearing off the wings of butterfly for their own amusement.

They are on leashes in human form, kneeling before her chair like dogs. Xander's eyes are lowered to the floor. Savage has a heavy black muzzle and is covered in lacerations and bruises, telling me his beating was recent. Lyle has his white teeth bared in much the same way his shifted form is wont to do, and he too has recent signs of injury. It makes me wonder if they had shifted and then been beaten back into human form.

Scythe sits on the floor by The Collector's knee, and her hand strokes his silver hair. In this heightened state, I see everything. Every drop of blood, every marking...including Ghoul sitting in the next lounge area over, the serpent's corner. There is something about his presence here that focuses me. His eyes on my face, the faint lethal red flaring through the shadows as if to warn me. I can almost hear him saying, *"Control, snakelet."*

The Collector raises her chin, red lips curved as her eyes flick to slitted and back again. Her voice drips with mockery. "They kneel for me, as they never did for you." *I would never have made them.* Savage for fun, Xander out of revenge, but never like this. "A *worthy* regina," she drawls, blowing out smoke in lazy rings.

I've questioned my own worth many times. In my own head, in my own actions. But not anymore. Not when I've seen the consequences of it. I had been born to face beasts like this. I had been born tethered to five of the most dangerous monsters, and today, they rely upon me to be their *apex* monster. This creature is nothing.

I level Katerina with a look. She smiles at me. I don't return it. Nor do I blink as I mark her. The particular shade of hazel in her eyes is a mixture of mouldy green and rotten brown—the colour of life bleeding away. Her heartbeat, fast when I'd entered her area, now settles. The pulse at her pale neck flutters, the vein thick with lifesblood.

She thought I'd attack her here.

The crocodile within me lifts her eyes above the waters of my consciousness. I know when my pupils change. I see her own dilate as she notes it with some surprise. Savage whines. That's what sets me off. The ground beneath us shakes. Then the walls. It extends to the ceiling. Somebody behind me yelps as glass smashes and liquid spills.

Out of all the beings in this terrible world, it's Xander who saves me. *"Not now,"* his voice is almost smoke in my brain. *"Not now, regina. You are outnumbered. Did you come alone? Fuck. Not now, Aurelia."*

I clench my jaw, and the power surge recedes.

"Struggling with control, Lady Boneweaver?" Katerina drawls.

How little her mind is that she doesn't understand she walks on a knife's edge. It takes a deep breath for me to centre myself, another to be able to speak. My voice emerges steady and deep, with a strange gravelly edge that makes all the predators in the room pay attention. "When I'm out of control, Lady Crocodylus, it'll be too late by the time you notice it."

It's Scythe who draws my eyes. It's an imperceptible change, but my psychic senses come alive in that moment. He blinks. His pupils move from his mistress to me. My heart all but leaps out of my ribs.

"Yes," Katerina drawls, pulling my attention back to her. "I've heard of your...instability. It's a shame you can't get any help for that, what with the Lily Institute *gone* and all."

"Oh yes," I say without hesitation. "In the same way you haven't yet been able to get help for the unicorn you keep beneath your house. Beautiful creature that Lorian. Such a shame."

Her eyes flash with rage as every beast in the Jewel of the Jungle goes still.

Ghoul cackles in my head. *"Oh, you sly, sly snakelet. Creature of my heart and soul."*

I rake my eyes over The Collector's perfect skin as she no doubt plots her revenge on me. Crocodile skin, impenetrable even to bullets.

"Lorian is dead," she says far too quickly, and I see the lie hovering around her like a black spot with my shark's eyes. "He succumbed to the injury you couldn't heal. Perhaps Boneweaver healing isn't as powerful as we all thought."

"Perhaps," I sigh wistfully. "Perhaps my other powers are starting to take precedence." I scratch the side of my mouth with my left thumb, the barest hint of my fangs showing as my lips part.

Clasping my hands in front of me, I try not to look at my mates, who only have eyes for the floor as they've no doubt been ordered. The rest of the beasts follow my every movement with bated breath. Just waiting for a weakness. Just waiting for blood to spill. I step forwards and hold out my hand. "Well played, Lady Crocodylus."

Her eyes drop down to my hand, and I watch her make quick calculations about my intentions. Would ignoring my hand be perceived as a power move? But if she doesn't, she might look weak. Might look too scared to touch me. She gives in, puffing out another plume of bitter smoke before lazily holding out her hand.

I grin with my teeth as I take her hand, squeezing just the polite amount. "A less than worthy adversary," I say softly. My palm tingles, and I watch the smile slide off her face before I let go.

As my heart squeezes with pain, as my soul screams with rage and torment for my mates, I do what must be done. I turn my back on them all and leave.

Chapter 17

Xander

Girl with One Eye – Florence and the Machine

It's hard to describe how I feel right now.

Aurelia had come for us. Come like some goddess of old. Like an otherworldly creature, her power thrumming in the currents of the air for all to feel. It had thrown Katerina, I could tell. Naked and glorious, with her eyes *aflame*, I thought I would pass out. It had been enough to pull Scythe out of the curse, just for a moment. Hell, it had made me want to tear off my collar and leap over to her, covering her body with my hands, so the disgusting creatures here would stop clawing their eyes all over her precious skin. She didn't even try to cover herself. Didn't even seem like she cared about her lack of clothing.

I've known love for my mother, my sister, and the hatchlings, but the way I *loved* Aurelia in the moments she stood there, the way I felt proud of her, is like something else. Something that was made in fire-blown stars far beyond this earth and now sits glowing in my chest. Something I feel solely for her. Even stripped bare, she was a force to be reckoned with and she stood alone, without backup, and stood her ground, goading The Collector, challenging her.

Then she shook her hand, and I thought the tension in the room would snap like sheet metal. Only it didn't. Until she left and everyone loosed a breath.

Now Katerina tries to collect herself. Her heart was pounding at first. Perhaps she was worried it would test the curse. Perhaps she was worried Aurelia would shed blood tonight. If it weren't for my warning and Ghoul's...whatever you call that, she may have.

And a fucking unicorn? More than one group is muttering about it now. I knew The Collector had rare creatures stowed away, but a unicorn is actually insane. The dragons will riot. I'd not felt any strange presences or magics back at the compound, unless this Lorian is far, far underground.

Annoyed that I have no one to problem-solve this with, I glance over at the serpent's lounge, where three of Mace's generals are pouring drinks like this is a party. One of them is cleaning his nails with a fang and I scowl.

"*Did you know she had a unicorn?*" I ask Ghoul.

He doesn't react physically, continuing to pour his whiskey. "*Are we friends now? Did you miss me, dragon? Shall we fuck our regina together again?*" I send him the mental image of a finger and he settles back in his armchair, those shadows smoking around him in lazy curls. "*God she was beautiful, wasn't she? Couldn't even tell your dad broke her leg clean off until she came up—*"

I don't know whether it's the tension or the curse of seeing Aurelia tonight, but I take my earphones out and throw them to the floor. Red fills my vision, and I lunge for Ghoul with a roar, yanking Katerina with me via my chain. Metal digs into my neck, but I savour it as I wrap my hands around Ghoul's throat and squeeze.

He chokes or laughs, I can't tell, but his fangs are in my face before the *other* type of red fills my vision. My head sears like it's being burnt and the scent and sensation triggers me. I rear back with a snarl, ready to rip heads off, but that pain comes again and I know it's the fucking basilisk eyes. I fall flat on my back, groaning in old pain that's bringing back memories I can't bear. Not without my brothers, not without my regina.

"Control your beasts," Ghoul says, brushing off his sleeve from the armchair he never left. "This doesn't look good for you. I'm telling Mace."

"Tell him all you want," Katerina says before someone shoves my earphones back into my ears. "We're leaving." She gives me a scathing look before addressing my brothers in a haughty command. "Savage, Scythe, Lyle, Xander, move out."

"*Ooh,*" Ghoul's voice jeers in my head. "*She's just been bursting at the seams to say that in front of an audience.*"

I snort in disgust and scrape myself off the floor to follow. Someone yells so the entire floor can hear. "Say hi to the unicorn for us!"

Katerina holds out until we reach the carpark. Then, what we see tips her over the edge. One of the three Jeeps we rode in is a tangled mess of squashed metal. It and a few other cars look exactly like a dragon used them as a landing pad. That explains the noise we heard before. It's a nice way to make an entrance and it makes my heart glow to see Katerina shriek into the sky, her hands rigid fists by her sides.

We were going to spend the night in the city. Some romantic vision of hers. But with her secret unicorn now out in the open, she can't afford to leave her property. She sends one of her males to procure a new vehicle and climbs into a surviving Jeep, taking Scythe's hand in a way that makes me want to rip hers off. Like they're newlyweds or something. I get beckoned to join her. Savage and Lyle have to squash in the back with Sav sitting one of his ass-cheeks on my knee, hunched over.

"This is ridiculous," I inform her.

"If you don't like it, you can ride on the top," she snaps, eyes slightly wild.

"Do you know what? I think I will." I shove Savage off me and slide out of the car.

But before I do, I can't help but notice the way Katerina keeps looking at her palm and frowning.

Chapter 18

Aurelia

The universe has strange ways of delivering justice.

I never intended to reveal the truth about Lorian. I didn't actually know if another one of the monsters of our city would have treated him any better than The Collector. Everyone wants a unicorn, and now I can just imagine Katerina's mental state. I hope they forget about me and go after her instead.

This is the main thing that's on my mind as I launch myself into the sky. I'm keeping my mind busy so I don't actually swing right back around to go and get my mates. I could have telekinetically whipped them up and launched into the air. I could have tried to test the stupid spell. I could have...

The list of things I trawl through is endless. The way Savage had been hurt by her. The way she might be hurting Scythe. Xander was fine, but he looked strained at the edges, and the glow in his eyes wasn't as bright as it used to be. Somehow, that scares me. I might not have noticed in his astral form, but in person, he was weary.

She's breaking them down.

My heart cracks through the middle, and I want to roar over the city. I want to set fire to it and destroy every inch. The plan needs to come together. Now.

It seems I haven't learned certain lessons because it's happened before—for someone to creep up on me when in flight. When I was distressed and deep in thought in what I'd assumed was freedom of the sky. Maybe someone had filmed me and put it online. Maybe they'd all been alerted as soon as I'd touched down. Because yes, they were waiting for me. And yes, they know my weaknesses.

Ten minutes after I leave the lights of the city and enter the dark of the outskirts, something sharp glances off my left hindquarter. I rear in midair, back flapping to find my assailant, my senses panning outwards. An Australian wedge-tailed eagle swoops away from me, then a second and third. They fly in and out, weaving around me like orchestrated flies.

Surely I can out-fly them. But out of nowhere, three helicopters zoom in from either side and behind me. Within them are felines with tourmaline chains, and—

Gunners? They have military-grade *gunners* riding in the open doors of the helicopters.

I have just enough time to notice the Naga sigil on the sides of them before I release an angry breath of fire. My father is banking on the fact that I'm not a monster. He's banking on me being kind and generous and...sacrificial. But I've given up on being prey. I want blood on my hands, flesh in my mouth, and bones between my teeth. I won't let them take me. I won't let them touch me. Not anymore. They'll learn that now.

Blue fire lights up the night, and male screams light up my ears. Something explodes in the engine of the first helicopter, and it pours smoke as it falls. But I have one mouth, and there are three flying machines. The second helicopter guns bullets into my rear, and it takes me a second to realise they're going for my *new* leg.

Pain in this leg triggers me anew. The electricity of it strikes my heart and mind and drives me wild. I flail, shooting blue in every direction. The smell of charred flesh hits my nose, but I don't care. I spin in a circle, exhaling heat and death.

Bullets fly, and from beneath me, another helicopter roars into existence, so I turn my fire downwards. But pain is eating up my leg like a monster of its own, and it eats up the rage as well, turning me into a bubbling mess.

I scream into the smoke-filled sky. This body of mine. The beastly forms that have served me can't face this pain again. The one that almost broke us. My body shifts without my permission, morphing, moving, changing. My eyes bleed, my vision turns hazy, and nothing so far, no form, has felt like this. That void that has been growing within me opens up wide, swallowing me whole.

The shriek of something inhuman fills my ears before shifting into something without a form at all. Everything disappears into the darkness. The stars blot out, and though I don't have wings, I *move*. Bullets fly right through me, metallic whizzes sounding in my ear before I move forward. My insides are screaming, my head is roaring, but I just move. To the nest. To the nest.

Somehow, the lights of Animus Academy appear on the horizon, but they look wavy as if distorted. Like I'm watching the world through a screen and not with my own naked eyes. There they are, twinkling like hazy jewels, and all of a sudden, they're around me and I land tumbling upon the grass, finding my feet and sounding a call.

The ground vibrates, and a single human voice carries across the lawn. "Lia!" Beak cries in alarm.

I collapse on the spot, but he's there, catching me and scooping me up, exclaiming when he finds my body sticky with blood. This pain is connected to only one form, and it's because of that, that I have no choice but to shift into it. I hold on with all my might. "Water," I choke out, gripping my thigh. "Under the anima dorm."

Beak wastes no time, nor asks any questions as he sprints with me. I lie somehow limp and rigid at the same time, clenching every muscle with all my might to halt the beginning of the shift. My vision winks out, and all I know is the thudding of his feet and a gravelly voice that must be Christine, the door gargoyle who sits on the awning above the entry.

"Third floor," I sob between clenched teeth. "Hurry." But he's already taking the steps three at a time, his breath heavy, his hands tight around me. Through the painting, I tell him. Down the winding stairs that make us both dizzy. "Throw me in," I croak.

Of course he doesn't listen, instead lowering me gently. But I shift as soon as I smell the salt water, and Beak, having never seen this form of mine before, shouts in alarm.

But I'm free. I'm still, and this form lets me *breathe*. Water engulfs me perfectly, completely. Scythe was always right about this. Under the water is the only real peace. Though my voice is silent as the darkness, its cadence but a ripple in this canal underneath the academy that shelters me so lovingly, I know it sends out its signal across the sky.

They can harpoon me. They can shower me with bullets. They can even take my family away from me. But each time, I will rise again and again. They will know why I am regina of the Boneweaver pack. My line will *not* end with me.

Chapter 19

Xander

By the time we arrive back at the compound, I know something is different. Savage has been whining low in his throat against Lyle's neck. And even growling, Lyle has his arm around our wolf brother, his hard gaze on the back of the driver's seat where The Collector sits, her foot hard on the pedal. I'm in dragon form, flying above the convoy as commanded.

I bet he doesn't even know why he hates her. The spell is strong enough that it's pulling at their psyche, but there's a layer under that it can't reach. Something soul-deep is telling Lyle he's in his enemy's domain. Scythe is cold in his seat, but there is a new rigidness to him that I observe as I fly low next to the road, at a deep enough angle that I can see him clearly. There is a crack in his dark aura now, something like light spilling out of it.

I wonder if there is a time limit on this curse. I wonder if it's wearing off.

My regina's bone is one of the strongest magical objects on the planet, most surely, and the way they've wielded it against her screams of injustice. Claws tear at my chest as I think about her, hoping she got home alive. From Katerina's discussions with Mace, I know someone came after her in the sky. Some plan had been set in motion. I strained my ears as we left, using all my senses to locate her. Perhaps she stayed close to see the after effects of her display?

But there was nothing to pick up. No gunfire. No roar in the night. I thought perhaps I'd felt something deep in my chest, but there was nothing out in the sky to back it up. Grimacing, we'd left in the opposite direction to the academy.

About half an hour out from the property, Katerina gets a text message that makes her slam the steering wheel multiple times. She swears loudly, and I try to use my enhanced sight to catch a glimpse of the text, but even for me, it's too small.

But I know what it means. Whatever plan she'd set up hadn't worked.

My smart, brilliant, regina. Elated, I gain some height, planning on reaching the compound before them.

* * *

There is extra security in The Collector's domain tonight, all claws on deck with enough armour and firepower to make the place look like a military base. The grunts have the audacity to aim their piddly anti-air force weapons at me as if I'll try something upon landing. Fortunately for them, my brothers are in the Jeep speeding through the front gates, so I won't be able to have any fire parties with them.

Katerina screeches to a stop, leaping out to speak with her head of security, a red roo, six foot six, and tanked with muscle. They both glance at me as I shift back and stalk over to check on Savage.

He growls under his breath the entire time we're put back in our sleeping positions. This time, I squeeze my way into Lyle and Savage's cage, concerned about the mental states of both. If they shred me in their sleep, so be it.

Both end up shifting back through the night, but neither ends up attacking me. They just sleep against each other as I watch over them and make sure Katerina's ongoing cooed commands over Scythe bear no fruit for her.

I wait for Aurelia to call me back into the astral realm, but to my utter and eternal dismay, she does not.

* * *

When the morning light spills through the small, high windows of her bedroom, Katerina lets us out to wash. It's then that I notice her hand is bandaged. Her *right* hand.

Delicately sniffing the air when she turns around, I notice a faint scent of...something delightful. Something bitter and sharp that makes me happy beyond compare.

The morning progresses as usual. She makes Scythe and I kneel by her side as she eats breakfast, feeding us morsels when she feels benevolent. But I must be in her bad books from last night's slip up, so bits of omelette get thrown in my direction onto the floor, where she has me lean down and lick up the piece like a dog.

She brings us around as she does her checks and has meetings with her avian breeding staff—the healers and scientists she uses to monitor her so-called programs. Connor gets his blood taken, eyeing me with alarm. One of the guards was showing him something on his phone.

"See anything from last night after Aurelia left the Jewel?" I ask into his head.

He can't reply, so he gives an imperceptible shrug, his eyes wide, which probably means everyone's seen footage from inside the Jewel when Aurelia arrived but nothing more than that. There were a lot of beasts in there who had their phones out, so I knew the entire meeting would end up online. It annoys me I'm not there to scrub it for Aurelia.

I'm placated by the way Katerina scratches her hand. I'm further placated when I see a faint line of red creeping up above the bandage. It oozes blood.

"Oh dear, regina," I drawl, swallowing bile as I use that word on her. "I think you'd better get that checked. Smells like it's festering."

Her head snaps towards me. "Does it?" She sniffs her own arm, frowning. "I only smell..." She snaps her mouth shut before she acknowledges what this actually is and gets out her phone, walking away from me.

Mace himself arrives that evening. I'm not in the room when he visits, but Connor gives me the gossip the next day. "Mace walks in, right? And he says, 'show me!' Lady Katerina unravels the bandage, which is up to her elbow by now, and Mace literally takes a step away from her! Can you imagine! His nose crinkles like he's smelling something gross. 'Your skin is breaking down. How did this happen?' Lady Katerina is all sweaty, and she snarls, 'You're supposed to tell me, it was your fucking daughter!' Mace raises his brow, right? Like, all dramatic, and I couldn't breathe, like, at all, but then he says to General Ghoul, 'pull up the footage.' They watch the video of the meeting and then Ghoul points, 'there it is. She's cut her thumb with her fang.' Everyone in the room goes quiet, except Ghoul, because you know how he is. 'And then she drew a sigil on her palm. When you took her hand, she placed the curse on you!' and the bastard laughs all crazy!"

Connor slumps against the wall, running his fingers through his long black hair. "Aurelia did something to Lady Katerina's hand. They're trying to figure out how to undo it now."

I want to beam. I want to sing.

I want to sing? Wild Goddess, I'm finally going insane. But my regina, *my* regina, has found a way to break the impenetrable skin of the lady crocodile.

She's created a weakness The Collector never had before.

Chapter 20

Aurelia

I have no way of knowing how many days it takes me to recover at the bottom of the canal, but at some stage, I feel a pull to look upwards and see the light with the rudimentary eyes at the end of each starfish arm. To see my friends. The ache in that leg of mine is soothed. I flex and stretch it out and find it to be strong.

There is movement of shifted bodies above the water. Then a muffled snort and a human voice. Shifting makes my joints creak and pop, which means it's been days since I've last been human. I grow tall, my arms stretch outwards and reach up, my head appearing where there was only the fifth arm of the starfish.

It's always weird growing a head and face out of nowhere. It feels like entering a new dimension and losing another at the same time. A bit like a portal. And when I step through that door, I kind of miss the other side.

I gasp as my mouth breaches the water, breathing cold air and wiping the water from my eyes. There's a lioness's chuff before I'm squinting at Minnie's human form and Stacey in her golden lioness form. "Oh, hey Lia!" Minnie pipes, stroking Eugene in her arms. "We thought we were doing rabid pack again, so Stacey was all for shifting now that she's feeling a little better."

Rabid pack is referring to the time where I shifted into my lioness form and wouldn't come out of it for days. This was after the council had declared I deserved execution. I'd hidden myself in here for months. My anima has different desires these days.

Telekinesis helps me get out of the canal and onto the cement landing. Rolling my shoulders to stretch them out, I grimace as I take the towel Minnie offers me. There are bags of food and bottles of water in piles about the stone landing, as well as backpacks with clothes and toiletries.

"I got injured," I explain, gesturing to my newer leg, still a slightly lighter colour than the other.

Henry levitates over to me from where he'd been perched on Stacey's head. Eugene gives a strained sort of cluck, and I grimace at him, shoving a finger in my ear and twisting it. "Maybe none of that for a while, okay, Eugene?"

He ducks his head, and I present my hand for Henry. The little nimpin sniffs the air, chittering with his beak before levitating himself onto my shoulder and settling there. He's assumed the position of mother hen again, and today, I have no complaints with that. "So what do you guys know?"

Minnie puffs out her cheeks. "We know you did something bad enough to have an entire squadron of armed officers from the council come and *raid* the academy."

"Bad enough," I repeat with disgust. "I was *defending* myself against bullets and harpoons!"

Stacey shifts back into human form and grabs her backpack of clothes. "They said you destroyed *six* helicopters, Lia!"

"Lies!" I exclaim, waving my arms, and then crossing them defensively. "I counted four."

Minnie chokes. "That's really great and all, Lia. Like...really great, but it means there's a very inconvenient arrest warrant out for you."

"Wasn't there already one in place?" Stacey says, re-tying her pigtails. "Or was that finished and they've begun another?"

"I can't bloody keep track," I mutter. "Arrest warrant *this*, arrest warrant *that*. Is there food?"

"Yeah, Beak left jacket potatoes with cheese and baked beans," Minnie says, heading to a small table with a foil-covered plate.

"Savage would be proud," Stacey chuckles.

That's what does it.

My vision blurs, and I grab my stomach as if I can stop it from dry retching. Something inside of me twists so violently I think I want to starfish-it again, but I can't. I just miss him so much. Miss *them* so much. He'd been hurt. They are all suffering. I'm sobbing and dry heaving and arms come around me and Henry squeaks in my ear.

"Who said what to Lia?" comes Sabrina's deadpan.

"It was me," Stacey says thickly. "I'm sorry, Lia. I shouldn't have brought Savage up."

Someone pushes a bottle of water in front of my lips, and I gulp the cool contents down. A hand pats my back, and somebody pushes my hair off my face. Three faces swim before me, and Minnie whisks a tissue into her hand so she can mop my eyes. "This is really hard," I whisper hoarsely. "I saw them. They looked awful."

"We saw the videos," Stacey whispers. "But you did amazingly."

"It doesn't matter." I hang my head back. "For all my bravado, I don't know if any of it made a difference. They're still captive right now. I'm still being targeted by my father. They're sending helicopters after me. I don't know how much longer I can go on doing this—"

"I've said it before and I'm going to say it again," Sabrina says through gritted teeth. "They are *alive*, Lia. And while they are alive, there is reason to go on."

"I'm sorry," I sniff, feeling ashamed that Sabrina had to lose her mates to death to be able to say this to me, here and now.

"Don't get sorry. Get even. Besides, your ass looked great as you walked out of the Jewel. Everyone's saying so on socials." I stare at Sabrina, and my leopard friend graces me a rare smile. "Girl, if the ass gives you followers, I say we milk that shit for all it's worth."

"Marketing campaign for Lia's ass, roger that," Stacey says, getting out her illegal tablet and pencil. "It'll be a movement."

Minnie hands me the uncovered plate of food, and I dig into the potato and beans with my hands. "Marduk was in a *state* when we realised where you'd gone," Minnie says, twirling her finger through a curl as she often does when talking about her oldest mate. "But somebody was filming *live,* so we had our eyes glued to that for a while."

"He said they'd come after me," I say, wiping my mouth and only smearing more of the baked beans sauce. "I couldn't have waited another second, Min. I just couldn't. All I've done is research serpent magic and just *thought* about things. It was time for action. That crocodile cunt forced my hand."

"I know," Minnie says gently, handing me a serviette. "We all would have done the same."

"Nuh-uh," Stacey says. "Lia has those big dragon ovaries now. None of us have *that* type of courage. I mean, naked too? Come the fuck *on.* People will be talking about this with their grandkids."

"Hopefully, for the right reasons," I say darkly.

Once my stomach is full, I feel capable of leaving the underground cavern and facing the light of day. We wave goodbye to the boat bopping on the canal waters and make our way up the spiral staircase and through the painting into the anima dorms. Beak has been trying to get into the cavern, but the girls refused to let him through. He, Marduk and Yeti had been on the phone with Rufus to manage a couple of things with Scythe's investments, and they are worried about another council raid.

No less than thirty armed guards had scoured the place, half of them serpents. They could scent me, but with so many other hormonal animas around, and Christine the gargoyle hurling profanity at them, they'd left with empty hands. Marduk had managed to convince them I'd gone off-grid with helicopter-related injuries, but we don't know how long that excuse will hold up.

There is one thing of importance on my mind, and I wait until the last rays of the sun disappear under the horizon before I call for my fifth mate.

Chapter 21

Ghoul

I used to have the urge to destroy the academy whenever I'd creep up on it. Execute everyone inside and send the walls crumbling. I'd wonder how much power it would take to turn it to ash. How strong were the dragons that made this place?

But then one night, when Aurelia was newly enrolled at the academy, I was pretending to patrol outside the anima dorm when the gargoyle above the door spoke to me. "Hello, sir basilisk," she said in a squeaky sort of voice. "My name is Christine." I said nothing back, smoking a joint and wondering if she spoke for the place at large. "Lovely night," she cooed. "Here to see the B—uh, the wee little lady inside? Long black hair? Blue eyes that light up your heart?" I'd put out my joint. "Sorry, can't let you in tonight."

Finally, I spoke and she jolted in her stone. "Are you... protecting her?"

"Of course!"

"Why?"

She squinted at me like it was obvious. Sticks for legs swinging straight out. "Uh, she's the most powerful creature here. Only the most powerful can be guardian of the house."

"So you're protecting her because she needs to protect you?"

"Got it right between the eyes, sir," she chuckled at her own joke.

"And why do *you* need protecting?"

She shut her mouth, twisting her lips as if she'd almost let something out. Christine waved her finger at me as if I were the idiot. "Why, there's books inside, my good lord! Important books."

Lying through her stony teeth. So I decided I wouldn't destroy the place after all.

Tonight, as I approach the academy, the cicadas stop chirping as they sense me, and all the little birdies in their nests huddle closer to one another. A lone brown snake slithers deeper into the bushes at the base of the tall academy walls, and the guards—a dingo and three wolves—send telepathic waves between themselves. The bald eagle who likes to hover around Aurelia, and one of his subordinates, a rare black cockatoo, patrol the cloudless night sky.

None of them notice me slithering through the air, my shadows a moving inkblot against the dark. Even if the sharp eyes of the avians do note a strange shift in the air, within a single blink, I'm already a part of the dark, invisible to everyone. Even to *her*, I've been unnoticeable this entire time.

I don't know when she started feeling my presence. Maybe she began to notice the rising of the little hairs on the back of her neck, or a cold feeling of dread coiling inside her stomach. Tonight, she's opened her window for me. And a girl who opens her window for monsters at night is my kind of girl. I catch a glimpse of her from a distance.

Wait, do I think *I'm* the baddest creature of the night? There she is, stark naked, with her hands on those delicious hips, pretty eyes narrowed like a predator as she waits for me. I know it when she sees me. Her eyes lock in and her edible lips part because I'm sure she wants to kiss me. There's a hint of fang under the moonlight, and *now* I'm hard as fuck.

Soundless, I slip through the window, around her perfect body, and assume my human form right behind her, the shadows bubbling outward into the shape of the man version of me. My beautiful monster does not flinch as I inhale the scent of her neck, and I don't fail to notice every goosebump that spreads across her skin, in the same way I don't fail to notice anything else about her. She smells like violence and dragon smoke, yet her heartbeat remained steady until now.

"Is there something you desire from me, snakelet?" I murmur against her ear, my shadows reaching around her waist to hover just over her skin. "You seem to be doing quite fine by all reports, but your text message was quite...*insssssistent.*"

She raises a hand, fingers curiously brushing against a lick of shadow. "They're soft, and yet...strong." Her voice is gentle, unlike her scent, and the way it slides down my spine is like something out of this world. "Do you have control over them, or do they have a mind of their own?"

Dying to touch her, I caress a gloved finger down the length of silken black hair lying against her spine. "They can be wild," I admit. "It's like taming a wild serpent. You think you have control over them, and then a second later..." Two licks of shadow slide around her throat.

The snakelet sucks in a breath, and the movement presses her back against me. I let my fingers hang down, trailing them against the soft skin of her bare thighs. Her arousal sweetens the air.

"If I touch you now, will you be wet for me?" I murmur in her other ear. "If I taste you between your legs, will your pussy be sweeter than your venom?" My fingers trail higher as her breath quickens, brushing into the soft skin above her curls of pubic hair.

"Touch me," she whispers, rubbing a thumb over the band of shadow at her throat.

Of their own accord, those bands apply a subtle pressure. Chuckling under my breath, I command them away, removing my gloves with my teeth and replacing the shadows with my bare skin. She exhales arousal, and I cup her throat, pulling her against my body, letting her feel how hard I am as I command my shadows to slide down the old scars on her stomach and caress the dark hair at the apex of her thighs. Down they wander.

"You've acquired a taste for danger, snakelet. I'm not sure if I should spank or fuck that out of you."

Snakelet gasps as those shadows find her wet heat. Find those pussy lips slick and deliciously hot. "Why do you care?" she pants, placing her hand over mine at her throat. "You've never fucking cared about me."

"Hmmm," I hum, enjoying the feel of her core, of her centre as I delve deeper for that precious hole. She cries out as I enter her, expanding the shadows and filling her up. She bucks in my grasp, and I band an arm around her waist as yet another lick of shadow joins in at her core, this time circling her swollen clit. "That's a lie," I say into her ear as the shadow inside of her expands further. "I've warned you many a time." She gives me a sweet cry, and I brush my lips across her jaw. "Breathe, snakelet. Breathe for me."

"It's growing," she says, running a hand down the thick length between her legs. "How is it growing?"

I hum again. "Is it?"

"You bastard," she pants, but it's half-hearted.

"This is what you miss, isn't it? The cocks of your mates in you. I can give you whatever you want all by myself."

The shadow grows, pumping slowly, lovingly, into her as her clit pulses under the second finger of shadow. She tilts her head back to look at me, and I surrender into her gaze before slanting my fangs over hers. "If you don't kiss me, I might leave," I whisper. She growls, reaching for the back of my head and hissing into my mouth. I toy with a nipple as her tongue slips past my lips, and now it's my turn to groan into her.

Snakelet's pussy floods my shadows, her desire growing around us. I move faster, the shadows fluttering against her clit in a sucking motion, the pulsing inside of her bigger, faster, and stronger than before. Her muscles tense, and she screams into my mouth, her fangs biting on my lower lip, venom shooting out. I grab her chin as she comes and cries out, sucking on her mouth for her delicious poison. "*I need every last drop,*" I tell her into her mind. "*Every last fucking drop of you.*"

Her hips buck under my shadows, and as venom slides down her mouth, I slowly lick it up, savouring the power and taste of it. She pants against me, and I circle her clit in a lazy motion to drag every last bit of pleasure from her. As she sags in my arms, I just have to bury my nose in her hair, wrapping her in my power, wrapping her in night.

"It's warm," she says curiously, "but cool at the same time." As she's looking back at me like this, I could drown in those gems she calls eyes. The one pair of eyes in the world immune to me and my lethal nature. "You can give me whatever I want?" she asks carefully.

"Ah, I'm wounded. You're using me." A glimmer begins in her pupil, spreading outwards as she turns around to face me. Her hand slides down my trousers, finding my hard length and squeezing. I tilt my head back in pleasure. "Oh, snakelet."

"Don't you dare think for a moment that I've forgotten Drakos Estate. You owe me for all my trouble." Her hand slides up and down, working me like an instrument.

"Yessss," I say with a sibilant hiss. "I forget nothing, snakelet. Ever. What is it you want from me?"

She unzips me, untucking me and letting that achingly hard length spring out into her hand. Her touch is nothing but torture on my needy skin. "I want some of that heat serum they injected me with at Drakos Estate. Six doses worth at least."

Even my darkness stutters. "Snakelet," I drawl. "Now why on the Wild Mother's forsaken earth would you ask for something like that? Do you not remember what happened the last time?"

"Oh I remember quite well, General," she returns, her voice soft and beguiling. Is it getting hot in here?

"All this time you wanted drugs from me?" I pout over my fangs. "I'm hurt, actually."

She removes her hand, shoving at my chest with enough power behind it that it actually makes me stumble back a step. "Can you get it or not?"

Enamoured, I have to stare at her for a moment. Stare long and hard enough that inside me, something long-awaited ignites. "Finally, she shows me her fangs," I say.

"Finally, I realise that the monsters in the jungle are no scarier than me," she purrs. It's definitely hot in here. She takes a step towards me, predatory intent in her eyes. "Finally, I realise that the only thing stopping me from being the bigger predator was *myself*."

"I don't know if I can keep calling you snakelet after tonight," I breathe.

"There is something else you can call me. Something you've been avoiding."

There is a glint of some type in her eye now. Her voice booms around me. "Give me what I want."

She just tried to regina-command me. Spells and secrets on my body burn like poison through my veins. My heart pounds in my ears, and my fangs elongate down past my lower lip. "You're calling upon something you're not ready for," I warn.

"I've been ready for a while, Ghoul."

We stare at each other, eye to eye. Basilisk to Boneweaver. Her pupils turn into serpentine slits, mesmerising me.

"I'll get you the serum." What am I even saying? "But—" I quickly recover. "You'll have to do something for me first."

She frowns. "Why? I don't have time for this."

"You'll make time," I say simply. "You've owed me for a while now. And I'm guessing you want these vials badly enough to do whatever it takes."

She doesn't scowl, doesn't give anything away, and just for a moment, I miss the old Aurelia, whose face gave away everything. I'm going to have to be on my game now.

"Alright, what do you need me to do?"

So level. So calm. That heartbeat is focused, her breath steady. Those pupils...still slits that hook me in by the cock. "Meet me here tomorrow night," I say, striding towards the window. "I'll get a dress."

Before she can respond, I'm one with the darkness and out the window.

I'm about to leave when something pulls my attention away from my exit over the academy wall, and I decide I'd better go pay my respects. I descend to the medical centre, opening myself up to whatever lurks here. Where I find Raquel. Where the wolf anim's astral form has been running around shouting for help this entire time.

"*Boo!*" I shout.

The anim skids to a stop right in front of me.

Chapter 22

Aurelia

He'll get a dress.

Whatever Ghoul was getting me to do was definitely not going to work in my favour. In fact, it's more than likely it's going to hurt. But unfortunately, he is right. I need the serum for my plan, and I'll do anything to get it.

I await him after dark, this time on top of the animus dorms, with not a stitch of clothing and a scowl upon my face. I've only told Minnie that I'm leaving, and though she wasn't happy about it, she gave me that half shrug that says, *I know you do what you have to, just don't get yourself killed.*

Ghoul arrives on the first cold wind of the night, heralded by the scent of poison. It's sharp but sweet, toxic but alluring. And when he un-dissolves himself from the shadows into a man, I cast him a level look. "You're aware they're hunting me. I can't go anywhere I'll be seen."

"You won't be," he says, his occipital lasers glinting that severe crimson. "You take dragon form, and I'll lead the way."

"I can do phoenix so we get this done."

"So impatient," he drawls. "But no, someone will notice. It gives off too much of a signal."

I hadn't really thought of that, but I don't show that I'm kicking myself. "This isn't going to be a trap, is it?"

There's no way for me to tell if the bastard is lying; he's so well protected by those shadows that I barely get to see his mating mark. "No fun in that," he says. "Besides, I need you."

Something ancient stirs inside me at his words, but I have to brush it aside. He has always been my enemy. "I just want you to know," I say, stalking forward. "That if you betray our agreement tonight, not even death will save you from me. Do you understand?"

He goes still, eyes flashing in something akin to anger. "Threats?" That sibilant voice is so dangerously soft. "Threats make me hard, snakelet." It's his turn to take a step forwards now. "Threats make me want to see what you look like bent over your precious academy wall, screaming because my cock is stretching your dripping. Wet. Pussy."

His lethally soft words *do* make me wet.

"You've been to the Jewel, with warnings from your shark and lion, no doubt. But where we're going tonight, snakelet, will make the Jewel look and feel a puppy playpen. I know you can handle it."

I clench my teeth at his assumptions about me. "Then let's get this done."

We head into the night, with me following the darkest part of it, an amorphous, shifting ball of the void moving like a missile just beyond my nose. We don't head into the city as I assumed we would, but southeast of it to the suburbs. Ghoul leads me onto an unassuming street, lined with regular domestic houses, and makes a beeline for one property in particular. This townhouse hits me in the chest—not the vision of it, but the scent all around it that screams to keep away. There's a tug in my gut.

"Whose house is this?" I say darkly, already knowing the answer.

"It's mine."

I let out a huff as he opens the front door without a key and leads me into the dimly lit entryway. It's clear he didn't decorate it himself because no monster except perhaps Xander has this much taste. From memory, the generals are all given houses of their own as gifts when they join my father as seniors in his retinue. Just as a king would grant land to his liege lords in the Old Way. A classy designer has decked this house out in burgundy and black, the occasional white of a lotus breaking up the dark hues.

We go upstairs to the master bedroom, where a king-size bed is decorated with black silk sheets. There is a trace scent of ash in the air. "You're going to be under disguise as a young woman called Jade Brown."

"That name is familiar."

"She's around your age, probably a peer when you were princess that one time."

I narrow my eyes at him. *That one time.* "I'm something much worse now."

He smirks. "You'll need to cover your power with that special ability of yours."

"Obviously."

Ghoul drapes a black gown across his arms. It's stunning, off the shoulder but long-sleeved, and it's not until he helps me step into it that I can see it has no back at all. It hugs my thighs before trailing down to the floor, leaving a short train. Being dressed by Ghoul is a mildly disturbing domestic experience. His hands are gentle but businesslike. It's nothing like his touch from last night.

He steps back, and those red eyes seem to gleam with a feral awareness that makes my heart quicken. "I want this colour on you," he says, handing me a small leather makeup case. I open it to find a concealer palette for different skin tones and a single, red lipstick.

I turn around to see him holding a black lace material. "What the hell am I doing here, Ghoul?" I ask suspiciously.

"There's a little event I need a date to, and, well...you are the perfect candidate." He shrugs. "Here, put this on. They need only see your lips tonight."

It's a tall headdress with a black lace veil. A traditional serpent kind that wealthy women wear to serpent gala functions. I've seen Aunt Charlotte wear something like it just *once.* My stomach turns, but I've come here to get what I need, so I take the thing from him and tie my hair in a bun. I wedge the tall black plastic arch shape in front of the bun, and Ghoul throws the lace veil over it, securing it in place with some clasps. It hangs low just below the tip of my nose.

The air suddenly changes around me. Around us.

"Fangs out," Ghoul says in a strange new tone.

I glance at him before obliging. "I think you like these too much."

"You'd better not speak tonight either."

"Luckily, serpent women don't talk at parties," I hiss back. "Why bother when all the males can do that for us?"

He gazes back at me, no retort on his forked tongue, only a heavy observation that I feel down to my bones. "What do you know about basilisks, snakelet?"

I'm taken aback by the question, so it takes me a second to respond. "Nobody knows anything about them."

"That's not true."

"You're the only..." I say, suddenly losing steam on my line of thought. Ghoul is like me. The last one of his kind. More softly, I say, "Unless...your parents or family are alive?"

It's the first time I notice any hesitation in him. A drop in the arrogance. His shadows lose some of their height, hanging around low at his elbows. "There's no sign of any other," he says. "The shadows would know if there were others."

"Where do you come—"

He abruptly turns and leaves, his boots clomping away into another room. When he returns, he's dressed in a finer version of his normal uniform. The crisp black shirt and jacket seem darker and of a newer make, a row of gold medals hang from his left breast and he's added a clean bone mask to his face.

The shadows reach like fingers, looping around me. "We're going to be late."

I should be annoyed at his avoidance of the question. I think I know the answer anyway, but this line of thought...this line of conversation is something I've not had time to think about before now, and I find myself ashamed of that.

Ghoul leads me to a black SUV in his driveway that looks brand new. I suppose he never has to use it due to his far more efficient mode of travel. He helps me and my dress into the passenger seat, and we're both quiet—him with military efficiency, and me with the poisonous sort of thoughts that only come upon a regina with an enemy as her mate. It only gets worse when the short drive leads to a gated mansion in a wealthy part of town. My heart starts pounding at the small tells as to where I am.

The fountain we pass up the long drive is unmarked, and so is the black rendered brick fence at the front. There are no name-plates or sigils. No big stone statues that proudly shout the order of the occupants. But everything looks suspiciously brand new. There are *a lot* of vehicles parked in neat rows by the entrance—military grade trucks with open-and-closed backs, some with canopy-style coverings. In stark contrast, classical music plays in the distance, carefully curated to present a certain image. I'm familiar with these tactics. I've practised this facade since I was a child.

A towering mansion sits like a king at the head of the property, with ornate finishings, a possessive archway, and stained-glass stone doors. With my heart in my chest, I glance at the ground beneath it, wondering if we're driving over the cells of any unfortunate prison-ers. At the front of the grand entrance, four military beasts stand, black Kevlar vests and automatic weapons at their backs. One wears a skull mask like Ghoul.

The basilisk parks right before them, gets out of the car, and tosses the keys to one of the guards. With my heart hammering, I flick down my veil and open my door to find Ghoul already there, all but carrying me out so I don't dislodge my tall headdress. His shadows wrap around me at the same time his arms do, a light veil of black smoke around my entire body, sheer enough to show my dress and form but not much else.

Now the only thing that will reveal me is my voice.

My world is obscured by black lace, as if this household requires yet another layer to disguise the dark origins of the funds that led to its purchase: me. The guards avert their gazes and don't appear surprised to see Ghoul's lady companion as she walks inside. Golden lights gleam on the white shiny tiles, and to my ears come the sounds of glasses clinking, excitable chatter, and Mozart in the background. A classic, but sizable serpent's party.

The basilisk does not clutch me to his side, but his shadows do the job of being commanding, telling all those who come across us tonight that I am his possession. I get a strange sense of déjà vu. As if by stepping into this house, I've stepped into an alternate reality where I get a glimpse of what could have been. Where nothing in the past ten years has happened. Like I'd never been exiled. As if I'd never been a Boneweaver, but a serpent princess and heir to my father's empire.

The fangs scraping my lower lip could have been my permanent cobra fangs. Ghoul could have been my high-ranking consort. I'm in a sort of daze as the sounds of the party get louder and two doors swing open to admit us.

Ghoul and I step inside, and we're greeted by a round of clapping that suddenly roars in my ears. Someone cheers. My eyes squint under the bright lights as I struggle to catch my breath, realities colliding in the most brutal way.

"Ladies and gentlemen," Ghoul drawls, holding an arm out to me. "I present to you my bride, Jade Brown."

An engagement party? *This* motherfucker.

Chapter 23

Aurelia

"**W**here's the real Jade Brown?" I hiss into Ghoul's dark mind.

"Dead, funnily enough. Smile."

That poor innocent girl. I barely remember her from primary school. The type of girl who didn't stand out amongst the rest of the hatchlings. Average grades, her ponytail always in a scrunchie. There are plenty of Eastern Brown snakes on this side of the coast, and while they are dangerously venomous, the ability to sell their venom to research has made a lot of them quite wealthy with a high rank in the serpent community. It made sense that Ghoul would choose one as his mate.

I bare my fangs as suggested, and the shadows part just enough for everyone to see my red lips and the sharp white tips. Everyone, that is, including my goddess-forsaken father, who is at the head of the crowd, tall and foreboding. My vision through the lace is fragmented, but I would know my sire on his power alone. It coats the air like oil, hanging above it and yet contaminating everything around it. It gives everything around him a subtle feeling of being choked.

I suddenly wonder how my mother ever tolerated it. How I, as a child, had ever tolerated it. But it had been all I'd ever known, and he had loved me at the beginning. Or perhaps it wasn't love, but possession and greed that made his touch doting. It's shocking and uncomfortable to feel betrayed in retrospect.

The other high-ranking serpents hang back, letting their king greet his general. To my utter and brilliant shock, my father embraces Ghoul, clapping him on the back just once before stepping back. He doesn't even look at me. "Congratulations, General," Mace Naga says. "Finally, you bring me good news."

Interesting; that feels like a jab. More interesting still is the fact that it sounds like they've been trying to get Ghoul married.

Aunt Charlotte saunters forward, her stilettos clicking, in a long black dress with a dramatic fur trim. Her blonde pin curls look a bit dry at the ends, and her red-lipped smile is strained as she glances me over, then turns to her only living mate, Uncle Ronald.

"Well done, General," Uncle Ron says. His smile doesn't reach his eyes.

"Thanks, Ronny."

Ghoul being chummy with my family makes my stomach turn, but it's not until Aunt Charlotte tries to usher me towards one of the black velvet couches off to the side that I break out into a sweat. "You must sit down, dear," she says, reaching out as if to sweep me away.

Ghoul's shadows make me scoot backwards into his body. "My bride will sit with no one but me."

A nearby anima that I recognise as one of Charlotte's besties laughs nervously. "Ah yes, the possessiveness of basilisks is said to be akin to a rabid dragon, is that not right, General?"

"If the rabid dragon had its eggs taken from him, yes," Ghoul says smoothly.

"We were all beginning to think you were impotent," a stout man with a thick moustache chuckles. "Are you sure it's yours?"

Light flashes and sizzling sounds. There's a scream before it's abruptly cut off. Everybody flinches, then immediately turn away and continue on like nothing happened. There is no trace of the man who stood there. Only a pile of smoking ashes and a joke that lingers in the air.

Wait. *Wait.*

"I'll be in touch with you about your pregnancy requirements,

Jade," Aunt Charlotte says formally before turning on her heel and clacking away.

Now I'm shouting furiously into Ghoul's head, *"You can lay your own eggs, Ghoul! What the hell."*

He only chuckles, pulling me to sit on his lap. *"Don't you want my hatchlings, regina?"* I go still. Suddenly, this dress feels tight around my diaphragm, and more sweat trickles down my spine. *"Easy, snakelet. I know the princess is in there somewhere. All of this could have been yours, remember?"*

I do remember, that's half the problem. I imagine if I had been my father's daughter, princess of Naga House. I had always been kept away from the generals, but as an adult, I would have had to interact with them. *"You would have had to answer to me,"* I tell him.

"It would have been perfect."

I frown at him, but the basilisk general is looking threateningly out at the crowd. They might not be able to see his eyes, but his posture in the seat, the set of his shoulders and thighs, and the slight cock of his head scream pure, lethal challenge.

Now I get to look out at the rest of the people in the room. A string quartet is working its way through the Four Seasons in the corner, and overlooking them is the Naga family crest in gold and silver, shiny because it's brand spanking new. I guess they couldn't save the original one.

My eyes scan to the right of them, where on a dais before a little crowd sit three people, gagged and chained with obsidian to three chairs. My gasp is involuntary. It's the tall figure of Ablo Obon; the wolf queen, Lunissa Darkfang, and Irma Goldwing, the avian queen. All three have glazed, unseeing eyes, but their breathing and heartbeats are rapid as if they're in pain.

He's done it. My father has actually done what he'd planned all those years ago. Mace Naga is preparing to take over the state.

I want to jump out of this seat and run. I need to warn Minnie and the academy. I need to find my mates. I need to get them back *now*.

"Settle," Ghoul warns into my head. His shadows slide down my arms as if to soothe me, and perhaps because he's one of my

mates, it works. The regina in me succumbs to his hold. The serpents in the room mingle and laugh. They point at their captives and shake hands with each other. Suddenly, I'm all too aware that every male in the room is wearing a formal military evening uniform. It looks official. Intentional.

It reminds me of images I've seen of another time and place where such things had happened, in another fragile decade.

My vision sharpens, and with that, my mind. Though I keep my gaze turned away from them, I allow my mind to stray to the wolf queen. What manner of serpent magic is this? That the avian queen with her refined healing powers could not fight off? That Ablo Obon, with his powerful telekinesis, could be helpless against.

The wolf queen does not respond when my power touches her mind and asks permission to speak. It's as if her mind is cast in darkness. In shadow. My head swivels towards the face of my fifth mate. Both of us, with our eyes covered from the world. Both of us covered in shadows. *"You did that?"*

"Did what?" he drawls. *"Cast a spell upon The Collector to make her skin fall off?"*

"We are not the same."

"We're exactly the same. That was a stroke of genius by the way. Very well done."

I won't get any type of answer from him, and I know it. *"Is this it?"* I ask. *"You want me to be your bride? Bear your seed?"*

"Is that too much to ask of my regina?"

"You've never been loyal to me."

He bares his fangs. *"Are you ready for what's to come, snakelet?"*

My stare is hard on the points that glint crimson. He's caught me off guard with his words for the second time tonight. *"Get me out of here,"* I say with disgust. *"I've played my part."*

When he rises, holding me close as if I am only made of shadow, my gaze finds my father sitting in a winged-back chair, his eyes fixed on me. My heart jumps like it's been shot but he *can't* know that it's me. A band of shadow wraps around my arm in a guiding fashion, and Ghoul leads me right over to his king. He bows, and I do a hasty curtsy.

As we turn to leave, a woman's voice rings across the room. "Jade? Oh Jade, how happy we are!"

A plump woman and an older man are hurrying towards me, their faces panicked, their arms reaching out. Maybe it's their panic, maybe it's *my* panic, but I too reach towards the flustered mother.

There is a strange and awful hiss, and a column of shadow bursts around me like a tornado. My world is a whorl of black and power. Wild Mother, all I can see now is the tornado of turning shadows around me. I stand in its eye, hidden from the entire room.

"Do *not* touch my bride." Ghoul's voice has taken terror to a whole new level. Within my tornado, he sounds like he's very far away, but even then, his wrath sends me reeling. "She is no longer yours. She is *mine*. As are the hatchlings. As is her soul. Do you understand me?"

There are other muffled voices from outside the storm of shadows, and before I know it, I'm being whisked away by dominant, possessive hands and being lifted into Ghoul's SUV. We're tearing down the street fast enough for the streetlights to be a blur.

There are too many things wrong with all of this. My father wants Ghoul to breed. Jade's mother doesn't know she's dead. The world doesn't know that the council is being held captive. There is a warrant on my head, and none of my mates can help me right any of these wrongs. Ghoul is an enemy. But why is it that he doesn't touch me like one?

No words are exchanged between me and the basilisk lord, but he undresses me with the same efficiency as he dressed me, then proceeds to lead the way back to the academy. The flight is strained, but not physically. I'm troubled as to why he hasn't chosen the real Jade Brown to be his wife. Nothing stopped Xander from taking Francesca as his for a while. But I'm not going to ask him any questions at all. There's no point.

When I'm finally back in my bedroom, feeling like I need to scrub this night off my skin, I turn around to address the silent giant. "How are you going to keep up this ruse?"

"You'll be coming back as needed, of course."

"Arrogant bastard," I mutter. "I don't want to go back there."

"Hush now, *wife*."

I round on him, but he's already gone, and in his place are six glass vials glinting like jewels on the open windowsill.

Chapter 24

Ghoul

"The Collector is taking quite the share of oestrous meds," complains our new chief scientist the next evening. "Her medical staff can't be using *that* much."

Chewing on the end of a stolen pen, I consider him, down in the lab of Naga mansion. "Maybe she's found a female unicorn. Maybe she's experimenting with that Connor anima. But she's not letting anyone within a kilometre of her land, so no one knows."

"You need to find out," Mace says from his chair. "We need to know what she's hiding in there before we make the decision."

"The girl will plan her attack soon, surely," General Taipan says from the door. "What if she successfully manages to kill her?"

"Then the choice will be made for us." Mace waves a dismissive hand. "But if there are rare assets in there we can trade overseas, I might consider that beneficial."

"They might end up killing each other," I say conversationally.

"She cannot die here," Mace says. "I will not waste an opportunity of that nature."

War is expensive. If he can make money by selling her, he will. It would be the smart thing to do. "Very well," I say, groaning as I get to my feet. "No rest for the wicked." Tossing the pen back to the chief, I watch him catch it before I bow to our king and take my leave.

* * *

The night above Crocodylus Estate is laden with magic, but my shadows slip past it like oxygen. So many guns. So many soldiers watching the night as if it'll attack them if they look away for long enough.

Scaredy little crocodile in her swamp.

It takes me a minute to find Katerina and her new toys, sinking down through the levels of the house and underground. She's gathered them in a room with a metal floor, low lamplight flickering in the corner, making for a garish scene. There are shadows abound, and Xander's tall form is the first I see, towering before the rest of them. His shoulders are stiff, and his arms crossed. His dark power buzzes around him like a live wire.

I sneak up on the dragon, low and slow like a cat ready to pounce, but a slight turn of his head tells me he knows I've arrived. *"Has she moved the unicorn?"* I whisper. *"I want to see if rubbing its ass will grant me a wish."*

"Rub my ass and see what that does," Xander replies.

I peer around the corner to see what has him riled up tonight. There's a female grunt, and if I had a human face right now, it would be twisted in disgust. I lay eyes on what the Lady Crocodylus is doing, and even my shadows recoil.

She wields a knife over the Great White shark, her eyes almost as wild as an aquatic shifter in psychosis. Scythe is strung up, both wrists tied to a metal hook on the low ceiling. Metal glints under the harsh lights, and skin opens up to red, but Scythe does not flinch. His naked upper body is covered in deep, bleeding lacerations, but cold and distant, he does not move.

Katerina's entire upper body is bandaged, crimson patches blooming like morbid roses across her arms and chest. Interesting.

"You are fucked!" Katerina snarls, panting hard as she wipes her forehead. "The lot of you are *fucked.*"

Savage lies curled in his wolf form, patches of white amongst his black pelt where he's been singed. The massive lion is unconscious next to him, his mane roughly shorn down to the skin, and so many darts stuck into his back he looks like an echidna. I turn to look at

Xander sideways. *"You're just standing there,"* I say. *"Just standing by..."*

His growl is for my head alone. We both watch Katerina dance around Scythe, the metal darting this way and that but not touching the skin. As if she's shadowboxing and can't decide which bit of tattooed skin to cut up next.

"Won't so much as *touch* me," she grunts. "Or look at me. What is the fucking point? You were supposed to be dead anyway. They all *want* you dead." She's muttering like a madwoman, and something tells me she hasn't slept for many nights now. I suppose the novelty wore off when reality was not as she imagined.

"Gah!" Katerina lunges upward, slashing far too close to the shark's eyes, managing a vertical slice to his cheek. "So beautiful, everyone thought," she spits, sweat dripping down her face. "They won't think you're *beautiful* after I'm done with you."

"Power corrupts," I drawl out loud. "Absolute power corrupts absolutely." Katerina whirls around, eyes wide, and for just a second, I think she's going to attack my materialising body. "Can I see the unicorn? Does it do rides?" She bares her pointed croc teeth and lets out the scary deep growling sound her kind like to do when they're angry. "Oh shit, is it that serious?" I ask. "Because I'm serious about the ride."

"Get the fuck out of here," she snaps, advancing towards me, that feral gleam in her eye bordering on rabid. "And tell Mace he can f—"

"Uh-uh." I waggle a finger at her. "Let's not forget who runs the entire state now."

Anger flashes over her face like a flame. "He can't even get this spell off me." She gestures to her bandaged arms. "Either he's not got as much power as he's advertising or he's not on my side at all."

"If he wanted you dead, you would be," I say soothingly. "You're so valuable to us, Katerina. With or without the unicorn."

Her scoff is pure disgust. "You and everybody else want what I have." She waves the knife at the three brothers behind her. "And—"

"What is it you have?" I ask with a soft hiss, stepping forward. "What"—I wave my hand at her charges—"*is* this?

Katerina's pale nostrils flare, slitted pupils flashing. Water splashes nearby, and I wonder who's watching us. Which of her mates she keeps in those waters is human enough to hear our words? "You would never understand. *You*, who prefers to execute anybody he has been given to mate. *You* who was given *everything* by Mace. You got to be saved. You were given your life on a fucking platter. I fought for power. I fought for my independence and grew my enterprise from the ground up when no one thought an anima could."

"You're more like Aurelia than you think," I muse. "Also like Scythe, in many ways. Is that what attracted you to him other than the pretty hair?"

Her face twists as she looks out at the river she made. "I was there the day Scythe made himself known and threw a tub with the splattered body of the cold cassowary patriarch on our table. We all thought he'd never last on land."

"Ah, that's why his rejection hurts so much," I muse. "Because he might have understood you. He might have *seen* you under those hard scales."

Her head snaps back at me, much like a saltie's whip-quick movement. "Go home and suck Mace's cock like a good general."

"It's so funny that none of them want you back. Even with your fancy hyena spell."

She holds up the knife. "The spell is holding. They are under my complete control. If *she* comes here, they will capture and shackle her on sight, and that will be the end of Aurelia Boneweaver." Her grin is all teeth. "How ironic for her own mates to be the end of her now when they were the ones who gave her up for execution to begin with."

"I'm impressed," I admit. "That's some kind of poetry there."

Scythe's wounds have already closed up, the blood pooling at her bare feet long clotted. "Why are you here, anyway?" Katerina asks.

"Mace wants to know if you're breeding Lorian the unicorn." She narrows her eyes at me. "Alright, *I* want to know if you're breeding Lorian the unicorn."

"Get out, Ghoul. You've haunted this room long enough."

"I came all this way for nothing?" I gesticulate widely.

She snarls at me in annoyance. "If I get the girl, the first fucking thing I do will be to stud Lorian on her. She was supposed to be subservient for the mounting rack after we took off her leg and I personally nursed her back to health, bonded to me as her saviour, but *somebody* got in the way of that process." She throws a glare at Xander.

An involuntary hiss emits from my mouth, my lips curling into a snarl over my fangs. But it's the smirk Katerina throws my way that gets me under control again. She knows exactly what she's saying. "I don't think she's subservient to him either," I say, showing her I'm unaffected. "Too stubborn."

"No, but...she's soft in other ways. Now that I have these four, I get three chances with a knife at their throats for her to agree to be bred. Twice with Lorian, at least."

"Three chances?"

"Oh, I'm not killing my pretty shark." She runs her fingers down his chest. "He's chained to me forever. Once Aurelia is bred to her maximum parity, she'll be executed and I'll wear him down eventually. I'm in this for the long game." She smirks at me. "Just like Mace was with you."

Chapter 25

Aurelia

"**D**on't ask me why I was there," I say firmly as we all meet in my pack's suite. "But half the council—and for all I know, all the council members—are drugged captives of Mace Naga at their new house."

Marduk regards me mildly from where he sits on the dining room chair. "That would explain why Ablo is not returning my calls."

My phone rings, and I yank it up to see Rufus' name. I glance at Beak before picking up. "Rufus," I greet. Beak and Yeti stray closer to hear better.

"My lady," Rufus says, and my hackles raise as I sense the tension in his voice. "Early this morning, there was an incident at the subdivision of the enterprise we refer to as Blue Bird. Council agents bearing Naga insignias raided five chain stores and took possession of all of them."

I can barely hear him over the war drums in my head. "What... subdivision is this exactly?"

Rufus lowers his voice. "We are cleaning money through Blue Bird, my lady. This is a chain of confectionary stores."

Money laundering. I shouldn't be surprised. I cast Minnie a dark look, and she goggles her banker-family eyes at me. "Right, so what do we normally do in situations like this?" I ask, feeling fully out of my depth.

"Just one extra thing. Those bank accounts are now frozen. You'll likely find yours frozen too, my lady."

I cringe. It's not like I was ready to go on a shopping spree anyway, and the academy provides everything I need already. "Okay, I can handle that."

"Funds are no issue due to Mr Xander's secured treasuries; however, normally we are able to negotiate agreements around this type of interference. It seems that's not an option at this stage. Our only option is to lie low."

I take a deep breath while he lets me process this. My father thinks I'm powerless without my mates. That he can move in and simply snatch our funds. He thinks I won't make a move. "Mr Rufus, lying low is not an option. Rest assured, I will take the necessary action. Is that all for today?"

"Yes, my lady."

"Very well. We will speak again in two days."

I hang up and calmly cast my eye about the room. "My father's plans are advancing. I need to execute the rescue tomorrow."

"Tomorrow!" Minnie exclaims, throwing a pillow across the room. "Where's the plan? *What's* the plan?"

"Shush," Stacey says, clutching Eugene to her chest like a hot water bottle. Henry is perched on her shoulder alongside her own nimpin. "There's a plan in Lia's Boneweaver eyes; I've seen it growing."

The rooster has been avoiding eye contact with me, his bejewelled goggles sparkling under the sun's light. On the other hand, since the Clawson incident and the Jewel of the Jungle incident, Stacey has relegated me to the position of Wild Goddess. I love her for it, but I'm not going to let it get to my head. There's a lot I don't know, after all. A lot that could still go wrong. She almost died because of me, but I'm trying hard not to think about that.

"I'll need all the nimpins," I say. "But otherwise, I'll be doing this solo."

Minnie leaps to her feet at the same time Stacey does. Sabrina pushes back her hood and narrows her dark eyes at me. "Absolutely the fuck not!" Minnie exclaims. "Lia, this is *not* a solo mission. This isn't the Jewel, where you're walking on neutral ground. You're going into her *lair,* where she has ammunition and guards who can jump high enough to pluck you from the sky. Not to mention her river full of gnarly crocs!"

The backs of my eyes burn as I meet Marduk's and Yeti's eyes before looking back at my best friend. "I expected to do this alone, Min. It's going to be dangerous. I can't risk more people I love." I look at them all pointedly.

"Well, you're people I love too!" Minnie stomps a pink-sandalled foot. "I won't have it!"

"She has a bloodlust now," Sabrina says, nodding at our tigress. "She wants more blood on her teeth after the Clawsons, and frankly, so do I. These fuckers have gone on too long with their power unchecked."

I stare at her. "I can't ask you to *kill* people, Sabrina."

"You've killed for me," she replies firmly. "If I get the chance to kill for *you,* I will. I have nothing left to lose, Lia."

"This has all taken a dire turn," Yeti tries to reason with us. "Who says you're killing anyone?"

Minnie rushes at me, grabbing my hand and addressing her mates in a tone of great finality. "We're blood sisters now, Lia and me. I'm going to help get her mates back."

I sigh, taking a moment to adjust my plans in my head. It *will* be easier with a team, even I can admit that. "Alright," I say to myself. "Alright," I say to my friends, bringing out the clinking bag. "This is my weapon of choice." I reach in and show them my prize.

Yeti takes the vial and looks at it. Eyes of the palest blue flick up to me, and he raises a white brow. "Really, Aurelia?"

"What is it?" Minnie says, plucking it out of his hand and reading the label. Her face sobers. "Oh dear."

"As a result, none of the males can come," I say firmly. "Even as backup."

"No males?" shout Yeti and Beak at the same time.

"No males," I say carefully, watching them pass the vial around. "I'm going to call Hyacinth Dabu and see if she's willing to help us break them out. Since Savage broke them out of prison, I'm guessing she'll say yes."

"You're going to use this," Sabrina deadpans as she holds up the vial, "as what, a distraction?"

"Naturally," Marduk says, though his eyes are glinting at the idea. "This is mad, Lady Boneweaver."

"Of course it is," Sabrina says. "That's why it's brilliant."

"Tomorrow night," I say, clenching the bag in my fist. "We do it tomorrow night."

* * *

When I get ready in my room the next afternoon, I look around the empty space. Their scents are still here, fainter than before. I refused to change the sheets this entire time, sleeping on a different spot every night, burying my nose in each pillow. Their absence has left a hollow yawning at the centre of me.

Soon, Savage's laugh will fill the space.

Soon, I'll feel Scythe's piercing gaze on my skin.

Soon, Lyle will be soothing my legs with Tiger Balm.

Soon, Xander will be moping by the windowsill, casting me longing looks.

But that can only happen if I get this right. Only if I can kill Katerina Crocodylus, The Collector.

My power drapes around me, its wings flicking outward, the tough skin settling firmly in place. I would be bulletproof with my dragon hide, but that doesn't mean a harpoon won't bloody hurt.

I close my eyes and send out a request, carried on tongues of mythical flame. Tonight, is the night that more animas than one might get their revenge.

My phone buzzes with a notification, and I glance at it before saying goodbye to the empty room. "We'll be back soon," I tell it. "Be ready for me and my pack, and until then, look after the students within the academy walls. If my father or Ghoul comes here, don't let them in."

The wind is cool on the animus dorm roof where Hyacinth and her mates—the slender Sifa and bleached blonde Teylani—await us under the late afternoon sun. With them, we animas make a team of seven.

Stacey and Sabrina wear stretchy black catsuits they stitched up in a hurry. Sabrina gets a hood on hers, drawn tight so only the moon of her face shows. Stacey's hair is in a tight bun, but she's dressed herself in black lipstick. She downs an entire can of energy drink and hands it to Eugene, who pulls it towards him with a claw. Stacey might have recovered from her ordeal, but she still feels the long-term effects of poisoning, including fatigue.

Minnie wears black leggings and a zip-up jacket. She's got a black strap to tie her pink curls back so she looks like a karate master. Hyacinth and her pack watch this with raised brows, but when they see me, they straighten as one. As if I'm some war general, ready to give them their orders. I hone in on their bodies, looking for any signs of weakness or lack of focus.

"Focus," I say. "The flight will be just under an hour by dragon wing. Five minutes from the compound, we'll begin."

They nod as Marduk, with the nimpins huddled on his shoulders, gestures for them to step backwards. He, Yeti and Beak frown from the sidelines, clearly not happy about being left out. Beak tried negotiating with me. He wanted to go in with a group of avian forces, attacking the property from the air. Yeti wanted to bring military trucks and surround the place with brute force.

Marduk, for his part, remained silent, understanding that I need to do this and obeying his regina when she told them to cease their protests. They listened thankfully, and Beak bowed his head when I stared him down. I was always going to do this my way.

My dragon form bursts from my skin, lungs sizzling, my blood heating as the building becomes mine. There is no roar for me to release tonight. I keep it all within. I save it.

Marduk and Yeti levitate everyone onto my spine, and I wait for them to settle, flexing my claws out one at a time. *"Are the earpieces working?"* I ask into their minds.

Marduk sourced us the FBI-worthy comm devices as easily as he sources everything. While I can talk into their heads, my friends not being able to respond has made things difficult in the past. Because animalia have excellent hearing, I have to make sure any communication is not heard by enemies around us.

"What does a dragon in heat look like?" Minnie's voice is clear in my left ear.

"I dunno, what?" Stacey pipes.

"Godzilla. Lia is going to be Godzilla tonight."

"It's giving Jurassic Park," Stacey snickers.

"*It's giving*, this is serious," Hyacinth warns. "People are going to get hurt tonight."

"We'll be invisible. It'll be fine," Sabrina drawls.

"I signed the consent form I made!" Minnie protests. "We all did."

"We're also all adults." I project to them. *"If at any point you want to get out of there, you're allowed to. You just have to tell us."*

"We're all good, Lia." The earpiece makes Sabrina's deadpan sound like it's right next to me. "Let's do this."

Without another word, I wrap them in my shield, bend my knees, and we're off.

Chapter 26

Xander

The air is silent as Scythe changes Katerina's bandages under her brusque instruction. There has been no change in the scent of the room. Blood and rotting flesh make for a foul scent to my dragon's nose, and yet I find it comforting.

My ears strain, and although I know there is nothing to hear, something ancient rumbles through my bones. Savage and Lyle open their eyes from where they are sleeping on their cell floor. Scythe's hands pause in their work, making Katerina frown up at him. A little smile twitches at the edges of my mouth moments before becoming full-blown laughter.

Katerina's head snaps towards me.

Our regina has come for us. And she is *furious*.

Chapter 27

Aurelia

We come upon the Crocodylus property at sunset, orange and pink bleeding across the sky at my left shoulder.

A pretty day to die.

Darkness gathers on my right, and it's the perfect amount of light to begin. I fly high so my wing beats don't create turbulence on the ground, alerting the many guards who patrol the barbed wire fence that surrounds the entire property. New guard towers have been hastily constructed out of the same metal scaffolding that still holds up the back part of the house—devastation caused by another dragon; that one black, not blue.

I shiver as I recall that day. Most of it is a blur of pain. My life narrowed down to nothing more than pure instinct and survival. My mates walk that narrow precipice now.

The animas on my back poke each other as they get their first real look at the area, muttering at the two manufactured long rivers on either side, like parallel highways. Even this late in the day, no fewer than twenty salties lie on the banks, their mouths open as they regulate the temperature of their cold blood.

"It's time," I tell my friends.

Plastic crinkles at my back as Hyacinth brings out the drawn-up syringes of oestrous-inducing medication. She injects Sifa and Teylani, then Minnie and Sabrina. I refused to let Stacey be dosed, given her recent compromised state. We needed a level head on the ground in any case, so our lioness and hyena regina are going to be the designated wranglers.

Two minutes later, Sabrina's voice grunts in my ear. "Oh wow. Yeah, I feel it coming on."

"Same," Minnie says. They've all experienced heats before, but a manufactured heat carries a heavier signature. I've warned them as much as I could, and it's going to be up to Stacey and Hyacinth to keep them in line.

"Then let us begin," Hyacinth says.

I begin my descent as the sun finally disappears below the horizon, leaving a purpling edge along the seam of the world. I needed the visibility of the light to make sure we weren't flying into a trap, but we need night to prepare our ambush.

I see them before anyone else, but it takes the others only seconds to notice.

"Oh look," Sabrina mutters. "It's the lion, the witch and the *cunt*."

My eyes catch on three figures walking out of the house. Connor, Katerina, and the Lady Hyena are leaving the house and walking, not to the vehicles but to the side of the house towards the river.

"We weren't expecting her to be here," Hyacinth says. "She's been AWOL since your appearance at the Jewel."

"She's come to see if the skin curse can be reversed," Sifa whispers. "Clearly, the serpents couldn't help her." Or *wouldn't*, if what I suspected is true. My father's only real ally is himself. I'd known that long before entering Halfeather House that fateful day so long ago.

Regardless of the trio walking towards the crocodile fence, I maintain a slow-moving spiral downwards until I'm just out of detectable range. Minnie and Stacey work together to bring down Hyacinth and her pack safely. Enveloped in my invisibility bubble, they are levitated down like assassins on climbing ropes. We can't see them, being in the shield, but Minnie's always been the strongest and most precise telekinetic of us all.

Regardless, I monitor for their safe landing in the gathering dark, feeling the slight weights of the three remaining felines.

Minnie's whisper sounds in my ear. "See you soon, Lia."

"Remember, if you leave my line of sight, you'll lose invisibility," I warn.

"Roger that."

Something wholly primitive calls to me. It's not a roar, not a screech, not a pounding in my head. It's a regina's hunting silence. And it settles into every artery, every vein, stretching alongside the shadows that follow the sunset. My senses become alive, become linked to my nerves, the spaces in my brain meant to strategise.

Blood will flow tonight.

Mid-air, I shift into eagle form, exchanging webbed wings for feathers and light bones, a snout for a beak. My eyesight shifts, not as violently detailed as the dragon's, but eagle eyes are something that I've always been used to. *"Let's make a lap,"* I say.

I shift into a cobra, removing my own invisibility so my friends can see me, and slither towards the guard towers. Low to the ground, the world looks bigger, but I know I hold these moments in the palm of my hand.

It's fully dark now, and big floodlights are turned on, aimed at the road before the front fence. There are two lighthouse-style rotating beams aimed at the sky. As Hyacinth leads her pack towards the gate, I monitor my feline animas as they levitate beside me. My forked tongue sneaks out to taste the air, and I scent them. Feminine, sweet, lusty. Like dripping honey, it coats the air, lustful and longing.

This scent is made to travel. Made to attract, draw attention, and drive males into a frenzy. It's a weapon that bypasses order powers, intellect, and military strategy. I suffered for the privilege of that information and now I use it as a weapon against the very enemies who sought to use it against me.

My friends pant under the force of its power, their heat signatures bright and hot to my serpent eyes. Minnie taps Hyacinth on the shoulder before driving all six of them up the first guard tower, where two guards hold automatic rifles.

"What's that smell?" a burly roo says, twisting around to scent the air. "It smells so fucking good."

"Are there any animas here?" another replies, unconsciously tugging at the collar of his uniform. "If she has Connor on that stuff again, I'm gonna be so...Yeah, someone's in heat." He rubs his dick because he can't help it. These roos are unmated, and it shows in the pants now tenting.

My animas say nothing, letting the scents wrap around the tower before Minnie draws them away. The guards sniff the air and frown to themselves before the first leaps right off the tower and lands on the dirt, kicking it up in a cloud. The second follows.

We continue on to the second and third guard towers, collecting three croc guards patrolling on foot along the way. The guards become distracted, losing their patrol formation and leaving their posts to track the scents of the animas. Two of my friends are reginas, and they're powerful, sweet treats for unmated animuses.

It's Sabrina, with a small knife, wielding it with the precision she's known for, who's responsible for the deaths of the two animuses who don't respond to the scents, likely because they are a part of a mated group.

The rest make up a group of twelve big, rifled males, and when Minnie flies the animas right over the main gate, the males have no choice but to unlock the gate and follow. Hyacinth and her pack lead them out into the night, while my felines jog back to me.

I don't know these creatures, but I know they guard The Collector so she can execute the most heinous crimes of our kind. It's not just Lorian. Who else has she got tortured and starved in the dark under her house?

Sabrina stumbles back to me, and there are tiny flecks of crimson on her cheeks. "Let's go," she whispers. "Hyacinth is taking them out on the west side." She retrieves the last syringe from her pocket and offers it to me.

I shift into human form and take it with a nod, jogging ahead of them towards the main house. The syringe cap comes off with the aid of my teeth, and I spit it into the dirt before stabbing myself in the left deltoid. There's a familiar sting as it goes in, and suddenly, the flash of bright halogens and white walls, lab coats and serpent sweat fills my nose.

But I'm not in Drakos Estate. I am free.

My feline sisters and I keep a fast pace as we jog up the long road to the house. I keep our invisibility around us all, with me being able to make out who's who by their heat signatures. About halfway, emerge a group of five guards in a Jeep, purposefully moving in the opposite direction. In the back seat is none other than the hyena queen.

I only have a split second to make the decision, but I do it.

My telekinetic power lashes out, and I halt the truck. It screeches to a stop, the wheels stuck in place. The driver revs the engine, but Sabrina must know a thing or two about cars because her power zooms past me and something blows in the engine, making smoke stream out from under the hood.

After multiple curse words, they jump out of the vehicle. Silently, we move in around them, and it takes less than three seconds for them to notice the scent. Except something unexpected happens when the group halts, sniffing the air like predators.

Stacey lets out a choked sound and stumbles into me. I grab her, but she violently shoves me away, barrelling past me and into the soldiers. "My rex!" the lioness gasps, gripping one of the males. "You're my rex!"

"No fucking way," Sabrina mutters.

Minnie clutches my arm. The male rears back, unable to see his assailant, and I have no choice but to uncloak Stacey.

When she's revealed, we all see Stacey clutching onto the arms of the tall male, peering into his eyes. He stares down at her as if he's seen a ghost, and I'm sure he's looking at her neck and the mating mark they both share. She reaches up with slender, trembling fingers, but he snatches them up. "Why are you here?" he frowns. "How are you here?"

The hyena queen stands from the Jeep. "If she's here, the others are scuttling around here too. Just like mice."

One of the guards closer to us raises a walkie-talkie to his mouth. Without warning, Sabrina ducks out from behind me, and I suppress a cry, keeping the invisibility around her.

"Take the front two," I tell Minnie. *"I'll get the middle two."*

As Sabrina leaps onto the guard, knocking the walkie-talkie out of his hand and making him stumble, Minnie's power lashes out, telekinetically wrapping around the front guards.

The males struggle to see the invisible assailant, and I charge my power into the chests of the two in the middle row, gripping their hearts and squeezing until they lose consciousness. Blood spurts from the throat of the man Sabrina has, while the front three have their feet swept out from under them, falling hard as if thrown and knocking the backs of their heads hard on the ground.

Stacey whimpers as her rex pushes her away and swings his gun around blindly, aiming for the rest of us. "Where are they?" he shouts.

"Are they dead?" the lioness whimpers, looking out at the rest of the guards.

"Yes," the hyena queen says, before calling out into the dark. "Finally got some backbone, did you, Boneweaver girl?" she cackles. "You won't leave this compound, and neither will your little lioness friend."

"You guys need to get Stacey out of here," I quickly tell Minnie and Sabrina, rolling my neck as I feel the heat dancing in my veins. *"Find the keys from the dead guards and keep an eye on the front gate in case she calls for reinforcements. I'll come and get you."*

"Like fuck!" Stacey shouts at me, fully hearing my conversation.

"They're here!" comes a shrill voice through the walkie-talkie on the ground. "Shoot them on sight!" The soldier swings his gun around and shoots Stacey right in the arm. Everyone screams.

Before anyone can stop her, Sabrina bounds towards the hyena matriarch, a fresh needle and syringe high in the air. Before I register what she's about to do, she stabs the hyena matriarch right through her dress sleeve.

Chapter 28

Aurelia

The old woman cries out, but Sabrina pushes down on the plunger before the hyena whirls around, the needle still in her arm. Sabrina dances back, but the hyena follows her with her eyes. The plunger continues to move downwards under Sabrina's power. The hyena queen cries out, yanking the needle out and tossing it to the ground. But more than half the drug entered her system. She shakes her cane, and hyena magic flies uselessly through the air.

"Shit!" Minnie cries, pulling Stacey into her arms.

"You fucker!" I cry, shoving back the feline guard with telekinesis as Minnie plucks his gun from his arms. I squeeze his heart until he falls unconscious with a heavy thud.

"We don't have time. Go!" I shout into their heads. *"Take them out to Hyacinth!"*

We go our separate ways. My friends whip up Stacey and her rex and run towards the front of the property. I give the hyena matriarch a wide berth as I head towards the house. Sabrina shouts, and the lady hyena gives pursuit, her cane working overtime as she hastens after them, muttering curses into the night.

What she plans to do, how she plans to catch up to them, I don't know. And Stacey's bastard rex is something we'll have to deal with later.

The constellations look different tonight as I jog alone to The

Collector's house. Tonight, they look like a hundred eyes on me. Ready to see my downfall or my rise.

I take off my eighth shield. I brought no clothes with me, and while I've spent the majority of the last few weeks buck naked, for the first time tonight, I feel exposed. The hormones spin through my system, making me sweat, flooding my core with wet desire that I'm struggling to control.

Violently pushing the lust away, I settle into my anima and the regina in me who's about to fight for her mates. Lowering my head, I follow my nose across the compound, following the scent of The Collector.

I come across her at the entrance, speaking furiously to the guards. The lights of the house spotlight Connor, standing tall next to his mistress, his dark mane in a big bun as his crown. He looks worse for wear; there's a darkness under his eyes, and fine lines around his mouth as if he's been frowning a lot. His eyes widen with fear when he sees me. Fear *for* me. He glances at The Collector, who stands with her bandaged hands on her hips, nostrils flaring.

Those slitted eyes drag up and down my naked body. I don't know how she'd expected me to arrive here, but I doubt it was naked, walking right up to the front entrance. "I'm going to have you killed," she hisses. "And I'm going to watch your mates do it."

I mark her slender form with every part of my being. From the dark bob of her hair to the red and bleeding marks my curse has made up her arms and torso. I cock my head before I make my promise. "Before morning, your blood will paint these floors."

Pure murder festers in those slitted eyes, but she steps backwards. "Connor!" she orders, harsh arrogance dripping off every word. "Bring my mates to me. All of them."

Connor scrambles inside, his fear perfuming the air. He glances back at me like he wants to say something, but we know any warning won't work now.

Katerina and I stare at each other, the very air tightening between us. I don't blink as I examine her and the new bandages wrapping around her body like an Egyptian mummy. I hadn't even known that the spell would work. Only that it was worth the shot and the risk to try. She knows as well as I do that her breached crocodile skin makes her vulnerable now.

Ancient instinct feels their approach before I see their feet cross the threshold of the entryway. The other pieces of my soul stalk out one by one, in slow motion, their towering, terrifying human forms taking up all the space, power and menace oozing from every pore.

They look in even worse condition compared to when I saw them at the Jewel. A weariness hangs about their forms, as if dragging them down into the depths of nothingness. The spell is taking its toll on them, and my instincts tell me they feel it creeping through their bodies like black poison. Before long, it would make them shadows of themselves, wandering behind The Collector like wraiths.

Their souls are screaming, and they don't have the ability to understand why. Savage's bare torso bears a sheen of glistening sweat, making the wolf head on his chest gleam under the floodlights. His dark hair is mussed, hazel eyes wild. Lyle's hair looks more like matted locks at the moment, the twists hanging limply around his bare shoulders, a tattered white shirt hanging uselessly over his arms. Scythe's shark eyes are ferocious behind the glassy film, shark teeth gnashing like he's trying to speak, and it stretches a new, deep gash on his cheek. And Xander. My dragon's eyes illuminate the night in painful contrast to the rest, his fists clenched at his sides. He alone looks groomed and aware.

Every bone in my body screams out for them and their pain. Just as every vessel in my body feels the heat serum kick in with full force. My breath comes fast, and it makes my head spin.

"Catch her," The Collector snarls from Connor's side. "Bring her to me; do *not* be gentle."

I force my feet to walk backwards, never taking my eyes off them as they advance towards me as a predatory, stalking group. Savage notices the scent first, the flare of his nostrils and the curiousness in his eyes that no spell could take away from him.

"You know me," I say to him. "Your body knows what I smell like in heat." I glance at Scythe. "And your heart knows mine."

I nod reassuringly at a worried Connor before turning around and sprinting. But of course, my mates are apex predators of the highest order, and the sudden movement makes them growl and snap. They lunge for me. And I let them.

Strong hands band around my body, and I groan softly in awareness of Lyle's body, hard and hot behind me. He growls in my ear, and a second animalistic growl enters the other. I close my eyes as the four of them surround me, noses sniffing, breaths hot, the combined scents wrapping around me like a blanket of bliss.

I squirm, those oestrous hormones sliding through my veins, making firm hands feel like heaven. Someone's nose touches my neck—Savage's, I think—and I let out a whimper of longing. "Savage," I whisper. Teeth scrape around my bicep, clamping down on the same muscle the injection went into. It's Scythe's teeth surveying the spot, and I sigh under the burn.

"I can't believe this was your plan," Xander whispers by my mouth, lips brushing its corner. "I can't believe you thought this would work."

"Shup," I sigh. "I mean, shut up, dragon."

But Lyle has collected up my legs and is bringing me bridal style into the house. I look up into his eyes, and though he's striding quickly like he knows where he's going, he does not take his eyes off mine.

His animus is in there, hungry, ravenous, and powerful. I feel his chaotic power on my skin. As if a fucking spell could take over *his* unhinged animus.

His gaze is terrible on mine, and I search for him within it. I can't help but smile at his proximity. At his focus. His fingers dimple my thighs, and I reach down to touch them. Such strong fingers that hold me. "Gods, I missed you," I whisper to him.

But then we're in a familiar room with cold white lights and a triggering smell of antiseptic.

My scream is involuntary and immediate. I struggle violently against my mate's hold, bucking and trying to throw myself out of his grip. Lyle is forced to band his muscle around me with bruising force, and I scream again. It makes The Collector laugh as she stands by the familiar medical bed. "I believe this is where we left off," she drawls, eyes bright and greedy.

But then Xander is standing next to me, his fingers lashing around my right wrist. *"Get your shit together."*

In my head, glass breaks. Gentle hands cradle me, and draconic power envelops my body. I clench the toes of my right foot and swallow the string of screams that wants to let loose. That wants to scream and not stop for breath like we once did before. The bright gold orbs of Xander's eyes burn into mine, his tight hold reminding me that we've already done this. That I have my leg back. That I am fine. That Flores Drakos is dead by his son's hand.

I take a shaky breath as Lyle brings me to the mattress that once changed my life. He removes his hands from around my body. I touch that ferocious, angry face, the blonde scruff on his cheek. *"Come out,"* I hiss to his animus. *"Come out, my big, angry lion."*

Lyle's pupils grow, and a cavernous rumble grows in his chest like a building storm. My most rabid mate. The mate least likely to fall prey to *any* type of captivity—not after what he'd been through, not after it claimed his family. Feline teeth elongate, and he bares them in a snarl. He inhales deeply, those big eyes closing for mere seconds as his lungs fill with the scent of me.

A hairline fracture appears in the spell around his mind, and I lunge for it, hungry. *"I did not execute Frederick Ulman only to see you captive by another's hand."*

In my head, a gravelly, barely human voice replies, *"Regina."*

Chapter 29

Lyle

The puzzle pieces that were flashes of clear sight I had gotten over the past few weeks now get put together. Now make sense. My brain emerges from the torturous fog that's burdened us.

Horror winds its way through my spirit in a way that hasn't happened since I was a teenager. I scramble to control my animus, and though I don't let him shift me into animal form in this small space, I feel the raw, terrible need take over.

There is red in my eyes and death in my heart.

And that sweet scent wraps around me, my regina's unique smell. And it hones my rage like a sharpening knife.

Chapter 30

Aurelia

A chink in the armour.

Lyle's lion bows his head to me before whirling on Scythe. He slams a hand around my shark's throat, thudding him back against the wall. The Collector screams at him to stop, but the growls of both males drown her out. Savage, completely ignoring the other two, sniffs at my feet at the edge of the bed. He wrinkles his nose before sniffing my ankles, my shins, and knees.

"Stop!" The Collector screams again, pulling open the cupboards, no doubt looking for her cattle-prod. But Xander is there, wrapping his hands around her arms, digging his fingers into the bandaged wounds. She screams in pain and fury. Meanwhile, Savage has worked his way halfway up my body, the muscles of his arms catching my eye as he supports himself using the edges of the mattress. His nose touches the apex of my thighs, nudging open my labia. He inhales with his eyes closed. I spread my legs with a moan, my hormones surging with need.

"Savage!" The Collector screams. "Get Xander off me!"

My wolf is frowning now, the command now at odds with his nose. He inhales my scent again and growls into my core. His tongue darts out, and he clutches his chest with one hand, moaning at the taste.

"Regina," he says raggedly. "Where is my regina?"
"Here!" come two voices—one moaned, one shouted in rage.
Savage shakes his head, confused, and I call his name.

Chapter 31

Savage

Fluffy brain full of bunnies.

Fluffy like cotton.

Fluffy like nimpins.

Why can't I see properly?

Why can't I remember where I am?

Smell. Regina. Pussy.

Wait.

Wait.

Pussy? Yes, pussy. My regina's.

"Princess?" I cry. "Where are you?"

"Here," comes a voice, soft and beautiful like a moonbeam.

"Mine," I say to the world. *"Where have you been?"* I demand angrily.

"It wasn't my fault!" she protests. Always so sassy. *"I came for you!"*

The black haze lifts from my mind, and when I see the room, when I see *her*, I roar.

Chapter 32

Aurelia

Savage bellows into the room, black pupils swallowing his irises. I roll over on the medical bed, panting with desire and trying to force my brain back into focus. The Collector's eyes are wild as Xander holds her still, the points where his fingers touch her bandages gushing blood. "Let her go, Xander," I say.

Savage leaps off the bed and pulls me towards him. "Regina," he whispers against my mating mark, his voice breaking. *"Aurelia."*

I lean into his face, cupping his cheek. "I'm here," I say. My eyes flick to Katerina, trembling with fury and *morbid* hunger. "Your regina is here now." It takes everything I am to disentangle myself from him and get to my feet. I stalk forward. On my right, Lyle is still struggling to keep Scythe pinned to the wall. "Xander," I say again. "Let her go."

He doesn't want to, that possessive mouth tightening before his hands come off her.

Katerina darts for the door, but I'm ready. I've been ready for a while.

Power floods my right leg, and I launch after the crocodile. She sprints down the corridor, kicking off her boots and running barefoot across the tile. I charge after her, watching her muscles for signs of direction change. She shouts for her guards, her servants, for anyone, and although I hear voices and other shouts, no one comes to her aid.

Katerina reaches the foyer and shoves the door open. Her servants blink with confusion. Connor's eyes go wide as I whoosh past him, my feet slapping hard against the tiles and then the dirt. I feel my mates charging behind, all four of them dogging my steps, snapping and growling.

I inhale a lungful of cool night air as Katerina makes a beeline for the river. For her crocs. It's then that I pounce, throwing myself through space and grabbing her by the back of her shirt, yanking her backwards and right into my arms.

"Scythe!" she screams. "Scythe, save me!"

The snarl that tears from my throat is pure, vicious fury.

My power snaps around her—serpentine, feline, canine, draconian, and shark all in one. Fear perfumes the air as I bury my hand in her hair and wrench her skull back, snarling into her face, with a lifetime's worth of people trampling me behind my rage. "Nothing will save you from me. Not the Wild Mother, not your crocodile skin, and certainly not Mace fucking Naga."

I bury my sharp canines into her cheek, ripping out a chunk of flesh and spitting it out onto the dirt. Katerina screams in horror and outrage, her legs kicking out against my power and failing as I rear back and slam my teeth into her neck. The taste of blood and flesh drives me near rabid, and I shift.

Four limbs, low to the floor, and terrible, long jaws with enough force behind them to break a skull. Katerina chokes on her own blood and scrambles away from me, kicking up dirt, but I *pursue*. For each step she takes, I take two, and I'm on her in an instant, my entire world focused on flesh, even my mates fading away into the distance. Elation fills my veins, golden joy spinning through my head. *"This is for Lorian,"* I tell her before my jaws clamp around her neck. *"This is for my mates."* Bone crushes in my mouth, the crack reverberating through my body and filling me up with utter, primal satisfaction. *"And this is for my leg."*

Chapter 33

Xander

My bloodthirsty, hungry, *vengeful* regina eats Katerina Crocdylus with all the relish of a full-grown crocodile. Long, scaled jaws tilt upwards as they crunch and snap and swallow.

Savage goes on his hands and knees to stay close and eagerly watch. He licks his lips and I just know he wants to join in, but I only worry about her stomach and what that flesh will do to it once she returns to human form.

Aurelia spits out Katerina's head and begins on her body, chomping down on her shoulders. I spare a glance for my brothers, not fighting now that they're fixated on Aurelia. Scythe is staring at Katerina over Lyle's shoulder, and I'm sure whatever remains of the curse is now just oxygen, but he'd descended into his shark so deeply that he's not responding to the lifting of the spell yet.

"Scythe," I say. "If you want a piece of this, I'd get some now; otherwise, your regina is going to have all of it."

The shark gnashes his jaws at me, and Lyle removes the forearm he's pressed to our brother's throat, allowing both of them to prowl forward with bloodlust in their eyes.

Apparently, I'm the only sane bastard in the room.

My brothers gather around crocodile Aurelia with reverence, in something akin to ritualistic prayer, except their Goddess is a guzzling croc and her sermon is the primal sound of her consuming the entire torso of The Collector.

Aurelia hasn't taken our captivity well, and it only hits me now how hard it affected her. The combined effect of her heat and murderous, regina rage has resulted in the most primal bloodlust. She's pushed her mammalian side completely away and moved down, right into reptilian.

Sighing dramatically, I attend to the next important thing, which is The Collector's messy head. I grab her by the hair, my eyes illuminating her Aurelia-punctured features. Her skull has been cracked in multiple places by Aurelia's teeth, but she's still recognisable.

A loud belch sounds from beside me, and I spin around, brows raised to see Aurelia with her jaws open over what remains of The Collector's legs.

"Must leave evidence," Savage agrees wisely. "Now she looks like the Witch of the East with her feet sticking under Dorothy's house, only—"

"She doesn't even *have* the rest of her body," I say, trying to hide my glee.

Aurelia slumps sideways before shifting. Savage reaches for her, but she thrashes as human skin appears and her snout retracts into her human face. The four of us instinctively reach for her, my animus roaring for her gaze to touch me. She gets to her feet, and when she rises in her human form, I feel like the entire universe has roused itself in my head. As if my centre has shifted into here and now and *her*.

Aurelia's fingers reach out for us, brushing along our chests, our faces, and Scythe's teeth. "Mine," she snarls. Her face and mouth are covered in blood. Her skin is hot, and her golden, honeyed scent fills my head. "Mine."

"Yours!" Savage cries with glee, grabbing her face and planting a big kiss right on her bloody mouth. Lyle rubs his nose against her cheek, while Scythe's tattooed hands reach for Aurelia's bare stomach as if he's soothing her old scars.

I'm suddenly aware of shuffling movements and hushed voices around us. Connor, Minnie, and Sabrina are huddled together and peering at us with a group of Katerina's collared servants. I don't say anything, I just raise The Collector's head. One of the servants faints, and Minnie clutches her stomach. Connor presses his hands to his face, shaking his head back and forth like this is a nightmare.

"I thought..." He covers his mouth. "We need to get the others out."

Aurelia suddenly appears at my side. "Lorian," she growls.

"Who?" Connor asks.

"The unicorn," I clarify.

His face, already ashen, seems to fall. "They moved him out of his cell a few nights ago, but..."

"But what?" Aurelia stalks forward, and her appearance makes her friends flinch. Minnie's eyes, however, light up. "Where are the rest of the guards?"

"Dealt with," Sabrina says, tugging the cords of a strange black cat suit. "Rounded up or dead by Hyacinth." She wrenches forward one of the guards wrapped in so many ropes I can't see his uniform anymore. Sabrina holds up bunches of keys. "Took these off Stacey's rex."

By the ever-loving gods.

"Take me to Lorian," Aurelia says to Connor.

"Free the rest of the captives," I say to the others. "And for the retinal scanners..." I hold up The Collector's head. "That should do it."

Minnie and Sabrina are more morbid than I ever gave them credit for because Minnie grabs the head by its hair and the two run off cackling, their captive between them. No wonder the anima girl gang gets along so well.

Connor, looking like he wants to vomit, reaches out for Aurelia. With a cute grunt, she takes his hand, and together the two animas lead the way. Scythe and Lyle try to shove past me, but I manage to elbow Lyle and hurry ahead of them.

The scent of blood tints the air as we pass the cages Katerina was keeping the Animal Justice captives in. Crocs thrash in the river on our left, and it doesn't take me long to see where Connor is leading us.

My eyes are like a spotlight beam on the metal hut in the middle of the thickest part of the river. No fewer than ten full-size saltwater crocodiles lie on the banks on either side, and more glowing eyes stare at us, half submerged in the water. Their kind don't usually come out when there's no sun to bake in, but the blood of the events of tonight has sparked their interest. At our approach, the fattest of them swings a mighty head to look at us. A Jurassic bellow resounds from the opposite side.

"This is their favourite spot," Connor says, gulping. "They specifically feed them here."

The carcasses of the humans I'd killed had disappeared rather quickly. No doubt their remains had been scattered all through here. "Is the top of the hut open?" I say, wondering if I can fly in and wrench it off its foundation.

"Yeah, but uh...they can *jump* ten feet into the air," Connor says, "and the top of it has a metal mesh. He can still see the sky, but no one's getting him out of that without opening the steel door with the retinal scan."

My regina wanders forwards, brushing the wire fence with her fingers. Another croc bellows in warning. Connor shivers.

"They sound like dragons," Savage says, also stepping forward to join her. "But even dragons can be killed."

There is movement in the water, a giant splash, then a full-grown, naked man crawls out of the river and straightens. He's thick like a bull, no less than six and a half feet of brown skin and huge muscle with slitted, yellow pupils. He points an oversized finger at us. Okay, so this just got significantly worse. Natural, even rabid crocs I could deal with, but a whole colony with human intelligence?

Aurelia snarls at the animus, baring her teeth and still-bloody mouth in challenge. "Let's fucking do this."

I have to do a double take at this regina of mine. Lyle and Savage also blink at her like they've seen a new dawn. A second later, feathers are sprinkling over me, and she's burst into her eagle form. She takes flight and swiftly makes her way over the fence, towards the metal hut.

"Wait for me!" Savage cries, hurriedly hooking his fingers into the fence and climbing.

"There's barbed wire at the top!" I warn. Savage cusses me out, his eyes only for his regina. But then Lyle's animus is blasting his power into the fence, and the entire thing bends over like an old man. Metal screeches, water splashes, and tails thrash. Aurelia gives a shrill cry, and I swear bloody murder.

"Lyle!" Aurelia admonishes, a regina command ringing through the air and making us all freeze.

Chapter 34

Lyle

My rabid lion gets shoved back behind his chained door at the sound of my regina's cry. My vision clears, and the night is suddenly open to me, along with the mob crocs thrashing in the water now that I've pushed down the fence. A metallic shriek pierces the air as some parts of it snap, but I've shoved it hard enough for the central point to lie useless in the water.

My rabid lion has always been...ambitious.

Connor lets loose a shout, and he sprints back to the main house like hell itself is after him. Xander groans in annoyance as five crocs charge at us, something scarily human flashing in their eyes. I lash out with my telekinesis, realising too late that order powers don't work on crocs. Savage lunges onto the back of one large animus, wrestling its jaws shut with his bare hands.

"Anyone got duct tape? I've seen them do this on TV!" our wolf calls excitedly.

"Yeah, sure, just in my fucking pocket!" Xander shouts, his fire whip snaking out and wrapping the snout of another croc.

The issue is that two more are coming for him. And for me. And for Scythe.

The shark in him is silent as he yanks off his belt with a snap and leaps right over the first croc charging for him, and heads for the second. I have no time to see how he manages to use his belt, but since I can't use telekinesis on the crocs, I use it to shoot myself towards my regina where she stands on the metal roof of the hut in the middle of the water. My bare feet land in a crouch on top of it with a heavy metallic thud. She's trying to wrench off the metal mesh that covers the structure.

"A little help here!" Savage demands from the bank, still on the thrashing croc. I pick up Savage and whizz him over to us on the roof, followed by Scythe, who had two crocs creeping up on him from behind. Xander...looks like he's managing fine, so I leave him be.

"Great!" he shouts sarcastically at me, no less than five glowing fire whips anchored to his fingers like a puppet master as he wrestles with the crocs he's bound.

"You're a dragon, remember!" Savage shouts, cupping his hands to his mouth. Xander drops his head back in annoyance before he shifts. Clothes tear, cartilage snaps, and the ground shakes as a mighty black dragon replaces the human male.

I always forget just how *big* the bastard is.

He wastes no time in opening that maw. Orange-yellow fire spills over the land, fence and river, roasting as it goes, steaming up the water and boiling the shallower parts on the bank. We all have to turn away for a moment, covering our eyes and faces as heat and light turn this part of the world into a small hell.

When the fire clears, I turn around to see smoke billowing into the sky. The metal fence is now nothing but a hunk of melted and twisted mess. This is not the case, unfortunately, for the fifteen very angry crocs who have now become hulking human males and females.

"They can't be killed by dragon fire?" Savage cries, clutching the sides of his face because even he knows we're outnumbered here. It's then that I notice the movement on the side of my eye. Savage roars and punches the leaping croc right in the throat. It splashes back in the water, but three others try their luck in quick succession.

"We need to get out of here, regina," I say, thumping the metal roof. "This thing is bound with hyena magic."

"I'm not leaving him!" my regina snarls at me.

Immediately, I'm ashamed of myself. But a commanding voice travels across the air like a spear, "Move aside!" and we all stare as none other than Celeste Agnis sprints towards us with Minnie, Connor, and Sabrina behind her. Celeste explodes into a ball of red fire, fading away to reveal her brilliant phoenix form.

The crocodiles charge at our friends, and Aurelia stands up with a cry of dismay. But the lady phoenix breathes fire over the riverbank. This time, it's magical phoenix fire that blasts the descending crocs, the sound nothing but a screaming cry.

The heat and magic singe the hairs on my skin and pulls my regina into the protection of us three males. But there is another female scream, and Minnie is soaring into the air in terror, a white-faced Sabrina in her arms, her right arm in bloody pieces.

And that's because the phoenix fire did not touch the charging crocs. I whip a frantic Connor up into the air, dumping him on Xander's back.

"Lia!" Savage cries, and it's then that I notice my regina is *vibrating*.

"Run," she chokes out, then takes a breath before she expands like a bomb. Savage, Scythe and I are blasted off the roof, right for the water, but I snap my power around the three of us, drawing us back to the hut's roof as our regina—

Does *not* sweep into the sky on dragon wings as I expect.

She has no wings at all. She is scaled and huge, just like in her dragon form, only her scales are a deeper navy of the pre-dawn.

"*Don't look!*" Xander screams into every head in the vicinity, and I get to see a glimpse of a blinding ultraviolet blue beam through the night.

There are multiple male screams and crocs' bellowing roars, and though there is no fire to be seen, acrid burning fills my nose, and a sound like nothing I've heard before. Like electricity. Like a live wire humming with lethal power, but on a large scale. My primitive instincts are roaring at the danger, at the pure lethal monster that has appeared before us.

Suddenly, there is a deathly quiet. Only Sabrina's sobs can be heard from Xander's back.

"It's safe." My regina's quiet voice is in my head this time. *"You're safe now."*

We find her on Xander's back, in human form, with Sabrina in her arms, an opposite power to the one she'd just displayed working on her friend's mangled arm.

Around us, where living bodies had just stood, now only lay piles of steaming ash.

Chapter 35

Scythe

I swim to the surface of my consciousness, my shark giving me a way to process the shock that broke his cold.

Savage gapes at the ashes on the river bank. "What was—"

"We'll talk about it later," I say.

Savage instantly forgets what he was worried about and grins at me, now clear-eyed. "You missed it, brother!"

"I'll find out," I assure him. Because I can feel the night's events in my bones. The shark's memories are mine, he just hides them when convenient. Now I'm back in control, the memories will unfog themselves, one by one.

My eyes search for my regina in the night, finding her on the other side of the river bank hugging Celeste Agnis. The backs of my eyes burn as I lay my eyes on Aurelia, the woman who has become the light of my life. Who has used her light to destroy our enemies.

She came for us, primal and raw, taking our fate into her claws, taking what is hers. I can't even describe what I feel right now. But my skin feels tight around my muscle and the dark whisperings have started back up. I blink hard against the hallucinations that want to make their way back in. I've been away from her for too long. I need the sea and I need her, but we have business to attend to first. Much has happened tonight, and much more needs to happen still.

Lyle has levitated himself toward a sweating Lady Agnis, and they speak softly to one another. She takes Aurelia's hand to steady herself, and together, the three of them make their way toward the hut whose roof Savage stands on.

I wrench my eyes away from Aurelia long enough to climb down to the platform the hut sits on and I use a power I don't often get to use, clearing a path in the water so they can walk up to the hut without getting wet.

Lady Agnis nods appreciatively at me, while Aurelia, her face flushed with adrenaline and bloodlust, Katerina's blood smeared on her face, meets my eye. I see only determination and a fierce will in those blue eyes and have never been prouder to be in the Boneweaver pack. A goblin hallucination appears behind her, dogging her steps like an ugly shadow, and I turn away to study the security sensor on the door.

"Hut hut!" Minnie cries, and while standing on Xander's back, she kicks something into the air like a football. Her aim is accurate, and Savage leaps up and catches the thing like a professional AFL player, before landing in the squelching mud. He holds up the head of Katerina Crocodylus by the hair like the Grand Final trophy before climbing back up to the platform and holding her up to the retinal sensor. The door hisses as it unlocks.

Aurelia and Celeste levitate themselves up onto the platform and surge forwards, pushing us males aside to nudge the door open. It swings inwards, revealing a silvery-white glowing beast, lying on his side in the dark. Celeste gasps and leaps for him.

"He's not dead," Aurelia says, reassuring herself and following her in.

"Lorian," Celeste chokes on her knees, her cheeks glistening. "Speak to me."

The beast breathes, his sides expanding with air. *It will take more than the likes of The Collector to kill me.* The voice is both light and heavy in our minds. *And the tears of my beloved will help.*

"Oh!" Celeste buries her face in his silvery mane, and a sick feeling twists in my gut. Healing wounds on his flank bear an awful scent, but I have a feeling they'd been much worse. I'm suddenly glad he found kinship with a powerful and kind anima such as Celeste.

"You need to see the moon," my regina says. "Let's get him out of this cursed place."

Aurelia and Celeste carefully levitate the unicorn out of the hut, through the mud, and onto dry land. Once we're all safely on the other side, I wave a hand to release the water back to its original flow.

Savage won't leave Aurelia's elbow, carefully studying the unicorn with a lopsided grin of wonder and delight. Lyle is more concerned about the remaining crocs in the river. There are more further downstream that might get brave and stray back here. Xander is speaking with Connor and some of the freed captives, some of whom look unwell. To my surprise, Hyacinth and her mates are also present, the hyena's sharp eyes surveying the captives in a maternal fashion.

As I return my attention to the creature before me, I'm floored by its presence. Rarely do I get to see something so pure in this world. Lorian bears the unique glow of his kind, precious and rare. His colossal, spiralling horn also sheds its own gentle light. This beast is something out of a dream. Impossible and...pure.

Like my regina.

It reminds me of my own impurity and how close I'd come to reliving an old past. But then Aurelia, as if she knows what I'm thinking, glances up, her eyes glistening with emotion. In this moment, every bad thought of mine tumbles away into the abyss. She has real love for me. And if a perfect, powerful creature like her can love me, then I must be worth loving.

A smile touches my lips, and she smiles back at me before attending to Lorian. He speaks to Aurelia quietly for a moment, though the words are hidden from me. I can't help but be jealous that he gets her focused attention. But then my regina steps back.

"Take us away," Celeste says to Lorian. "Get us out of this world, my love."

Power cycles around the two of them, and that fabled horn glows brighter as the air around them spins, then warps and melts. To my psychic eyes, they sparkle and gleam in the way of other-worldly powers.

Then they are gone, only a faint opalescence painting the air in their wake. We all stand there for a moment, stunned at having witnessed something so unexpected. *Out of this world,* Celeste had said.

Aurelia sucks in a breath and turns around to survey what's left of this night. I want to reach for her. Want to press her to my body and never let her go. But there is something dark clinging to my body. Something that demands to be scraped and bled off.

Connor and Hyacinth approach us. "We've released everyone," Connor says. "Some are unwell, but there are a few avians who can help."

"We have Lady Hyena in...custody." Hyacinth's lips twitch. "She's not coping with the oestrous injection."

"Will you kill her?" Aurelia asks, and I glance at her proudly.

"Not yet." Hyacinth nods at me. "She may be of use." The hyena gestures to her two mates, who bear the ex-hyena queen between them, her elderly body bound in obsidian chains.

"We need to clear the area," I advise. "Mace and the others will come looking for Katerina and opportunities for livestock. I will call for vehicles. May I use your phone, Hyacinth?"

"Of course."

I make a quick call to Rufus, informing him of the current state of things and my imminent return. We'll need some buses and medical staff, and I'll finally get to make use of the new safehouse I had built after the Lily Institute attack.

Connor seems to enjoy taking the lead, and I shake his hand in thanks. "Keep them safe," I tell him. "Once you're at the safehouse, you shouldn't be disturbed. I will send you more security."

"We'll be here to help," Minnie pipes. "And my mates are almost here."

Of course the Caspian and Siberian tigers aren't far away. They'd no doubt followed their regina at a distance, in case their insane plan didn't work out. I give Marduk a call too. My regina is at my side the entire time, and after I return Hyacinth's phone, I run my hand down Aurelia's black length of hair, now unbound and wild from all the shifting. "I need to leave with Xander," I say softly. "I need to go to sea, regina."

Something shifts in her bright blue eyes. Fire and water and *rage*. "No," she snarls.

Lyle brushes a knuckle along her cheek. "Everyone is tired, angel. And we are saved. You can rest now."

"No," Aurelia snarls again, her power booming in my ears, gravelly and deep. "You are mine. Mine only and mine to take. I will bear you, and I will *kill and consume* all others who try."

The bloodlust in her eyes is stunning me speechless, and then her power wraps around the four of us and reels us in like four fishing hooks. Savage lets out a hoot as we're all pressed together in a tight circle around our regina. She reaches out to clutch my and Lyle's shirts on her left and right, a low constant growl rumbling from her chest. Blue eyes dart left and right as if looking for an enemy. Lyle and I exchange a glance.

"Uh-oh," Xander says, but there's a strange, gleeful yellow around his aura that I've never, not once in the time that I've known him, seen before.

"What's happening?" Savage asks, looking between the dragon and our regina.

"This," says Xander with fascination, "appears to be a treasure haze."

PART TWO

Chapter 36

Savage

My strong regina carries us over the land and far, far away where the rest of the world can't hurt us. Scythe and Hyacinth organised everything with the captives so they can get to a safe place, but when Scythe started frowning into the dark, I knew it was time to leave and herded everyone up.

We ride into the sunrise, and it feels like Aurelia's flying us to heaven, which is very, very different to what we had in the last few weeks. Each of my bones feels sore, and my skin is all itchy and gross, like I haven't showered in months. Have I showered? Everything I remember of The Collector's house is all blurry. I shake myself out.

"I need you to kiss each body part," I say to my regina. *"Many kisses on each one to make them better."*

"Yes," her voice is all dragony in my mind-ears. *"Each one, my wolf."*

I swing my legs in happiness, making Lyle grumble behind me. I'm riding shotgun at the front and centre. Scythe is behind Lyle, and Xander is behind him, but The Collector's head is riding in Aurelia's front claw because she's refusing to let it go.

At one point, I lie down on her warm, hard shoulders, wanting to be close and skin to scales. I love her so fucking much, and if the treasure haze means she'll love on me even more, I'm so excited and ready for it.

By the time daylight is bright in my eyes, Aurelia cloaks us in her special invisibility shield. Too tired to talk to my brothers, I snuggle into Lyle's arms for the rest of the ride.

* * *

I smell the sea, and my eyes fly open as we arrive on the coast. Aurelia tilts her pretty snout down, and we veer toward the ocean itself. Putting my arms up in the air, I enjoy the rush of the wind on my skin, the feeling of infinite freedom after being cooped up so long like a battery hen. Aurelia's claws skim the water's surface, and her wings snap out in a paraglide across the water as we head a little out to sea where humans won't accidentally see us.

She flicks her wings up like a sail, and we slow down. "Are we —" Lyle asks before Aurelia levels out as we breach the ocean's surface, the droplets of sea spray sprinkling on my cheeks.

"Yes!" I cry as she settles on the ocean, and I imagine her little legs paddling like a duck under the water's surface. There's a splash on my right, and I see the soles of Scythe's feet disappearing into the water. I too get to my feet and dive in after him, and I feel Lyle doing the same.

I swim to wash the night's sweat and blood off my skin, but the problem is that I immediately miss my regina's touch and I have to swim right back to her, gasping for breath at the surface right near her side.

Pressing my cheek against her wet scales, I breathe in her smoky scent. *"I hated it, regina,"* I tell her. *"Hated every second not being near you."*

"Me too, precious wolf," she says, making my heart swell to the size of the moon.

A black blob, which is Xander's body against the sun, still sits on Aurelia's back, staring at the water as if it might hurt him. I catch my regina's eye. "He may start to smell, regina."

She snorts before a 'gust of wind' knocks Xander right off her back into the water. I cackle with happiness, diving under again, only this time, I come face to face with the mighty ol' shark that's

Scythe. I boop him right on the nose before following the mass of bubbles to Xander's flailing body.

We break the surface at the same time as he gasps dramatically for air and I thump him on the back. Lyle appears out of nowhere, his blonde hair plastered to his face, looking happier than I've seen him in ages.

Our regina paddles around us, suspiciously surveying the water for enemies. *"We must go soon,"* she says. *"But I will not leave Scythe. Lyle, hold this for me."*

The Collector's head flies out from under the water, and Lyle catches it with his telekinesis. Aurelia shifts, shrinking until she's only a grey dorsal fin above the water. I dive under again, only to see the two sharks circling around us like hungry predators. Above the surface, there's just two fins chasing each other.

"So cute!" I say to Lyle. "Remind me to get a fin for next time."

Xander is floating on his back, looking sort of glum and over the entire situation. He was awake the whole time and The Collector made him do all sorts of awful things, and I think it's affecting him now. I scowl at the black mark on his neck because it's not even shining like the rest of his wet skin is. Like it sucks all the light from outside and swallows it. Lyle treads water next to me, also staring at the floating dragon. We exchange a look and leave him alone.

An hour later, Scythe is calm, and Aurelia paddles the rest of us to the beach. There are a few tourists here, so we stay invisible as we climb onto the shore. Nakedness, the humans can deal with, but the severed head maybe not so much. Rufus is waiting for us in the carpark with a black Jeep and bags of supplies. Aurelia snaps her teeth at him and possessively draws Scythe away when he tries to speak with our jaguar manager.

"Home," she snarls. "We go home now."

I love her so much.

Aurelia blocks Lyle when he goes to take the driver's seat. "No," she scowls, grabbing his hand and pointing to the sky. "We fly again where it's safe."

"Sweetheart," Lyle says, cupping her salty cheeks. "We need to go to a safe building for today where we can eat and shower."

Her face lights up in the most adorable way. "I can get food! Lots of it for my big mates."

"We can get it together," I offer, stepping forward and taking her hand. "All of us."

She shakes me off and crosses her arms. "No, *I'm* getting it."

"Regina," Scythe's rasp gets her attention as he pushes me aside and tries to talk to her. "We have an apartment here. It will be safe for all of us."

"No," she says firmly. "We go back to the nest where it is surely safe, then I get food, we feast, then I clean my mates. End of story."

"Step aside," Xander drawls. "Aurelia, going to the academy nest will take too long, and I feel unwell. We have a closer nest here that we can use. I need healing." We all turn to stare at him. Xander runs a hand through his wet hair, flexing a bicep as he does.

"What?" Aurelia says sharply, shoving past me and pressing her nose against Xander's chest and rapidly sniffing all over his body. "You're unwell?"

"Yes," Xander says fakely. He even presses a hand to his forehead like he's going to faint. "I feel ill. I think I'm going to pass out."

"No!" She reaches up to his face and kisses him on the cheek. Now this isn't so fun anymore. "Okay," she says sharply to me as if it's my fault. "Where is the closer nest?"

"I'll take us," Lyle says, catching on and playing pretend too. "Put the ill one in the car."

"Yes." My regina, *my regina*, takes Xander's hand and gently leads him to the car as if he's elderly! I gape at Scythe, but he just shakes his head and nudges me into the back seat with them.

"I was wondering what the smell was this whole time," I announce as I slide in next to Aurelia, who takes the middle. "Xander must have gastro."

"What!" Xander and Lia say at the same time, which makes me more annoyed.

"Actually, I think I've caught it too, blah!" I pretend to retch, and my regina cups her hands in front of me as if she's going to catch my vomit. "You're the best regina ever," I say, copying Xander's voice. "I'm running a fever, I just know it."

Xander and I enjoy Aurelia fussing over the both of us as Lyle drives to one of our beachside apartments. When we get there, Aurelia demands to inspect the property first so she can assess for predators. I follow her closely around the three-bedroom apartment, and she sniffs better than any wolf I know, checking every surface, every curtain, and tests all the windows. Then, she finds some antibacterial wipes and runs them over every surface, *including* the light switches.

She makes me and Xander sit side by side, and she takes our temperature with the measuring device from the medical kit she hunted out in the bathroom. Then she assigns Xander and me one 'contamination' toilet and the rest of them get the other. Then she checks over Scythe and Lyle. She tuts over Lyle's matted hair, and her eyes glisten when she sees what remains of the healing wound on Scythe's cheek. She gently eases her power into his skin, kissing him better, leaving his skin unmarked like it was before. She runs her fingers over the rest of his body, healing every little wound and scratch The Collector made.

After that, she tries to shove us all into the big shower *together*.

Lyle's cock is pressed up against my ass, which is all well and good until Xander's cock comes swinging my way. I let out a high-pitched feral wolf scream, which has Aurelia jumping a foot in the air, baring her teeth, ready for an enemy. When she sees I'm pointing at Xander's dick, she rolls her eyes and yanks me towards her and the soapy loofah she's swinging like a mace.

"Ow!" I cry as she yanks my head down by the hair and scrubs the back of my ear with the aggression of a pissed-off wolf mum.

"Bad wolf!" she says. "I have to clean you properly."

She works *fast* and hard, scrubbing me all over, and I don't even get to enjoy it because she moves on to Lyle, who grins at me while she attacks him. Scythe has moved into the corner, steadily cleaning himself, and I squeeze past Xander to go look at him.

"Don't," he warns me as I open my mouth.

I pout. "Okay."

He uses a bar of soap and the sink while he waits for the shower head, scrubbing the back of his neck. Even though Aurelia healed him, I know he's scrubbing more than skin right now.

Back in the shower, Aurelia turns on the spray, and with the removable shower head in one hand, washes down Xander and Lyle like they're cars. They rotate like good boys when she tells them to, and then they have to wait because she refuses to let them dry themselves.

Xander watches her so closely while she does all of this, a strange, distant look in his eyes. I think he's back at Drakos Estate in his head. My heart feels less hatred towards him these days, and I don't feel like vomiting when I look at him now, but I still can't stand that darned black mark on his neck. It gives me the heebie-jeebies.

I shiver, and Aurelia is on me in a flash, dragging me and Scythe into the shower and shoving Xander and Lyle out of the bathroom with strict instructions to wait for her. Our regina has singular, dedicated focus on rinsing the soap off us, her movements so fast it's like she thinks we're running out of time somehow. Maybe she's making up for lost time.

I'm alarmed when I notice she's panting a little, a tiny frown between her brows. Scythe notices it too, and pulls the shower head out of her hands when we're all soap-free. He cups her cheeks and ducks his head, pressing his forehead and nose to hers.

"You felt helpless, didn't you?" my brother says softly to her. "So did I."

Her cheeks pinken. "I have to take care of you," she whispers. "Please don't stop me."

My eyes burn, and I scrunch up my face because this hurts so much. "I'm going to make fairy bread," I announce. "I'm going to... to...do something."

The biggest surprise ever is when Scythe says, "We should get popcorn and watch a movie."

"And put pillows on the floor?" I ask hopefully.

Aurelia's face brightens only a smidge. "Only if Xander and Savage feel better," she eyes me with the suspicion of a doctor.

I pat my eight-pack. "Yep, I think you fixed it."

She grabs the towel and starts to dry us. "There's a lot to do, you know. I don't know if there's moisturiser and underwear for you here."

Scythe yanks a new towel from the shelf beside the shower and dries our regina's hair. "We only have men's clothes here; you can wear my clothes until we can get back to the academy nest."

She nods, chewing her bottom lip because I just know she's writing a mental list. Then she absently rubs her stomach like it hurts her. Scythe glances at me. It's not every day you get to eat a whole human. The Collector was not a big person, but I think it's the biggest thing my regina has ever eaten. Bones and all.

"Do you need Gaviscon?" I ask. "Tums?"

She waves a hand, but the frown remains, and she rounds us up like sheep back outside. Xander and Lyle are already dressed and Xander's found our stash of phones, already ordering a bunch of takeaways.

"And Gaviscon!" I shout at him as Aurelia tries to yank a T-shirt over my head the wrong way around. Unfortunately, she gets it in her brain that I also need socks and a scarf for my fake illness. *I hate* socks, but I let her tug on the white ones she chooses for me anyway, ignoring Xander's smirk as I wiggle my toes.

After what seems like forever, we gather in the living room, fresh and clean, with our pizza laid out in front of us and Shrek on the TV.

We all need something harmless tonight.

Chapter 37

Ghoul

The air over The Collector's property feels...odd.

Aurelia's friends, their mates and surrogate-mates, gather with the infirm and traumatised captives. Those who aren't dead or ill are setting the place on fire and destroying it. A mound of guards lies outside the wire gate, their bodies bloodied and marked with hyena witchcraft. If I hadn't seen it for myself, I wouldn't have believed the carnage.

There's a portion of the riverbank blackened and still smoking. Aurelia and her mates are gone, but her scent still lingers in the air along with that strange smell. Some of Aurelia's friends remain. The powerful tigress Minnie, who sits with the lioness Stacey in her lap. The girl has a bandage over what looks like a gunshot wound to the upper arm. She is staring at someone—the sole remaining guard, chained to a chair with Sabrina watching him closely. She, too, has a bandaged forearm.

The hyena matriarch is also sitting on a chair bound in black chains. There are two Dabu pack hyenas watching over her, but they wander forwards to speak with their regina. I take the chance to dive down and whisper in the old woman's ear. "I've never seen you so *tied up.*"

She scowls at waist level, determined not to crane her neck to look at me. "I knew you'd be the first to arrive. Are you going to stop them?"

"No."

"Thought as much."

"They turned the place upside down, didn't they?" I muse, watching two ex-slaves throw their silver collars into the river with a cheer. Someone has brought out fire crackers and two go off, reverberating into the night as the freed beasts jump and cackle with glee.

"You mean *she* did," the old woman says. "Aurelia Boneweaver killed Katerina Crocodylus. Gobbled her up *whole*."

"She actually did it, huh," I deadpan. "She's become quite the little monster."

The hyena actually glances at me then, a tiny smirk on her mouth. "You all underestimated her. *Mace Naga's* daughter? Bah! Lot of idiots."

A feeling like fireworks resounds in my own stomach, and all I can do is sniff the air to feel the residue of her bloodthirsty presence. I take my leave of the ex-queen of hyenas, noting down Hyacinth Dabu, the queen apparent, commanding the area. My shadows are twitchy as we get back into the air, and I open myself up to the plane of things-better-left-untouched. More than a few spirits hover in this area. Some will find the light, but others...

A whisper of menace slides around me, a low moan of discomfort. The Collector's soul slinks through the air as if looking for a way back to the world of the living. "I'm glad you're dead," I say cheerfully. "Feeling alright?" Of course, she has no body with which to feel, so the question is just to pour salt. "You'd better continue on to where you're called."

Katerina's spirit hovers before me, suspicious till the end. *"There are screams in there."*

"Yeah." I shrug. "They do that sometimes." All the time actually, but I'm not telling her that. She carries on, obsessed with her old property for the moment. She has no body to mourn, so it might take her a while to move on, and Hyacinth Dabu and her mates have made markings all around the property, warding it against malevolent spirits. I've got to give her credit; she knows what she's doing and moves fast.

Exiting the shadow realm, I survey the twin rivers running on either side of the property. There are still crocs in there. It's likely Katerina's rex still resides in there with his other animas. I wonder how much he knows. What he'd seen and who'd done it.

I fly lower, wanting to get a look at the rabid croc, rumoured to be a completely changed beast. No one had seen him in his human form for decades. It's then that I see the mounds of ash dotting the bank like miniature funeral pyres, and what is left of my old, rotten heart quivers.

Chapter 38

Aurelia

A part of me knows I'm nuts. The other part of me doesn't care.

It makes me sort of feel better knowing what a treasure haze is like. That Xander was actually aware when he was under it. How much he struggled with control during, I'm not sure, but I sure as hell am giving in to it completely. My soul needs this. And from the way my mates preen under my care, I know they need it too.

I brush Lyle's dried hair with a specially made lion's detangling brush. There are knots all through it, and fixing it takes time. She hadn't even tried being a real regina. She'd just wanted to play at it. Just wanted the power and satisfaction and control of it. Katerina Crocodylus' flesh churns in my stomach as I sit on the pillows before the TV. I'm going to enjoy every second of digesting her. Destroying her so completely that there is literally nothing left of her existence except her head, which is presently in a plastic bag in a closet where I don't have to look at it.

Savage is cuddled up behind me, and Scythe is behind him. Xander is on Lyle's other side, eating sweet potato fries with a knife and fork, because of course he is. Lyle periodically feeds me a chip, which I try to evade, but he grabs my cheeks and tucks the food into my mouth with a grin. My urge to feed *them* is so strong. I love watching them eat. I loved washing them and taking care of them.

It's soothing a crucial part of the wound that was left when they were taken.

I smooth down Lyle's hair with a smile, and he wipes his fingers on a serviette before setting his empty plate down. "Come here," he demands.

And I have to listen to their demands now because I have to take care of their every single need. Xander *especially* knows this, and I watch his glowing eyes perceive me with the sharpness of the greedy dragon that he is. "What do you need?" I ask, sliding to my lion's lap.

Lyle runs his hands down my arms, then down my thighs, my bare skin enjoying the feel of him enough that I have to close my eyes. He gives a little puff of satisfaction, leaning forward to scent me. "I need you," he whispers against my lips. He smells like food, and I'm happy he's eaten his fill. Gentle lips brush against my mating mark before he slides the loose black T-shirt up my body. I raise my arms as he tugs it entirely off. "I need to feel your skin against mine so I know you'll never be away from me ever again."

"I'm not going anywhere," I sigh, cupping his face. He needs to shave, but we haven't gotten around to that yet. I'll have to do it tomorrow after I brush his teeth in the morning. My lion buries his face in the crook of my neck and inhales, wrapping his arms around me and holding me close. It makes me turn towards Xander, who's looking down at his empty plate. "Do you need more?" I ask loudly. Lyle growls into my neck, and Savage takes up my discarded brush and starts running it through my own tangled hair.

"No, I've had enough," Xander says, not taking his eyes off me.

"How much did you eat exactly?" I ask suspiciously.

He fiddles with his earphones. "Six burgers, two pizzas, and that bag of chips."

"Where does it all go?" I ask, staring pointedly at his flat stomach.

"Good question." He smiles at me, and I'm stunned for a moment.

"P-Pass me that brush, Savage. I have to detangle Xander's hair." It's gotten even longer, now the same length as Lyle's, brushing his shoulder blades.

"It's fine," Xander says quietly. "I'm just going to braid it." He gets to his feet.

"No!" I growl, looping my power around him and bringing his body back to the floor.

Xander falls to the floor with a heavy thump, his brows shooting up in surprise. "I forgot how strong you are."

"I'm the regina," I snarl. "I'm doing your hair."

He grumbles about it, but I don't care, carefully getting on to my knees behind him and plaiting the long black strands so they lie prettily down his back. Xander turns around, and the look he gives me makes me ache. He feels like he doesn't belong. Like his pain isn't worthy. My vision turns blurry as I feel the weight of his emotions. The weight of the black mark he carries.

"No," he whispers, touching my face. "Aurelia, no."

"What did she make you do?" I whisper. "If I could take it away, I would."

"I know," he says, the corners of his mouth turning down. "I...I don't want to talk about it." Those words from *his* mouth make me crumble. I fling my arms around his neck and press myself into his body, sliding my legs around his waist as if I can squeeze myself into him and push all the other evils of the world away. "She's gone now," Xander says into my hair. "You made her go away."

"Call me regina," I sob. "Say it right now."

I feel him struggle with it—the word, the implication, our other mates hearing it. But eventually, I get a quiet "*Regina*," in my head.

"Out loud," I sniff, pulling away to look at him in the eyes. I slap him on the shoulders. "Out loud, damn it."

Pain flashes across his features. "Regina," he breathes.

I sob again before I crush my lips to his. Xander slides his hand behind my neck, the other hand banding around my waist as he kisses me back. Our mouths open to each other, and it's so different from being in astral form. He is real, under me, his breath hot on mine, his touch demanding but gentle. I can actually feel his assaulting darkness as his tongue seeks out mine, feel the undercurrent of the rage his animus always carries in the groan that rumbles through his chest.

Savage snarls in annoyance behind me, burying his fingers in my hair and forcing my head back around. The burn of his hunger feels *right*. I am met with the eyes of a furious wolf. "I did not wait all this time just to see a fucking dragon hog my regina."

I'm about to say that there's enough of me to go around, but he slams his mouth against mine, impatient, hot, teeth and tongue consuming and demanding my attention. His frantic hands pull me from Xander's lap and dump me onto the soft pillows strewn around us. I try to roll off my back, but Savage's hips pin me to the pillows, his pants kicked off, his massive erection hard against my stomach.

"Don't deny me now, regina." His voice is rough with need as he pulls the loose shorts off my hips. "Don't say I can't have you."

"I'm always yours!" I say as Lyle pulls the fabric off my feet.

Savage presses his forehead against mine. "Then spread your legs like a good little regina and let me fuck you like I need to."

I think I'd forgotten who he is. Who they all are. But then they're all towering over me, with need and devotion saturating their gazes, and I melt into the pillows and gush all over Savage's fat cock as he enters me.

My wolf proceeds to put away his fairy bread side as if it was never there and fucks me hard and fast, with a desperation that takes my breath away. I shout with need, and he bites my lip with deep rumbling growls. Oh, Wild Goddess, I need this with everything that is in me. I cry my wolf's name as his eyes glow just before our powers kiss at our cores, twining around one another in the playful dance that is uniquely me and Savage's.

He lets out a desperate sound and pulls himself out before flipping me over and yanking on my hips so my ass is high in the air. I push myself up on my hands and come face to cock with Xander, but his pants are still on and he's moving away, not toward me.

Savage shoves himself back in me with a satisfying sound, and I cry out in pleasure. My hand snaps out and snags the elastic of Xander's track pants, drawing him to a stop. He looks down at me before back up at Savage. "One chance, dragon," Savage says wickedly. "One chance to prove yourself."

Xander's jaw clenches in a sexy way that makes my mouth water, and I tug down his pants, letting his massive dragon's cock, already hard, spring free in my face. I waste no time, taking that gigantic head in my lips and sucking hard on the tip, just the way I know he'd like it. He tilts his head back with a feral groan. "*Regina.*"

I make a happy sound, and the look of bliss on his face almost makes me come.

"I'm glad I get to see how you suck while you're getting fucked," Xander says down at me. "Now we get to see who can make you come the hardest."

Savage lets out a snarl at Xander, and the dragon bares his teeth right back, making a purely draconic sound. Smoke wafts over me, and I swallow Xander's cock with relish. I never thought I'd see the day when I'd get fucked by both dragon and wolf at the same time, and it lights up something in me to know that they're both snarling at each other while I take care of them.

Lyle, stroking his cock off to the side until now, won't be left out and comes up next to me on his knees. I let Xander's cock go with a pop, pre-cum slipping out of my mouth. Xander swoops down and grabs my chin, kissing me possessively before I turn to my lion. Lyle snaps his teeth at Xander, and I see his animus is out, those amber irises huge.

"Don't fight," I say, although I know it's useless.

"Regina," Lyle's animus says in his gravelly voice. "I missed you."

It makes my heart glow that I can be with three of them at the same time. As I take Xander's cock in my hand and Lyle's cock in my mouth, my eyes slide to Scythe just a little ways away. His eyes are alight as our gazes touch and he rubs his bottom lip with his thumb, letting me know he only wants to watch right now.

I'm then distracted by Savage playing with my clit, and the movement of all three of us winds me higher, sending me soaring into the sky on the wings not made of feathers, but something more ethereal. Lyle's cock tastes like a salty sun, his pre-cum blooming on my tongue as I draw it out of him. Pulling back, I tease the big veins at the side of his cock before swallowing him whole again.

Lyle's thumb strokes reverently over my jaw as Xander brushes his hand over my hair. I close my eyes, lost to the sensation of the three of them until I feel like I'm made of nothing more than feathers and light. My body arches under it, and suddenly, I erupt into a million stars, clutching onto Xander and crying out my release. I've waited so long, so fucking long—

Savage withdraws from me, his fingers wringing out every ounce of pleasure from my sensitive clit. I grab his hand, my eyes flying open as I vibrate around him, suddenly aware that it's still not enough, that there's three pairs of hands wringing me for all I'm worth and there is still someone missing. I look over at my shark. His lips are parted, his lids lowered as he stares at us, the bulge in his pants telling me he might want more. *"Scythe,"* I pant, reaching out a hand. "Let me..."

My voice fades away into breath. Savage withdraws his hand, drawing his fingers up my spine as he crawls to my side. I straighten to look at Scythe.

There is infinite sadness in those sky-blue eyes as he stalks toward me. "Not tonight, regina." Then his voice lightens, turning coy. "You told us *we* get to feast tonight." He nudges Savage aside and drops to the floor. He pushes me onto my back, lowering his head between my legs. I'm suddenly lost for words then, lost for demands as that perfect masculine face looks up at me, all apex predator, all ruthless don. "And I am still *starving*."

Chapter 39

Scythe

I lick Aurelia's clit like a thirsty beast. While the ocean satisfied my animus' physical need for the ocean, Aurelia's sweet pussy provides me with the ephemeral waters I crave. I lap up what she gives me, fluttering my tongue over the swollen nub and enjoying the way she cries out.

But my jealous brothers are not to be left out after so long without their regina. Lyle grabs Aurelia under the arms and pulls her up his body. She instinctively spreads her legs as Lyle's cock, hard as steel and pulsing with his desire, springs up between her core. Lyle fists his cock, and Aurelia grinds her hips until the lion presses himself against her asshole, all ready from Savage's ministrations. I beckon to Savage for the lube we had delivered alongside the food and he dutifully brings it for me so I can help my regina take her lion.

Her head tilts back in pleasure, and Lyle presses his lips to her mating mark. Growling with impatience, I shove Lyle's legs apart and surge forward, finding my regina's clit again. Aurelia cries out as I lap at her clit, helping her ease the burn of Lyle's cock. She relaxes under me, her hips settling lower, allowing Lyle to slide into her. I suck at her pink, swollen lips, dragging my tongue up and down until I find her entrance.

She's already gushing with pleasure. I tongue-fuck her until she squirms. Her scent, her sweet cries fill me up in a way nothing in the world can. Everything else seems to fade away until it's just us, just her pleasure and my greedy need to see her scream in submission.

She is entirely open to us, and I'm only dimly aware of Savage's equally greedy mouth on Aurelia's heaving breasts, his hungry growls as he sucks and licks at her dark nipples. Xander finds his own position on her other side, and Aurelia reaches for him, sliding her fingers over his dragon's cock.

We can't get enough of her. In fact, I don't think we'll be able to get enough of her for the rest of our lives. Not this perfect creature who saved us—minds, bodies, and souls. It only fuels my desire to see her writhing under our mouths and cocks. I let my tongue wander where it wants, exploring her wet perfection, the way she is sweet and powerful under my tongue, the way her power moves and begs for entry. I shove my tongue in her while Lyle eases himself in and out, grunting under the way she tenses around him. Her muscles close around my tongue as well, and I'm delighted when her power fills my mouth with golden, swirling patterns. I groan as my own power responds, and she gives me what I need to stay sane, and I give her what she needs to be content.

Lyle's cock moves faster before me, Xander's hips stutter as Aurelia takes him into her mouth and her hips buck as I flick my tongue over her clit and enter her with my fingers. She accepts me like the impatient regina she is, grinding her hips against me. I move faster, curling my fingers and finding her G-spot.

My own desire is hard between my legs, but he wants to wait tonight. I need more time. My spirit is still rigid where he swims under the happenings of the last few weeks.

I tap Savage on the shoulder, and he raises his head. I nod at him and move aside, letting him take over. A feral smile takes over his face, and he dives between Lyle's and Aurelia's legs before shoving his cock into her.

All four of them groan as they fuck our regina together.

Seeing Aurelia in pleasure, watching her succumb completely in the safety of three males who love her unconditionally, heals an old, broken part of me that reared its ugly head. I love watching her. I can't take my eyes off her heaving chest, the pulse at her throat, the way her head is thrown back in vulnerability. She is safe. And we are safe. A strong pack keeps each other safe, and as our leader, she'd demonstrated why she had been made our central mate.

Savage thrusts desperately into Aurelia, shoving both her and Lyle back towards the couch. Lyle and Xander snarl at our wolf, and this must set off Aurelia because she comes again, bucking, her back bowing as she screams around Xander's cock. I can see her clenching around both lion and wolf, and this makes both groan, Lyle's cum spilling out around them, followed by Savage's. They both pump it back into Aurelia with smooth, long strokes, and Xander comes third, his hands around Aurelia's face as her groans no doubt vibrate up his shaft. The dragon tilts his head back, the powerful muscles of his chest bunching under his own release. Aurelia's loud swallows are almost enough to make me come, but I sit on the armchair and watch my pack pant against one another.

Aurelia's head flops back onto Lyle's shoulder, and her bluest eyes find mine, a sleepy, satisfied smile gracing her shiny lips. There are few things in life more satisfying, more healing, than watching my regina's eyes flutter shut, her heart full of satisfaction and her body full of our pack's cum.

Chapter 10

Lyle

It's just after dawn that I wake, my first night in an actual bed in weeks. My regina is curled around me, with Savage curled like a sloth around her newer leg, and Scythe at an angle so he's by her head.

A long-fingered hand rests on my chest, and I marvel at it. I marvel at her, and the deep breaths of sleep she takes. The long, dark lashes that brush her cheek, the soft, pink lips. She makes a small contented noise and snuggles further into me, setting my heart alight and making everything feel like it's all in the right place. Like the universe has been set straight once again.

It hits me then how much I love her. How much my heart had ached when we were apart and how healing last night had been. The Collector's spell had felt like being buried in cursed mud, and none of us were to understand the effects of it until after it had been removed.

Feeling my rabid lion take possession of me once again feels like an old wound being torn open anew. We'd lost control and let others take control of us. This is something that will take me a while to process, but being together with my conscious brothers and my fierce regina is surely healing.

Small lights from over my shoulder let me know that Xander is watching. As he'd watched over us every night at The Collector's property. I don't remember specifics, but I remember those lights and how constant they were. How aware. It must be a habit of his now.

For the first time since he severed his bond to us, I broach his mental communications. *"Did you sleep at all?"*

I feel his attention on me. And his hesitation. *"A little. And no, I don't wish to be counselled on this matter or any other."*

"I wouldn't dare try."

"I would like your counselling, Lyle," comes a sleepy, wolfish voice. *"I have a lot to say."*

"We all know that," Xander drawls.

"I don't think anyone can help you," Savage replies, but it's so faint, I don't even think he's fully awake. Xander rolls out of bed with a huff and storms into the bathroom. I half expect to hear the door slam shut, but instead, he's so careful that there's only a soft *snick.*

There is something about this that deeply affects me. I look down at my regina and am pleased to see her still fast asleep. This is perhaps the first moment of peace we've had in a *very* long time. I hold her close to me and enjoy it while I can.

* * *

In the living room of the apartment, Aurelia narrows her perfect blue eyes at me, looking my body over as if searching for signs of illness or disease. Her demeanour is sharp, determined and...if I didn't know any better, anxious. I've heard of a treasure haze before, but dragons are private and so few and far between that I doubt any other orders have witnessed one first hand. The mental health clinician in me is fascinated, while the rabid animus prowling in my mind is snarling at the injustice of our role being stolen from us.

I put my arms out to the side, opening myself up to her inspection. "Do I scrub up okay?" The aware part of her makes her eyes bright, and she smiles coyly at me, sauntering forward. She reaches up and cups my face. Reverently, I lean down and accept her lips on my mouth. Her mouth and body might be soft, but under her skin, her power vibrates like a live wire. It reminds me of the electric currents that run along the prison wall of Blackwater Penitentiary. She's made to tame beasts. Made to make powerful creatures bow.

It's so uniquely her that I can't help but gather her into my arms and pick her up. She chuckles against my lips, and I fall in love with her just a little more.

Setting her down, she promptly turns away from me, inspecting Savage in the same eagle-eyed way. I shove down the urge to keep her for myself and instead find amusement in Savage's beaming smile and the little dance he performs for her inspection.

Our regina kisses him too, before moving on to Xander. The dragon is tense this morning. There's a stiffness to his shoulders that now seems permanent. I was hoping the pack sex would have bonded us together, but he still holds himself apart. Forgiveness is something that takes time, and I don't know whether I will fully forgive him for his transgressions. But I don't exactly hate him anymore.

How can I after what I suspect he did for us? Unlike the rest of us, he'd been aware the entire time. Watched over us, guardian of our memories and...I glance at Scythe, who also bears the tenseness borne of old trauma. The Collector had not achieved what she wanted to with Scythe. That much is clear in the angry wounds he bore when we'd all 'woken up.' I have a raw feeling that Xander played a part in preventing that too. He could have simply left us in The Collector's compound at any time. But he'd chosen to protect us. For some reason, this stings.

Savage, the most adaptable and forgiving of all of us, seems to have come to terms with having his autonomy removed for a time. Or, at the *very* least, Aurelia's current presence takes precedence over any historical difficulty. Aurelia gently takes Scythe's hand in hers and guides him to the kitchen bench where she's prepared breakfast.

There's toast, scrambled eggs, and bacon piled on plates. A fried fare that we watched her cook, growling at us when we'd try to help. Luckily, the freezer was stocked with some salmon and she'd baked it to perfection. This she carefully plates for Scythe, a slight crease between her brows as she slides the spatula out from under the fillet. Scythe obediently sits down on the barstool opposite her.

Aurelia picks up the silverware and cuts a small piece, offering it to him. His lips twitch, and he opens his mouth to allow his regina to feed him.

She watches him carefully as he chews. "Is it okay?"

Scythe gets off his chair, rounds the bench, and reaches for her, delicately kissing her mating mark. "It's perfect," he says quietly. "Just like my regina."

Aurelia seems mesmerised for a moment, her lower jaw loosening, those cheeks flushing. I take an involuntary step forward as her arousal perfumes the air.

"Me next, me next!" Savage demands, excitedly skipping behind the counter and picking up a plate.

Once breakfast is done—during which Savage makes Aurelia wipe his face—and we've washed the dishes together, Aurelia goes to the apartment window, peering out suspiciously. "We can leave after sunset," she declares after a moment. "I must secure the building."

I exchange a glance with Scythe. "How do you plan on doing that?" I ask.

She glowers at the view of the ocean. "That's for me to know."

Savage puts his finger in the air like he's in class at the academy. "But *I'd* like to know!"

Our regina finally turns back to look at us. "Has everyone moved their bowels today?"

Xander chokes on air before throwing himself down on the couch and flicking on the TV. "That's none of your damn business, Aurelia."

"Everything is my business now," she snaps back. "If you need a laxative, you have to let me know now, because we can have it delivered. There are lots of different types."

Savage grins at me. It seems our regina's avian preference has had an effect on her treasure haze. The four of us males watch her as she paces back and forth before the front door. She seems to be debating something within herself, chewing on her bottom lip as she comes to some sort of conclusion.

To my great dismay, she heads to the kitchen and selects the biggest knife from the wooden block next to the stove. Then she takes it and heads back to the front door, where she sits cross-legged on the floor before it. We all immediately pursue our regina. Savage sits in front of her, causing her to grumble, climb over him, and seat herself between him and the door as if protecting him.

"Regina," Savage says slowly, leaning forward to try to get eye contact. "Why do you have a knife in your sweet paw?"

Aurelia growls at the front door as if there's an enemy right behind it. "I have it so I don't scare the humans."

We wait for her to elaborate, and she huffs impatiently, waving the knife in the air. "If it's an animalia, I can shift to fight them. But if it's a human, my shifting will scare them, so a knife makes more sense. There are humans on the levels beneath us."

Savage nods. "Oh, that makes a lot of sense now."

Aurelia guards the door the entire day, leaving only when she needs to use the bathroom. By the time the sun starts to set, she gathers us by the door and we prepare to leave.

Chapter 41

Scythe

Riding back to Animus Academy on Lia's back is something I never imagined I'd be doing. I am well practised at riding Xander, but when he suggested he bear us, Lia glared at him like she was going to lash her teeth around his throat.

"Over my dead body," she snarled.

It made the rest of us snarl to hear her talk that way, instinctively gathering around her. She looked us each in the eye with such determination, then began to shift. We'd all had to sprint to the corners of the apartment roof to avoid her massive blue limbs. Savage was the first to recover, as he often is, treating this like it's some great game and climbed up her body with enthusiasm, seating himself in shotgun position.

Lyle pats Aurelia's foreleg before levitating himself up onto her back. I glance at Xander, who holds Katerina's head in a plastic bag hanging from one hand.

"*Is it strange riding another dragon?*" I ask, heading towards her hind leg.

"*Yes, it's pretty fucking weird,*" he replies. "*You go on.*"

Katerina's head soars through the air, and Lia raises her forepaw to receive it in her massive grip. I bear climb up my regina's hind leg, hand over hand, until I'm on her flank, at which point I walk down her spine and settle behind Lyle. Her scales are pleasantly warm under me, and it's reassuring to feel that through my trousers. It's the only type of warmth I crave these days. The only type of touch I want.

Compared to the touch of The Collector, which had filled me with such…poison. The Wild Goddess knows the type of toxicity that would have plagued me had she gotten her way with me. Deep instinct tells me she didn't. So when Xander pulled me aside last night, with a quiet voice and earnestness in his eyes, a part of me had already known.

"I didn't let her, Scythe," he'd said, gaze flicking down to the floor. "I stayed awake and made sure you wouldn't do what she was asking. Connor didn't fasten my shackles properly, so we have to thank him for that when I see him next."

"Thank you, brother," was all I'd been capable of saying. How could I have said more, when the very thing I'd hated him for had been the thing to save me? It was only the severance of his bond that led him to have a clear mind while under the spell. The Wild Goddess was more likely to be a twisted, laughing crone if *this* is the type of fate she deals out.

Lia's power now envelops us in a bubble of warmth just before she launches into the night air. A moment later, a black dragon joins us in the sky, flying low, directly under us as if protecting Aurelia's underside from those below.

Earlier today, Rufus informed me of the goings-on in my absence, including the ambush Aurelia received after leaving the Jewel of the Jungle and the way she'd destroyed multiple council helicopters.

My regina has grown. She has matured into a full-grown Boneweaver, and now the world knows what she's capable of.

In just the same way, her sire's plans are also maturing. His investments are claiming full interest. Mace Naga *is* the council now. He can wield full political power and has been steadily using it against us. The loss of my cleaning businesses is a heavy blow, but nothing we can't recover from. I'd built my enterprise to be resilient in that way. But one thing is now clear, Mace is getting bolder.

Last night, there was a council raid of warehouses owned by some other underworld crime lords. It had appeared on human news as a great success by Mace. Some propaganda about cleaning up the corrupt animalia community. This had been his end goal all along. A way to get the serpents' full power over the other orders he'd perceived as their enemies.

He'd not forgotten the Great Serpent Purge of 1970. Not forgiven the council and all those in it who had persecuted his people for their powers. Who had marked their faces for carrying venom and executed all feral serpent families. But what does Mace intend to do with all that power? How is he going to exact his revenge?

Marduk reports that he and his pack, along with the other animas are back at the academy, except for Connor who has taken the rest of Katerina's captives to safety in the accommodations I've provided. I've utilised my contacts from the Lily Institute to send them the staff to ensure their proper medical and psychological treatment. This is important to me because it's important to my regina. Marduk also has a captive with him by way of Stacey's newfound rex. This news, while inconvenient, might come in use.

"How long does a treasure haze typically last?" I ask Xander.

"Mine was three days," Xander says. *"But Aurelia has four treasures, and she killed for hers. So I don't know if that will extend it."*

"I'm enjoying it," Savage says. *"She's so cute and powerful. But if she wants to wash us all every single night, that might get difficult."*

"Agreed," Lyle says. *"For her sake, I hope she comes out of it soon."*

Aurelia huffs beneath us, probably aware we are conversing without her. She is a seasoned flier, and I marvel at the command she has over her own unique body. Her ability to shift into different beasts and seamlessly adapt to them in essentially no time is astonishing. It takes beasts of regular orders a while to learn how to use their animal body, and Aurelia looks like she was born to be a dragon. She had fought as one not long after shifting into one for the first time. And then what had happened on the riverside bank of Katerina's property...

Xander flies on ahead as if he's scouting for us, no doubt listening for any sign of a faraway helicopter or anti-dragon weapons. There is little chance anyone knows where we were for the last two days, but the closer we get to the academy, the closer we get to visibility and predictability.

We reach the dark turrets of the academy deep into the night. I never thought I'd feel glad to see the place. Guards move in their towers, and I sense Aurelia's telepathic communication with them as she circles the perimeter of the academy grounds in a wide arc, as if looking for signs of anomaly or enmity. Once she completes her circuit, I expect her to veer towards the animus dorms, but she doesn't. Instead, she angles her nose towards the road before the front gates.

Her landing is slightly different from Xander's, her newest leg unable to take the full brunt of the required weight. But we're only jostled a little before she commands us to the ground. To my surprise, she shifts into human form. I watch her long-limbed figure kissed by the light of a gibbous moon, her eyes glinting with something wholly primal. Something that makes my primitive shark gnash his teeth and pay attention.

All four of us follow our regina's every movement as she takes Katerina's head from its plastic bag and walks up to the front gates of the academy. When I see my regina levitate upwards and slam the head of our enemy onto the central spike of the school gates, the only appropriate thing to do is smile.

Chapter 12

Aurelia

I usher my four treasures into our nest. My wolf sighs deeply when he returns to the familiar rooms, the sound of a tired male coming home. I allow them only a moment to appreciate this before bustling everyone into the bathroom to ensure they clean themselves properly in the shower.

They can look after themselves. They can clean their hair and wash their bodies, but I cannot stop my need to oversee it and take care of them. While they finish up with fresh clothes, I clean up the nest—changing out the sheets and fluffing out the pillows. I even spray the eucalyptus oil I found in the cupboard because I know Savage likes the smell and it calms Lyle's animus. I place a glass of salted water on Scythe's side because I worry he'll dehydrate, and I even find Xander's stash of cigars and put them by the single bed he used to sleep on.

The rest of the academy is quiet, with only snores and occasional coughs sounding on the levels beneath us. Yet my blood is agitated. I step from foot to foot as my mates file out of the bathroom, and I only stop a moment to inspect their condition before nodding my satisfaction and heading back out to the roof.

Enemies may try to find us. Enemies always seem to be after us. With the death of one enemy, others may follow, and this nest, filled with so many of my other charges, might not be safe. The wall around the academy is strong, filled with my own energy, but there are always many strategies, many ways to attack a nest.

"Regina." Scythe's quiet voice stops movement, his eyes tired but alert on me. "Where are you going?"

"Patrol," I say simply, climbing up the stairs to the roof.

He follows. "You need not do that. The guards will keep an eye on the sky and road."

The night is cold on my skin, the smell fresh in my sinuses. All is quiet, but I need to make sure it stays that way. I turn around to find they have all followed me out here. They need to understand. "I am responsible for them *all* now. This place is mine."

Lyle steps around Savage. "What do you mean, angel?"

He thinks *he* is guardian of the school. Perhaps he can still be guardian of the education of the students. There are lots of beasts here who need him and his teaching after all. "Celeste Agnis is gone," I say clearly. "I am appointed guardian now. The school is loyal to me."

Understanding comes over them, especially my mate with the glowing eyes. Impatient now, I step away from them and shift into dragon form.

My wedge-tailed eagle form will always be my favourite, but there is something in my spirit now that craves the draconic power. The covetous, greedy for blood and hungry for flesh part of me still calls to my anima. Into the night again I fly, the wind no longer cold on my scales, but instead something like an invigorating bath in the sky. Rather quickly, I sense a second presence join me, and it is not Beak, like I'm used to.

I ignore him at first, executing my usual circumnavigation around the academy as I survey the roads leading in and out of the area. Nothing unusual moves between the trees that speckle the land between the human-made paths. It soothes my heart a little to see all is safe and the rapid racing in my chest slows down. The black dragon with the glowing eyes follows my movements like a monstrous shadow, and at times, over the past few days, it's been hard for me to believe he is one of my treasures. That a beast of such power and heat belongs to *me*.

I make an abrupt turn, rounding on him. He mirrors me, and it's like a dance where we perform in a tight circle. I break away, tucking my wings and shooting towards the ground. He pursues me. Metres before the tree line, I snap my wings out and glide over the highest branches, before angling my nose upwards and beating powerfully to gain height.

Xander chases me, copying my every wing movement and following my climb towards the stars. But he gains height faster, and now we're both vertical, belly to belly with our wings beating downwards. We twine around each other, and having never done this before with a mate or other avian, I'm mesmerised. It's a delightful new dance. And maybe, a new hope. "*I dreamed of this,*" he says, breathless in my mind.

I veer away, blinking hard, shaking my head as the open sky suddenly seems like a new thing altogether. Pointing my nose toward the nest, with its magical lights only I can see, my blood heats up, but not in the same way as before, and a tingling in my chest makes me take a deep breath. I come to land just outside the academy gates, stretching out my right leg as I do.

Xander lands behind me, the ground trembling in fright under his heavier weight. I tuck my wings in and turn to look at him. A stunning creature made of night, his eyes are like the glowing stars themselves. Like he's a piece of the puzzle of midnight, and in his . eyes, I see one simple wish.

I stalk forward and he meets me, lowering his head to mine like he'd done once before while I sat on the academy wall. I raise my long neck to meet his face and gently press my snout to his. A low, gravelly rumble resonates from his chest, soft and yet hard. Like rocks groaning under the ancient earth. He slides his snout against the side of my face, and it's so warm on me. He nuzzles down the slope of my neck, and I chuff in response to the sensation. But there's something sad in his movements. Something that still feels like loss. "*You will be okay,*" I say to him. "*We will all be okay.*"

He doesn't reply, instead stepping away from me and shooting up into the night as if he weighs nothing at all. "*You rest, regina. I will patrol until dawn.*"

It's a true weariness that drags at my bones. I haven't rested in some time, and I should check on my other mates. In a pensive silence, I shift into eagle form and make my way up to do a final check on the guard-towers—just to make sure the guards haven't been slacking off in my absence.

It's then that I see the roiling shadow travelling towards the animus dorm. With a sharp cry of protest, I shoot toward him, beak at the ready like a spear. The shadow reaches the open window of my pack's dorm, pausing just outside. I pummel right into him, snapping a piece of shadow and tackling him into the dark room beyond. He shifts into human form on the floor, and I clamp a sharp claw around his neck. *"And just where the fuck do you think you're going?"*

"I go where the fuck I want, snakelet," he drawls, the paint on his face glowing white in the low lights of the room.

My mates leap out of bed and surround us, but I wave a wing at them. *"Not here, you don't,"* I tell him, snapping my beak at his red eyes. *"Get out."* I shift into human form and climb off him, pointing to the window.

"And what if I don't? Are you going to fight me?" Ghoul asks, extending himself to his full height.

I laugh darkly. "Without hesitation."

Savage cackles. "I love this so fucking much!"

"I thought we shared a moment before." Ghoul turns to my mates and says over my shoulder. "We shared a *few* moments in your absence, actually."

Savage gasps dramatically. Lyle growls under his breath. "Did you hear about your friend?" I ask sweetly.

"I saw Katerina's head sitting on your academy gates, yes," he says smoothly. "Impressive work, I must say. Such *style*."

"Thanks," I say. "Now you must leave before I hurt you."

He puts a hand over his heart, the shadows parting to allow his hand. "Who, me? You'd never."

"We know what serpent court is doing," Lyle says. "We know Mace is out for our blood."

"But the snakelet and I have an agreement," Ghoul says evenly. "She made me a promise."

"The thought of leaving my mates now makes me want to

murder someone," I say through gritted teeth. "And I will. Don't test me."

He scratches the corner of his mouth as if thinking. He takes a step to the right, and I mirror his movement. "So protective," he hisses. "And all they had to do was be weak enough to get caught?"

"I'm detecting a little jealousy," Savage pipes as I register the same.

Ghoul's red eyes flash behind the swirls of darkness. "Do they know you're carrying my offspring? Do they know you're my fiancée?"

All the males in the room go still.

"Oh, stop it," I snarl. Turning to the others, I reassure them. "He's just joking. I'm not pregnant. I wouldn't do that with him." But it doesn't seem to help. Scythe's eyes have gone navy. Savage's mouth is suddenly full of canines, and Lyle is stalking towards me, his amber irises blown out.

Ghoul cackles. "Wonderful."

"No," I say, holding my hands up to Lyle. "Smell me. I'm not pregnant. And I'm definitely not engaged to a *general* of my father's court!" But Lyle doesn't stop his advancing, and I have no choice but to step in front of him and block his path with my hand on his chest. "Stop this," I say. "Listen to me."

But now Scythe and Savage are advancing forwards, and to my great concern, they are lethally silent. No growl, no snarling. Only deadly focus.

"We've fought before," Ghoul says lightly. "They barely won. Even three against little old me."

I huff without looking at him. "You're not helping. What did you come here for anyway? You need to leave."

"We had an agreement," the basilisk lord says. "You need to come with me."

I let out a short laugh. "Not tonight, buddy."

"Want to know what's funny about this?" Ghoul says darkly. "You'll be begging me by the end."

"What?" I swing around to confront the bastard, but he's already gone.

Savage, Scythe and Lyle rush towards the window, sniffing and growling in the wake of the shadows. Lyle tries to leap out of the window in pursuit, but I lash my own power around him, shoving him backward into the room. "Don't mind him," I say quietly. "I...had to pretend to be his pregnant fiancé to get the heat serum, but it was all just a ruse."

Savage rounds on me, his nostrils flaring, his eyes purely wolfish as he gets on his knees and sniffs at the apex of my thighs and my lower stomach. Instinctively, I bury my fingers in his hair, until both Lyle and Scythe come on either side of him and wordlessly do the same. I sigh up at the ceiling because I thought I was the one under the spell of the treasure haze, but if I'm feeling irritated, then it must be fading away...only to be replaced by my three mates crashing out at Ghoul's taunts. Lyle presses his face into my side, inhaling deeply.

"See?" I coo. "There's no hatchling in there."

It's odd to see Scythe on his knees, rubbing his face into my side in a way that tickles. But when he looks up at me, any giggle, any response to being ticklish fades away. Those navy eyes, dead serious, bore into mine. He gets to his feet, the other two following. I take a step back at the fury in their eyes. The sheer possession. That all-consuming hunger. My breath catches as they stalk me, my heart racing with anticipation. I get the urge to run. To be pursued by them.

Oh yeah, the treasure haze has well and truly worn off.

Then the entire building shakes with the force of a dragon slamming into the roof, and it only takes seconds for a naked Xander to cut off my exit from behind, his eyes lighting up the room. "Tell me it's not true," Xander snarls, smoke streaming from his nostrils.

I turn around. "I—"

But that's all it takes for Scythe to seize me by the waist. He takes me to the pack bed. Setting me down, he pushes my thighs apart to look at my core. All four of them gather at the end of the bed to stare down at me. My four towering, angry giants.

"Ours," Scythe's shark whispers, before giving me one long lick from ass to pussy. I cry out at the abrupt pleasure. "Ours to suck," he says before nudging my labia open with his lips and tonguing my insides in a way that makes me arch my back.

My lion appears by my side, a firm hand around my throat as he whispers across my lips. "Ours to fuck." He claims my mouth with scorching lips and tongue, the combination of both lion and shark's mouths on me nearly forcing me off the bed in my writhing.

My wolf's fingers find my chin and force my mouth against his. "Ours to play with," he growls before nipping at my lower lip.

Xander appears at the head of the bed, and I'm lifted up, completely off the bed, a tangle of limbs around me as the dragon buries his hand in my hair and tilts my head back, dragging his lips up my neck. "Ours to possess," he snarls softly.

I come with a simpering gasp, gushing onto Scythe's face. But they're not nearly done with me—not for hours more.

Chapter 43

Ghoul

Is it my fault I'm ready to kill someone tonight? Definitely not. That little interaction with the Boneweaver pack was worth the look on those faces as I'd gloated my latest comeuppance on Aurelia's mates. I growl darkly to myself as I arrive at Naga mansion. Pottering about in the foyer, Charlotte glances my way, disturbed. But then her eyes flick expectantly past me, and my mood grows fouler still. I flick at her with my fingers. She's much like a fly—flitting around me incessantly, unwanted.

"Where is she?" the fly squeaks.

"My fiancée has had enough of public displays," I say, striding past her. "I don't want people giving her the evil eye."

Charlotte makes an ugly face. "She had just the one!"

"And it was enough."

She shakes her head. "You know our people need to see her to boost morale." I glower at her, and she sticks her jaw out. "I'll be sure to take it up with my brother."

"You do that."

"And I'll have the next batch of girls ready tomorrow night."

So much for my fucking reprieve. I give a mocking bow with both arms sweeping out. "If my king wants me to have a harem, I'll be *so* glad to oblige."

"Such a chore." General Adder sidles up next to me with his hands in his pockets. "To be breeding so many women every week."

I brush at my shoulder like I'm proud of myself. "It's for the cause."

Charlotte bristles because she's lost more breedable serpents than she can count due to my so-called style. "I'll be sending a physician to your house to check on Miss Brown."

Fury makes my shadows rustle around me. Power fills my eyes, and I watch the hairs on her arms stand on end. "I'll be the first to know if she is unwell," I sneer. "She is *my* bride. *My* property, and *mine* to care for."

She wrinkles her nose before turning on her heel and leaving. I walk through the house until I get out the other side and into the backyard. It's a broad expanse of grass, covered by military vehicles parked for our nefarious uses. It's empty of other souls for a few rare, sweet moments. My shadows twitch with agitation as I look up into the infinite void. All things began in the shadows, and so all things end in the shadows. The very air has changed, the void dancing in awareness of what is to come. Darkness approaches, and I am the one who will bring it. They will call me by my real name in the end.

"Are you ready for the truth, snakelet?" I whisper. "How long I've waited to show you."

Chapter 44

Aurelia

I wake up with a start, a feeling of dread winding its way through my chest. I rub at my sternum and find myself sweaty. Morning light glows around the border black curtain as I blink at my surroundings. My pack is here: Savage, Lyle, Scythe and Xander all lie in a tangle on the bed. They are returned to me, alive and with all their limbs.

Savage growls and licks my knee, nuzzling me as if he senses my sudden discomfort. I can't help but see and feel that my heart is *almost* complete. That my pack is missing its final member. Its worst member?

But his hands had been gentle on mine that one night. His voice soft. His shadows softer. I grimace, struggling to understand this feeling—a feeling that cannot be right or true. Ghoul is my father's most prized possession. His most effective weapon. The highest of the seven generals. He would be sworn to him as all his servants are sworn to Mace Naga. To obey *every* order to the death. And yet he can't help but seek me out. Like I can't help but...regret not going with him last night.

Lyle rolls into my lap, his long, golden hair draping across my legs. I run my fingers through the light threads, and it soothes me as much as it does him. My lion's purr rumbles across my thighs.

"You're thinking hard about something, I can tell," Xander's drawl is heavy with sleep. "Don't tell me the basilisk bastard got to you."

I cast him a side-eye from where he rests behind Scythe. "How did you even know?"

He smirks. "When you think you're not being watched, your face is an open book. When you first got to the academy, I thought it was just a side effect of you being isolated for so long. But now... well, when you're as powerful as you are, why bother hiding anything?"

I scowl. "There are people after me—the bastard basilisk being one of them." And I definitely guard my face when I'm around him.

"He's going to betray you," Xander says flatly. "You know that, right? Whatever regina feelings you end up having for him won't matter in the end because he's sworn to your father."

"I bet these were the types of things you said to Scythe and Savage when I first got here," I grumble. In a deep voice, I mimic him. "Don't trust her, she's crazy. She'll betray you. She's nuts and evil." Xander is silent for so long that I turn to stare at him. "It *was*, wasn't it?"

He closes his eyes. "You're right. But we didn't know you then. We *know* Ghoul. And he *is* nuts and evil."

I rub my face. "I'm so confused."

"*Aurelia*." The note of alarm in Xander's voice makes me raise my brows. It's not often that Xander panics about...well, anything. The dragon sits up and reaches over Scythe to grab my wrist. "At Drakos Estate, my dragon...well, he punished me for rejecting you and showed me things from other lives we had as pack. Other times."

I sit up straight. "What? What the fuck did you see? Why haven't I heard of this before? Tell me everything."

Xander scratches his chin awkwardly. "It was only fragments, and at the most inconvenient times. We all looked different in each one, but I just knew who was who. It was a feeling. A lot of it wasn't good. The other times and places were violent. It seems our pack trends on the trauma side of things."

"Well, fuck."

"And in each one," Xander presses, "Ghoul's soul *always*

betrayed you. Mine seemed to swing back and forth, but *his...*" Xander shakes his head in disgust. "Even his soul has real problems." This information only troubles me further. "This appeals to your regina instincts, doesn't it?" Xander groans, covering his eyes. "I shouldn't have said anything."

"No, you did the right thing," I say, carefully climbing out of bed and heading into the shower, alone.

We spend the rest of the day locked up in the dorm in each other's arms. Minnie and Stacey ask to visit when they hear that I'm back, but I tell them I need to stay with my mates. They need me. None of them say it with their words, but their eyes, their stroking hands and desperate, straying lips tell me all I need to know. They ache from their time with The Collector and some wounds can't be bandaged directly. I move from one lap to the next, and more often than not, there's two or three sets of hands grazing my skin where I sit on the couch or dining table. We watch TV, Scythe, Xander and Lyle talk on the phone to various people, and Xander gets out his laptop.

At one point, I watch him frowning over his screen and I can't help but leave Savage's sleepy embrace and stalk over. He glances at me, and without a word, I nudge myself into his lap, straddling him so we're chest to chest. After a moment of surprise, he holds me, breathing in deep before looking over my shoulder at his laptop and getting back to his work. "Are the share prices down or something?" I murmur, examining his lone dangling cross earring with gentle fingers.

Xander huffs with discontent. "I'm only concerned with the price of gold—and that's always good."

"Then what are you frowning about?"

"Selena has been sending me emails. Updates about Mother and the hatchlings every other day."

I recline backwards to look at him. "She didn't want you to miss anything."

His Adam's apple bobs up and down as he nods. "They're alright, so that's the important thing."

"And Lady Drakos?"

The corner of his lip quirks. "She's re-taken her maiden name.

She's Lady Darkcleaver now. One of dragonkind's most ancient names."

"That's an incredible name."

"Indeed."

But something niggles at me. "So what's *your* name going to be?"

Xander's expression turns sombre. "I don't know. I guess I'm just Xander now."

* * *

As night falls and Lyle arranges our dinner, I can't help but look around the dining table and the five plates Savage is carefully setting down. It pokes at something in my soul. Nudges the deep-seated regina instinct in me that knows it should be six places. Suddenly, there is a hole in my chest that gapes far and wide, and it only seems to widen as I sit down for dinner in Lyle's lap, and he feeds me pesto fettuccine and garlic bread. After dinner, I announce that I'm going to my shift for sky patrol.

"Can I come this time?" Savage asks hopefully.

"No, it's my turn," Lyle says.

They both turn to me as if I need to make the decision. I smile softly at my mates. "I think I need some alone time tonight. Is that okay?"

Savage pouts but nods all the same. Lyle pulls me into his body and kisses me on the crown. "You don't need permission for that, but as soon as you get tired, promise me you'll pass the watch over to Beak and the others."

"I will."

Scythe is watching me closely, but I give him a smile as I head out to the roof and send a quick message to Beak that I won't be on patrol tonight. I put on my invisible shield as soon as I take my phoenix form and launch into the air, high above the clouds. I fly for a kilometre before collecting my power and slingshotting across the land right towards the house of my fifth mate.

Was finding Ghoul supposed to be difficult? Because there are a few lights on inside his house, and my phoenix ears catch his heavy footfalls along with multiple others. Now, the stalker becomes the stalked.

Landing on gentle claws in the darkness of the house opposite his, it's three breaths before I let myself take a new form, the elastic strap of my bag shrinking with me. It's not often I have to use the possum, but they're great at climbing and seeing in the dark. Plus, they can hold things in little hands, the absence of which is a big setback for most animal forms.

Scuttling into Ghoul's front yard, I climb up onto the fence between his property and the next, and listen in. There are two black SUVs parked on the street in front of his house, and it's then I hear the multiple female voices murmuring within. Heels click down the stairs, and at least four pairs of the other shoes clomp down after it. Shadows move behind the front door before it swings open to reveal—to my great disgust—my aunt Charlotte, followed by four young ladies in black silk dresses.

"Get in," Charlotte snaps, waving them towards the cars. She stands aside and turns to the large figure of Ghoul now taking up the entire doorway.

"I *expect* to see her next week for her checkup," Charlotte says shortly. "Basilisk guard or no, she is a pregnant serpent, General, and you *will* do what's best for the hatchling's health, upon His Majesty's orders."

"I'll do what needs to be done, Mrs Naga," Ghoul says, but it sounds mocking to me.

Charlotte turns on her heel and follows the girls into one of the SUVs. One of them is sobbing inside the car, and I can't help the way my stomach roils. Ghoul heads back inside as the cars take off and I consider my options.

He probably has human-type security on his house to stop both human criminals and other serpents from slithering in when he's not home. But video motion detectors only work on *visible* prey. General Ghoul is *not* the type of beast who spends a lot of time at home, especially at night, so within ten minutes of his guests leaving, he's out the front door. Man becomes shadow, and the mass of power zooms up into the air like a corrupted helium balloon before zipping away.

I head around the back to the laundry door, and the sudden mental image of Ghoul scooping up laundry powder makes me snort through my possum nose. Shifting into human form, I finally reach into my elastic pouch and take out the lock picks Sabrina gifted me so long ago. She would be so proud right now if she knew what I was doing. I can't tell her yet, of course, but I just know she'd be cheering me on.

Under my ministrations, the door opens in less than a minute. Quiet as a shadow of my own, I slip inside. The laundry is spotless, I note as I pass through it. From what I remember from when I was a child, my father's seven generals had small teams of serpents who maintained their personal needs like laundry, cooking, cleaning, and grocery shopping so they could spend their full time on their work.

The quiet corridors show signs of being recently cleaned, and I narrow my eyes at the shiny black tiles, wondering which serpent he trusts enough to come into his personal space. He turned off the lights before he left, so it's with my eagle eyes that I make sure I don't trip as I make my way up the lacquered wooden stairs. A floorboard creaks as I step onto the second floor, and I take a moment to cringe before continuing on to his bedroom.

Though I've been in here before, being in someone else's bedroom without them feels like a special sort of intrusion. It's probably why my body hunches in on itself as I creep through the dark, as if I'm cringing against the feeling of being a criminal. It's so funny that I'd been accused of being a criminal for so long, accused of doing things I never did, that when I actually do them, it feels like nostalgia. It feels like I'm coming full circle.

In the end, I *did* become an arsonist who burned full mansions down.

I *did* become a murderer of multiple beasts.

I escaped capture by the council and others multiple times.

And I regret none of it.

I really do belong at Animus Academy after all. Beak had been right in his assessment so long ago when we'd first met. Lyle will be so happy to hear his assessment had also been right when he'd caught me with his bazooka net. *Gods,* I'd hated him then. How things change.

So I channel my inner criminal and think of the places Ghoul would hide his prized possessions. Gazing upon the king bed that takes up the back of the room, I wonder if the basilisk lord has any prized possessions at all. Where *had* he come from? I run my fingers in the air over the bedspread. It's expensive silk, the dark pattern notably South Asian. Perhaps the better question is, where had my father *gotten* him from?

The headboard and side tables have the distinct colouring of heavy mangowood, and when I open the drawers, I find nothing at all. Frowning, I head over to the inset wardrobe, sliding open the matching wooden panel. As expected, there are multiple sets of his serpent general uniform. Black shirts and pants, and Kevlar vests with little pockets that I think he must wear for fun. On the bottom sit rows of black boots, some more worn than others. With nothing more of interest here, I leave this room and find the bathroom next door.

It would be foolish to turn on the light, so I settle for my eagle vision, startling myself when I see my own big eyes in the mirror. The cabinet over the sink contains shaving paraphenalia, an electric toothbrush and toothpaste, along with dental floss and mouthwash. It's the same green liquid of the brand we had in the Naga household. Something about this is unsettling, perhaps humanising the beast I know so little about.

He's just a person. And yet, he's anything but.

I shove the door shut, making a face at myself in the mirror as I turn away to inspect the shower. There are three matching black bottles—generic shampoo, conditioner, and body wash. Another reminder that I've never actually seen Ghoul's bare face. I quickly dart out of the bathroom and inspect the other rooms. They are bare like his own with the strange, ghostly feel of disuse. It almost seems like he's a visitor in his own house.

Huffing, I make my way out using the same way I came in, careful to lock the laundry door before shifting into phoenix form. I learnt nothing tonight except that Ghoul has exceptional hygiene.

Chapter 15

Ghoul

Fifteen years ago

I had been alone in the cave for a year when he came for me. Darkness had become my friend. Silence had become a familiar melody. People don't wander close to this area. Something about the malevolent power I gave off warned everyone, including other animals, to say away. So when the murmur of adult male voices hit my ears, I sit bolt upright, my eyes burning into the far light over the cave's small opening. I crawl towards them with caution, in case they're people with weapons again. But then the voices fade away, the sounds of the feet crashing into the jungle headed in the opposite direction to my cave.

I let loose a breath, and sniff the air in consideration. A scent hits me. Barely able to believe my nose, I scamper out on hands and feet, rubbing my eyes with one hand. Warm food. Placed right before me on a clean, green banana leaf. I sniff all over it, seeking any poisons or bad magics, because *those* have been tried before too. But all I can smell is something similar to my mother's cooking; the spices she used, the warmth of rich ghee. There is no other thought in my mind as I tear into the meal, the flatbread warm on my tongue, the potatoes and cooked meats melting in my mouth, hitting me right in the heart. My groan is pure bliss as I sit back on my haunches.

Hunger has become normal for me. Sometimes I try to hunt after sunset, but there's never any game around my cave, and I can't risk going into the village. Can't risk seeing someone I know and having no choice but to hear the sizzle of flesh and the scent of ash. Death so fast there isn't any time to scream and I never have any control over it. My heart is already broken, I fear another injury to it will kill me. So with my belly full, I crawl back into the depths of the cave and sleep contentedly.

The next day, the deep voices reach my ears again, and I'm curious enough to want to see who would dare come here with food when no one else had ever bothered. Who would ever be nice to the monster in the cave? The monster of the village?

On hands and knees, I creep up to the entrance, eyes closed, listening closely. One of the accents, heavier, commanding seems foreign. The local voices are frightened, but his is not. "Good afternoon, child," he says in my mother tongue. My eyes fly open and I scamper back, in case I hurt this person who brought me food. "Don't be afraid. My eyes are covered."

Frowning, I creep out again, cautious for any attackers. But only a single man stands there, in an English suit, coloured like cream, and a patterned white strip of cloth tightly bound around his eyes. He is tall, his skin darker than a white man's, and instinct tells me he's a king cobra. My mind fills with questions, but most importantly, "Do you have any more food?"

Two minutes later, we're sitting down opposite each other while I shove my face with spiced rice and chicken. "I have been looking for someone like you all my life," he says quietly. "A serpent with great power."

He still can't see me, but I nod vigorously, because my cheeks are full of food. I have been alone for so long. So unwanted that I'm starving for any connection. *Hungry* for mere conversation. "Do you want to live, child? Live without fear? Live like a king with many serpents at your command?" Chewing, I listen carefully. "I come from a place like that," he says. "Where a beast like you would be worshipped. Where you could learn how to use your powers."

My spine straightens. "Really?"

He smiles. "You want to do that? Learn to use your powers?"

"If I can stop killing people, yes!" I exclaim. "Everywhere I go, people die."

"Very well. I can help you...if you will do something for me in return."

To leave this cave? To have a normal life with food? "Anything!"

He reaches into his pocket and takes out a small jewelled pocketknife. "Just a small oath to swear yourself to me," he says gently. "That you will always obey and never betray or lie to me. And then you are free from this life of nothing."

* * *

We make it to the docks in the middle of a tropical storm, at the peak of monsoon season. Rain falls like bullets upon the sailors, making the sound of a war drum upon the wooden boards of the big ships that sail across many oceans. And in this turbulent weather, I couldn't be happier. I feel like a new boy. My eyes are closed and bound shut with fine, comfortable cloth, and I'm in new clothes and shoes that fit me with room for growing.

"Will you help me, child?"

The king has helped me so much already, it feels like grace to say yes when he whispers the instructions in my ear.

And undoes my blindfold.

They don't see their death coming on the ship that's taking me to my new life. The first one drops like a sack of heavy rice. I come upon the second from the side, the next from behind. They fall one by one, after one last terrified twist of their faces. The last look at my monstrous form, then they jump right into the sea.

"I missed that one," I grumble, closing my eyes and hurrying back to the tall figure of my saviour as his own men take over the ship.

"No matter. You are a good boy," the King Cobra says, stroking my hair. "Such a good boy."

I lean my cheek to the side, savouring the feeling of the human palm on my face. The feeling of having done something *good* for once fills me up like sweetened milk. I believe him. Every word.

The journey is long, but the cobra king and his serpents make the time go fast with grand stories. The place we're going is heaven. It's the land of opportunity for a child like me, full of wide-open spaces where I won't have to hide. Where there's no need for a secret cave in the jungle. He told me that those days are behind me.

During the dark of night, we reach the new world, and it feels so different from my old one. The air is dry and cold. There are so many automobiles, so many new sounds and wondrous scents. But I pick up on these things, and I pick them up quickly. I want to learn. I want to be free. My king promised me a warm place to stay with a real bed and a television and he delivers it with a smile in his voice.

The small house is at the back of a big property, with big trees standing like protectors beside it, their leaves like friends. It seems new, the smell of new paint and fresh lemons inside. "You'll live here," the serpent king says. "You'll be safe and cared for while you learn your skills."

By the time I leave this house and am unleashed on the world, it becomes corrupted by my power. The beams begin to splinter under my shadows, the windows cracking under the strain. And during one errant shift, my tail lashes a hole in the ceiling. My clumsy attempt to patch it up means that every time it rains, it leaks.

It's years before I return to this place, and when I do, someone else is dwelling in it.

Chapter 16

Aurelia

I wake up with a start, tangled within four sets of naked limbs, the last image of the dream burned into my mind's eye making my heart pound at a thousand miles an hour.

That dream. My bungalow.

Sharp awareness roils through my veins at the realisation that this changes everything. And yet somehow it changes nothing at all.

My bungalow had originally been Ghoul's house.

My father had brought him there from a land so far away I don't know how much more of it he remembers. When his powers had come in, he'd likely not known how to control them and had done great damage, forcing his family to isolate him.

Ghoul had been alone from the beginning. Had been the only basilisk anyone knew from the start. He had been just like me. When Ghoul arrived in town, I would have still been living at Naga House. Still going to school, living a normal life. My mind flashes back to the night of the fake engagement party and the basilisk lord's possessive arm around me as we walked into Naga mansion together. The strange feeling I'd had in the depths of my being. That feeling of another life, another time. Another possibility. The unexpected ache in my heart makes guilt slide through me.

Scythe sits bolt upright, Savage not a moment after. "Your breathing," Scythe says, putting a hand on my shoulder. "Regina, was it a bad dream?"

Savage's hands find my skin too as I look at my shark. He searches my gaze and seems to understand, like he always does, that this dream wasn't a dream. I reach for him, banding an arm around his neck, and he pulls me into himself, that perfect tattooed naked skin like a soothing haven on mine. He brushes my hair aside and grazes his lips against my mating mark. I shiver in his hold. Savage shuffles closer to warm at my back. Between the two of them, I feel more at home than I ever have anywhere else. It settles my racing heart and the sting of the knowledge I'd just received.

Ghoul's memories are different from the others. Sharing of memories is a serpent order power, and while my dream-memories from my other mates have been clear enough, this dream bore a stark brightness to it that I can't ignore. Does *he* see his world like that? So bright that it's painful?

For the rest of the day, I'm quiet with my own thoughts, coming to terms with what I'd been shown. I get to see Minnie and my other animas in Raquel's hospital room. It's our meeting place these days, and it turns out we're all upset. Eugene hops into Stacey's lap, her eyes as red-rimmed as mine are. Henry returns to my shoulder, cooing his own reassurances in my ear. "Stay with me," I whisper to him.

My little nimpin buries himself in the thick strands by my shoulder as the vision of my dream runs itself through my mind on a loop.

Alone. We'd both been alone at the start. Both vulnerable to the powers looming over us. The difference is that while my life has changed dramatically, Ghoul is still alone. Still on the outskirts of things.

Stacey tearily tells us about her rex, Etienne. How Marduk has him tied up under the school for questioning. She brought him food under Yeti's supervision last night, but the bastard refused to eat from her hand. Refused to even look her in the eye. She touches her healing shoulder, grimacing under the pain of it.

"He's just ashamed, I think," Stacey sniffs. "That he hurt me and didn't mean to." She swallows as we listen in earnest. "I...I don't think I'm going to go back there tonight."

"He said," Sabrina says angrily, "that he wanted to go back to

The Collector's property. That the pay was good, and now he has no income. That *we* ruined that for him."

Stacey trembles, clutching onto Eugene, who looks at her with worry. "He's just confused. It's not the meeting either of us dreamed of."

A single tear slips from my eye as I stare at the blank wall behind Stacey. Another follows it. A sob escapes my mouth, making Minnie's head snap towards me. Stacey and I leap for each other, Eugene darting away just in time. I squash Stacey to my chest, and she clutches onto me so tightly my ribs creak. Minnie and Sabrina rub both our backs and we cry, loud and broken.

Half of me can't comprehend it. Stacey's heart had been pining for mates she'd never met, and the moment she'd met her rex, also alone, he'd *shot her* like a pussy.

My little house had been my home for seven years, and I thought I had been alone. I thought it had been Charlotte's abandoned guest house, but it had been there before Charlotte's house had even been built. My mate had been there before anyone else. The final piece of my soul had lived there, slept in that bed, showered in that bathroom, and sat on that very same couch. I clutch onto my friends with all my might because I don't know what to do with any of this. How to process it. I can't even say it out loud. How old had he been when he'd arrived there? Thirteen? Fourteen?

"Dear Wild Mother." Except it's not me saying it. It's Minnie. Someone hands me tissues, and I wipe my face.

"I know why I'm crying," Stacey asks. "But why are you crying, Lia?"

"I think it's just everything," Minnie says soothingly. "Isn't it, Lia? This world is just too fucking much sometimes."

I hear their own burdens in their voices, and it pulls me out of my misery for a moment. Standing back, I huff a breath. Maybe I should have known. Some part of me should have felt that my mate had been there. Shame creeps through me like old poison. "It's just dumb regina things," I say thickly. "Feeling shame about things I had no control over."

Minnie sighs into the ceiling. "Tell me about it."

I groan and rub my eyes. "Do you think we'll look back on this when we're older and laugh? Or will we just sit in our rocking chairs and cry about it again?"

"My vote is for cry," Stacey says darkly.

"Well," says Minnie, "Eugene and I think we'll have learnt a lot by the time we get to rocking chairs. We'll all have our mates and have parties for our grandbabies—" Minnie abruptly shuts her mouth, glancing at Sabrina sitting huddled inside her hood. "I'm so sorry Sabrina, I'm a fucking idiot."

"It's fine," Sabrina says in that deadpan. "I'm fine."

I blow out a heavy breath against the tension you could cut through. Fucking hell. Meanwhile, I'm supposed to be pretending to be pregnant with Ghoul's imaginary progeny. "One step at a time," I mutter, grasping Stacey's hand. "We do this one fucking step at a time."

Stacey and Sabrina are booked for their counselling sessions with Theresa, so we split up for the afternoon, each of us finding our thoughts in the darkest of places. When the day draws to a close, I eat an early dinner with Savage, who's planning a moonlight run with the other wolves of the academy. It's a full moon tonight, and the others are at the gym before it closes for the wolf-exclusive use of the grounds from sunset to sunrise.

"You sure you don't want to come?" Savage asks, wiping his mouth on the back of his hand.

I shake my head. "I need to fly to clear my brain."

"More alone time?" Savage nudges me. "That's perfectly fine by me," he says, trying hard to appear nonchalant. "I'm not upset that I can't fly *at all*."

Kissing him on the cheek, I lower my voice by his ear. "I'm gonna suck your dick so hard when I get back."

Savage's cheeks bloom pink as his eyes brighten on me. He goes to reach for me, but I dance out of his grasp. "Bye!" My wolf's deep laugh follows me out into the night.

Once again, I instruct Beak to cover for me, fully aware that his narrowed eagle eyes follow me north where I need to go again.

I check Ghoul's house first, and finding it vacant, stretch my wings in the direction of the new Naga mansion. Ghoul had shown me the way in his own car—inadvertently or not, I'll have to figure that out—but it also makes me realise there are no hyena magic protections against my entry like there were in the old house. Ghoul had brought me right in without incident. Which means I can potentially spy without incident too.

Serpent heat sensors make it difficult for me to simply walk in there under my invisibility shield. Not all serpent shifters have thermal detection in their human form, only the most powerful or feral ones, and there are definitely those around in Naga House at night.

As I approach the house from the air, the many golden lights making it a beacon amidst the grand open lawns that surround it, I note the activity around the back of the house and give the property a wide berth as I come at it from its back side, and manage to land in the tall trees that line the fence, bushing branches aside with my beak so I can see better.

There are several serpent generals gathered on the white gravel, including what looks like a whole team of armed forces, organising themselves into military vehicles. A shiver runs down my spine as Ghoul, the tallest of them all, takes a long drag on a cigarette before discarding it on the ground and digging his heel into it. As he heads into the first vehicle, a small serpent ducks behind him and scoops up the cigarette with a dustpan and brush.

I recognise the thin, dark-haired boy immediately. Thomas Krait had been at Animus Academy a while back and had been responsible for outing Sabrina and me for sneaking into Titus' room the time we stole his laptop. It had all been worth it in the end, but he still hated my guts for the death of his twin brother, Theo. Now Thomas is here, picking up trash and it's only a disgruntled feeling I get through my gut at the sight of him.

The trucks rumble off down the long drive and out the front gates, and I follow in the sky, keeping a distance and watching Ghoul's vehicle in the lead. They travel a little way down the highway and turn into serpent territory. So this is not some mission for an enemy attack; this is court business. Ghoul's vehicle rumbles to a stop, but he doesn't get out of the car. Instead, another general gets out and knocks on the door. There is a conversation before two boys exit the house—no older than thirteen—shouldering duffle bags. They are led into the trucks.

The convoy rolls up to the next house and, in the same manner, a young boy and girl get out with bags and load up the vehicles. My stomach turns.

By the third house, I know exactly what this is.

Ghoul doesn't get out until the next house, when there is an extended conversation and a man's raised voice. I swoop down low to get a better look. An elderly male holds a young granddaughter around the waist. The pale hatchling has a barcode and ID number on her right cheek, marking her as venomous. "You're not taking her!" her grandfather exclaims. "Sophie, get back in the house."

"I don't want to go!" Sophie cries. "You can't make me!"

But then Ghoul strides up to the door, and the little girl lets out a shrill cry. Ghoul's voice booms through the night. "Get in the car, unless you want your granddaddy branded as a traitor."

Sophie shakes her head, and on shaking legs, bravely steps out of her grandfather's grip. Satisfied, the general turns away from the house, letting Sophie walk up to the convoy.

"Monster!" the grandfather cries after them. "The lot of you are monsters!"

Ghoul halts and slowly turns around. My heart beats rapidly. The basilisk lord makes some signal, because from the vehicle, four serpents spring out of the cars and march into the house, dragging the man with them. The door shuts, and all I hear is a scream as Ghoul casually gets back into the vehicle.

Moments later, the house is silent and the serpent militia exit the house, knuckles bruised and stained with blood. I can't stop watching as the night wears on.

Chapter 47

Ghoul

My little snakelet wants to know about me. Well, of course I will oblige her.

She'd entered my house stealthily, and I just know it was the little leopard who taught her how to pick locks. She'd done it brilliantly too, no doubt thinking that any motion sensors inside the house wouldn't pick up her sneaky invisible shield. Except I had motion detectors on all the doors and windows, and when my phone pinged a warning, I got it out to check the hidden cameras all along the townhouse. It showed nothing, of course. But all I had to do was turn on the thermal imaging and there she was. In the most perfect silhouette, my snakelet crept along, snooping at my things.

Naturally, I was honoured.

My physical needs are minimal. Have been since I was cast out by my adopted family as soon as my animus had made itself known. I'd had to survive on nothing for so long. Old habits die hard, and once Mace brought me to the 'new world,' I'd not felt the need for anything exactly material. Mace called my ways 'ascetic,' and it had always amused him that a boy who'd come from so little, like himself, never wanted for anything more by way of physical possessions.

But he doesn't understand what I do.

And I think Aurelia may be the only creature who understands it too. Who has the right to. Maybe that's why I've always been fascinated by her. As I'd watched her go through my townhouse, I'd wondered what went on in that brain of hers. What thoughts she was turning over and what conclusions she was drawing. It only felt right to show her something clear that night in her dreams. And naturally, it made her return. Made her want to know *more*.

Presently, she follows us high and back in the air, but I know she's there. My skin prickles in awareness of her. My dark soul cries out with longing that I snuff out and put away, making my fangs snap out of my gums. I lick a drop of venom off a sharp point, savouring my own toxic taste. "Continue on without me," I say to Natalia, my driver tonight. "I have business to attend to."

"Yes, General," she says obediently.

I pull down the window and dissolve into the night, slowly gaining height to make sure my snakelet sees me deviating from the road.

Shall we play a little game?

It doesn't take long to lead her to the gritty part of the city, where a choice nighttime venue lies nestled between two strip clubs. I sense her caution, but nothing about this should be new to her. Reconstituting into human form as I land, I can barely contain myself. The two burly python guards at the door bow as they see me, and a smaller green tree snake hands me a neatly rolled joint. "Good evening, General," he says, lighting it for me.

I straighten, exhaling smoke into the air. "And what a good one it issss," I hiss. Sauntering inside, the darkness engulfs me, the dramatic smoke machine humming away in the distance, so that when I walk through the entry corridor and out into the open space beyond, it looks like I've stumbled upon a dream. Or a pretty nightmare.

The sign on the door says, in dripping toxic green: *We drop our fangs, and you drop your panties.*

A mixture of animalia and humans writhes on the dance floor and couches within, most of them with some type of face covering. Anonymity is encouraged at Club Venom, and the mixture of masks, shimmery veils, and balaclavas under the strobe lights create the perfect place for a mysterious and secret fuck. As soon as midnight hits, the place transforms into something from the devil's dreams. The other orders might make a show of hating serpents out in the open, but when it comes to their dirtiest fantasies, they come to us for fangs and fulfilment.

The crowd parts like the sea for me as I stroll through it, exhaling smoke above their heads, to the roped-off VIP area off the side. It works as a stage some nights; other nights, it's just a place for the generals to watch with their own animas. Relaxation time for us all is becoming scarce these days, so the black velvet couches sit empty and waiting for me. A bikini-clad working girl nods at me before un-latching the rope and letting me through. After a word, she runs off to fetch me a drink, and I sit. And wait.

I can sense when she enters the building, as I always have. Even with all of her shields in place, even without my thermal sensors, that golden presence—wild like the gods who made us and powerful like nature herself—is always so clear to me. It's changed with time as she's come into herself. Her power when I'd first laid eyes on her is *nothing* compared to her power now.

Pretending to watch the crowd, I turn my face away from the snakelet. I can tell without looking at the time that it's approaching midnight. Beasts have shifted into serpent form, clothes have come off, and a woman with bare breasts tries to catch my gaze. She carries a banana python around her shoulders and grinds her hips into the girl standing behind her. As I watch them, she runs her tongue over white teeth, her lips, black like her hair, curving up into a seductive smile.

I note that my snakelet has paused off to the side. Smirking, I raise a hand and beckon to both women. They look at each other in surprise and make their way over to me. Settling back into the couch, I spread my legs out, awaiting them. The two serpent animas approach me with their necks bared, getting on their knees before the bisecting rope. Wrists come out, baring the black cursive 'B'. The attendant allows them in, and they shuffle forward.

One glance at the snakelet tells me she's stalked forwards so much she's almost at the rope herself, and now she's producing enough heat to make her light up my thermal vision. I chuckle, beckoning to the first woman to get onto my lap. "Your hair reminds me of someone," I say, rubbing some strands between my fingers.

"Really?" she purrs. "Who? Is she pretty?"

"She's ethereal," I murmur, turning the woman's face to the side. She closes her eyes, enjoying the attention I'm rarely known to give to any female. I turn her face back and lean towards her ever so slowly.

A hissing voice I love so much slides into my mind, sharp as any fang. *"Don't you fucking dare."*

The anima suddenly tumbles from my lap, landing on the floor with a thud. She then proceeds to slide off the stage along with the other woman, both of them getting dumped into the receded pit below the stage. It's then that the rest of the lights in the place turn off, leaving only laser green strobe lights in the pitch black.

A snakelet-sized weight drops into my lap, and a small hand bands my neck as her voice whispers across my lips. "Trying to make me jealous, Lord Basilisk?"

My fangs extend in arousal. "Not at all. Just a usual Friday night for me, snakelet."

"Liar," she hisses, her power thrumming around me like a boa constrictor's muscled grip. She reveals herself, naked and supreme in my lap, and my pulse races, its beat almost in time with the music. "Gods, you are stunning."

The hand around my throat squeezes before she drags a tongue up my right fang. I let out a cursed moan, my hands coming around her waist to hold her close. Aurelia's fangs slide down from her gums, the white points coming to rest on her full, delicious lower lip. She looks at me with flaming hot desire and anger in her bluest eyes before she leans down and strikes me right in the neck.

My body slumps back under her ministrations, my eyes fluttering shut as her lips and fangs attack me, those dangerous points injecting toxic venom right into my bloodstream. Her unique venom burns through my veins, and under my thundering heart, it delivers its nectar to my entire body. For the first time in my life, I feel the effects of a serpent's paralysis.

Chapter 18

Aurelia

A teensy, delicious sense of power trickles through me as I pump venom into Ghoul's firm neck. My tongue draws a circle over his flesh as my fangs enjoy the sensation of finally being embedded in living flesh.

I've never done it before, but I think I like it. My senses are suddenly heightened in the dim light, and as the fumes of arousal saturate my nose, I realise my heart gallops alongside Ghoul's. Suddenly, his entire body relaxes, and he slumps under me, nothing but a dead weight. My head snaps back as I release him, my fangs dripping with venom and blood. Fascinated, I watch as his head falls onto his right shoulder, a small sigh escaping his lips. The shadows move lazily about him, as if they too are affected by the paralysis. Unbidden, a smile creeps along my lips, and I envelop us both in my invisibility, lifting him up with my telekinesis. In the darkness of the club, not a soul sees us.

Quicker than a striking adder, I get the both of us out of Club Venom and its writhing, fucking bodies, a smug grin—that I absolutely deserve—plastered on my face. Outside, the cold air slapping me brightly, I quickly consider my options and turn left, walking us down the street. I'm dragging him through the air behind me, careful not to bump into the beasts and humans of the thinning crowd.

"I captured the basilisk lord," I sing into his mind, channelling

Savage and knowing full well he can't respond to me. "*I can do whatever I want with Mace's mighty serpent general.*" Maybe I'm a bit high from my first ever fang-paralysis situation. Or maybe I'm a bit high from my second time stalking someone, but I'm giddy inside and shaking my ass as I dance down the street with my paralysed captive, the most dangerous beast in the city.

This late at night, the streets on the outskirts of the city are empty, and there are parklands with pretty trees and botanical gardens. Primitive instinct leads me away from the concrete jungle into the real bushes and trees, where the smell of pine, eucalyptus, dead leaves and animal scat is fresh in my nose. There, behind some bushes in the dark, away from all prying eyes, I remove the invisibility shield so I can see the basilisk general properly. Dumping him on his back upon the dry grass, I crouch next to his near seven-foot body.

Lazy shadows bump and coil against my knees, like smoke from a dying fire. Red points, faintly visible behind the eyeholes of his half-skull mask stare up at the sky, his gloved hands resting by his sides. I remove the glove closest to me.

Curiously, I pick up the large, tattooed hand in two of mine. It's darker and more calloused than my own, the fingers long and thick, the nails short, and I have to use my eagle eyes to see the dark ink decorating them. Two males, with their top half human and the bottom half serpentine, their long tails coiled around themselves in ancient patterns. I trace the design in wonder. I'd seen artwork like this before, in old temples of faraway lands. I wonder what other tattoos he'd chosen to put on his body.

I place his hand down and examine his neck and visible chest. The brown skin is unmarked up here, except for the celestial glow of our mating mark, dimmed under a thin veil of his shadows. I touch his skin here, shooing the veil away so I can see our mark properly. "The Wild Goddess was having a joke, wasn't she?" I say, sitting back and staring at it in full view for the first time. "She had a dark fucking sense of humour when she gave you to me." I lean forward and touch the edge of his mask. "Now I finally get to see your face."

But a hand snaps out, lashing around my wrist. "Naughty,

naked little snakelet." Ghoul lunges for me, and before I know it, I'm flat on my back with him above me, holding me in place with strong hands. "You've never bitten anyone before," he says with a note of surprise.

"Fast metaboliser aren't you?" I grit out. "I thought I'd at least have half an hour."

The alabaster mask hovers over me for a second longer before he leans down and a fang brushes against my pulse. I suck in a breath, ready for the sting of the bite. "If I were anyone else, my venomous little vixen, I'm quite sure I'd be dead." He holds himself aloft, his body barely touching my skin, and I find myself craving his weight on me, his muscle flush against my hips. Warm lips flutter at the skin under my ear. "You should try to bite your other mates, see if the effect is the same."

"You'd love that, wouldn't you? To see them hurt."

"Oh yes, snakelet. Dead, maimed, bloody—I'd love to see all of it." I scoff, disgusted by his words. He rears back to look at me, the red lasers flaring. His deep timbre rings with accusation. "You love them."

"Of course I do!" Ghoul leaps off me as I gape at him, clambering to my own feet to confront him properly. "They're my *mates*, remember? Your bond brothe—"

He's before me in an instant, a hand covering my mouth. "Do *not* remind me."

I narrow my eyes at him, and he slides his hand away, exhaling through his nose. My brow cocks. "Oh, is that it? You want me all to yourself?" He shakes his head, and a new sort of tense energy settles over him, making the shadows twitch as if ready to battle. "You sent me a memory last night," I say quietly. "I want to see another. I want to know what happened after my father brought you here."

There is no emotion in his voice when he says, "You are not ready to see more."

"I promise you I am." He gazes at me. The heaviness in the air between us thickens like congealed venom. "I can take it."

Backwards, he begins to walk away from me. "Do not come crying to me, snakelet," he hisses. "Do not look at me with *those* eyes. I will only have you, pupils slitted and defiant with rage. I will have nothing else. Do you understand?"

The regina in me understands what the human will not. That my darkest mate needs me hot. He needs me wild. He needs me dripping with venom. So, even as my heart squeezes so hard, I bare my fangs at him, feeling my pupils changing. "Do you not know who I am?"

There's a wavering moment between us, full of something more than electricity. Something that turns hardened beasts to ashes. "I know where you came from," he says. "I know who made you."

"I made my *fucking* self," I spit. "Bone by bone, wound by wound, I grew myself into what I needed to become."

Ghoul raises his chin. "The end is coming, snakelet. And it does not include the things you want. Know that. *Feel* that."

My face gives an involuntary grimace, but I set my jaw. "We'll see about that, General Ghoul. We'll see about *everything*."

His lips curve into a cruel smile, fangs extending past his bottom lip as he walks away, the shadows engulfing him as he disappears completely. "Sssso we will."

Chapter 49

Scythe

Xander and I fly out on a much delayed visit. We have a lot of business to attend to, but my regina's needs always come first. The Wild Mother gave her a rough fate in this life, and it does not seem to be easing for her. She remains troubled and unsettled despite our combined efforts to soothe her. Even now, my shark gnashes his angry teeth at me, not wanting to leave the nest. But a darker time approaches, and we must all be ready.

It should be strange to be on Xander's dragon-back again after so long being estranged from him, but it's not. It's like being home again. It's like being embraced by a brother. I may never truly forgive him for what he did, but I understand him in a way no one else, except Aurelia, ever will. Our hearts are dark, and our spirits strong. Those two things are a recipe for difficult mates, and all we can do now is try to make it up to Aurelia for our past sins.

Xander and I check on Connor and Katerina's ex-captives in the new safe house, a wide double-story duplex with plenty of rooms for privacy and nest-building. Connor looks better than the last time I saw him, and he appears to have found his calling in managing the care of the many occupants of the large house. He's been coordinating the doctors and social workers, making sure the younger animalia are showering, and ensuring the food gets distributed evenly. I made a note for Xander to ensure Connor and his grandfather get the appropriate funds to make sure they are both looked after. Connor deserves it, after what he did for us and we make sure he knows it.

The lioness asks about Aurelia and his other anima friends, expressing his worry for all of them. I reassure him they are all tired, but healing from their injuries, emotional or otherwise.

"Some of the younger girls drew this for you guys," Connor says, handing Xander an A4 envelope. He opens it, revealing hand-drawn thank you cards full of love hearts and rainbows. There is one for each of us by name. Xander takes his own, a small crease between his brows as his fingers brush over the letters of his name in pink and yellow. Connor clears his throat. "There's something else for you and Lia in there as well, but you can open it at home." Xander makes some notes about what more is needed, and after making some calls, we head back into the sky.

Not far from the regional safe house, Hyacinth Dabu and her pack hold the dethroned hyena queen captive in an isolated town where no one asks questions. The house is aging, but it suits its purpose as a negotiation outpost. Hyacinth is a shrewd leader, and though she hasn't announced her capture of the matriarch yet, word of her disappearance has unsettled the hyena community. They know what it means when a leader goes missing.

"I've set her up in the dining room," Hyacinth says as she lets us into the house. "I haven't gotten everything I want yet."

Lady Hyena sits tied with obsidian chains to a steel chair. There's strain at the edges of her eyes, and the air is rank with her sweat, pain, and anger. They have allowed her trips to the bathroom and minimal food, but not much else. "Would you torture an old woman, Scythe?" she says, her cunning eyes beady and dark on me as Xander and I come to stand before her, dwarfing the room. "I know that is your preferred method. Have you finally found your boundary with an old woman?"

"The thing is," Xander drawls, "that it works very well. And the issue we find ourselves with is that you won't talk."

"Of what use is *talking* when the deed is done?" she spits. "My rule has ended. I will be killed for my part in it." She means the spell she put on us to exchange reginas. Katerina Crocodylus may have instigated the spell, but the hyena queen made it possible.

"What's Mace planning?" Xander asks. "We know he's recruiting for his pseudo-military. Does he want a dictatorship? Does he want to overthrow the humans and make an empire for himself?"

My guess is that this is Mace's fantasy. To claim recompense for the serpent purge of the previous generation and gain the ultimate power. While the power fantasies of most beasts are rarely achieved, Mace Naga is not most beasts. He has already eliminated the state council and made bonds with the human leaders. For animalia, we keep territory business private. Other countries or states will likely not interfere with changes in power. They will simply watch and wait for the outcome. That's the way it's always been.

"You don't know what dark powers you're playing with," she says. "Powers Mace kept private even from me. Even from most of his generals."

That piques my interest. "If he's kept it so secret, how is it you know about it?" I ask.

"He's been hinting at something grand for years now. Some ancient serpentine weapon."

Xander glances at me. Serpent magic has always been mysterious. Blood magic, venom magic. These are things serpents keep close to their chests, and we already know basilisk magic was used to gain power over the council. What other secrets does the basilisk have? Things seem to point back to Mace's most powerful general. "Do you think he'll come for you?" I ask abruptly. "Do you think he will come and save you from me?"

A cold smile curves her lips. "No."

"Then why protect him?"

She searches the air around me. "Tell me what you see when you look at me."

I consider for a moment and am happy to tell her the truth. "A poisoned aura. You've taken many lives and don't regret it. Many secrets and many lies."

She nods. "I imagine it's much the same when you look at the other underworld leaders. Ha! It's probably the same when you look at yourself in the mirror."

I smile without humour. "There are demons in my mirror."

She sobers. "He's going to come after you. He's not going to let you get in the way of his plans...which I'm assuming you are going to try."

"If we know what they *are*," Xander says, throwing his hands in the air, "we might get to choose."

"If I were him," she says. "If I were bitter and hateful about the way my people were treated for the last fifty years, then I would want to kill them all. Wouldn't you?"

"I have a regina that wouldn't let me do that," Xander says.

The lady hyena tilts her head back and cackles. "Exactly!" She quietens, regarding us. "Only a regina knows what a regina is truly capable of. *That* was Katerina's downfall." She grins, crooked and gloating. "She never was one, after all. She had a rex." Xander stills as he realises what she means. "And the only thing worse than a rampaging, revengeful regina is a rampaging, revengeful *rex*."

When Hyacinth Dabu closes the door quietly behind us, she gestures to something she's set on the small dining room table. A clear glass canister, filled with a dull white powder.

My heart jolts in my chest, rage and fury and agony mixing into one maelstrom in my mind. Xander goes as still as stone.

"We found this in The Collector's secret stores," Hyacinth says gently. "It's Aurelia's right to have it back. In the wrong hands it could do great damage."

She doesn't need to say what the bad powers in the world would do with powdered Boneweaver bone. Reverently, I take the canister, cradling it to my chest. "Thank you, Hyacinth," I say. "I'm not sure what my regina will do with it, but at least she will get to decide on her own terms."

Xander and I leave the old house and its occupants behind in silent contemplation. Our flight is also filled with an icy silence, laden with the implications of Lady Hyena's words. But it's because of our late and silent return to Animus Academy that we see our regina returning from the far north in her phoenix form, where she'd no doubt been all night, without anyone knowing.

Chapter 50

Savage

"**M**y little chompy pie has been sneaky sneaking out every night?" I exclaim with great anguish.

"Calm down," Xander snaps, throwing a football at my head.

I angrily swat it away, and it bounces off the Rec room wall and lands clean in an armchair. I give Xander a significant look when that happens because, see how great I am? Scythe sits in another armchair away from us, staring into a glass of whiskey as Lyle stands with his arms crossed, frowning out the window. Aurelia is back upstairs now, and the other students aren't allowed in the Rec room this late. The rest of the wolves are still outside on their full moon run. Scythe and Xander gave her the urn with what's left of her powdered femur. She went still and soft and asked to be alone with it for a while. I love her so much, it hurts to see her hold something that came with such great pain and I told her I wanted to kill Flores Drakos, only he's already dead, which is great. So instead, I can help her build a shrine for it maybe. "I grew it back just fine," she'd said, patting her new thigh. "With Xander's help." she smiled at the dragon bugger. "This was a part of me once. I want to keep it."

Now in the Rec room, I want to hurt someone.

"You don't get it." I point at Xander. "She's only *just* started liking you, but she tells me *everything*. In fact, this might *be* because of you. I'm going up to ask her right now!" I ram my shoulder into

Xander as I make my way past him, but he blocks me with two hands.

"Think about it, Sav," he says gently. I narrow my eyes at him because why is he cooing to me like I'm a rabid dingo? Xander's glowing eyes glow brighter, and that only happens when he has an idea. "She's been secretive lately, don't you think? She might not take well to us asking her outright. If she's wanting to try covert manoeuvres, maybe *we* should try covert manoeuvres too."

I rub my chin. "You mean like...play the same game as her?"

Xander grins. "You get me."

"So we follow her!" I say excitedly. "We see where she goes and spring out of the bushes and be like, "Gotcha!"

"Maybe," Xander says.

"I liked it better when you two were enemies," Lyle grumbles. "I don't like this approach, but I agree she needs a gentle hand. She's been sensitive."

"My chompy is not *sensitive*, she ate a whole crocodile!" I say to Lyle, holding my hands out to remind him how big crocs are. "There's a lot going on, is all."

"She's holding her cards close," Scythe interjects. "I can't blame her. While I would prefer she came to us with every and any issue, the truth is we are still working out our dynamics as a pack."

"And there is that basilisk-sized outstanding factor," Xander mutters.

"She's having dreams again," Scythe says. "I can't imagine what memories she's being shown."

"I bet they're not mermaid dreams," I say darkly, peering out the window as if the gum trees will give me some clues.

"She really should have come to us," Lyle mutters under his breath. "I don't like that she's keeping secrets."

"Worrywart," I say. "And what would you have done? Sabrina's twerking therapy would work better than *talking* about it."

Lyle rounds on me, offended, just like I wanted. I dance away from the window, heading towards Scythe for safety. "We're going to find out, don't worry your big lion's mane over it. Xander and I will *stalk* Miss Chompy tomorrow night, and Bob's your uncle, we'll know everything."

"She's not going to be happy about being followed," Lyle says. "It may ruin the foundations of trust we've worked hard at setting."

I groan, but Scythe nods. "You make a good point, Lyle." But then the corners of his lips twitch, and my brows fly up in surprise. "However, our regina also knows *us* very well."

Chapter 51

Savage

I spend the *entire* next day giddy with excitement. As expected, the queen of my heart is tired after her nighttime hunting, and she sleeps in until midday. I wake her up with a grin two inches from her face and warm cheese croissants. She's *starving* and wolfs them all down with cute, happy sounds. Scythe appears with a bottle of water and electrolyte powder, and Lyle rubs Tiger Balm into her newer knee. Xander even appears with a lavender-scented heat pack.

We are nothing but supportive mates. And if our regina wants to secretly go out in the middle of the night doing unknown things and then lie about it, then I will *happily* support the entire business. I'll get her an ABN number *and* draw a logo.

Aurelia's Secret Interesting Organisation. A-S-I-O. Completely unique.

During the day, I wonder about ways I can help her. My regina is very quiet for her part, and I feel like she's in pain about something and I don't think it's her bone powder. I discreetly sniff her all over to check for physical injuries, but nothing comes up, so I know it's either a brain-pain, or a pain of the heart. My vision goes blurry as I realise her little heart might be hurting.

"You can't kiss hearts, that's morbid," I say out loud as we sit in Raquel's room where the wolf anim still sleeps.

My regina frowns at me. "Spell morbid."

"Easy one," I say. "M-O-R-B-I-D."

"Good boy."

I grin at her. She's so good with me, and it's because she loves me so much. I feed her again, and when we take the nimpins for health checks with zookeeper Rick, Blair and Blade and I pluck some flowers from the gardens for our reginas. The cheetah twins pick some for Raquel and Stacey as well to make sure they're not left out, and I approve. They are good surrogate mates.

But it's when it starts to get dark that I notice my regina is glancing up at the sky and to the north. She rubs her arms as if she's warming up her wings and stretches out her pretty neck. There's lots of thoughts behind those perfect blue eyes, and I want to know all of them.

"Are you staring at me, wolf man?" she says quietly as we eat dinner in the TV room of our floor. My bond-brothers are in the gym, and she's been playing with her broccoli for the last minute.

"I can't help it," I sigh, sitting my chin on my fists. "You're far too interesting and beautiful and talented." She presses her lips together, trying not to smile. "I want to know what it's like to be you."

My regina rolls her eyes. "Well, it's shit half the time and great the other half."

"I have a lot of questions," I say, getting out my notebook where I've been writing things down about my regina.

"Really?" she asks, cutely trying to read my notes upside down.

I hold the book closer to my chest. "Hey, be careful! My new song is in there."

"What's it about?"

"It's a secret until it's finished."

She laughs and scoots her chair back, and I see that she's more than ready for her secret mission. "Okay, well, you be ready with your questions tomorrow, and we'll go through them."

"Thanks," I say. "Are you going on patrol now?"

"Yep."

Gods, she lies so prettily. I beam at her. "Okay! See you later, regina."

She leans in to kiss me gently on the mouth, and I inhale her in, barely staying in my seat.

As soon as her long mane of black hair disappears into the stairwell that'll take her up to the roof, I leap up from my seat. *"Xander, it's go time."*

We meet outside, under the shadow of the animus dorm. Xander is watching Lia when I arrive, as she does a lap around the school borders before disappearing into the clouds. There is a silent sound that presses at my skin and brushes at the loose strands of my hair. Xanders swears under his breath. "She's used a phoenix sonic boom."

I turn to him. "How fast can you fly?"

"Pretty fucking fast when I want to, you know that. But—" I whip something out of my pocket. Something red and lacey with the supreme, godly scent of my regina's pussy all over it. Xander swears again. "Let's go."

He shifts right on the lawn, and I jog towards his face, holding up the thong to his nose.

"Wait," he says into my head, tossing his head back. *"Take my earphones."*

I grin. "Are you sure?"

"Make sure you put them back in when we get there."

His earphones come flying out towards me, and I catch both tiny black pieces in one hand. Xander's glowing eyes turn scary black, and he starts vibrating like the world's biggest phone. "Here!" I cry, waving the thong like a flag of peace.

His big dragon's head clocks me, going predator-still. Nostrils flare as he catches the scent before leaning down and snatching them right out of my fingers. I cuss really loudly before scrambling up his fat leg and up onto his back. It's just in time too, because Xander gives an almighty leap and we're shooting into the sky like a rocket.

I have just enough time to put Xander's earphones into my own ears before the breath is snatched from my lungs.

Caribbean Blue – Enya

We charge through the air at an insane speed, all the while this strange song plays in my ears. I wonder why Xander was listening to it before we left, but it might be a stress management thing he learned from one of our classes since twerking therapy isn't going to work for him. My skin is plastered to the bones of my face as we ascend into the chilly night, and I'm crouched low on his back from the G-force, but I refuse to close my eyes. I don't want to miss any second of this chase.

Once Xander reaches his favourite height, he sweeps his mighty wings forward and then snaps them back. I get to take a deep breath before a speed I've *never* known takes Xander. We rocket through the sky—

I fly off Xander's back from the sheer speed but grab his tail at the last second. With both hands, I grip on for my life, my body horizontal as Xander powers through the air on the scent of his regina's pussy, all the while this lady is singing a soft, happy melody in my ears. My heart almost pounds out of my chest because I can't really breathe and the wind is pulling my pants down, but I think the song is making it better.

Now I know how a footy ball feels when it's kicked in the backside.

Berserker Xander likes Lia's pussy, and that's really good information to have. When I get back home, I'm going to tell everybody. Because if he ever gets tired of wearing the earphones, he could probably—

Xander slows down, tossing his head angrily. I hope he doesn't try to launch me off his tail because my hands are getting sweaty now. I can see the shining lights of the city like little jewels on a dress. Berserker Xander snorts and growls, likely looking for a fight. Or I wonder if this works like Scythe's shark mate drive and there's not much thought happening in there, just instinct. He's scenting her out, and that's great because my nose is not in a position to work right now as I fight for my life on his tail.

He starts to descend and I let out a groan of relief, thankful the earphones managed to stay in my ears under whatever dragon magics Xander put on them. Landing a grown-ass dragon in the suburbs is going to be an issue, but Xander scopes out a park and thunks down, shaking the metal playground at the centre of it. I'm jostled about and have to let go of his stupid tail. Flying through the air and with no Lyle to cushion my fall, I shift into wolf form and land tumbling across the turf.

Xander has shifted into his human form, panties held up to his face as he storms across the park. I've caught up to him on four legs in an instant, feeling in my heart for my regina's location. But then the earphones hurt my ears, so I shift again into human form and take them out, jogging naked after the bastard. It's a whole lot easier to let Berserker Xander find our regina until we reach a street with lots of houses and people noisily having dinner. Xander is growling and snarling loudly at them, so I have no choice but to jump piggy-back on him and shove his earphones into place. Once they're in, his eyes brighten into golden-white, and he shakes himself.

"I almost died," I say seriously. "But we're here now, so it's fine."

Xander looks around, still fisting the panties that I'm trying to tug out of his grip. "She's in the bushes over there," he says. "It smells like serpent territory."

I sniff the air, and sure enough, a scaly, slithery scent fills my nose. Xander crouches down, and quiet as a cat, disappears into the bushes. Quickly, I scamper to follow. We creep up on Aurelia slowly, doing what we do best as predators stalking prey. Quiet in the night, softly on our feet, hunching my back to keep low. Xander climbs a strong tree in someone's front yard, and I jump up after him.

Aurelia crouches between the bushes and the brick fence of a small unit, staring at the house on the opposite side of the road. Her invisibility shield is off for some reason. I want to remind her to put it back on, but then I won't be able to see her. From our higher position, I can easily see what she's looking at. The big townhouse has a dim light on upstairs.

And just a little ways from the window stands a big beast. I scowl as I recognise him and scowl even more as he takes off his shirt in one clean movement. My eyes flick back onto our side of the road. Aurelia's lips are parted as she stares at him. Back on the other side, Ghoul rubs a hand down his six-pack before reaching down and tugging his pants off.

What the hell is this!

Xander covers my eyes.

"I want to see!" I whisper-yell.

"Pervert!" he whispers back. But he lets me go all the same.

Ghoul has turned around and is starkers, ass and all. I sit up straight as I stare at Lia watching this *display* with her mouth open, a hand reaching up for her throat. Xander is grumbling under his breath, a hand shielding his eyes so he doesn't give us away with their light.

"Lia is perving on Ghoul," I exclaim into Xander's mind. *"She didn't have anyone to teach her not to do that!"* Scythe taught me this long ago.

"Ghoul is facilitating it," Xander replies darkly. *"He fucking knows she's watching."*

I squint back at Ghoul, but he's turned around again, a hand rubbing low down the ripples of his hard stomach. He reaches for his cock, stroking the length of it slowly. *"Is it warm tonight?"* I say, reaching for my forehead.

"I'm as cold as a corpse," Xander says with disgust. *"I don't want to look. What's he doing?"*

"He's jerking off."

"By the Gods."

Lia is covering her mouth, and I can't see where her right hand is. Ghoul now has a hand braced high on the window, showing off his biceps and he's leaning over, pumping his cock faster and faster.

"I thought this would be something interesting," Xander says, disappointed. *"If I wanted a striptease, I wouldn't be coming to serpent territory for it."*

"Yes, but Lia wants one. Why has she never asked me— Wait!"

"What is it?" I squint at Ghoul carefully. The basilisk lord is stroking his snake strongly now, gaining speed, his abs tensing. *"What?"* Xander presses me.

"I actually think his dick might be bigger than yours."

"Impossible," Xander says. He risks a glance, narrowing his eyes so the lights are thin crescent moons. We both watch Ghoul, pumping his cock faster and faster until he goes rigid for a moment and—

"*Did he just—*" Xander chokes.

"*He came all over the glass, yeah,*" I say, impressed. A quick glance back at Lia tells me her hands are between her legs. My mouth drops open into a big O as I salivate and my own cock stiffens. I want to help her, but then the game would be up. "*Well, at least Lia's having a good time.*" I tell him reasonably. "*That's the most important thing.*"

Chapter 52

Xander

Aurelia's midnight stalking turned out to be an utter joke. We return to the academy right behind her, at which point Savage meets her in the bedroom and I get to watch him spread her legs and devour her.

I lie a little way from them, on the single bed under the window, one hand in my pocket, gripping her red thong. She has many like it, I've learned, the lacy, frilly type, and in many different colours. There's just something about the red that sends my organs racing. My cock twitches, but I don't give in to the urge, rolling over to give them space. Aurelia lets out a breathy moan, and I close my eyes. She and Ghoul were...getting to know each other in the worst possible way. From afar. Where the yearning grows more strongly. I would know, after all, having kept her at arm's length myself for so long. Before I knew it, the obsession grew, and I became addicted to watching her.

We know little about the giant worm except that he came into contact with Mace a very long time ago. Whatever memory-dreams Lia is having is only drawing her closer to him. I don't like this. Not with our real enemy. Not when Ghoul is as close to her father as he is. A *daily* consultant. A *daily* weapon. Sworn to him, body and soul as all his generals are.

And she's thinking about him almost as much as I think about her.

* * *

During the day, Aurelia is pensive.

There has been something ineffable about her since we were all reunited. There has always been something otherworldly about Aurelia Boneweaver, but now, in her full power and short only one mate, she is more alluring, and more mysterious than ever. I'm sure it draws in the basilisk too. How much he is resisting her I can't even be sure, but it's not as if they're sneaking off on a tryst. They're both holding back.

Any time I think I'm ready to ask her directly about her dreams, she seems more closed off than ever. There's a strain to her shoulders, and a pain in her eyes I cannot unravel. And that assaults me the most. All I can do is ply her with electrolytes and make sure her physical needs are met. I catch her taking paracetamol that afternoon, and she smiles bashfully. "It's just my neck."

It's not her neck, and we both know it. I wander close to her, enjoying her scent as I brush my fingers across the bare skin of her thigh, sending my healing through to her tired muscles and bones. She sighs, eyelids fluttering shut like the wings of a butterfly. I'm drawn in and I catch myself leaning down as she melts backwards into me. My lips find her shoulders, and one of her arms reaches around, burying her fingers in my hair.

It's the small sound she makes at the back of her throat that does it. I grab her face and invade her mouth with my tongue. She moans into me and then we're tearing at each other's clothes. My shirt comes off, and I wrench at her blouse. My pants pool at my ankles, and she hikes her own skirt up. Before I know it, her hand is around my rock-hard cock, and she's guiding me into her dripping pussy.

She slides back onto me, arching her back, crying out and clutching onto the dining room table. "Xander!" she cries.

I seize her around the waist and fuck her. "My treasure," I growl over her mouth. "Tell me how much you need me. Tell me how much you love my cock in you." She moans loudly in bliss, and I

332

don't realise how much I needed to, but I've been fantasising about this for days. I bury my nose in her hair as her sounds and scent invade my mind and demand that my body comes deep into her.

"Yes!" she cries with approval, and I empty my balls into her heat in stuttering thrusts of my hips. She takes me wholeheartedly, her gripping hands and dripping pussy telling me how much she wanted me too. When we're done, I take her to the bath and clean her up like I did one time so long ago when I'd been half out of my mind. But this time, I'm completely focused on her and what she has come to mean to me. She accepts my care with a soft, knowing smile, *this* time allowed to enjoy my wandering hands. I dry her off and apply moisturiser on her face and body. Lyle won't let anyone else dry her hair, so I let him take over for that.

This time, when Aurelia goes out as per her new stalking habit, Savage and I find her following a convoy of electric serpent trucks in the far outskirts of suburbia. They are silent and purposeful in the way of a seasoned military operation. Ghoul is definitely in one of them because I see an oversized boot sticking out one of the windows, followed by clouds of white smoke. I keep my distance because I just know Lia will sense me if I get too close.

Our destination makes itself known. Like a diadem in the dark trove of some old, cranky beast, the warehouse appears, illuminated by high, blaring white floodlights. It's brand new, and the convoy of vehicles heads up to the gate where they are stopped and checked before proceeding onto the property beyond.

"There's something important in there," Savage says unnecessarily. *"Do you think that's the new venom factory?"*

"It doesn't feel the same," I say, making a wide berth around the place.

Power crackles over it, much in the same manner as Animus Academy's protective dome, except I don't think it'll ignore me in the same way. My heart pounds as Aurelia's eagle body swoops perilously close to the dome. But she's smart enough to stay in the shadows, away from the sizzle and the powerful lights. Mace Naga has learnt a thing or two about protecting his goods. No doubt my father had lent a hand in that.

"We need to find out what's in there," Savage says.

"Even the hyena matriarch didn't know," I say. *"But there's got to be another way."*

Aurelia circles around the facility a few times, and I remain high above, monitoring her movements. When it becomes clear Ghoul isn't leaving anytime soon, she decides to leave, heading southward towards the academy. But something strange happens not five minutes into our trip back.

She disappears.

Savage gasps. Both of our eyes are keen in the dark, mine even more than Savage's, and we don't take our eyes off her when we're following. One moment, her mahogany wings are sweeping powerfully along the currents, and the next second, the night swallows her into nothingness. On high alert, I search the night, but there is no sign of wings nor feathers. It's not like her invisibility shield; my magical eyes don't see her heat signal either.

"Where is she?" I snap at Savage.

"She's here," he replies more calmly than I. *"I can feel her."*

Those words gnaw at me like teeth on bone because I don't feel our regina in the same way the others can. I feel her power, but that inherent, ever-present soul tug Savage has is only a ghost to me. I know it's there, but it slips beyond my grasp. And that's entirely my fault. But Savage's words slow my heart all the same, to know she hasn't just blinked out of existence.

"There!" Savage shouts into my mind. Far ahead, moonlight glints silver on eagle wings, and I speed up to see her better. At the tips of my regina's feathers, a black smoke lingers before evaporating. Savage mutters under his breath.

Well, well, well," I say. *"I wonder what Ghoul is going to have to say about that."*

"I don't give a fuck what he has to say," Savage snarls. *"If my regina wants to be a shadow princess, she gets to be a shadow princess."*

"Do you know what? You're right, Savage."

"Huh?" Savage says out loud in utter shock. *"Since when do you agree with me?"*

"*Since...Since I realised you're right.*"

"*Well, fuck me sideways,*" Savage chuckles, slapping me on the neck with glee.

Chapter 53

Ghoul

Fifteen years ago

Mace Naga has filled my house with clothes and food—special sweet treats, warm rich foods that remind me of my homeland. He also gave me many books with words and pictures and told me to read them. He sang my praises. Told me he was excited for me to meet the rest of his people.

One day after sunset, he brings those people to my house. Through the thin bandage around my eyes, I stared open-mouthed at the tall serpent animuses, who wear interesting clothes the colour of the landscape at night. Their faces are covered in white masks, making it look like they wear the skulls of other people.

"These are my friends," Mace says. "They have come to help you control your powers."

I don't see it coming. Don't completely understand what's happening to me. They take me by my arms and pin me to the floor. Their fangs bite into my body, sharp, toxic, and devastating on my young flesh. Venom pours into me, its burn entering me like poisoned fire. My screams tear through my throat until the venom makes my heart slow. Makes my lungs stiff. Makes me a prisoner in my own body.

"Fight it," one of the old generals says. "Let your beast take over."

All I can do is stare in horror as the grown beasts stand over me and tear my skin to shreds with their fangs. I can't move. I can't even talk.

"The last basilisk," they jeer. "Where are his scales? Where are his fabled shadows?"

I don't know! I want to scream, but my voice won't come. *Why are you doing this?*

It goes on into the night, me nothing but a prisoner in my body to their violent ministrations. By dawn, the house is empty, and Mace returns with the rays of sun. He cradles me in his arms, speaks gentle, soothing words, and wipes my tears and blood with a black handkerchief.

"They hurt me," I whisper to him.

"Yes, they did," he says seriously. "And I will make it better."

And so he does. He feeds me from his own hand, smooths down my hair, and puts me to bed. In this moment, I feel safe.

But when night comes, so do the generals. I cower inside my wardrobe, but they find me and drag me out, setting me on the kitchen table before turning all the lights off. They shine torches under their chins, and through my blindfold, I can see the creation of ghastly shadows along the planes of their masks.

"You see this?" one of them says, moving the torch this way and that. "These are shadows. They go wherever you tell them to go. Wherever they are, there is no light. We want to see yours."

Fangs sink deep into me once again, and I know they enjoy it. My pain, my fear. It only makes them more feral to see the struggling of their prey. I don't understand what they want me to do, why they're attacking me. I only want to hide. I want to hide in the dark where the monsters can't get to me.

Mace comes with the dawn, and I'm glad to see him because it means day has come. He picks me up from the table to clean me. He holds me in strong arms and puts new clothes on me, then feeds me again. Finally, I pluck up the courage to ask him why they come for me at night.

He frowns. "Why do you not fight them?"

"But I did. I fought until the venom made my body stone. They are stronger than me."

"But how is that possible?" he asks, appearing confused. "Are you not a monster? Is that not why your people sent you away?"

It's true. All these things are true.

On the seventh night, when they come for me again, dragging me out from under my bed, I crave to see Mace. I crave for day to come and to see him walking through the doors with hot food and a gentle hand. But when I tell them Mace will come to save me, they just laugh and dig their fangs deeper. His words echo in my mind.

Are you not a monster?

Fire tears through my body, my screams fading and folding within the cage of my soul until only I can hear them, bouncing between my bones.

Are you not a monster?

Something catches my scream in the dark. The great maw of something that opens wide in a lazy, fanged yawn. Dark scales, and something else darker still. My blood turns cool. My fear turns off. This soft heart of mine is held in a dark fist

I am a monster.

Power lashes out in multiple directions, dark and spiked. Hollow shouts sound before the hard thuds of big bodies. In the dark, I sit up and remove my blindfold, wrapping my body in my power like a shawl of armour.

When dawn comes, Mace finds me standing amongst the bodies of his generals, their necks broken. He smiles at me, and though every time before it gave me a feeling of happiness, this time, I feel nothing.

"These shadows," he says, gesturing to the power banding around my body, keeping close. "If you put them before your eyes, you no longer have to wear your blindfold." I try it and find that I can see as clear as day through them. "Good boy. Now shall we see what more you can do with them?"

Again, I feel nothing at his praise. "I can do a lot," I say, looking between the cobra king's smile and the dead serpents. His own men. "Will you teach me? Will you show me?"

"Of course." I sense the change in the serpent king. And where his voice was once before doting and gentle, now becomes more careful, now takes on the tone of a reminder. He sees the monster now. The serpent king gestures at the mark he made over my navel and calls me by my real name. The one my family gave me. "You are mine. Remember that. Now, come with me."

Chapter 54

Aurelia

I wake up in a panic, fighting off my bedsheets like a caged animal. I scramble off the bed, kneeing Xander in the side and smacking Lyle's face in the process.

"Regina?" Lyle says in alarm.

But I'm already running. I hit the floor with my good leg and get out of the room. My newer leg cramps up. I don't let it stop me as I hobble out of the suite and up the stairs that takes me to the roof. I need air. I need cold. I need—

How do I even fucking know what I need? Cold air slaps me across the face as I clear the top stair and reach for the wall lining the roof. Stone under my fingers and the cold air finally let me *see*. My chest heaves as the images burn themselves into my mind. Four of the pieces of the soul gather behind me, and as much as I love them, the one that I want to see is not here.

Ghoul may have been right. Perhaps I hadn't been ready. Perhaps my heart had torn apart enough. Had been battered and beaten so badly the bruises still smarted. I know my father is a monster—a cruel and malevolent creature who crawled from the depths of some hell and had fooled us into thinking he was a regular person. But this level of manipulation over an innocent child is a new level of evil. And how I reconcile Ghoul's child-self with the adult beast I know today seems impossible.

We are all damaged beasts. Never broken, but somehow still in pieces. And my pieces seem to be trying to fit Ghoul into us. But whichever way I turn it, try to jam him in, he resists. There is no real way to undo his blood bond. Only death will free him now. My regina's heart shrieks out at this loss. Shrieks in pain and hate at the beast who did this to us.

A large hand plants itself against my own, a gold ring on the thumb. "Do you want to fly, regina?" Xander asks.

Something about his deep voice, so often holding a bite, now soft, soothes my pulse. His eyes beam their light from the corner of my eye as I look up into the heavens. The spaces between the stars remind me of Ghoul. That void-like darkness. The regina in me wants to be closer to him. Wants those velvet shadows to cloak me as they cloaked him. They had been drawn out of him through pain. His animus had not taken *over* exactly, but had come to the front to take away the pain of torture. To bring forward the monster because he recognised that an apex predator stood before him. He had done what he needed to do in order to survive. He had become dark-hearted to save himself.

Xander turns around and leans against the stone next to me, letting his head hang back as he breathes deeply. I feel the others lingering behind me, letting me know they are near but giving me space. My dragon closes his eyes. "What did he show you, Aurelia?"

"Don't 'Aurelia' me," I snarl, even though I can't take my eyes off the way his muscled throat and Adam's apple look at this angle.

The corner of his mouth turns up. "What did the basilisk show you, regina?"

"Something bad."

"I wouldn't expect anything less."

"Still an asshole," I mutter.

"No one will take that from me, not even you."

For some reason, that makes me want to smile, but I'm determined to be furious with the world and the bad things that happen in it. Scythe's presence is like hoarfrost behind me, and it's enough to make me turn. My shark looms, his silver hair even more beautiful under the stars, his impossibly perfect beauty cutting through my vision and drawing me to him. He places his hands on either side of my cheeks, tilting my face gently upwards. "We must not let the past control us, regina."

Half of the time Scythe speaks, I want to cry. "We can't let the bad men win," I whisper.

"We have to make sure we don't become bad men in the process," he counters. "Ghoul is a bound beast, regina. He made agreements. He must carry them out."

"But he was a child when he was blood bound."

Scythe's eyes search mine as this new information registers, but he never hesitates. "Children pay for the choices of the adults around them. It's not fair, regina, but it's the truth."

I look into his ice-chip eyes and sigh, thinking about the choices that had been made for me. A choice that tore my heart into five pieces. "I want to kill my father, Scythe."

He nods, his hands sliding down my arms to hold my hands. Lyle's shadow, his hair unbound, his wild eyes wrangled into tame irises, steps next to us. "That is a burden you'll carry for the rest of your life, regina. Are you sure you want that?"

I glance at Scythe and Savage, then at Xander, who stares at me with something burning in his gaze. I look back at Lyle. "Not a burden," I say with lethal softness. "A privilege. A right. The fulfilment of a vow I made in my mother's name."

"You want your pack to be complete, regina," Lyle says. "That is your right too. We just don't know how possible that is."

"We don't know much about basilisks," I say carefully. "I need more information, and the source isn't giving us much."

"I'll try the old Drakos library," Xander says. "I want to see my family anyway. I can check if Selena knows anything."

"Thank you." Selena is a wealth of knowledge, having spent so much of her adult years in the dusty archives under Drakos Estate. She'd been a great comfort to me when I'd been alone.

"And I'll help you check the academy texts tomorrow," Lyle says.

I turn north, looking over the dark school grounds and the bushland beyond. My hand finds the stone again, a strange expansive sense travelling up from my fingers and spreading through my hands. A bid for attention. "I feel the academy. I feel like it's trying to tell me something."

Savage appears next to me, pressing an ear to the stone next to my hand. "What's it saying?"

I feel it out, trying to parse the sense of imbalance. "It sounds like a warning."

Once the adrenaline wears off and I get cold, everyone follows me back inside. This time, I crawl next to Xander, who carefully puts his arm around me and fills my legs with his healing power. It's still new, being this close to him, but his power is so familiar and calming that I nestle into it. I think it's new for him too, because he doesn't melt into me the way my other mates do. He still...holds himself. As if he's worried he might hurt me in his sleep and needs to watch me breathe.

Chapter 55

Scythe

The mornings feel heavier these days. When Aurelia doesn't sleep, I don't sleep either, and neither of these things is good for the pack. My regina puts on a brave face, fuelled by her need to learn about her most mysterious mate. Sharks are creatures familiar with the darkness, but basilisks *are* the dark, and Ghoul revels in the ancient powers he was gifted. Or cursed with.

Rufus is thorough with his morning run-down of operations. I'd culled much of my business a few months ago before my planned departure, but my enterprises are as robust as ever. There have been no further moves on my property. The other crime lords are all lying low after Mace's sudden elevation and Tiberius Clawson's demotion. It was a shock to everyone, even Marduk and Yeti. It's for this reason that I seek out a meeting with the Devi pack this morning.

Marduk greets me in his suite with a tumbler of apple juice. "Looks like whiskey, shark-friend," he says. "But without my regina's disapproval."

"Thank you, Marduk," I say, accepting the glass. He waves me over to a seat at their rounded wooden dining table, where Minnie sits with a mug of what smells like chamomile and honey tea, her yellow nimpin Gertie on one shoulder. She's nervous, and I don't blame her one bit.

"Good morning, Scythe," she says in a happy voice. "Lia is occupied in the library this morning."

"So she is," I say conversationally, sitting down opposite her. "There's a lot on her mind lately."

"Hence our covert operations."

"I do not hide anything from my regina," I reassure her. "But today's events concern the Devi pack."

Minnie nods. "I've been avoiding my parent's questions." Yeti places a hand on his regina's shoulder in moral support and she covers his hand gratefully.

"I think that is wise," I say. "But hopefully not necessary for much longer." She audibly swallows. Finally, I ask the question. "Are you ready, Minnie?"

Something comes over the little tigress' eyes. Something I've never seen from her before. I'd seen her the day Titus broke her bond and the way she'd come out of it. I'd seen her stop an entire unit of military bullets with just a thought. But this is something new. It's dark and still, like the surface of an ancient lake that hides danger beneath. Suddenly, I understand why this is Marduk and Yeti's regina. Why she is *my* regina's best friend.

Because I can only describe this look as frightening.

"Yes, Scythe. I'm ready."

Chapter 56

Aurelia

After breakfast and a quick text to Stacey, Savage and I head down to the library. Minnie is busy with her mates this morning, and so is Scythe. Lyle promises to meet me after his morning class with the third-year students. He said it would be good for everyone to try to get back into some semblance of a routine; try to find some stability after the upheaval in their lives. Eugene won't meet my eye, but Henry sails over on his tiny power, chirping a friendly hello and settling on my shoulder.

"How have you guys been?" I ask Stacey as she pulls out a seat for herself and sets Eugene down on the table. We watch Savage shake Eugene's wing with amusement. It's such a *normal* question that it sounds odd to my ears.

"Oh, you know," she says, waving a hand. "I'm trying to keep busy while we work on my rex. He's given Marduk some useful information about The Collector but *still* won't talk to me."

"Keep at it," Savage says. "We'll break him down in no time, and he will learn to love you like Aurelia learned to love me. Do you remember when she tried to reject me? But I convinced her."

Stacey presses her lips together. "I don't think any of us is going to forget that Goddess-forsaken time."

I clear my throat. "This place is a collection point for assholes. Just another day at Animus Academy." Savage nods sagely.

Stacey snorts as she opens her laptop. "Tell me about it. We're researching real-life *basilisks*! I bet the humans don't even know we have one."

Savage chuckles. "Do you remember when they found out about phoenixes? That was funny." I had only been a child, but the media went crazy when they found out the animalia population included phoenixes. Dragons and the rest of us they'd known about for so long, no one even remembers when we came out of hiding.

"They know about Boneweavers now," Stacey says. "There were newspaper articles about it when you were on the run after Drakos Estate, and they had no choice but to tell the authorities. But..." She looks at me sheepishly. "You missed all the fuss, of course."

"Probably for the best," I say darkly. "And even for me, it was hard to find information about my kind. There was just that one old tome we found. Maybe we should check that first." I wander to the locked cabinet where older, fragile texts need permission to be looked at. Luckily for me, this cabinet is academy-wrought, so when I go up to it with my fingers stretched out and say, "Open, please," the old lock obediently clangs open. The handle is cold under my hand as I open it, the inside dusty and dry. I reach for the familiar leather-bound tome and take it out to the table.

"Take a picture of anything that looks important," Stacey says. "I'm gonna look up the other serpent texts we have. The internet is useless for this."

I leaf through the yellowed pages of the book and quickly find that most of it is not in English but another swooping language I've never seen before. The section relevant to me, about Boneweavers and their extensive powers, has a regular A4 sheet of paper stuck inside with an English translation that Minnie and I presumed was from Selena when we first saw it. Eventually, I give up on trying to make sense of anything else and search through the mythical creatures texts while Savage and Eugene doze on the table next to me.

"I've got to go check on Etienne," Stacey says, closing her laptop. "I'll come back straight after."

"No, we've been at it for hours," I say, nodding at the wolf and rooster asleep next to me. "We'll take it back up tomorrow." Stacey waves me goodbye, and Henry chirps his farewell to Stacey's nimpin. My current book is a compendium of the mythic orders, ancient and modern, and includes some really strange creatures I'm almost certain that someone like Katerina Crocodylus Frankensteined in a lab somewhere. I pat my stomach thoughtfully. "But not anymore."

It's then that I feel it—an icy draft. I sit up, my head snapping to the right as if I'll see the culprit standing there. But of course, it's only the library wall, black brick and solid with no open windows. It wasn't like Scythe's hoarfrost, nor any other power I'm familiar with. It's alarming enough to make me stand up, and after a glance at Savage and Eugene, still unmoved, I pat Henry on my shoulder and move to inspect the area. The shelves end a metre and a half before the back wall, giving enough walking room so you can round the corners. I turn to the next row and narrow my eyes down the length of empty space. Everybody is at class and even the librarian must be at a meeting because I'm the only person who sees the new addition on the back wall of the library.

An ancient door.

It's arched and made of black wood. Charcoal bricks form an arch around it in the same Gothic manner as the rest of the school. Sitting at the apex of the arch is a gargoyle's head, with cheeks so large they droop, bat-like ears, and a rounded button nose. He looks like a brother to Charlotte and Bastien, but he has no body.

"Hello?" I ask, stepping forward. "You are new, sir."

Black eyes follow my movement, and a low, sonorous voice greets me with severe seriousness. "Great Lady Boneweaver. So we meet in this time and place, but I am not new."

"And so we do," I agree slowly, stepping before the door. "What is your purpose here?"

"My purpose?" he says as if offended. "It was around *me* this noble house was built, after all. It is for *me* that you are guardian." Something strikes me in my gut—a shooting memory—of the day Celeste left and gave me the title. I hadn't been entirely sure what it meant and had assumed she just meant that a building made by dragons required someone powerful to oversee it. And since I'd returned as a dragon, it only made sense that it was me. But...

"Is it your wish to enter?" the gargoyle asks.

I stare at the door, at the strange, old power that seems embedded into it, and quite suddenly I don't think I want to see what's on the other side. My foot takes an involuntary step back. "What's behind it?"

He blinks at me. "Do you wish to enter, my lady?"

I ask the question again, and the gargoyle repeats his answer. "What is your name?"

"Ashfang, my lady."

"That's an interesting name."

"I was named after the beloved of the enchantress who made me."

The name tickles something in me now. It suddenly gives me courage. "Open up, then, Ashfang."

The gargoyle bows his head as much as he is able, and the door swings silently inward. There's darkness beyond. Solid, everlasting. My heart pounds as power spirals through it, pulling me in, drawing my feet forward. It's *powerful*. I want to go in, but equally, I do not. This is not a power of this world, and yet something about it is irrevocably familiar. Torn between wanting to peek in and wanting to run in the opposite direction, I rock back and forth on the balls of my feet, gasping under the force pulling me. Henry shrieks on my shoulder.

"Angel?" Strong hands fold about my waist. "Close it!" Lyle commands, and Ashfang swings himself shut. The icy air cuts off, and so does the drawing, twisting power.

"It...It was like a tornado, pulling me in!" I say in awe and horror as Lyle tugs me into the stacks and away from the black door. I tear my eyes away from it and look into the grounding face of my lion, whose mouth is pressed into a harsh line.

"What happened?" Savage asks, jogging over to us. "The air felt strange all of a sudden."

"Looks like Aurelia just discovered a new door," Lyle says.

"C-Can you make yourself invisible again?" I ask the gargoyle. "I think I'd feel better if you were a wall again." Ashfang bows, and the black stone melts into the brick, becoming nothing but a seamless wall.

Chapter 57

Aurelia

The next morning, Minnie meets me for breakfast in the dining hall. For the first time, I notice a strain in her eyes, her nimpin Gertie jittery on her shoulder. She just shakes her head. "We have things to talk about, but I just saw this." She slides the morning newspaper under my nose.

MACE NAGA MAKES STRIDES WHERE NONE HAVE BEFORE

My stomach roils as I stare at the blow-up front-page photo of the man who'd raised me, waving at the crowd, a benevolent smile moulded to his face like plasticine.

"That was a press conference," Minnie says quietly. "He's giving a speech tonight at one of the blended universities in the city."

"He's recruiting," Xander says darkly, leaning into me to read it.

"The generals will be there," Minnie says pointedly. "The younger ones go around getting emails and handing out meet-up details."

"Recruiting for what?" Stacey whispers.

Xander, Minnie and I remain quiet because it hurts to say it out loud. But I know I need to see this for myself. The warehouse last night...the house visits. I need more from Ghoul. He's breadcrumbing information in my dreams, but giving me zero in waking life. I understand that he *can't* do anything against his blood oath, so *I* need to be the one doing something. Maybe I could weasel my way into one of these meetings and see exactly what they're up to. There have been no consequences for our destruction of the Crocodylus property or my murder of the crime lord. The only thing that explains this is that my father is preoccupied with other things. Things I need to know about immediately.

I want to maintain the image that I'm perfectly fine. Xander is suspicious of me, and Savage has been particularly exuberant, so I make a great show of actually going to classes for once. No one actually expected me to attend them since I came back from Drakos Estate, but Lyle was right—having a sort of routine may balance my jitteriness while I wait for night to come. Minnie, Sabrina, and Stacey make an effort to come as well, and it makes Theresa's eyes light up to see us all, Eugene and the nimpins included, waltz in and take our seats like we used to. Our first class in this room feels like so long ago.

Unfortunately for me, the topic of the day is 'Building Trusting Relationships with Mates.' I squint at the board as if I'm concentrating, but honestly, I don't know what the fuck this means. How do you build trust when your mate has a blood oath to be your sworn enemy?

"Try to find some positives," Theresa says, waving her whiteboard marker and glancing at me and Stacey. "There are always positives in our relationships with our mates, just sometimes you have to look a little harder."

To my surprise, Savage raises his hand. "I support my regina in everything she does. Even if it's not very smart."

I gape at him. "Savage!"

He gapes back in surprise. "What did I say?"

Minnie snorts. "Lia is highly intelligent! Nothing she does is 'not smart!'"

"Hear, hear," Sabrina says in a low voice. "Take it back, Savage."

"All I meant," Savage says slowly, like he's explaining something to a bunch of idiots, "is that I'll do anything for her. Why is that bad?"

"Savage is trying to describe loyalty," Xander says crisply.

Theresa looks like she's about to quit teaching. "Well, *that* I can write down on the board."

"What about..." Stacey screws up her face. "If your mate has to be loyal to someone else other than you?"

"Mates come first," Savage says dismissively. "Nothing else matters. Anyone who says otherwise should have their head eaten." His eyes pointedly move in the direction of the school fence, where Katerina's head still sits, even though some of the teachers wrote Lyle emails about it. We're not taking it down anytime soon. The native birds are still working their way through her soft tissue.

I watch Stacey sink into her seat, and something like a searing iron strikes my insides. "Sometimes there are conflicts, right? That's life. That *happens*."

"These are difficult conversations that are important," Theresa says calmly. "Open conversations between mates are the only way forward. Honesty without judgement."

Xander sighs next to me and says into my head. *"Don't try to justify Ghoul's actions. I don't even care what memories he's showing you. He wants you to feel sorry for him. He will betray you."* I don't reply to my dragon, whose eyes flash when he glances at me. He watches me closely for the rest of our classes, but of course I quit the day early and head back to our dorm to take a nap.

That evening, I duck out earlier than usual. At this stage, I don't even care if anyone sees where I'm going. I don't need permission from them to see one of my mates. The sunset washes the world in red, and as I ricochet across the sky, it makes it look like the world is spilling blood. Stacey was able to tell me which universities were on the meeting list, and one of them is south of the city: a gigantic campus with sprawling buildings and concrete pathways. I shift into my eagle form as I come upon it, finding the gathering crowd immediately.

This time, I'm prepared enough to bring a set of clothes, and it takes me a minute to change inside the ladies' toilets and come out like I'm any other student, shouldering Savage's small backpack. It had been my dream once to leave my bungalow and hide away in a blended university where my mates would never find me. The fact that I'm now in the centre of one, looking for a mate, feels cathartic. I had planned to take my blue beetle Maisy, all my belongings, and flee here, pretending to be an eagle and learning to be a healer-nurse or doctor. I was good at healing. Now it seems like most of the time I'm doing the exact opposite.

How times change. How *I've* changed. The person I am now looks around at the tall, clean buildings of this college with a soft smile, knowing we've outgrown this dream. It makes me equal parts happy and sad. How little I thought of my life. My skills. How much *more* I am now. I hope my mother is proud of me.

Feeling a little mellow, I hang around the back of the crowd gathering at a quadrangle area with a concrete platform made for such events. There's a lectern standing ready and a couple of serpents with professional video equipment and someone with a livestream set up. They're people I don't recognise, and it makes my heart beat a little slower for the sake of my spying. More people join us, and I smell barbecue somewhere nearby. Pretty soon, I'm locked in with people excitedly pressing in behind me, and the loud buzz of their combined voices winds through the air. I adjust the strap of my backpack, but when I sense *his* presence approaching, a sudden, deathly focus overcomes me.

And I don't mean Ghoul.

Time seems to slow as my father strides up to the lectern on the back of a loud cheer from the crowd. I don't clap with them as he raises his hands in welcome, nor as loud screams vibrate through my body when three of his generals appear behind him, face masks in place, black camo gear pristine. Fixed to the spot, I stare, the predator in me clocking the other high-order predators who've made themselves known. Ghoul's shadows are thick around him, lazily making swirls as if he wants to show off. My father launches into a round of thanks to the people who invited him here and lists the things he wants to do to help the college.

"My efforts will not go in vain, I assure you of that," he says, voice deep and provocative. "Our voices will finally be heard. We are not creatures who skulk in the dark. We move proudly in the day, without fear. My first move will be to abolish the barcoding system." The crowd roars its approval. "If you would like to join the campaign, the sign-up sheet is going around. I am here to make a change for the better."

My heart sinks in my stomach because I know what this sounds like. It's then that a faint red gleam catches my eye. Ghoul's darkness is on show like a creature of nightmares, but no one seems to care. It excites the crowd as he stands there, so tall and so proud. And yet I know his attention is on me. I know where those deadly red eyes point. Like a waking dream, an image flashes before my eyes, and my jaw goes slack with shock. I see my old bungalow, but I am young—only slightly older than the year of my exile.

Red fixes on me. I blink.

Surely not.

But my bungalow is lit up at night, the familiar buttery lights of my living room lighting up the panes of glass beyond my TV. Four-teen-year-old me sits cross-legged, tears in her eyes. This is impossible. Ghoul tilts his head ever so slightly.

"*Yes, snakelet,*" he says to an unanswered question.

A high-pitched buzzing pierces my ears. I can barely breathe as I ask him, "*All this time?*"

The floor seems to slant underneath me. My body leans forward, trying to counterbalance, but it utterly fails.

"*All this time,*" he confirms, just as I black out.

Chapter 58

Ghoul

Aurelia's Bungalow
Seven years ago

I felt you before I saw you.

In my early days of serving as a trainee in Mace Naga's court, my favourite thing to do was to head out into the shadows of the night. There were many secrets to see when the world fell under darkness, and I travelled above it all, watching for my own amusement. It soothed my violent animus after a day's harsh classes with the young generals in training. Now I have to live with them in a secret boarding school and learn their ways. Now the classes are fourteen hours long, five days a week, and we're forced to learn everything from proper hygiene to literature to combat.

But one night, somewhere in the quiet under the stars, I feel a presence that's somehow both old and new. It draws me in, and I point my shadows toward a familiar neighbourhood. I know Charlotte Naga's house like the back of my hand, because I lived there when the slab went down. But where I expected to land in the shadows of the tiny house, I find the warm lights on within.

Falling to the ground like I've practised many times in class, I creep forward, the grass silent under my boots. Hunched low, I'm surprised to find a dome of power around the house, humming with awareness. I regard this new, strange shield with raised brows, cloak myself in my own dark protections, and breeze right through. Undetected, I crouch against the bushes beside the front door to find out what manner of order could have produced such a thing.

I saw you sitting on the threadbare couch, a thin blanket around your shoulders as you watched TV. Your cheeks were wet as you dug into the cup of two-minute noodles, and you sniffed as the lights flickered across your teenage face. Never before have I felt the urge to blast into the room and scoop a person up, take you into my shadows and keep you safe from the harm that made you cry. My frown deepens as I watch you wipe your nose on the back of your hand, then wipe your hand on your track pants.

Mace Naga has put another creature in this house, and instead of feeling possessive over my old house, I want to help you. *Are you like me? Is Mace Naga training you to join his army like he trained me? Torturing you like he'd done to me?* But my nose is telling me the cupboards in the house are bare. That the fridge is on its last legs and the leak in the roof has returned. *Are you a prisoner? Is this... some punishment?* This house was worn down after I'd corrupted the place and left it for boarding school. So there could be no other reason for you to be living here unless you've displeased the serpent king.

And I'm very interested in people who displease the serpent king.

But as I observe you over the next few nights, I see that you're just a child. A child who misses her family like I once did. A child who's alone, like I once was. There are bags under your sad eyes, your smiles were scarce, and sometimes you forgot to brush your teeth before you go to bed. And no one ever comes to visit you like they did with me. So on the third night, when I return just after sunset, I steal into Charlotte Naga's house and put some of her spaghetti and meatballs onto a paper plate, cover it in foil, and leave it on your doorstep, making sure I trigger your shield on the way out.

I watch as you suspiciously open the door, wrapped in a blanket, peering out with your eyes like brilliant jewels in the night. I can't help my grin as you smile and pick up the plate. You giggle like it's a good day.

From then on, as often as I can make it, I steal food from Charlotte's house and put it on your doorstep. You think it's your Uncle Ben, never realising that he's too cowardly to take food from his regina and give it to you, the exiled girl of serpent court. *Ben* sees the food on your doorstep and thinks his regina is feeding you. Imbecile serpent.

I got my revenge for that eventually, of course, because Ben is now dead.

He needed to die for not helping you more.

And you need to know that it had always been me.

Chapter 59

Scythe

It was past time that I joined Savage and Xander on their nighttime stalking of the stalker. As we followed Aurelia to the college campus, not once did she cast her keen eyes back towards us pursuing her. Perhaps a part of her knows we'll always be there for her protection. That we will always have her back. It may also be likely that she's so intent on her purpose that she's *forgotten* about us. My insides revolt at the thought of that, but I know we are too important to her.

Aurelia had packed clothes, ready to be seen this time. We followed behind her at a great distance because the three of us are noticeable, if not for sheer presence alone, but also height. Savage lingers the closest, hunched under a baseball cap and tank top as he surveys the crowd for any signs of danger. The auras of the crowd begin to pulse in joint enthusiasm moments before Mace comes on stage. My regina is always like a beacon to me, and her still form is noticeably rigid, her eyes unblinking. Her shields are up, but I just know she's watching her sire and marking her prey. I too have been curious as to what this new power has done to Mace.

But as we watch Mace's speech, something changes. The air around Aurelia becomes dense as mud. Ghoul has sensed her.

Savage catches Aurelia as she keels over and pushes out of the pulsing crowd low and hunched so no one notices the commotion. Around a corner and onto the athlete's oval, Xander gets us up in the air and as far away from the university as quickly as possible. I sit backward so Aurelia's unconscious form is cradled between the arms of both Savage and me. He strokes her face. "Regina!" he cries. "Wake up!"

Her heart beats a rapid pace against her ribs, her breaths even, but there is a deep crease between her brows, as if she's in great pain.

Blue eyes fly open. Some thought grows in her eyes as she blinks up at me, trying to focus. Her legs scramble dangerously.

"Regina," I command in a low voice. "Be calm." Still, she fights me, flailing, her face contorted in a mixture of shock and horror. I grip her shoulders firmly. "Focus, regina. Breathe. Think."

But she shakes her head, gasps, and shifts. Her eagle form leaps off Xander's back and we're travelling so fast that she doesn't get purchase on the wind and her small body slips out of my fingers and away from me, tumbling all the way down Xander's body and into the air behind him.

"Xander!" Savage screams.

Our dragon rears up in mid-air, back-flapping with a strangled noise, but Aurelia is far behind us now, her wings folded into her body as she dives towards the earth.

"Down!" I command Xander. He sees her and obliges, nose-diving right behind her.

Chapter 60

Ghoul

One year ago

In a small coastal town, I watch my snakelet hopping towards the cafe in crow form. She doesn't see me sitting at the table behind the four elderly humans. She didn't notice me following her the entire way.

So fixated on her goal of food, she cocks her little head, and blinks those fascinating blue eyes. She's starving, dehydrated, and about to lose her fight for freedom. But she needs to come back. She needs to go to Animus Academy where I can continue to watch her.

Black wings flap. Women scream. An elderly woman swings her handbag.

I leave my takeaway bag on the table and leave, only looking back long enough to make sure she grabs it.

Chapter 61

Aurelia

The world roars in my head.

Memories and feelings and emotions scramble their claws against my mind. I can't believe any of this. Do I even *want* to believe any of this? But it's all there, clear as crystal. The smells and sounds of my cottage. My teenage self. The desperation on my face.

Ghoul is telling the truth.

The ground nears with frightening speed.

Multiple male voices scream into my head. *"Stop!"*

I snap my wings out, catching the current and levelling out. It's jarring. All of it is jarring as land runs beneath me aggressively fast. I don't even care where we are, but there is greenery and land and trees and I glide into it, tumbling to a stop on cool, dead leaves. I lie sprawled in my human form, then drag myself to my feet.

Xander's mighty wing beats batter the branches above me, and I wait for my mates. Scythe and Savage drop down into the dark behind me, limber on their feet, coming close but giving me space. The sudden quiet tells me Xander has shifted, the heavy thump of his bare feet echoing in the small clearing.

They always come for me. My mates. The backs of my eyes burn, and I find the rough bark of a tree, grounding myself as I close my eyes, screwing my face closed to the world. It's Scythe's gentle voice that pierces the silence first. "What have you learned, regina?" he asks. "What did Mace's general show you?"

There's so much weight in that sentence. A weight I want to cast off like old armour. They need to know.

I swallow. "Ghoul has known me for a very long time." Another swallow. "Longer than I ever could have guessed. He was the first occupant of the bungalow I was exiled to as a teenager. He...came across me shortly after."

A moment of shocked silence passes. I don't turn around. I keep my face turned to the dark.

"And you never knew?" Savage's voice is so soft.

"Never." There's a sharp bite to my own voice.

"Turn around, Aurelia," Xander says. Unlike the others, there is an edge to his voice. I cross my arms and remain turned away. I don't know if I'm embarrassed, furious, or hurt. Perhaps a combination of all three. Perhaps one leads to the other. Where is Lyle when you need him? "Aurelia," Xander says, stepping closer. "Look at me."

I shake my head bitterly. Then heat, furious heat, lights up my back as Xander's power spills from him and floods the area. My body stiffens, but I refuse to face them.

Xander's guttural dragon's voice strikes me where it hurts. "Why do you punish yourself for every fucking thing, Lady Boneweaver?"

I grind my teeth together. I whirl around, stabbing a finger at the naked chest that stands close to me. "Why does everyone think they can *fucking* hide everything from me?"

Xander's eyes flare gold, heat making the air ripple around him. Making the loose strands of hair fly on their own power. He looks like a furious, wild dragon god. "You have secrets of your own," Xander says, his guttural voice rippling over my skin. "If the basilisk lord hid things from you, that was his choice. You must respect that."

"Oh, so he's the basilisk lord now and not my father's lackey?" I lean around him to stare pointedly at Scythe and Savage, who watch on with narrowed eyes.

My shark stalks forward to stand next to Xander, his own power flaring against the dragon's heat. "Call him whatever name you desire, regina, but he cannot be trusted."

"Are you implying that what he is showing me isn't real?"

Scythe cocks his head. "Is that possible? To manipulate memories?"

"I've never heard of it. But he showed me a memory that would be impossible to fake. He was watching me from outside my bungalow window. I was fourteen, and it was the right brand of two-minute noodles. He wouldn't be able to know what I looked like if he hadn't seen me in person. It's real. Everything was accurate."

Suddenly, the pressure in the clearing escalates, and Savage's low growl fills the air. Scythe stops breathing, and Xander's nostrils flare.

I too go still, trying to figure out where this is coming from. "What?" I ask.

Xander cracks his neck. He reaches out with a finger and caresses my cheek. "I've never had the privilege of seeing you as a child in any life. What did he do to deserve that?"

My heart clenches, and I have to look away from him. I've seen them all as teenagers or younger in their memories. Savage had been in kindergarten in my first memory of him. "Can we stay out for a little bit before we go back?" I ask, glancing around. Savage, now in wolf form, rubs himself against my legs, and I scratch behind his ears.

"As you command, regina," Xander says.

I have to side-eye him at that, but Savage then demands that I ride astride him like a horse while we walk through the empty bush-land, and I have to oblige.

Chapter 62

Xander

Aurelia is asleep in Scythe's arms by the time we get back to the academy. My senses tell me she's not physically tired, but emotionally, as her mind tries to compute so many years of reframing. It's the *only* reason my brothers and I ceased our fuming when she'd revealed Ghoul had been watching her as a mere *child*.

What a nasty shock. This whole time? This whole fucking time he'd been there? Watching her from the shadows, giving her food. He'd never touched her, by the sound of it, but the singular thought of his mere presence in the shadows of her past had us vibrating with rage. The minute we step foot in our suite and Scythe sets her down in Lyle's arms, he rounds on me and Savage.

"Whatever you want to do to him," he says, eyes near aflame with anger. "Do it."

Savage almost leaps out of his skin in excitement. "Whatever we want?"

The shark's face is pure, lethal cold. Anything that concerns children or innocents will send Scythe into an Antarctic fury, and his regina being in the eyesight of the biggest predator as an innocent fourteen-year-old is possibly the worst possible version of this. He confirms. "*Whatever you want*, brother."

Savage slaps me on the back, and in seconds, we're charging

downstairs onto the wolves' corridor. "Pickle!" Savage shouts. "Pickle, I need you!"

The skinny wolf stumbles out of his room just as we get there, his glasses askew. "Yes, my lord?" he says, eyes wide with fear. Savage chatters excitedly, waving his hands wildly in the air, and marches right past him into the room. I follow, listening closely. Half an hour later, we're back out on the roof and into the sky, zooming towards Ghoul's townhouse like the clouds are my own personal zipline. Savage wears the backpack Aurelia used tonight, holding tightly onto the straps like it's his first day at school.

"We're not even going to get in trouble for this!" he says excitedly into my mind.

"Well, one or two people might have something to say about it."

"The only person who actually matters is Lia, and she *did something similar not long ago, so I think she'll approve."*

I snort into the night air, the thought of revenge warming me from the inside.

Chapter 63

Ghoul

A pre-dawn blue lines the horizon as I re-materialise on my doorstep, getting out my keys from my pocket. But something smells off in the air beyond my mask. Pausing with my keys inches from the lock, I tilt my head upwards and sniff. The skin on the back of my neck prickles as the hairy scent of wolf fills my nose. Savage was here. But my motion detectors hadn't registered movement inside the house. My key finds the lock, and I twist it right to open.

A tiny *snick* is the only warning I get.

My body is engulfed in flames as I fly backwards, my skin bubbling and boiling, my uniform melting into flesh. Half a thought later, I'm in the air, inhuman, watching the carnage from above.

"SAVAGE!" I telepath towards Animus Academy. *"YOU'LL FUCKING PAY FOR THIS."*

It's only an echoing cackle that replies.

* * *

Ten minutes later, I'm striding into the drawing room of Naga House, where Mace sits with Generals Brown and Taipan. I tear my melted clothes off, taking sheets of skin with them, and dump them on the tile for the servants to clean up. I'm already healing, but even basilisks don't heal instantly. Blood drips on the floor from every limb; blisters pop on my burning face. The generals leap to their feet.

"Permission to destroy Animus Academy, Your Majesty," I snarl.

The serpent king regards me with disdain. "We've already discussed this; you know we need the location intact. Why did they catch you off guard?"

He already knows who it was. Why would it be anyone else? In this moment, the hold I have over myself slips. Ancient fangs buried deep, deep, deep lose their purchase and hatred pours out of me. My eyes burn and I—

Mace's voice is sharp when he speaks my true name. My mind snaps to attention, those fangs clenching around my proverbial neck, and I'm blessedly psychopathic again. "Permission to destroy anything at all, then," I say darkly. "Especially Savage Fengari."

Mace steeples his fingers under his chin, eyes alight with running thoughts. He's always been emotionless, something that's just gotten worse over time. Part of what makes him a formidable enemy is that he doesn't react out of anger. "He didn't act alone, of course. The security system did not alert us to intruders, which means the electrical signals were disrupted. That would be the work of Xander Drakos." I curse under my breath. There had been no scent of dragon on my porch, so no doubt he had done his work from a distance away.

"Disappointing," General Brown purrs. "The famed General Ghoul thwarted by a wolf pup."

"Hardly a pup," Mace says coldly. "The wolf is undefeated in battle, and we've seen why on the footage of the Drakos battle."

"The Silver Tooth pack will take care of him," Taipan says. "We need not worry about any of those brothers for long."

I hiss, turning away from them all as my shadows violently charge about me. My house. My trunk. This stinks of retaliation. They're making a point. They think I'm not a member of their pack and I never will be. Perhaps it's time I asserted my dominance.

"Calm yourself," Mace says. "Their time will come. We're

almost ready. The units are coming along as planned. I need you to contain your strength so we don't have a repeat of last time."

Of Halfeather's dungeon, I only remember darkness. But I turn and bow all the same. "Yes, Your Majesty."

"You will lodge here from now until Phase Three," Mace continues. "You are due for a milking in any case."

"As you wish."

I have to wait until the next night to fulfil my own desires. But to my utter delight, my regina once again seeks me out. Her constant stalking of me is a thrill like no other. I have her full attention, her every breath is poised on my movements, and her wing beats are drawn to me like I am the darkness and she the high priestess of the night.

My healing skin prickles as she watches me from the backyard of Naga mansion. No doubt she has seen the ruins of my townhouse and came here to check on me. My weary heart flutters just a little at the thought. I saunter around the lawn like a peacock being appreciated by a peahen, smoking a new joint before handing it to General Adder and dissolving into the air. The winds speak of change tonight, and my shadows whisper their own vow. My dark soul-brothers cannot be allowed to think they have laid full claim to our regina. I won't allow this insubordination. I was born to reign over men and beasts alike. *Some* of them have forgotten that.

She is mine. She was mine first and foremost. I had looked after her first. I had cared for her, pined over her, *fed* her first. And as she follows me now, her eagle eyes fixed on my shifting mass of dark power, she finally knows it. I lead her to the place where it began, where her soul shone to me first through the natural shadows of the cottage behind Charlotte Naga's house. I re-materialise under the eaves of the double story, quiet in its vacant state.

Charlotte Naga, her remaining mate and their three children have long since been evacuated from this property, and the adults now reside at the Naga mansion for their own protection. The hatchlings live separately, but that is less for their protection and more for Mace's convenience. I lean against the brick, simply watching her, simply enjoying her attention. This night, this space is one only we share.

She appears from between the acacias that line the fence in her human form. And on a night with no moon, there is no light to touch her skin, only me and my covetous, crimson gaze. Bare olive skin, long dark hair, and...fangs that poke out under her plump upper lip. My body stiffens to attention then, my spine bouncing off the wall as my attention hones in on her blessed mouth. She walks with languid perfection, like a serpent in human form, smoothly across the grass. There is a new grace to her, seeded and then grown by the adversaries she's crushed. By accepting her own power.

How long I've waited.

She turns toward the cottage, looking at it contemplatively. I am drawn to her side, though my limbs hardly know how they get there. Her scent on the breeze sobers me instantly. "It looked a lot better when you lived in it," she muses, her eyes fixed not on me, but the house.

"My presence has always been a corrupting force," I say, my gaze only for her.

She inhales through her nose, and I allow my shadows to fall back, to let her see the man beneath. Hardly a man. I've earned the name *Ghoul* time and time again, but I crave for her to see me as I am.

"There's still something missing, isn't there?" she says. "Even after the memories you've shown me, I feel like I'm missing something crucial."

Her soul senses it. What is about to come. The horror that will come to pass by my hand. "You can't tell me," she sighs. "The blood bond—I know, I know."

"Look at me," I hiss.

Her lips press together in agitation, but she complies, albeit narrow-eyed. A scarlet sheen crosses her pupils, and I blink, stunned for a moment. "They tell me you'll betray me," she says. "That you'll hurt me."

Betrayal. Pain. Torment. These things are mere words in the face of what it is we must do. Here, where it all began, in the dark outside our cottage window with my heart trying to bite out of my chest, I finally demand of her what I've always wanted.

"Let me claim you publicly."

She stares at me, her heart beating with desire, eyes narrowed in suspicion. "Why do you want this?" she asks. "You've never wanted to claim me before."

"Oh, the things you don't know."

"Then tell—" She scowls at herself. Aurelia swallows, and I can see the accusation in her eyes. *You would be with me if it weren't for a blood oath, I know it.*

"You don't know what the shadows know, snakelet." She doesn't know my destiny.

But my snakelet is a stubborn regina. "I'm not doing it. I did what you asked. I repaid the favour. You'll need to take someone else as your pretend pregnant wife."

I see the gleam in her eyes, the set in her jaw. "I don't want to take anyone else, snakelet. Not a pretend Jade Brown but as you are. You are my regina."

Her pupils flare as I say it, her hair billowing out under her own brutal power. "You're baiting me," she hisses, dark and low. "Don't you *dare.*"

I lean back, sucking air through my teeth. "I didn't want it to come to this, but you've forced my hand." I let that sink in between us before— "I have Raquel."

She frowns. "Raquel has always been at Animus Academy."

"Their body has, yes," I say smugly.

"Minnie and her pack *freed* Raquel's mind."

"And then I found the little wolf anim's consciousness wandering around the halls of the medical ward. They were screaming, you know. I imagine it's frightening and painful to be separated from your body for that long. It was easy to bring them with me. Tortured souls are drawn to the shadows."

"Don't you dare lie to me, basilisk."

I bare my fangs. "If you want Raquel to wake, do as I ask."

Aurelia leans away from me as if disgusted. "So this is what it's come to."

I grin with my teeth. "This is what it's always been."

"You selfish bastard."

The chuckle escapes me on a breath. "So much like your other mates." She can't argue with that, and doesn't. All five of us are selfish, awful bastards.

"And what does this public claiming involve?" she demands. "Is it another orgy?"

"Where I come from, I would have been a king. So I will claim my bride in the way that befits a king."

Chapter 64

Xander

There is something different about tonight. Aurelia returned in the early hours of this morning from her night-time stalking with a frown between her dark brows. We didn't follow her this time. For some reason, it felt intrusive. For much of her life, she was left isolated, and it was something she'd become used to. Something she still sought when her mind was unsettled. I understand that; it's something dragons naturally crave too. A part of me burns to know that while Scythe, Savage and I had each other, and Lyle had the lady phoenix to help him, Aurelia had no one.

"I think that's why it hurts her so much," I explain to Savage as he, Eugene and I smoke at the top of the Animus dorm as the sun sets. "She never knew that someone *had* been there after all. It's almost like a betrayal."

"It *is* a betrayal," Savage says viciously. "I hate that she thought it was just her. No one to pat her back while she slept, no one to check if her coffee was too hot. It's not fair, Xander. It's not fucking fair, and I hate the planet."

"Me too," I sigh. "Because I was the one who kept making it worse."

"Yeah," Savage agrees, patting Eugene on the head and offering his joint to the rooster. "But you tried to make it right. Ghoul is just a plain old nightmare." We sit in silence for a moment as Eugene puffs on the joint. "Where do you think she'll end up tonight?" Savage wonders, pulling the weed away from the bird. "I gave her an extra-strong coffee so she wouldn't get tired again."

"I gave her vitamin B supplements earlier today, so that should help," I say, blowing smoke into the sky.

"I don't think we should give her coke." Savage shakes his head. "If I'm not allowed to have it, she can't either." Savage had tried wolf-strength cocaine all of one time before we put a ban on it. We don't talk about *that* night.

"Always making good choices, Sav," I say. "Nope, we're—"

A little cobra slithers by the school wall. It looks left and right before ducking into the bushes and disappearing completely. Since the university lecture event, she'd figured out that we were following her, and she's going to extra lengths to stay concealed tonight. A second later, both of our phones buzz, and I look at the notification on mine. It's from Minnie:

> Club Venom 10pm

Of course she'd told her little tigress bestie before us. I scowl at my phone just before Scythe and then Lyle's feet storm up the stairs. "Eugene," I say. "Get your goggles. The monsters are hitting town tonight."

I don't think any of us were prepared for a summons from Aurelia. Delivered via Minnie, no less. I video call the tigress immediately, of course, and she picks up with a sheepish smile.

"Sorry, Mr Pardalia." She shrugs. "Aurelia told me to text you where to meet her tonight, and that was it."

"She didn't disclose anything else?" I try not to sound disbelieving.

"Nope."

Marduk inserts his head into the call. "I am under the impression she is initiating covert manoeuvres tonight, lion-friend. I would be on my guard."

"Always are," Xander mutters from next to me.

"Especially," Marduk says pointedly, "since your own manoeuvres on a certain basilisk a few nights ago. Retaliation is expected, no?"

Scythe exhales through his nose on my other side, but I say quickly, "Club Venom is a serpent's den, right? What do we know about it?"

Marduk strokes his dark beard. "It's a place of generalised debauchery, however, the higher-up members of Mace Naga's court are known to meet there together. We think they use the club as a cover for exchanges and business meetings with other serpents."

Marduk hesitates then. "It's the only known place other than the Jewel of the Jungle that Mace Naga visits."

"He's having orgies there?" Savage says excitedly. "I thought he was celli-bat."

"Celibate," I correct.

"Not orgies," Marduk says seriously. "But he petitions members of his court there. Does announcements and such."

"I'm seeing something interesting." Xander points to a light-up map on his phone. "They have their own methods of communication, but there's increased internet traffic in that area. They're getting ready for something. That has to mean there's an announcement tonight."

Scythe and I glance at each other in dark awareness. "Why wouldn't she tell us beforehand?" I mutter after saying goodbye to the Devi pack. "Why does she want to surprise us?"

"We can only guess," Scythe says. "But I'm sure she has her reasons. Xander, let's go."

"Whatever would you do without me?" the dragon says, pulling off his jacket.

"Lyle would fly us through the air," Savage says, nudging me affectionately with his shoulder. "Wouldn't you, Ly?"

Xander makes a face. "You could hold on to his mane, I suppose. How far do you think you can go?"

"Luckily, we don't have to find out," I reply tersely. "Savage, you'll need shoes, this is a club."

"Snakes don't even have feet!" he protests, but excitedly jogs towards the stairs all the same.

* * *

It's 9 p.m. by the time we land in Xander's favourite patch of grass on the outskirts of the city. Rufus and some of Scythe's wolves have brought two cars, and we take one while they take the other. We're not about to walk into a serpent's den without reinforcements ready on the outside. Scythe has always taken care of his own business without extra muscle, but in this case, the sheer numbers Club Venom is attracting makes us wary of traps.

Before we get in the car, Rufus hands Scythe something I can't see, but my shark brother slides into the back seat before I ask. I take the driver's seat, and Savage leaps into the passenger side, strapping himself and Eugene in place before Xander can get there.

The drive is quiet and tense. We're all in a state of disquiet. When our regina is hiding things, it puts my rabid lion on edge, and even though the shackles that bind him are long gone, sometimes I get the phantom impression of chains rattling. This has increased since our time at The Collector's property, likely because my memories of our captivity there are reduced to murky darkness. It was the only way the spell could work. Xander has been forthcoming about what happened, forming our memories for us, but I don't like not remembering things. It reminds me too much of another time.

I feel my lion's paws squeezing the steering wheel over my own hands, and by the time we get into the big lights of the city, the tension coming off all of us is like treacle in the air. Xander directs me to a private carpark, and Rufus comes out to meet us, his body tense. Savage slaps him on the back, handing over Eugene. "I'll shout out if there's any snakey business," he says. "Don't worry about it otherwise."

"We should all be on alert." I give the wolf a disapproving look. "They had plenty of time to make more venom bullets."

Rufus nods. "We'll be stationed exactly where we discussed, and Beak is already in the air with his owls. We'll be ready to extract if necessary." Savage scoffs and reaches into his backpack, pulling out a length of multicoloured sequinned material.

"And what the fuck is that?" Xander chokes.

"My pants!" Savage says, shaking it out. "See? We're going to a rave, Xander."

"Oh sorry," Xander rolls his head in a way that suggests he's rolling his missing eyeballs. "I don't know why I didn't bring mine."

Savage frowns. "We could've been matching!"

"This matches," Scythe says, holding out a full-face mask. It's black with an opalescent sheen. Savage immediately grabs it and puts it in place with a cackle.

"Where's mine?" Xander mutters.

"We're too noticeable." Scythe hands another mask out to Xander, and this time, it's a light-up one with red X's over the eyes. "You'll need to take your shirt off, Xander. Most people don't know you don't have your family tattoos anymore, and maybe hunch a little."

"We should split up as well," I note, tugging at my ponytail. "What?" I gape at the awful lime green wig Scythe is holding out to me. "I hope you're joking."

"I have to leave my shirt on because my tattoos are too noticeable," Scythe replies. "And your hair is equally noticeable. You need to cover it, and I assumed hair dye was not an option."

Savage is side-eyeing me as I take the green wig and clown mask. "I'll help you," he says excitedly, reaching for my hair tie. I allow it, thinking of my regina. "For Aurelia," I mutter to myself.

After my wolf-brother wrestles my wig into place, we assess each other. Scythe wears a dramatic black robe with the hood up and a scream mask, the long white face and open mouth actually making me shiver. Xander is now only in black pants and the light-up mask. I tie the green hair into a long braid because I don't want to deal with it any more than I have to, and I take off my suit jacket so I'm in my white shirt and suspenders. It leaves me with the scary clown mask, which suits me just fine.

Savage stops us to take a photo before we say goodbye to Rufus and head down the street and go our separate ways in pairs. Xander pulls out a joint as he follows me to approach the club from the southern end of the street. By the time we line up to get into Club Venom, the line is down the road, and we can hear the music pumping from inside. We're surrounded by serpents, all dressed in utterly insane rave outfits and all with various morbid masks.

Savage chatters an excited monologue into our heads so we know what to expect when we get inside by the time Xander and I reach the fanged archway entrance.

"There's a man in a thong!" Savage says gleefully. *"And oh, look, Scythe, there's glitter on that anaconda slithering around on the bar!"*

The music only gets louder. *"Someone call reptile rescue,"* Xander mutters in my head. *"Have you ever been in a club before, Lyle?"*

There was a period in my life after Ulmans' Sanctuary where I roamed freely on the streets, most of the time homeless and confused about my animus. In those times, before my incarceration, I *had* wandered into clubs once or twice. *"My animus liked the noise,"* I admit. *"He was drawn to them."*

Xander snorts in my head. *"I should have known."*

The bass vibrates through my shoes as Xander pays the ten-dollar fee to get us into the darkened space beyond. I clock Savage and Scythe immediately in the corner, mostly because Savage is already dancing like a madman near the front where a large stage is set, heavy black curtains setting the scene for something interesting.

The bar is busy on the left-hand side, teeming with writhing bodies. A girl in only a black thong and Catwoman mask slides past me. Revulsion whips through my body, and I turn away from her to Xander. The dragon notices this, and I just know he's smirking under that mask, but I jerk my thumb towards the bar and make my way over there.

The alcohol is just a pretence, of course, but Xander knocks his whiskey back like he needs it. It's serpent strength, and will be the equivalent of water in his big body, but to my surprise, he joins the crowd jumping up and down to the beat. *"Gotta look the part,"* he shouts in my head. *"Does the headmaster dance?"*

Suddenly, Savage appears out of nowhere and grabs my hand, pulling me into the throng. It's a trance version of *Paint It Black,* and under the anonymity of the mask, I give in. My lion purrs under the beat, the electricity in the air, and a scent that sits on the edge of chaos.

Moments later, at exactly 10 p.m., the beat changes.

The fast pace melts into something slower. The crowd is in tune with the change, almost as if expecting it. There are more people jammed in here now, and they move in a lilting, twisting motion more akin to a mosh pit. It's easy for Xander and me to adjust our movements, and ahead of me, Savage is moving along too, a fine sheen of sweat on his muscled back catching the strobe lights above. Scythe's voice slides into the group chat though I can't see him. *"I'm counting six serpent generals on tiers behind you."*

Adrenaline spikes in my blood once again, and I subtly glance around as the music morphs into *Angel* by Massive Attack, turning the scene even slower. *"And where is the seventh?"* I muse.

Everyone turns towards the stage just as Savage makes a choked noise. Serpents are heading towards a designated pit I can now see in front of the stage. They discard their scant clothing and costumes before shifting and entering the mass of serpentine bodies. We're swept forward by the space created as they shift and more people enter the club behind us. The pit quickly becomes filled with nothing but serpents, and I see more than a few attempting to copulate.

"Serpent orgy," says Xander with resignation.

But then the black curtain behind the stage ripples, and I grab Xander's arm—

Just before a fully grown basilisk slithers out from between the curtains.

More than a few people cheer and whoop with excitement as Ghoul shakes out the spines of his head that almost reach the ceiling. There's a black band of shadow around his eyes, protecting the crowd from the death of his gaze, and he towers over us, the black scales of his body gleaming under golden lights directed at him. His serpentine body seems to go on forever, the hard muscle joining the rest of him on the stage. He's as big as a dragon. And even without the wings and limbs, you get the distinct feeling of colossal, mythic power.

We all see it at the same time. The naked woman on his back, her bare legs astride him, breasts and stomach pressed against the black scales. The crowd's noise lulls to a hush as they see Aurelia. Her face and back are covered by a glittering, sheer black veil. The veil is fit into something that could only be described as a tall black diadem and falls to cover her eyes and nose, leaving only red painted lips and white pointed fangs for us to see. The veil is long enough that it drapes around her shoulders, seductively trailing down to her lower back.

I feel like I'm in a dream, because this cannot be *my* reality. Aurelia is a known figure amongst the wider community. They have seen videos and newspaper articles time and again, and the entirety of Animus Academy knows exactly what she looks like. Her body is distinct. All creatures of the mythic orders are. And if she turns only a little, the unique scars on her stomach will show. Her face is *barely* obscured under the material.

Aurelia looks like a basilisk's dark bride, and my entire body stands to attention as I register the message that's being sent. My regina bares her teeth at us, a clear hissing sound filling the air before she's joined by the hissing of the serpents roiling beneath us. She presses a cheek affectionately to Ghoul's serpent body, reared up and baring his own fangs at us. His long tail circles protectively around her before he lets out a hissing, growling sound that ripples over my own skin.

This is a declaration.

This *was* a trap after all. Just not the type we'd expected.

Chapter 66

Aurelia

It's hard not to get caught up in this moment.

The music, the hard body beneath me, the scent of lust and excitement in the air. This...announcement.

With Ghoul, I see a glimpse of what my life could have been. What the love of a family of my serpent community could have felt like—in the traditional clothes of the Naga, a serpent claiming his regina as his own, proudly telling the world that she is his. But I know this is an illusion. This is theatre, and I have played my part well.

The long veil and my angle, pressed up against him, shields my body. For all intents and purposes, I am Jade Brown, and this is a power play between the generals of the serpent court and its wider people. My father needed a display of power to rally the beasts of his court. A display of hope for his campaign. That is why he'd needed Ghoul to show himself with his bride. A court with its own powerful mythical creatures—the heralds of death, no less—makes him a formidable enemy and a powerful ally. None of the other courts would try to defy him after they realise he's breeding his basilisk.

The warm, humid air of the club caresses my skin as the combined hissing fills my ears, a satisfying, communal sound. After so many years of feeling like I belonged nowhere...this does something to me. But the regina in my bones suddenly notices that she's not alone with her basilisk. Points of light appear through the dark of the crowd and gauze of the veil.

Savage gapes up at me from the snake pit. Lyle and Xander look on seriously. And in the far corner, Scythe's raw Antarctic power tunnels its way toward the stage, never one to be left behind. I feel his piercing gaze on my skin *and* my actions tonight. *"I'm sorry,"* I whisper through the air. *"I should have told you."*

"But then where would all the drama be?" Xander's voice is dark in my head.

"And I wouldn't get to wear my sparkly pants," Savage says quietly. *"It's okay, regina. You're allowed to have fun."*

"Don't let us stop you," Lyle says, but he can't hide the jealousy and possessiveness in his voice.

Suddenly, I'm aware that my mates are *seething*. Ghoul's chuckle is vicious in my ear because this is exactly what he intended. I look to the spot of cold in the far corner that is Scythe, but he says nothing. He merely stares at me. It makes my heart pound at a fast, feral beat. My fingers twitch towards Ghoul's neck, and I raise my hand, letting my fingertips trail down his scales in a soft caress.

The basilisk goes still under me, his head swaying like I've hypnotised him with my touch. Enamoured, I try it again, caressing him by the skin up near my face and dragging my fingers down in a sweeping motion. *"So pretty,"* I coo into his head. *"So dark."*

He shivers then, and that mighty head lowers and bends around to face me. I caress him a third time, but the opposite way and more lightly. His big forked tongue flicks out, the tips licking my cheek. Below us, the snakes writhe, the DJ plays a languid beat, and the beasts in their human forms cheer. My inner thighs clench around the powerful body beneath me, and a low hiss rumbles from his throat in response.

"Tell me why I shouldn't fuck you right here," Ghoul hisses into my mind.

I give him a lazy smile, baring my fangs. *"I don't know, maybe you should."*

A long, slow chuckle comes. *"Aurelia."* It's Scythe's voice, icy cold and dripping with malcontent that says, "*Mace Naga has just entered the club.*"

Every cell in my body is gripped by the force of my own adrenaline. "*I hope you're joking, Scythe.*"

"*No, I see him too,*" Savage says. "*Regina, you need to get out of here.*"

Ghoul's body slithers over the stage, and I'm paraded across it for all to see. I can't see my father, but I feel the change in the air, the sudden tension as the king enters.

"*Let's go,*" I say quietly to Ghoul.

"*Are you frightened of the king cobra, snakelet?*"

Lyle's warning growl enters my head. Both of these things anger me. Send my blood thrumming to an old beat of long suffering. *Am I scared of Mace Naga?* So I do the only logical thing.

I stand up.

Placing one foot from my good leg on Ghoul's thick body, I rise, getting my second foot under me and placing my arms around the basilisk's upper body, throwing out my veil dramatically behind me, showing my thighs and ass. Putting both arms around him, I caress the basilisk like a lover, before lifting the knee on the audience's side and pressing it against his body.

If showing my ass to my ex-father doesn't prove I'm not scared of him, then I don't know what will. I'd once fantasised about being a stripper to make money when my father forbade me from working outside of Charlotte's shop. Looks like this is the closest I'll get to my dreams coming true. I drag my fingernails down his scales, and that mighty hiss fills the stage again. Suddenly, the music fades, and so does the light. Ghoul winds around me, his tail coiling almost protectively.

"*Uh oh,*" Savage says.

"*What?*" I ask.

"*Is there a door behind the stage?*" Xander asks quickly.

"*Yes,*" I say.

"*Guards are coming for the stage, regina!*" Savage cries. "*Go, go, go!*"

Shit.

I leap off Ghoul and throw back the face piece of the veil,

expanding my eyes into my owl ones. The curtains are right in front of me, and I feel my mates' heavy footfalls on the stage as I run on ahead to show them the way. Ghoul kicked out everyone backstage so it's empty now, but there's still a way to go toward the entrance he brought me through. When we get to the first door, I turn around. Savage, Lyle, and Xander are wearing the most ridiculous costumes I've ever seen, and a hysterical laugh bubbles out of my mouth as Lyle tears off his clown mask.

Xander scowls at me. "Get it together, regina."

There's no time to scowl back. "Where's Scythe?"

Savage is already peering behind us. "He was pretty far back."

More heavy feet sound on the stage.

"Shit!" I say.

"Go on," Savage says, reaching past me to open the door.

"Not without Scythe!" I snap.

Something heavy falls behind him, and we turn around just in time to see Scythe walking towards us like the grim reaper—correction, *as* the Grim Reaper, pulling off the scream mask to reveal his beautiful face aglow with a sheen of sweat. "Three dead. Let's go."

I don't need telling twice. We're through the door in a flash, and Lyle picks me up, throwing me over his shoulder with a hand over my naked ass. "Punishment," he says, slapping my flesh in a way that vibrates through my pussy. "Fucking punishment."

Savage and Xander run ahead of us as I shout instructions, but the back corridor doesn't have too many crossways and makes for a clean path. It's not until we get to the exit to the street outside that I realise we might be in trouble. Savage and Xander are ready for it though, because heat and light warm my legs as Xander blows open the door. Screams resound outside along with screeching tires and Eugene's greeting squawk. Male shouts and one scream greet us as we enter the cold open air.

More quickly than I can imagine, we're loaded into a car, and I find myself on Lyle and Scythe's combined laps as our SUV screeches down the road. Eugene squawks excitedly from the front seat, and Savage kisses him loudly on the head as we speed away.

"Oh no they fucking don't!" Lyle roars before winding down his window and waving his hand through it.

A massive bang sounds from behind us, and I cry out, scrambling to my knees to look out the back window. Two cars are upside down on the road, still bouncing on their roofs and blocking the street. Lyle growls and tries to open the car door, but I grab his hand.

"Stop!" I cry. "What are you trying to do?"

"Kill them!" he growls into my face.

I open my mouth to reply, but instead he slams his mouth over mine in a bruising kiss. He then pushes me aside and pulls open the door yet again. I leap for the handle and slam it closed. "No, Lyle!" I cry, pulling his hand away from the door and planting my weight in his lap.

"You better deal with him, regina," Scythe says from behind me, his voice abyss-dark and silver eyes glittering with rage.

"Seriously!" I cry in anger before reaching down for Lyle's zip.

My crazed lion stops his fussing as I undo the button of his trousers, making his hard dick spring out. I position my knees in the middle seat and lean down, taking him into my mouth. Lyle groans, low and gruff, his hips lifting off the seat, those big hands slamming against the window. I accept his length into my mouth, and as pre-cum spills onto my tongue, and he grows to his full, massive length, I moan around him.

Scythe moves behind me, slapping my ass. "Safe word."

I don't want to risk taking Lyle's cock out of my mouth, so I cry, *"Fairy bread!"* into the group chat. My shark slaps my ass, and I jerk at the contact. Wet fingers find my slit, bracketing my vulva, sliding up and down in a sweet caress before he slaps my ass again. Oh gods, I don't know what type of punishment this is, but I fucking deserve it.

The sound of Scythe's zipper coming down makes my insides clench, and I suck hard on Lyle's cock, laving my tongue along the thick veins. He growls breathlessly above me, stroking my hair back with one hand. Scythe's cock nudges at my entrance as he says into my head, *"That's the first and last time you taunt us with the basilisk, regina. Do you understand me?"*

He stretches out my entrance, and any protest fades as I grab Lyle's thigh, groaning around his fat head. There's a sharp smack to my ass and I'm writhing my pussy against Scythe's first piercing. "Please," I say over Lyle's cock. "Oh gods, please."

"I don't recall telling you to stop, angel." Lyle grabs my chin and pulls me up for a fierce kiss, dragging his tongue across my lips and then biting my lower lip in a greedy, punishing way. I sigh and bend over him again, flicking my tongue over his slit.

Scythe eases his cock into me, piercing by piercing, and I make my ass still, savouring as his inches give my pussy the attention I always crave from him. "Scythe," I beg.

He fingers my ass with a thumb. "Did you understand what I told you?"

"*I give the commands,*" I tell him.

"Not today, you don't." He sheathes himself fully. I cry out, arching my back before Lyle places his hands on either side of my head and fucks my mouth furiously fast.

Scythe fucks me without warning, grabbing my hips and thrusting with equal ferocity, my inner walls vibrating with pleasure. My mates slam into me from both sides until my eyes roll into the back of my head and I'm screaming around the both of them. My pussy convulses, drenching Scythe's cock while Lyle's pre-cum fills my mouth. Stars glitter in my vision, and my body coils into tighter and tighter circles until I'm lightheaded from the sensation.

"Hold my regina's ears!" Savage cries as he winds his window down from the front passenger seat. "Xander, take Eugene!" Lyle's hands shift to cup my ears just as three gunshots ring out.

I squeal around Lyle's cock, wrenching away to stare out the back window. Three motorbikes, each with two armed riders, fishtail and crash into each other, their front wheels blown out. I turn the other way to see Savage drawing most of his body back into the car with a satisfied grin on his face. He returns the black handgun into the glove box and puts his hands up as if to say, 'That's enough for today.'

"That was the last of them," Xander says, checking the rearview mirror.

Lyle makes an animalistic sound, and I quickly take him back into my mouth, my heart pounding in my head. Xander takes a sharp right turn that makes the tires screech, and I ram back onto

Scythe's cock. My shark groans before coming, pushing me back onto Lyle and rutting his release into me with hard, jerking movements. Lyle comes a moment later, roaring and holding my head in place as his hips move in stuttered, broken thrusts.

I come, swallowing Lyle down, my body vibrating around the both of them, my hips jerking around Scythe as he reaches around for my clit, fast fingers knowing exactly how I like it. When our breathing has calmed down, they both pull me between them, arms cocooning me as Scythe drapes his Grim Reaper costume around me like a blanket. They hold me like they wished they'd never let me go tonight, noses buried in my neck from either side. My heart swells between them, just as my soul trembles with anticipation... because it's cool black scales and a deep guttural hiss that I dream about.

Chapter 67

Ghoul

The club lies in an eerie silence in the wake of the departed crowd.

It's the type of silence that holds its breath. I still feel Aurelia's skin on mine. Her heat, her fingers, her hot pussy pressed against me like sweet heaven. The way her hiss vibrated through my body will forever be wrought into my memory. In those few moments, she had been mine. My bride. My queen. Whatever came after that doesn't matter. It was all fucking worth it.

So when three generals swagger towards me, their masks gleaming white-blue under the black lights above us, I allow the death from my eyes to shine through the shadows just a little. It makes their steps falter. How lucky they are that I protect them so dutifully. How *benevolent* I am as basilisk lord.

"Quite the display, Ghoul," General Taipan says, placing a joint in his mouth in an effort to look nonchalant.

"His Majesty and I thought I'd give the people a little boost in morale," I reply smoothly. "I daresay I think it worked."

Taipan snorts and wanders away to the bar where a lone woman wipes the wooden surface with low strokes, pretending not to listen to us. General Brown knocks back his rum and coke before tugging his mask back in place. His voice is quiet when he speaks to me. "Your girl had some interesting scars on her stomach," he says, not meeting my eye. "How did she come by them?"

I shrug. "Sometimes our enemies get the better of us."

"Leave." The command rings through the club, deep and definite. Mace Naga strolls into the light from the dark corner, one hand in a pant pocket. "I wish to speak with my basilisk lord alone." The other two generals bow to him before they leave, and I know they have dark looks under their masks. They've always been jealous of me.

Oh to have the full attention of a serpent king.

Oh to be a beast with *more power* than the serpent king.

Mace draws a deep breath as he looks about the club, surveying the lights above us and the empty stage. Remnants of the night remain: splashes of cum and alcohol on the floor, a glass bottle rolling off to the side. All of that fades away in the presence of the beast before me. The darkness he wears like a garment draws me and my shadows in. It always has. His power is a lure to the darkest beasts. Even without the many blood covenants I have with him, he would hold my malevolent attention.

Mace rubs at his lower lip with his thumb before he unsheathes his verbal fangs. "You think I wouldn't recognise my own progeny?"

The words hang in the air between us like a corpse swaying in the breeze. It sucks all the air from the room. It makes my darkness twitch excitedly.

"You've always played little games with me," Mace says. "Always tested my boundaries." Finally, he turns to me, his voice even and dangerous. "And you know I enjoy testing you right back." I incline my head. "But of course, you knew I would notice." The corners of his thin lips lift in malicious cadence. "She draws beasts in, my Aurelia. It's why I had to set her aside as a teenager. I started noticing the lingering looks beasts were giving her. The way they'd track her scent across the room even before she came into maturity." He shakes his head. "Her mother was never quite the same. I take that to mean my own blood played a part in the power she wields."

Now he calls her his. Now he tries to claim his actions were for protection. There is a power at the depths of me that tries to part the shadows. That claws his blunt fingers at my ribs. But he will not win today. I've made sure of that in a permanent way.

"I always knew one of her mates would be a serpent. How could it not? I'm just surprised that you've hidden it for so long."

"I'm surprised you never guessed it was me," I say.

The king of serpents doesn't take his eyes off me. We both know he's made the mistake of underestimating his daughter one too many times. One mythic shifter made sense in his mind. But two mythic mates was unfathomable to him. He thought I would be a rex of my own den. How little he knows about the powers that move the world.

"You are tied to *me.*" This is the first note of emotion in his voice for years. "You are tied to *my* blood. She may have your soul"—he shrugs, toying with his detached serpent around his wrist—"but your blood belongs to me. Together, we will turn this world into ours. You've known that from the start."

"So I have," I say, drawing myself to full height. "This world will know the sovereignty of serpents, and we will be the ones to pave the way."

Mace nods, his eyes assessing me. He sees the basilisk. He sees the lack of emotion, the psychopath behind the crimson glow. "Aurelia has served her purpose. I have the funds I need from her sale. The number of buyers for her dwindles as she makes her... wildness known. It's finally time we ended her."

"That's been the front for a while," I remark carefully. "Wanting to execute her."

"No longer a front. It's a certainty, because you are going to be the one to do it." Mace brushes a finger over the mark on his forearm. "I call upon our blood bond. I command you, Lord Basilisk, to execute your regina, Aurelia Boneweaver."

The mating mark on my neck screams.

The blood covenant over my navel pulls as tight as a noose.

My eyes burn, calling for ashes and death. I bow my head in submission. "My will is yours, Your Majesty."

"Oh, I know," he says smoothly. "Once you kill your regina, you'll be free for the more important task ahead of you."

PART THREE

Chapter 68

Aurelia

I wake with a shout.

"He knows!" I cry. "My father knows Ghoul is my mate. He's ordered him to kill me!"

There are multiple arms around me, and I throw them off as I leap out of bed. I reel from the movement, swaying a little as I reorient myself. We are back in our animus dorm room, and it's still dark. Xander flew us back, and Lyle carried me to bed. But now my pulse is hammering a war beat inside my skull.

"He knows!" I cry again to Scythe, who is the first to leap out of bed and come to me.

"How can you know this, angel?" Lyle asks, pushing himself up to sit.

"Serpent magic," Xander snarls, rolling to stand. "What exactly did you see, regina?"

I relay what I saw in quick sentences as my mates rub their eyes awake. Ghoul in the empty club, my father and their conversation. The tug of the blood covenant.

"So you could see memories before, but now you're seeing it in real time?" Savage checks the sky outside, and I look too. The first rays of sunlight peek over the mountains in the distance.

I pace the length of the room. Ghoul made sure I saw this. I don't understand how I know this, but I can feel that knowledge in the part of me held just for him.

She might own your soul, but I own your blood.

The pain in my chest is like a gash. There was a reference to his cold heart and a task to come. Something important only my basilisk mate can do. He wanted me to hear this full conversation. Wanted me to know, so I could prepare.

I will have you with your fangs out or not at all.

"Regina—" Lyle begins.

"I can take him."

I come to a halt before the window, turning to face them, and am met with silence. "Scythe, you were wrong." My voice is heavy as a corpse. "Ghoul is not the most dangerous member of this pack." The weight of my power fills my bones. "I am."

The truth stretches out like beams of light between the five of us.

"Aurelia," Xander says, "are you sure about this? That you want to do this?" I give him a small, grateful smile. Out of the four mates here, he is the one I can count on not to stop me. His respect for me lies on a different level. He's the one who's seen me at my worst. My most vulnerable and frightened. He's seen me come back from the impossible. Gold flashes through my dragon's eyes, almost as if he's reminding me of words said before. That he'd been my own general in wars so long ago.

And Ghoul.

He wants to see what I'm made of. He wants to see that I'm strong enough to face the truth and what goes along with it. Jaws snap inside me, seeking my attention. A whisper of a smile curves my lips as I sink into the icy cold depths that is my shark. The temperature of the room drops. My heart slows to a methodical drumbeat. Clinical. Precise.

"Yes." I turn to look at Scythe and Xander, and to me, my voice sounds like it echoes in an empty, dark chamber. "I will do what needs to be done. Our enemy moves in the dark, but so do we. There is something else to be done when night falls again."

* * *

"I don't like it when she's like this," Savage admits. "She won't give me cuddles."

"I think it's cool," Minnie chirps, eyes wide as she considers me from across the dining table. "She's like an assassin or something."

Scythe agrees, my big shark animus always keeping close to me and enjoying the power we share. Somewhere inside him, the Great White gnashes his teeth and lashes his tail in joy. Henry levitates before my face and chirps experimentally.

"Small, pretty creature," I say, my voice flat. "You will stay with me today."

Obediently, he sits himself on my shoulder, pushing his tiny body up against my neck as if he can push warmth into me all by himself. Xander watches from the corner of the room, and I turn to him, gaze unblinking.

A stomping up the stairs tells me Sabrina and Stacey have joined us. But when Sabrina appears, she throws her hood back and marches towards me. "Is it true?" she pants, her voice uncharacteristically harsh. "That psycho general is your mate? It's all over social media, that video of you in Club Venom."

"I know what he did to you," I reply in the same flat-as-wood voice. "Tonight, we fight to the death."

Brown eyes blink back at me. "What do you mean?"

"The basilisk general has been ordered to kill me, Sabrina. I am going into battle."

"Let's not get carried away," Savage says, leaping to his feet. "It's not to the death! I'm going to be there to make sure it's not!"

I give him a slow nod before turning back to Sabrina. My leopard friend sighs and takes the seat next to Minnie at the dining table. "Something big is going to happen," Stacey says. "I can feel it. The serpents have never been this riled up."

"The council is basically dead at the door," Minnie says with disgust. "We can't rely on them to do anything. We have to take action now, right, Xander?"

"Right, Minnie," he says. "But that also includes making sure Aurelia doesn't get herself killed."

Savage puts his hand up. "I'm on duty for that at all times, and so is Lyle tonight and so is the Devi pack."

"The basilisk will not come alone," I clarify, gazing out at them all. "More darkness gathers with him."

Stacey makes googly eyes at me. "Who, Lia? And where?"

"I will lead him to the place we will fight," I say, folding my hands on the table. "He wants to see my power. Tonight, we will finally see why I am regina of the Boneweaver pack."

The room is silent once again. And I revel in it.

* * *

In the night, I move.

I descend into something darker than my shark self. Something scarier than the depths of the dark ocean. Something closer to nothing at all. One second, I'm standing on the parapet above the animus dorm, being watched by my mates and friends, and the next, I'm...

It feels like flying, only I have no wings. I'm in the air and under the stars, but there are no wind currents guiding my body. Not even cold on my face. I am not human. Not animal. It's a wholly dark power, and my emotions feel invisible.

Now I see why my fifth mate is the way he is.

My dragon mate launches into the air behind me, many travellers on his back as his powerful wings sweep, unbalancing the air. It doesn't affect me though, for I am above such things in my current form.

They follow me as I follow my spirit through the night. *Things* call to me in the air, trying to divert my attention, but my purpose is all-consuming, my focus pinpoint. My heart calls for violence. It calls for the malevolent things in the world. It calls for death. This prickles something in the human deep inside me, but I brush that aside for the moment.

At this point, we split ways. My dragon mate flies northward, and I fly east. I am led towards the gathering dark, as familiar to me as my own soul. A broken piece in the void. A coiled piece of power, ready to strike. There in the dark of the ruins of the old Naga House, he slithers. Like a black, writhing tree-trunk, he moves through the ash, forked tongue tasting the air. I land in a crouch on the dirt ground that was once a lush lawn.

A head snaps towards me, eyes red through the dark. *"The snakelet is out to play."*

"There are no games here." Once again, I become darkness, shooting into the sky like a ball of pure power.

The chase is on.

Ghoul's power rises into the night, following me northward. In this form, we are both fast, and I am careful to be unpredictable. I zip this way and that, but all the while moving towards one precise location. When we come upon the group of warehouses, lit up with heinous white floodlights, Ghoul cackles in my head. I cannot see Xander, but I know he is there somewhere.

As nothing but shadow, I breeze through the protective bubble of dragon power that forms a boundary around this place, and it's barely a tickle to me. I come to land on the roof of the central warehouse. In human form, I rise to my feet. Ghoul lands, re-materialising into his near seven-foot form of muscle.

"It's just you and me, basilisk lord," I say, feeling my power gathering in my veins.

My father's general towers over me. "It was never just us, snakelet." He glances upwards where Xander circles carefully. I can't see who's on his back now.

"They have their orders," I assure him. "They will not interfere. This began with you and me, although I didn't know it at the time."

"And yet we find ourselves here. Would you kill me, snakelet, if it came down to it?"

I take the question seriously. Mostly because I've already thought about it. If Ghoul were a danger to my mates, to my friends, to everything that I loved, what would I do?

"You are a piece of me," I say evenly. "And I've killed parts of me to become who I am. To save the ones that I love. Yes, Ghoul, I would."

For a moment—infinitesimal in time, but long enough for a regina—I see a flash of something in those crimson lasers. Something I will think about later, and definitely for the rest of my life.

Ghoul glances over his shoulder to the ground where the serpent military has gathered in the distance. Then *through* them comes running Raquel, the wolf anim's eyes wide, their arms pumping as they sprint across the concrete.

Chapter 69

Savage

Flying high on Xander's back, I'm jittery with excitement to see my chompy kick basilisk ass tonight, but when Raquel appears sprinting down the open space in front of the warehouses, it feels like my brain is going to explode.

"Raquel!" I shout into her mind.

"Where?" Xander snaps in my head.

"Can't you see them?" I crane my neck to look. *"It's Raquel!"*

"Mr Fengari!" comes a faint cry in my head. *"Are you h-here?"*

"Yes! Above the dome! Aurelia has us invisible!"

Raquel looks up, eyes trying to find us. *"You n-need to see what they're d-doing here. I think I can g-get you in."*

"How?" I cry back to them. How are they even here?

My chompy and Ghoul are still talking on the roof, and I'm not sure if they've seen the spirit of the wolf anim yet. Why are they not in their body! This explains why we haven't seen them wake up yet. *Wild Mother,* this is so bad. Xander and Scythe must have shifted their sight because now they're tracking the anim's movements toward the middle warehouse. Lyle and the Devi pack won't be able to see them because they're felines, and Lyle grumbles unhappily about it behind me. Raquel disappears into the warehouse on the left.

"To the ground!" I command Xander, whacking my heels into his scales like he's a horse.

Xander dives for the ground, and Minnie lets out a little yelp. Next minute, I see three blobs levitating themselves to the shadows of the woods that surround the place like a Christmas wreath. Looks like dragon G-force isn't for them, and I think that's fair.

But now I have a problem: there's nowhere for Xander to land, so why is he speeding towards the ground like this?

"Lyle!" I shout into his head.

"I've got you, wolf," Lyle growls, before I feel myself lift off Xander's back. Xander shrinks rapidly beneath us, and in seconds, he's not under me at all, and we're all flying down in human form into the trees like a bunch of baby birds who can't use their wings. Luckily, Lyle is a good mother hen and captures me and Scythe in the love of his power and glides us down.

When my bare feet touch down onto firm soil, I jump up to standing with excitement. Scythe brushes his silver hair off his face and is already walking towards the blue glow of the dome. The Devi pack is already there, and Lyle and Xander jog towards them. I'm the last bloody one!

A mighty roar splits the air just as I reach them. Two massive basilisks rear up on the middle warehouse just as the blue dome fizzles out.

"Mr Fengari!" Raquel shouts in my head.

Chapter 70

Aurelia

It's an effort to keep both Xander and the Devi pack concealed when Xander rudely dropped to the ground like that. I'm sure Savage has seen Raquel by this point, but I can't give them any more attention as the battle for my life is about to take place.

I cock my head at the enemy basilisk. "You promised me you would return Raquel."

"And so I have," he says, shrugging. "You are here, they are here. Hence, the wolf is returned." He takes a heavy, meaningful step towards me. "Are you buying time, snakelet?"

I also take a step forward, showing him I am not afraid. "Do you know me at all?" He freezes then, and I get the impression of a flash of fury through his shadows. "You think watching me all that time means that you *know* me?" I hiss. "You watched me from the darkness like a coward. Like a worm wheedling through soil."

He bares his fangs at that. "I am here to kill you," he says, and I cannot hear an ounce of emotion in his voice. Just like mine. I wonder how long he has hidden his emotions behind the darkness.

"And I am here to stop you," I say. "Shall we do this, shadow man?" I raise a hand, and a wisp of black coils around it. Lazy like smoke, black as midnight. "Oh, would you look at that?" I give him no warning as I explode outwards. Growing huge, growing scales and terrible eyes. Eyes like death itself burn through my skull. I've only done this form once before, and at that time, I'd been wholly unprepared for the way the blue lasers shot through my eyes. It happens again now.

Ghoul goes flying backwards from the force of it. Twin beams of heat score the concrete, chasing him, and a sound like electric humming fills the air. The concrete smokes. I taste an acrid burning on my tongue, and Ghoul shifts into his basilisk form before he hits the ground. *"You need to cover your eyes,"* he hisses into my mind. *"Unless you want to kill every soul here."*

Oh, right.

My new shadows seem to want to play, but they are an extension of me, and move to my command in the same way a tail would. They are a new muscle, but I'm used to learning about new muscles. I pull the shadows up, plastering them over my eyes like a blindfold. My world becomes dark.

"Not too thick," Ghoul says, *"or you won't be able to see."*

"Thank you," I say, removing thin layers of the shadow until it lets light in like a pair of sunglasses.

"You're welcome." Suddenly, he's in front of me, rearing that big head backward before he strikes. This body might be new to me, but I had been *raised* to be a cobra. Dodging the attack comes naturally to me, and I swing left before rounding on him, striking his thick hide. Thick basilisk fangs tear into his cool scales, and the regina in me screams to see us hurting our mate. Venom surges through my fangs, blood fills my mouth, and flesh submits to me. He roars to the sky.

"You never told me how you found yourself in Halfeather House," I say, releasing him and launching myself off the roof of the warehouse. *"I've become very familiar with your spine. If I win, you have to tell me."*

Ghoul says nothing as I turn and see him staring down at me from the rooftop, his tongue slipping out to taste the air. From the side of my eye, the blue dome disappears, and my mates sprint towards the warehouses.

Chapter 71

Xander

The Devi pack remain in the tree line while Savage and I sprint to the far warehouse, following the translucent, astral form of Raquel. Scythe and Lyle make for the central warehouse that Ghoul is presently using to host his standoff with Aurelia. I have a nasty suspicion as to how the wolf anim ended up here, but we'll need to analyse that later.

I have to tell myself that Aurelia will be okay, because the urge to fly up there and tear out the throat of that scaled monster is far too strong. We can tell they are telepathing to each other, but whether they are taunts or flirtations, we may never know. Minnie promised me she will intervene if something goes untoward in the battle, and I fully believe she has the power to throw the bastard off the roof if she wants. This is the only thing that allows me to have patience as we infiltrate warehouse one.

"*Cameras?*" Savage chimes in my head.

"*Down.*" I'd already sent the electronics scrambling the moment the dome had dissolved. Mace has spent a lot of blood money on this place, and expensive warehouses rely on electronics. Blow those out, and they revert to backup generators. Blow the backup generators, and they revert to the tertiary generators. Blow out the tertiary generators, and everything reverts to manual, as they do now. The fire doors slam open of their own accord, and Raquel frantically gestures us inside. I turn the power back on to avoid suspicion, leaving only the cameras scrambled. Whoever is inside will chalk it up to the fighting basilisks.

"This better not be a trap," I mutter to them both. *"There better not be some serpent wolf hybrid experiment in here or something."*

Raquel runs on ahead of us, passing right through me as they do —an uncomfortable, shivering sensation—before they slow down. *"Keep quiet!"*

Savage glances over his shoulder to make a confused face as we stride after the wolf anim into the dark corridor. We take one flight of metal stairs and then another, coming out into a well-lit corridor lined with glass. Raquel presses a finger to their lips and points into the first window. Multiple voices sound from below us, one of them familiar. Raquel crouches down and proceeds to crawl on all fours. Savage and I copy them, crawling under the windows to peek through to the warehouse below.

Charlotte fucking Naga stands with a baseball cap and a whistle in the centre of a row of firm blue gym mats while children run around her with very real military-grade rifles. I swear under my breath.

"Is this a school?" Savage whispers.

"They're running d-drills," Raquel replies. "They have real g-guns. But look o-over to the side." I follow Raquel's tattooed, transparent finger to the far right of the gym where a smaller group of teenagers, barely of mating mark age, hold dark, translucent serpents in their hands.

"Why do they have tiny snakes?" Savage asks. But my magical eyes see they're not physical snakes at all. If I were a religious beast, I would have crossed myself.

"This can't be happening," I mutter. "How did they even learn to do this?"

Raquel's wide-eyed look confirms it to be true. "I thought that t-type of thing was a m-myth."

"It's the darkest sort of magic," I say. "Of course they'd be using it now. But for children—"

"These are *hatchlings*," Savage whispers. "We can't kill them."

Raquel presses a finger to their lips before gesturing for us to head back down. Dutifully, we follow. I want to get out of this place straight away, and so does Savage. Mace is using child soldiers. I shouldn't be surprised but I fucking am. There are supposed to be rules in warfare, but I guess anything goes in Serpent Court now.

Savage can't hold it together any longer, and when we get back down to the dark corridor that leads outside, he turns around to Raquel. "Why didn't you fly back to us?" he asks, clutching at his hair. "We were so worried, Raquel!"

Raquel rubs their arm uncharacteristically. "A-about that..." A deep rumbling growl sounds from further up the corridor. Four wolves prowl out, teeth bared, saliva dripping down open maws. "T-turns out," Raquel says awkwardly, "I'm regus of the pack that guards this p-place. The Silver T-tails. And they're...attached to me now."

I grab Savage around the waist and run.

Chapter 72

Aurelia

The basilisk lord leaps right off the warehouse roof, jaws wide open, fangs angled at me. Excited that he's taken my bait, I release the shadows over my eyes, letting loose the blue lasers. My power hums through the air once again, hitting Ghoul square in the face. His head snaps back before he veers away, rolling off to the side, his landing making the very ground shake.

The serpents watching us from nearby flee in their vehicles, shouting into their comm devices, tires screeching. I cover my eyes once again as Ghoul recovers and rears up. We circle each other on the concrete, the harsh floodlights showing me every centimetre of burned flesh on that mighty snout.

"*Does it hurt?*" I ask. "*When your mate wounds you?*"

He doesn't take his eyes off me, the faint red glow focused behind the shadows. "*I would say you're the expert on that. Must be a record. Four of the beasts you call mates tried to hurt you.*"

I watch his every muscle as we continue our circle. "*You really hate them?*"

His tongue tastes the air, big and forked. I remember how it had licked me in Club Venom. "*How could I not? They did nothing to deserve you.*"

My mind reels in pure shock. Shadows shoot out from his body, and not expecting this movement, I fly to the side and they simply follow me. Bands of shadow wrap around my body, trapping my muscles. I writhe against them as Ghoul advances, the red of his eyes powering up.

I shove at him with a telekinetic blast that sends him spinning backwards like a horizontal tree trunk. The shadows binding me loosen, and I shake them off to make my pursuit. Ghoul lands, rolling over the concrete, and I leap onto his back, spiralling my tail around his, wrapping my body around him until I am taut, trapping him entirely. He hisses in protest.

"An excuse to get close to me?" he taunts.

"No," I snarl. *"And keep your hemipenis away from me."*

"You can put your cloaca wherever you like."

There was once a time when I let a mate make a mistake. Allowed a mate to take advantage of me. *"Xander might never recover from what he did. His regret means nothing to him. I'm not going to let that happen again."* I squeeze my body around his, like an anaconda around prey. *"I feel your lungs,"* I say viciously. *"The air that's trying to get in."*

"I feel the beat of your heart," he whispers.

I try to unwrap myself, but it's too late. We are tangled, and Ghoul, sensing my intentions, begins to spiral himself around me. His power coils around me, dark and intense. His scales against mine, now warm, sliding and loosening something inside of me. Suddenly, I want to breathe that dark power into the bases of my lungs and let it consume me until I'm drunk on it.

"I waited for you," he says, just before my vision blinks out and everything goes black.

Chapter 73

Ghoul

She's in our cottage, but this time, there's a duffle bag on the couch, and she's carefully counting the things inside it. She lets out a big sigh and rubs her eyes. I knew it was coming, but the sudden realisation hurts in a way nothing has before.

She's going to leave.

Leave *me*.

I've never been able to see a mark on her neck, but I know she's mine. I let myself realise it as soon as she came of age. As soon as Mace Naga came to our bungalow and made her submit. That sealed things for me.

It's finally time. And I have no other choice.

* * *

I'm a monster in a cell of all darkness, all silence, all cold.

And that's a good thing.

It reminds me of when I was young and my family sent me away from the village to be alone where I couldn't hurt anyone. Where my eyes wouldn't kill my friends. All I remember of my guardians are whispers of "I'm sorry," carried on a desperate breath. A frightened breath.

And now, in another type of confinement, I lie safe and sound, when *she* comes in.

I feel only relief at the power breezing through the steel door. That golden power holds a promise against my aching soul. An expert mind brushes against my spine. It twitches in surprise at first, then gently handles the power I bound around myself.

My regina has come for me.

It worked. Everything would be alright.

Chapter 74

Aurelia

Ghoul's scales slide against mine, and I realise he has me in his complete hold, the full length of his powerful body completely wrapping mine. He's supposed to be trying to kill me, so why does it feel comforting after what I'd just seen?

Every memory of his makes me reel. Makes my world spin on its axis so I don't know which way is up or down. Like being caught under a violent wave that sends you tumbling in the undertow.

"What—" I manage to choke out.

Every time I see him watching me in his memories, it's like another knife to the gut. Even in my darkest moments, he'd been there. As I'd packed my bags, he'd been there. I remember that moment, counting tampons in my bag. Counting my meagre possessions. If only I'd raised my head and turned a little, I might have caught sight of him. The edge of a shadow, maybe even the glow of a mating mark.

But how had we gotten from that first memory to the next?

What had he done?

"There's something between you realising that I'm going to leave and then being locked in Halfeather's mansion with that shadow around your spine. What was it, Ghoul? What worked?"

Suddenly, he's gone. In a poof of black shadow, the pressure on my body releases, and the basilisk is before me. I rear up, ready to attack, but my head spins from being blacked out. *"What are you hiding from me?*" I hiss, tasting the air on instinct, trying to get a read from him. What does it mean? How does a beast go from being death incarnate to at death's door in Healfeather House?

But I taste only adrenaline in the air, serpents and felines. Fury bubbles up my spine, and I snap my fangs before lunging at him, maw first. He's ready for me and disappears into black shadow, making me slide right through him. Ghoul appears behind me, striking with his fangs out. But now I've learned something new and disappear into shadow. It sends him striking for the ground, but he rights himself as I appear behind him.

I strike, he disappears and reappears behind me.

As he strikes, I disappear and reappear behind him.

Faster and faster, we move, trying to out-shadow each other. I'm vaguely aware of shouts from the ground around us, but I need to maintain full focus to keep from getting bitten. Ghoul is fast, but I get the feeling he is enjoying this. When was the last time he fought someone his size?

Finally, I've had enough, reappearing a distance away and wrapping him in telekinesis so he can't move into darkness again. I fly him up into the air, and he thrashes against me. "*I am your regina*," I hiss as he struggles against my hold. "*I will always be stronger than you.*"

"*I know*," he wheezes. "*I know, snakelet. It's my only solace.*"

If I had brows, I would frown at this. At the whole thing. "*What is your plan?*" Abruptly, I let him go, and he crashes to the concrete with a thump.

"*Ah, snakelet.*"

I circle him from a distance. He disappears again, and *this* time, I don't move when he strikes me, right in the neck with his big, sharp fangs. My hiss of pain is very real, and for some bizarre reason, the bastard shifts. His human form wraps his limbs around my neck, fangs still sinking deep, a hot tongue flicking out and scalding my skin. My reality hones in on that single point. Until it's just me and him. Until it's almost a decade of pain between us, cutting deeper and deeper. How alone we'd both been.

So achingly close. So agonisingly separate.

My breath stutters before I, too, shift. I shrink and he moves with me to the ground, until his body is curved around my naked one, his breath hot on my neck, his fangs still piercing my skin. He releases me with a hiss, and I whirl to stare at him. I don't know why, but my eyes fill with tears at the sight of him. The memories he's shown me crash together like fractals in my brain, and it's suddenly too much. My vision blurs. My heart pounds the beat of a sad, lonely song.

"No." His growl turns into a breath. "*No.*"

My heart hurts so much. My heart feels like it's dying under the weight of this. *My* mate. *Mine*, my father's property, just like my mother was. In my head, a thousand angry shrieks sound, enraged, livid.

I need you with your fangs out.

He doesn't want my tears. I raise my arm to slap him across the face—only he grabs my wrist in a steel grip and stares me down with those red eyes.

"*I am here to kill you*," he growls. "*You think a slap was the best way to stop me?*"

It's the first time I've seen his naked body, and the realisation hits me like its own type of slap. My eyes can't help but drag down the length of his form, hard and lethal. Made for battle. Made for war if what I guess about my father is right. Around his navel is the convenant. Like an elaborate snare around his belly button. "I know what's coming," I grit out.

Ghoul goes still. "Eugene finally told you?"

"What?" I frown.

The basilisk lord sighs, tilting his head back, and the movement irritates me. I gather my power in my left fist and punch him right in the blood covenant. Ghoul lets my wrist go with an "oof," his body curving inward. But he recovers way too fast and tackles me to the ground. Too late, I realise my mistake because we're both naked, skin pressing against skin as I writhe against him. His cock is hard against my stomach, and I cry out in fury as the urge to fuck him drives me near *mad*. I shove at him, but he grabs my wrists.

"I signed your little contract, you know," he grits out over my mouth. "The one that said we could fuck you at any time. Anywhere."

I bare my fangs.

And spread my legs.

"Put your cock in me before I cut it off," I hiss.

A very male smirk curves along his lips as the head of his cock kisses my entrance. "Does it make you wet to fight me?" He drags his fangs down my neck at the same time he grinds his cock against my wet, pulsing clit. "Does it make you *drip* to know that I know your power is superior to anyone else?"

I cry out in fury, lifting my hips and pushing him inside of me.

Ghoul arches his neck and hisses to the sky, and it's then that I notice shadows cover us in a cloud of darkness. We could be in another realm for all I know. But Ghoul doesn't move inside of me. Frustrated, I grind against him, urging him in further. I've sucked his cock before, and I know its shape.

Something in me snaps at that memory, and I growl, using my telekinesis to throw us sideways and over, slamming Ghoul onto the concrete. He grunts, his eyes growing wide as I climb on his dick and sheathe myself on his length. We both cry out, and shadows strike out like serpents, wrapping themselves around my thighs, my waist, my breasts. My neck.

As if he wants to consume me whole.

I ride him, moving my hips over that massive length. Ghoul's eyes glow crimson as he arches his neck, and I can't help but bend over and run my tongue over the corded muscle until it hits the corner of something that is not skin.

That mask. That fucking mask. He's not paying attention, so when I slide my fingers under the edge of it, he doesn't stop me as I rip the thing clean off.

His face is revealed to me. Perfect, brown-skinned, sharp-jawed and straight-browed. He has a brutal sort of beauty, one made equally for looking down on his enemies from a high throne and snarling on a battlefield. But it's currently twisted in shock because I don't think he ever intended for me to see the many lines of the black tattoos covering his face.

I would recognise my father's markings anywhere. Because it's a precise, elegant hand that wrote lines of control over this face of death. Symbols for *control, slave, leash, prison. Obey.* My father struggled to control Ghoul so much that one covenant had not been enough and he'd needed to cover him in them.

I'd ponder this more, but Ghoul's cock swells inside of me, pushing against my inner walls. "What is that?" I pant, looking down as I gush around him.

"Hemipenis, remember?" he pants, gripping my waist. "It grows into a lock."

Something jolts through my stomach. "A serpent mating lock?" I say, suddenly panicking.

"Yes," he says slowly, not blinking as he watches me.

I try to remove myself, planting a foot on the ground and tugging to standing, but Ghoul's cock firmly and completely has me by the vagina as if we're glued together. My heart beats so fast I think I'm going to faint. "How long?" I whisper.

Ghoul lifts his head to look between us. "Only the Wild Goddess can say. It's never happened to me before."

I sit back down on his hips, staring at this new face in a sort of wonder. I don't know why I never expected this. Serpents lock when they mate; anywhere from twenty-four hours to three days is completely normal. I'd just...not expected it to happen in human form.

"Well, shit," is all I can say.

Ghoul grins at me around his fangs and between his glowing eyes...the only way I could describe is, well, *crazed*.

Chapter 75

Scythe

Lyle and I leave warehouse two, exchanging a glance. There is nothing at all in there. The place is empty—a concrete box with no windows and only one door. Or that's what I would believe if not for my shark-sight. I had stopped at the door, refusing to step foot or let Lyle cross the threshold into that place.

"There's nothing in here," Lyle had said.

"And yet I see death in it."

My lion brother looked at me with concern as I stared at the space with an impression of a whirlpool, faint to my eyes, but it was more the aura of the place. Death had come here. And something worse than death. It made my shark scream. It fascinated my dark heart.

Lyle had to drag me away from it, but I am glad he did. Soaking up any more of the dark power would send me to a place better left untouched. But it meant that as we came out of the warehouse, we were distracted enough to bump into Xander and Savage. The latter being hoisted up by his dragon brother so his feet dangled above the ground.

"Oi!" Savage said to us. "Run, you nutters!"

We don't ask why as Xander sprints on ahead of us, into the alleyway created between the first two warehouses. I can no longer hear the basilisks fighting, and I sprint across the concrete right behind him, ready to rescue my regina. But as we round the final corner, it turns out we don't need to rescue her. She and Ghoul are in a ball of shadow, and as we come up to it, it fades away to reveal Aurelia sitting on Ghouls' cock, staring at the spot the two of them are joined. She turns to see us, her face brightening.

"We need to go!" she says, pointing to the gate where multiple cars are speeding through. We knew we only had so long before the cavalry arrived.

"Then let's go!" Savage says, running over to her and grabbing her from under the arms as if to lift her off.

"No!" she and Ghoul shout. Savage's mouth drops open in dismay as he removes his hands.

"Serpent lock," Aurelia says, her lips pressing together as if she's embarrassed. She plants a foot and shows us, tugging herself upwards. The base of Ghoul's cock moves with her. "It's magical. No way to undo it."

Xander's head drops back in dismay. *Really*, Aurelia?"

"Don't start on me, Xander," she snaps. "It might take three days."

Savage yelps like he's hurt, clutching his face. "Nooooo!"

"We need to go, now," Lyle grits out. "We have to take both of them."

"No." Ghoul shows us his fangs. "I'll take her for now."

Aurelia sighs. "Alright."

Ghouls' fangs glint in the moonlight. "I'll make sure she comes, boys, don't worry."

Black shadows scoop them up like gathering clouds, and then they're gone as if they were never here at all. I clench my teeth together in dismay. He still has his orders to kill her. My regina knows how to look after herself, but that doesn't abate my fury.

"Problem!" Savage says, pointing to the incoming trucks. Titus Clawson and a team of felines are currently zipping towards us on the back of trucks.

"Xander, shift!" I command.

Suddenly, a humming breaks through the air, and the protective dome reappears, shining bright blue above us. A mad cackle sounds as Titus, standing on the open back of the Jeep with a gun in hand, points a fat finger our way. "You're not going anywhere, fuckers!"

Chapter 76

Lyle

My animus is roaring inside of me, and I won't even bother placating him. We have every right to be angry when it should have been our cock fixed in our regina's pussy and not the enemy's. The fact that he's taken her away is an utter failure on all our parts. That Titus is now whooping his way toward us is a further failure. We should have been out of here by now.

"Lyle," Scythe growls, gesturing towards the oncoming military vehicles. "Focus."

I growl in reply, locking in and focusing on the truck. I reach a hand out, sending a telekinetic blast towards them. The vehicle rocks, losing speed, but there are no fewer than six felines in there, staring me down and counter-acting against my power.

"Not today, Pardalia!" Titus roars back.

"There's too many of them," I say, gritting my teeth because it's not in my nature to run.

"It's too small for me to shift," Xander says, summoning his fire whip. But they're too far, and now the convoy of trucks splits, three vehicles driving side by side, loaded guns aimed at us.

Savage turns and sprints past me towards shelter behind the warehouses. "Run, everyone!"

"Run where?" Xander snorts, turning and sprinting after him. "We can't get through the dome anyway."

"The second warehouse," Scythe says, turning to follow. "They can't get their trucks in there."

Someone shoots, the bullet missing my foot by an inch, and I scoop everyone up with a hand of my power, thrusting us all behind the second warehouse. Engines roar at our tails as Savage opens the big metal door, leaping inside. Xander and Scythe follow, pressing themselves against the wall. I slam the door shut once I'm inside. We want to bottleneck them inside for a fairer fight on foot. Even without weapons, the four of us will then stand a chance.

"Titus is hanging back," Xander says, using his sight to look through the door. "He's sending the others through first. Scythe? Get the second guy."

"On it." Scythe closes his eyes, feeling out the electrical impulses of those outside.

Xander lashes a fire whip around the handle of the door, making the metal glow. A pained scream sounds from the other side as the man who went for the handle gets third-degree burns upon touching it.

The door rattles on its hinges, and Xander flies out of the way just as it explodes inwards under telekinesis. Felines leap over the fallen males, guns first, and open fire. Xander and I lash out, waving the bullets away as fast as we can while Scythe squeezes hearts, dropping those behind, and Savage knocks out the one in the lead with a punch to the head and grabs his rifle.

A bullet hits me on the shoulder, and the blow forces me to take a step back with a grunt. It triggers me to shift, and I allow my animus to take over. He announces himself with a roar, but now Savage is shouting, wrestling with another rifle. Power thrums through the air as my telekinesis meets five other feline powers. It makes the air charged, dampening the sound and forces.

"Fall back!" Titus shouts from what sounds like far away. "Clawson beasts, fall back!"

Telekinesis takes the beasts wrestling with our powers, and Savage has no choice but to let his enemy go as they are whisked away. "Come back!" Savage shouts through the door. "Come back, you fuckers—" Something skids through the door and Xander recognises the grenade before anyone else does, shoving it back out the door.

Except it's joined by five others.

"Run!" Scythe roars, possibly for the first time in his life.

Xander all but throws Savage through the door outside, and I take Scythe with me. The telekinetic power in the air hums for a millisecond before the explosion.

BOOM!

Light and heat explode into the air, and metal goes flying as we all roll onto the concrete outside. Something big shields me from the heat, and I growl in annoyance, pushing myself to my feet. Xander lets me go, the back of his shirt nonexistent after he covered Scythe, Savage and me.

"Looky what we have here," Titus snarls, and the barrel of a gun shoves into my cheek. The Clawsons have us surrounded, guns pressed to temples. "A pussy, a reptile, a fish, and a dog."

Savage snarls in dismay, and I want to warn him not to get us all shot. But then a voice, sweet and high but ravenous with fury, screams, "Titus Clawson!"

Every head swings around to see Minnie, Marduk and Yeti flying towards us, the little tigress' eyes alight with adrenaline.

Chapter 77

Savage

Just when I think we're all about to die, little Minnie appears, shouting her ex-mate's name. With one sweep of her hand, we all go flying away from each other. My ass skids against the concrete, giving me carpet burn straight from hell, so I'll have to talk to her about that later, but it means everyone is given a time out of maybe...ten seconds.

Bullets fly, but the Devi pack send them up all uselessly to the sky. Angry feline roars fill the air as many of the Clawson grunts shift into a mix of tiger, lion, panther, and cheetah. But Titus stays in human form, swinging his rifle right at the Devi pack.

Xander and I cry "No!" at the same time, but Minnie is better than all of us combined because she screams at Titus and waves her fist, sending the bullet *and* his automatic rifle flying high onto the warehouse roof. Guns go flying as Marduk and Yeti fall upon the other felines, knocking them out with telekinetic blasts.

I bet Titus regrets using feral beasts because they can't hold their human skins long enough to keep a gun. But the felines are too many, and they get split up under the sheer number of charging animals. Marduk blasts one lion into the sky, and Yeti punches another right in the face, sending him to the ground. Minnie blasts two away just as I start running to help them.

No one sees Titus come up from behind Yeti.

The Siberian Tiger's eyes widen as something strikes him in the leg. Time seems to slow down as I shout Yeti's name, but he just falls over, his mouth yawning open in the beginning of a shout. And then comes the sound of crunching. Titus claws Yeti to the ground, and my legs just won't move fast enough as Titus holds Yeti's foot in his metal-mouth and spits it out onto the concrete.

Minnie screams in a regina's outrage just before she shifts, clothes tearing off her body like tissue paper. Power booms out like a powerful ocean wave, rippling over our skins, raising the hairs and fur on everyone's bodies. Titus rises into the sky, his arms outstretched like an angel, and both his arms break at the humerus *and* forearm on their own. His big body crumples in on itself as his metal mouth opens in agony, eyes wide as if he can't possibly believe this is happening to him. Then Minnie is on him, leaping through the air and trapping his legs in her big tiger's jaws, pulling him down to the ground, claw over claw.

Nothing can stop her as Xander whisks Yeti and Marduk away to safety, but we don't need to deal with the other felines. Everyone stops.

Everything stops to look on in shock as Minnie mauls Titus Clawson to death.

Chapter 78

Scythe

We'd been preparing Minnie for this, but nothing could have prepared the rest of us for the way Titus screamed as he died. Screaming his fury, his rage, his misogyny as Minnie—his tiny regina whom he thought so beneath his consideration—overpowered him. Her superior power had always been there, she'd just never had the audacity to wield it in a way that could hurt people.

Marduk looks on with horrific adoration, holding a white-faced Yeti in his arms as his regina silences the last Clawson lord. The Devi regina's growls quieten as she shifts back, crouched over her ex-mate's mangled, bloody form, feline eyes glistening, her face consumed with feral bloodlust.

With her mouth and neck covered in Clawson blood, Minnie rises to her feet with Titus' metal jaw dangling between her fingers. She stares the other felines down with a look so terrifying, more than one beast takes a step back. She throws the metal onto the concrete, and it clangs as it bounces before coming to a definite, final stop.

The felines of Clawson House drop to the ground in submission, but Minnie only has eyes for her mates.

There is nothing else left of this night.

Chapter 79

Ghoul

There is only one place to bring my regina.

Only one place hidden in plain sight where no one will think to look for a little while, at least.

We rematerialise in the darkness behind Charlotte Naga's old house, and I hold my snakelet close as my feet touch the grass. She wraps her long limbs around my naked hips as I shove open the front door and carry her into the house. It's not bridal style, but it's close enough, and with my cock this deep in her heat, her skin on mine, and her scent in my nose, I cannot complain about anything. Even now that my mask is off, she's not looking at me, but at the living room through the darkness, her little nose sniffing the dust and old, familiar scents.

"Still smells the same," she huffs. "I think there's still two-minute noodles in the cupboard. Those never go off."

"Is that what you want to eat?" I ask, taking her to the kitchen.

She's still avoiding my eyes. "I'm not hungry."

She won't be. Serpents don't eat during a mating lock. "But you will be thirsty," I say, carrying her to the sink.

Her muscles clench around me as she turns to face me once again, and I hiss. "You've been waiting to do this," she says accusingly. Her breath is warm on my face. So sweet. So much power. If I could spend the rest of my days simply drinking her in, simply tasting her scent on the air, I would die happy.

So I say nothing as I reach up into the cupboard where I know the glasses are. Taking one, I set her ass on the sink, looking over her shoulder to wash it out behind her back and then fill it with water. She takes the glass from me, licking her lips thirstily.

There was a time when I never thought we'd get this close to one another. When I thought that contact with her would be relegated to a faraway dream. Where all I had to keep me going through the gruelling days was hope. Hope carried on blue eyes and shadow-black hair.

"Do you really think this will take three days?" she asks quietly, swirling the water in the glass and peering down as if it contains the answers. I want to tell her that *I* have the answers. And that only one *other* soul has the answers she needs to save herself. Long dark lashes flutter as she drinks the cold water, only emptying half of the glass before handing it back to me. I take it from her and place my lips where hers were, and knock the water back. She watches me drink it, her eyes on my mouth and nowhere else. I soak up her awareness like a desperate man.

She doesn't raise her gaze again. Is she shy all of a sudden? "It may take three days, yes," I say quietly, setting the glass down on the bench.

She swallows. "When did you know I was your regina?"

I put a finger under her chin and tilt it upwards. *Look at me*, I want to say. *My mask is off. Look back at me.* Those eyes, blue as an ultraviolet beam, meet my gaze without blinking. Without breathing. "In the early days, I thought you were like me. A kindred spirit, lost and alone. I couldn't figure out your order and understood that you hid yourself in a similar way to how I did with my shadows. I had...a strong need to look after your welfare. But as we both grew up, I began to understand that what I was feeling for you was a soul-tie."

"What about your family?" she asks. "Your parents and their den?"

I inhale a deep breath, letting her scent wash over me as I place my arms around her ass and lift her up again. Her bed will be too small for me, so I set about gathering her purple blankets to lay them on the living room floor like a nest.

"No one was able to tell Mace when he enquired, and I grew up with my adoptive family, believing my real family were dead for unknown reasons. Perhaps they were executed for what they were. I'll never know how many basilisks were in their den or if they were a mixed pack like the Fengaris."

"I'm sorry," she says, as I lay the both of us down on the layers of blankets. She gazes at my face, studying me, and I cannot move the arms I have around her. Her inner walls clench again as she adjusts her hips, and this time, she grunts under the stretch of my cock.

She frowns, looking down between us. "Does that hurt you?"

I snort at that. "I am doomed to the shadows of hell, snakelet, but at least I get to see heaven for three days out of the darkness of eternity."

Chapter 80

Aurelia

Without his mask, with the full force of his presence upon me, I suddenly find it hard to breathe. Find it hard to think being *this* close, cervix deep. Ghoul's presence has always been overwhelming. Like the stifling dark in a small room, you can feel that basilisk lurking so close to the surface.

He really is pure, coiled, malevolent power.

I can tell he wants me to look at his face. I don't know if he feels relief, or if he feels anything at all under the power of his basilisk. Being able to shift into different forms, I'm not subject to the order powers in the same permanent way as the other orders. Ghoul cannot or does not want to escape the dark powers of his monster. They are too crucial to who he is.

The monster is me and I am the monster, he'd told me when we'd first met.

It's just unfortunate that the giant serpent is even more psychopathic than a shark.

I have to breathe through the stretch of his cock, now that the heat of my initial arousal is cooling me down. And as we lie here, I suddenly can't believe we're back in my little bungalow.

When I'd left it the night after my wedding to Halfeather, I'd never thought I'd see the inside of it again. My eyes burn, and not in the lethal way. Ghoul leans in and scrapes his fangs across my bottom lip. His cock is still hard as diamond, but it twitches just a little as I suck in a breath at his touch.

How the fuck am I going to spend three days with this beast? Who only answers the questions he wants to, whose power sends infinite tingles across my skin? He flexes his hips, and I moan as my clit is jostled into pleasure.

"Are we going to spend three days fucking?" I ask wryly.

His tongue, this time forked, slips out to taste me. My eyes widen as the crimson glows. "If you are mine for three days, then I get to do as I please, do I not?"

"Well, technically," I say, "if your cock is stuck in position, you can't really do all that much, can you?"

I'm on my back before I know it, my legs over Ghoul's muscular shoulders as he thrusts into me. I cry out at the sudden pleasurable fullness, tingles spiralling through my clit. So he *can* move inside me. Just not all the way out.

My eyes warm as power collects behind them in response to the crimson glow above me. My fangs snap out of their own accord. Shadows snake out from his shoulders, gripping me around the wrists and pulling them all the way up over my head. My own shadows draw out, just slower and more clumsy with the new, smaller movements, and I touch the sides of his face with them. A face I want to get to know.

"Fuck me like you've wanted to this entire time," I hiss. "Fill me with your cum like you've dreamed."

Black brows twitch in amusement as he shoves himself balls deep in me. "I should make you beg for it." Something tickles my ass, and I know it's his shadow, ready to wind me open and fill me with everything he has.

I arch my back in pleasure, laughing at my own amusement. "We're beyond that, shadow-man."

Ghoul licks the column of my neck, up my mating mark and up to my ear. "Tell me how good it feels, snakelet. Tell me how much my cock makes you want to come all over me."

My body tenses around him, slow pulsing motions I don't even know if I can control. A finger of shadow slips inside my ass, toying with my entrance, making me gasp his name.

"I wish you knew my real name," he breathes. "You'll be using it before the end."

Ghoul fucks me hard and fast, like a serpent striking over and over again. His hips snap in and out, moving us both across the floor. He growls into my neck, hands tightening over mine as I scream his name to the broken ceiling, taking him and his furious need *and* his power that comes barrelling forth like a dark tornado that pulls and sucks and writhes within me. I let it twine around my own golden power, let them dance in a manic cyclonic wind of their own making.

I'm dizzy and breathless; we're both sweating and crying out as Ghoul comes inside of me. My cervix is flooded with him, and he fucks his pleasure into me in hard, brutal movements that I revel in. "Give it to me," I pant, squeezing his hands. "I want all of it."

He lifts his head, and our gazes lock, our faces truly meeting for the first time. "Aurelia," he says. Another first, and I come from the need in that single word. Come from the feeling of our powers finally touching. I come from the sudden unrestricted emotion I see in that face.

Because there, in the dark, with blue and red glowing between us, the thing I see—profound in its beauty and wholly unexpected— is pure devastation and devotion.

* * *

I wake the next morning to a heartbeat in my ear. My pussy is sore from the girth currently occupying it, and with a sudden jolt, the harsh light of reality comes crashing down on me. Ghoul's chest is warm under my ear, and I blink up at the light. Familiar dawn light streams through tattered curtains. My eyes fix on the yellowed material in wonder. How many times had Ghoul stared at me through them?

"*Regina,*" comes a faint voice in my head. "*Regina, are you there?*"

"*Savage?*" I reply, rubbing my face. "*Are you alright? I'm alright. Is Minnie okay? Is everyone alright?*"

"*You sound far,*" he says in dismay. "*I want you here.*"

My body pangs in multiple places, and I try to stretch out my stiffened joints. My leg protests, and I grimace. But a hand, brown, tattooed and large, runs down the seam of new and old, and I sigh, looking up at him. Shadows linger about his head like a dark halo. Like one of the angels that fell from heaven to walk the dark path. Hot crimson lasers regard me.

"*I won't be long,*" I tell Savage. "*But tell me you guys all made it home in one piece.*"

"*Um...*" Savage sings. "*Maybe not fully in one piece.*"

I sit bolt upright. "*Who is it? Who did it?*"

Scythe's faint voice, hard as rock and dark with unhappiness, whispers into my mind. "*Regina. Yeti is injured. Everyone else is whole. Where and when can I pick you up?*"

My heart twists as I look down at Ghoul. Yeti should have been the last person injured. Poor Minnie. They'd only come to help us. Guilt twists in my gut. As if he knows what I'm feeling, Ghoul cocks his head, his fangs snapping down beyond his lower lip. He rises onto his elbows, and I give him a meaningful look.

"*Two days,*" I say. "*But it will be faster if I come to you.*" Dark brows furrow over flared nostrils.

"*Every day without you, I suffer.*" Scythe's voice is almost a hiss in my mind. "*Every day without you I want to kill someone, regina.*"

It almost makes me smile. "*I love you too. But you need to go to sea.*"

"*Xander is taking me tonight. The next day we will come for you, and I will not hear another word on it.*"

A low hiss comes from Ghoul's mouth, and I lean over to kiss one of his fangs.

"*Yes, sir,*" I say to Scythe.

"*Good girl.*"

I have to let out a sigh to release the tension as Scythe disconnects. Instinct makes me lie back down on Ghoul's chest. The basilisk lord is forced to lie flat as I press my weight against him.

A deep-rooted awareness in my marrow knows that these next moments I have with Ghoul might be my last chance to feel my fifth mate's skin on mine, so I close my eyes and simply listen to his sounds. Simply feel his warmth seeping through me. We sleep like that for the next day and a half. Serpent bodies are made to sort of hibernate during this time, so neither of us needs to use the bathroom. And while I need only sip water, Ghoul will only drink my venom.

I have so many burning questions, but from the tattoos on his face and body, I know that he cannot betray Mace, can't plot against him, or lie.

"My father worked so hard to make sure you wouldn't rise up against him," I muse, tracing an old sigil for 'obey'. "He knows you're more powerful than him."

Ghoul doesn't smirk at this. It's knowledge he's had for a long time.

"What were you doing with Raquel?" I ask.

"It's a funny story actually," he drawls. "I knew they are sworn to Scythe so I stole them away, thinking I could use them for one thing or another. But when I arrived here, the Silver Tail pack recognised them as their Regus so I had to turn Raquel over."

"The Silver Tails," I say, frowning down at him. "They're a nasty, feral lot aren't they?" I sigh. "So naturally my father is working with them. I hope Raquel has been okay."

Ghoul's laser bore into me. "Central mates are born to take charge of their pack." His thumbs rub circles in my thighs. "It's a heavy responsibility."

I can't deny that. "But that only means the rewards are greater."

Ghoul does not reply, and it hammers home the realisation: he doesn't think we can ever resolve this. He doesn't think he can ever be free.

I'm not so sure of this either.

For the rest of our time together, we sleep in each other's arms, talking very little, sometimes only looking. Ghoul holds me like he's waited a lifetime for it. Like he never wants to let me go. Because we both know what comes on the third day: he will likely never hold me again.

* * *

I can feel when the lock ends. It's a loosening. It's a deep sigh at the edge of all things. Sleeping on Ghoul's chest, I listen to him as I have this whole time. His heart dances solidly beneath my ear, and I focus on it, forcing it to go slower.

He fights it at first, a sudden hiss erupting from his mouth. But I lift my head to look up at that face, so new to me, yet already so familiar. My vision blurs, and I squeeze my fifth mate's heart under significant power. His body goes rigid with awareness, his eyes holding mine with the knowledge between us.

That because of his multiple blood oaths, I can't trust him.

That he has been ordered to kill me.

"Give me one last taste, snakelet," he whispers. "Your venom."

His eyes flutter and droop under my hold, but I force my fangs out and angle my mouth over his. Venom drips onto his tongue, and he swallows it gratefully as his heart slows even further.

"Thank you," I whisper. "For what you did for me when I was alone. The food. Everything."

His breath heaves. "You need to break my legs," he pants, his lungs trying to compensate for the lack of oxygen.

"No," I say softly.

"You need to maim me in a way that will make it impossible for me to follow for a few days." I don't want to hurt him in the same place my father's generals hurt him as a boy. "Do it, Aurelia," he grunts.

I clench my jaw before I strike, my fangs slicing through his throat and pumping him full of the venom that is unique to me. I dose him more than I did that first time—doubling then tripling it. His slow heart will make for slower processing speed.

"*Not enough*," he whispers into my mind. "*I'll heal, snakelet.*"

I think fast, my heart racing, the regina in me protesting against my chest. Tears fall down my cheeks as I shift my hand into a claw. "*I don't want to do it.*"

"*I know*," comes the reply. *I will have you wild, with your fangs out or not at all.* He'd meant what he'd said.

For the first time in three days, I lift myself off Ghoul, freeing his cock. It's still hard and wet when I come off him, the hemipenis aspect shrinking to allow me release. But the large, engorged head is still swollen, still beautiful. Despite everything, I miss it immediately.

But there is a time to mourn, and this is not it.

I grab his right foot and slice through his Achilles tendon, then do the same with his left. I grab Ghoul's paralysed head and summon my telekinetic power. My vision is gone to tears, my heart bled dry. But I know he's looking up at me as I crack his skull just enough to give us all time.

I leave my bungalow without looking back, because I just know if I do, I won't be able to walk away. I leave him there on my purple coverlet. Injured. Alone.

"Regina?" I almost cry hearing Scythe's voice in my mind.

"I'm at my bungalow," I rasp, clutching my broken heart. *"Come quickly."*

The dry grass crunches under my feet as I stumble across it towards Aunt Charlotte's old house. I wonder where my little cousins are because this house looks long abandoned. The daylight stings my eyes as I hurry into the shade of the house, but another set of feet, too light to be Scythe's or Xander's, crunch over the grass just ahead.

A female serpent in military uniform raises her gun, pointing it at my face. I squint at her. Dark hair, a pale, angry face.

"Natalia?" I rasp. "Is that you?" Three male serpents in the same uniform rush up from behind her, swinging their guns up, aiming them at my sorry ass.

"Hold!" Natalia shouts. Her finger hovers over the trigger, and then I notice the black mark on her hand. I'd seen it before: a cursive B. I couldn't guess what it meant before, but I can guess now.

"Captain, shoot her," one of the males behind her says. The others growl in assent.

"I said *hold,*" she snaps at them, not taking her eyes off me.

"You're *his* mate," she says accusingly.

"I'm his regina," I hiss back. Of course they'd all seen the video. All recognised me despite my attention to the disguise.

They all bristle in surprise. Natalia even takes a step back, despite her gun and training, her eyes widening. "We should have fucking known," she mutters. "Who else could match his power?" The others curse under their breaths. I notice they have black marks on their hands as well. "I haven't forgotten that you saved me from your mates," she grits out.

My brows can't help but rise. "They were wrong to do that," I say darkly, remembering the time Scythe, Savage and Xander held Natalia captive and tortured her in our suite. That was after Natalia and her cronies had jumped me and tried to cut off my mating mark, but still. She was just a girl, like me. At the time, anyway. Natalia grimaces at the memory, glancing over my shoulder at the bungalow behind me.

"She's probably been giving him her venom!" One of the soldiers snarls. "She's probably controlling him!"

"What?" I say vaguely. "How would—" It hits me then. How Ghoul has been demanding my venom. Since Drakos Estate he's been drinking from me. Does that mean he's been—"

"She's not a basilisk," Natalia says. "She's a Boneweaver, her venom can't work the same."

I stare at Natalia for a moment. They haven't seen footage of our fight yet. "He's injured in there," I say quickly. "You'd better go help him."

Her dark eyes flick to me again. She assesses me and seems to make a decision, lowering her gun. "Stand down."

"What the fuck—" the males begin, but she puts up a fist and they shut up. "She fucking saved me when she didn't have to. We owe her. Let her go."

"Thanks," I say, rubbing my neck.

"You're different from the girl I remember," she says, continuing on past me. "Get the fuck out of here, Boneweaver."

I don't need to be told twice.

Chapter 81

Savage

"There, there, sweet baby," I coo at Toastie. He's the wombat joey I was taking care of as ordered by the council all the way back when Damien Agnis tried to be headmaster of the academy. That didn't last long, and neither did my moment as father to Toastie, but I do miss him. Lyle decided that since I might cause trouble while I waited for my regina, I might as well help Zookeeper Rick with the pups.

"You're doing a great job, Savage," Rick says, chuckling as Toastie guzzles down his bottle. It has a really long teat on it, and I wonder if mummy wombat nipples are that long too. Seems a bit dangerous if you ask me.

"I got really good at it, Rick!" I say. "Also, I look after my regina really well, so that's given me a lot of important skills, you know."

"I bet it has," he says, nodding while he puts a kangaroo joey back into his pouch to sleep. "Reginas can be a right handful."

"Not mine," I say proudly, handing Toastie back to him. "She's so perfect."

He nods like he knows what I mean. "All creatures are perfect in their own way."

"Except Titus," I say quickly. "He needed to die for *sure*."

Zookeeper Rick tries to think of something to say, but honestly, it's better not to say anything at all in situations like this. I'm about to tell him so when I feel *her* as she crosses the boundary into the academy.

I spring to my feet like a kangaroo, and Zookeeper Rick jumps back in surprise. I grab his shoulders and shake him like a tree. "She's back!" There's nothing else left to do except run out the door of the wildlife centre at the back of the Academy. "I'll come for a feed later!" I shout over my shoulder.

I sprint around the buildings at the side of the school to the front, where I scan the sky for a sign of her. She likes to do a lap of the grounds every time she returns from somewhere so she can check everything is safe. She's amazing like that.

Finally, I spot her in eagle form, massive wings spread out as she glides along the academy wall. I jump in the air and wave both arms at her. "Regina!"

Everyone needs to know she's back. *"Lyle!"* I shout into our group chat. *"Where are you? Our regina's back!"*

"Coming," he says quickly, probably stuck in a class.

I don't even care where Scythe and Xander are, all I know is that I'm sprinting across the field to the wedge-tailed eagle now touching down on the grass. She gives a sharp cry, and it makes my legs pump faster.

Aurelia shifts into human form, and it's always so fun to see her human face pop out and her beak shrink away, except now she's smiling *and* crying, which is very confusing.

Now I'm smiling and crying too. "Regina!" I shout again.

She tests her legs, moving forward slowly before she starts running towards me, but I'm faster and barrelling into her. I scoop her up, and she laughs and sobs as I spin her around in the air. Her breasts bounce in my face, and I quickly release her so I can kiss her mouth a hundred times.

"I love you," I say. *"I missed you, and everything is always shit without you."* Suddenly I remember some things and hold her out at arm's length to check her body. "Is your vagina okay?" I widen my eyes as I look at her pussy area. I drop to my knees to take a better look. That bastard was in there a rudely long time.

"Savage!" Lyle's angry voice flies across the field. "That's a private activity!"

I kiss those sore lips anyway. "I'm going to carry you now because you've been through the wars." To Lyle, I privately say. *"Her pussy is sore, dammit! You don't know anything!"*

Lyle growls as he reaches us, tugging at the tie at his neck. "Regina, are you alright?" He reaches for her, and I let them kiss while I scowl.

My regina sighs, wiping at her cheeks as she inhales Lyle's scent. "Not really."

"Good girl for being so honest," Lyle says. "Now, take my jacket and let's get you inside."

We carefully put Aurelia inside Lyle's suit jacket, and I try not to look at her red-rimmed eyes or the dark circles, or listen to the growling of her belly. *"She's not injured,"* I tell Lyle. *"But she's hungry."*

"I'm going to ask her if she wants a medical exam later on, but it's not the right time. I'll wash her hair first. I think she's dehydrated."

"I'm going to find Henry." Xander's voice is strained in my head, and I don't know why. *"She'll want to know everything, but don't overwhelm her, Savage."*

"I won't!" I cry. But I've said it out loud, and Aurelia smiles weakly at me where she's being carried like a bride in Lyle's arms.

"Are you guys talking about me?" she says softly.

"Only good things," I reassure her. "Everyone keeps telling me off for some reason. Like *I'm* the problem, you know?"

"Where's that dragon-sized worm?" I ask the group chat. *"What if he comes after her right away?"*

"He won't," Scythe says. *"Aurelia made sure of that."*

I look at my regina again, but her eyes are on her fingers where she clutches them together. The backs of my eyes burn like a basilisk's, and I want to kill the fuckers that caused this. Instead, we get Aurelia upstairs and take care of her.

She is teary when we bathe her, so we sit her in the bathtub. Her hardworking legs are a bit weak today, and Xander sends his power into them, making her sigh and close her lids. Little tears slip out from under her eyes, and Scythe, who puts himself on the other side of Xander, kisses them away. I'm pretty sure he's collecting them for himself, but he's looking bright from his trip to the ocean, but all our faces are hard with worry.

I know my regina is so tired because she hasn't asked about Yeti and the Devi pack yet, and everyone jumps when she starts sleeping in the tub. Lyle quickly washes her hair, and we rinse her and get her right out to dry. She can barely stand up, and Lyle has to levitate her so we can dry all her parts and then put her pyjamas on.

"You need to drink water, regina," Scythe says as we tuck her into bed. "Otherwise I'm arranging for an IV."

She grumbles in a cutesy way while I carefully rub moisturiser into her forehead but when Lyle presses the straw up to her lips, she drinks the whole thing down. "Tired," she whispers.

"Food and loving," I say, tucking myself in next to her. "And then you'll be bouncing up and down again."

She nods tiredly as Xander hurries out to get proper food from the kitchens.

* * *

My poor chompy sleeps the whole day away and wakes up in the middle of the night, *starving* for food. Xander puts all the food we have on a tray and brings it to her in bed, and she downs every piece of meat and vegetable, then asks for pasta.

When she gets up to pee, we find a dark spot underneath her. Scythe almost leaps over me to sniff it, but we quickly realise she's not hurt, but just on her period again. She sighs dramatically, and we all go into the bathroom together. I bring the pads because I'm the pad monitor. Scythe gets his box of painkillers, and Xander is on wheat bag duty.

Once we've got her set up, she tears her T-shirt off and sleeps on my chest with only her knickers on, which is just brilliant for me. We all sleep until morning after that, except Xander, who has been patrolling every night with Beak and the new guards we've brought in. Mace has been creepily quiet, and it's put everyone on guard.

Somewhere in the night, my regina whispers, "I love you."

I don't know who she's talking to, but I'll take every gift she gives me. "I've always loved you, regina. From the first day I met you in Halfeather's dungeon."

"I'm scared," she whispers. "And tired. I think I've had enough, Savage."

Her cheek is so soft beneath my thumb, and I look down at her face, pointed downwards. She's taken too much on her shoulders. "It's not fair, regina," I whisper. "But we're gonna fix it if that's the last thing we do."

"That's what I'm worried about."

Chapter 82

Aurelia

I wake up the only way I want to, cocooned between three mates. Xander is in the shower, steam coiling through the open door, the sound of the water like a pleasant drum in my ears. Scythe and Savage are on either side of me, and Lyle is hugging my legs in his sleep, a discarded jar of Tiger Balm off to the side. The dull pain in my stomach has returned, and I need to use the bathroom.

Carefully, I extract myself from between my mates, but it only takes seconds for everyone to be awake and on alert. Is this our life now? Looking over our shoulder at every turn?

Once I've taken care of hygiene and eating, Lyle takes my empty plate, and Scythe sits down next to me at the dining table. "We have a lot to talk about, regina," he says, ice-blue eyes glittering in awareness and observation of me.

"I agree." I put my hand over his. "Can I see my friends first, please? I need to catch up with them."

His lips twitch, and he caresses my cheek with the back of his fingers. "You don't need permission from me for anything, you know that."

Tiredly, I smile back. Xander and Savage offer to accompany me down to the school. It's mid-morning by now, and we follow Minnie's scent, something like sweet incense and cardamom, through the vacant corridors to a row of rooms I've never been in before.

In the lead, I peek through a square glass window cut into the door, and I see that it's not a classroom but a counselling room. Sabrina, Minnie, Stacey, Beak, and a group of students I only know by sight sit in a circle of chairs. There are three boxes of tissues on the table.

Savage points to an A4 printed sign next to the door. "M-O-T-F," he spells out proudly. "I don't know that word, regina." But all the breath has emptied from my lungs and I find I can't get any in. My vision blurs again, and I clutch at my stomach to try to prevent from throwing up my breakfast. "We can come back later," Savage says in alarm.

Xander has gone stiff next to me, and I frown, trying to blink my tears away. "No, I think I should go in. Meet me back here later."

"I want to come in too," Savage says quietly.

"Mates of the Fallen," Xander mutters. "That's what it stands for, Savage."

"But you haven't lost a mate," Savage protests.

It feels like I have. Xander steps away from me, and the corridor suddenly feels cold. "Let her go, Savage. It might help."

"You go," Savage's voice is suddenly irate. "I'll wait for my regina here."

"Very well." Then Xander is gone.

I push open the door, feeling like my head is stuffed with wool. Like something is trying to drag me through the earth and trap me there. My friends all look up as I come in. Minnie stands and comes over to take my hand.

Roland, one of our class counsellors, waves at me. "Aurelia! Good to see you. This is our Mates of the Fallen meeting group. Are you joining us?"

I tuck a hand around my waist. "Am I allowed to?"

"It's not just for beasts who have mates that have passed away," Beak says quickly. "There are many types of loss."

"That's right," Roland confirms. "There are other reasons why members of a pack cannot be together."

Minnie whispers up at me. "You can just sit and listen if you like." Shame creeps up my spine as they make space for me. They start a general chat, because I didn't even know my friends met in a group like this.

"We've spoken before about how grief can come in waves," Roland says. "Sometimes it'll hit you harder in different seasons of your life. Other times, you might be triggered by seeing something that reminds you of that person."

"Mine feels like it's there all the time," Sabrina says. "Like a heavy jacket I can't take off." The group shifts. "I didn't know my mates when they died, so I keep wondering about what my life could have looked like. It's everyday things, like eating dinner or going to bed. There's only one toothbrush at the sink. Only one set of clothes. *Everything* is triggering."

Beak nods in agreement. "I feel like there's too much empty space in my life now and nothing to fill it with. Nothing can match up to my mates."

"Nothing will replace them," Roland agrees. "But you can certainly fill your life with positive things to—"

"That's bullshit, Roland, and you know it," Sabrina deadpans. "You think crochet is going to *fill my time?*"

"It won't, Sabrina," Beak says. "But we don't get a choice. Either you let the loss make you into a living corpse or you try to spend your days doing what good you can."

"That's a bit harsh," Minnie admonishes. "Do you think the surrogate program is working for you, Sabrina?"

Our leopard shrugs. "It helps, but only because I didn't know my mates. I don't know if it would work for beasts who knew their mates well."

Minnie gnaws on her lip, and I watch her from the corner of my eye. Scythe had only told me that the Devi Pack had come to save them, and Yeti had been mangled in the process, but I don't know the details. But there's a dark sort of energy I'm sensing from her, and I need to know where it's coming from.

"My rex is still rejecting me," Stacey says, after some silence from the group. "He's giving me all sorts of reasons, but mostly he won't talk at all." She gestures to her arm, and her voice grows thick. "I don't even know if he feels bad about shooting me."

"Would you even want to be his mate after he did that?" Beak says, his mouth twisting with distaste. "No central mate should be able to come back from hurting the people they're supposed to look after."

Suddenly, I want to vomit again. "Sorry," I blurt out, shooting to my feet. No one says anything as I make a beeline for the door, my arms around myself to stop my sudden shivering. I shut the door behind me, and take three steps down the corridor before pressing my body against the wall and closing my eyes. My mates are not dead. Ghoul is not dead. Ghoul is still here. If I'd accidentally killed him, I would know; I was so careful about his injuries.

"Regina." Strong hands wrap around me, and I know it's Savage without looking, but I don't feel like I deserve a hug right now.

The door opens and shuts behind me. "Aurelia?" Minnie's trembling voice makes me whirl around again. She clutches shaking hands in front of her and takes a deep breath. Alarm bells ring in my mind, and I rush to her. "I killed Titus," she blurts out on a sob. "I killed him for attacking Yeti and—Goddess, I think I'm going to faint again."

I grab her, shoving her body against mine. "Fuck, Min. I'm so sorry. Just breathe."

Gertie, her yellow nimpin, hoots a beat in Minnie's ear, reminding her to breathe slowly. Titus is dead. I should feel relief or shock about this, but instead, I feel nothing. Like the emotions inside of me are living on fumes.

"I think Sabrina hates me now," Minnie says, her voice muffled against my shirt.

Pulling away, I wipe her tears with my thumbs. "She hates everything at the moment. He forced your hand. She can't understand that right now. Yeti could have died."

"He would have," Savage says, keeping his distance by the wall. "Titus would've gone for it if you hadn't gotten between them, Min."

Minnie lifts her head to nod at him gratefully. "I think you're right. I just don't like any of it."

"Wait until you hear what I did," I say darkly. "You should

come to my meeting with Scythe. Distract yourself from *your* problems with *my* problems."

My best friend and I smile weakly at each other. "Yeti doesn't want visitors at the moment, otherwise I would have taken you to see him first. They're going to have to do more surgery on his leg, and he's mourning his foot right now."

I grimace at the thought. Yeti was the head of the felines at the academy. Missing a foot is a death sentence for beasts in the wild. His gait will never be the same again. He'll never be able to run properly. The Clawsons had done such horrible damage to both Minnie's and my own family.

We walk back to the animus dorms in silence until Savage shares his thoughts with us. "Shame he can't turn into a starfish," my wolf sighs. "I went to see him yesterday and took a helium balloon. I drew a get-well card with a wooden stool and a smiley face."

"Why a wooden stool?" I ask.

"Because they only need three legs."

We make it back to our suite, where Scythe, Xander and Lyle are waiting for us. We sit down at the table, and they tell me exactly what happened after I left with Ghoul. The story is ghastly. The fact that my father has rounded up the children of Serpent Court and is training them up as soldiers is shocking. Teaching them to separate their animuses and animas like he learnt to is something I never expected.

"How is he planning on using them?" Minnie asks.

Scythe and I exchange a look. "My father was willing to use *me* as a teenager," I say. "I have no doubt he'll use them in every distasteful way he can."

"We can't kill hatchlings," Savage says earnestly. "That's the problem."

I shake myself of an awful feeling of dread. "Ghoul didn't reveal all that much during our time...together." I say slowly. "But it's clear to me he's been *trying* to help me for a very long time." Everyone is quiet.

"Well, he didn't do a very good job, did he?" Savage says angrily. "All those things you went through? Where was his help with that?"

"He was still sworn to my father," I say calmly. "I've seen the markings on his face. They are ancient enslavement markings, meaning he cannot defy, betray, or plot against my father in any way. He can't reveal his secrets either. What he could do was limited. He's been bending the rules as much as he can. I had to—" Nausea roils up my throat again. "I had to hurt him to make sure he wouldn't come after me for some time."

"Oh, Lia," Minnie says, squeezing my hand. She is the only person in the world who understands what I'm going through. Stacey's face flashes in my mind for a moment, but it passes.

"It's fine," I lie. "I mean, I'm sure he'll be *fine*, I just...He asked me if I'd kill him if we needed to." I have to swallow. "When I told him I'd put him down if it came to it, I... saw *pride* in his eyes." I look at Scythe in disbelief. "He was...proud of me."

"That fucker," Xander mutters.

Minnie frowns. "He's confusing."

"I think he gets off on being confusing," Lyle says. "There are clearly things he knows that we don't, Aurelia."

I nod at my lion. "One thing is clear to me for now. We need to talk to Eugene."

Chapter 83

Aurelia

Eugene has been roosting with Stacey and Yeti on alternate days. So when Savage fetches him that evening, he arrives trailing an eager Stacey. "I'm happy for any distraction right now," she says as I sit her down with a cup of tea. "Etienne and I are making zero progress, and I don't think he even wants to see me, but I go down with Beak anyway."

"Make sure you never go alone," I say worriedly. "There's something in the air that's making monsters out of beasts."

She nods sadly and pats the arm her rex shot. "I'm not going to forget this anytime soon."

Savage sets Eugene on the dining room table, though Xander mutters and insists on wiping his feet first. We all wait patiently until Eugene is ready. He stares out at us all, his bedazzled goggles missing some diamantés now that Connor hasn't been here to replace them.

"Eugene," Scythe says, sitting at the head of the table. Eugene's claws clack as he turns himself to look at his boss. "Do you remember that you are sworn to me?"

Eugene cocks his head before ducking it. Savage makes an excited noise before fetching a piece of A4 white paper and drawing three words, surrounded by uneven circles—YES, NO, and UNSURE.

Scythe continues. "And do you remember what happened in the days before you swore yourself to me?"

Eugene pauses, glancing at me, then Savage, then Xander before pecking the NO circle.

I sit back in my seat. "Poultry are known for memory loss," I say. "They think it's a side effect to do with the fast-forward flashes they get. And I'm guessing he's been a bird for so long that it's eaten up his memories."

Eugene pecks YES.

I perch on the edge of my seat. "Do you remember the basilisk, General Ghoul of Serpent Court?"

YES.

"He let slip that you might know some things that will help us solve a mystery. Ghoul was at Halfeather House before it burned down. But we don't understand how he got there. Do you know anything about that?"

UNSURE.

I glance at Scythe, nodding for him to continue. "Eugene," my shark says. "Do you give us consent to look through your memories? To see if there is something in there that can help us?"

YES.

"Wait, you guys can do that?" Stacey breathes.

"It's not normally done," Savage says. "But between my telepathy, Scythe's psychic powers, and my regina's Boneweaver powers, it's possible."

I nod, gesturing to Eugene to come to me. "It shouldn't hurt." Eugene hops into my lap, and I hold him close to my chest. Scythe and Savage pull their seats on either side of me and place their hands on Eugene's back.

"Gently," Savage reminds everyone. "He's only got a widdle brain."

Eugene lets out a warble that sounds like something in between "no I don't," and "yes, exactly."

We go one at a time, with Savage connecting first. Scythe goes second, and I feel his psychic power like a beam of moonlight on a cold evening, passing me and heading into Eugene. I join them last, closing my eyes and trying to connect to the bird before me. Because I'm still new to my shark powers, I let Scythe take the lead.

"Eugene." Scythe's gravelly voice sounds far away to me. "I want you to think about your first memory of Halfeather House. Then we'll try to follow a thread from there."

Eugene makes a sound in his throat, and I feel it vibrating through my arms

The image comes to me like telepathic images do, not quite as clear as a TV screen, but vibrant enough to make out all the moving parts.

Chapter 84

Eugene

Just over a year ago

I peer through the bars of my cage into Mr Halfeather's office. They've set my cage over the fireplace so I'm in easy reach, but it also means I get a good view of everyone who comes in and out. Tonight, Mr Halfeather welcomes a tall male with red hair, a white suit, and matching glasses. I peer at him from between my bars because his scent is very interesting.

Halfeather continues a conversation from outside. "Not even curious?"

"I refuse to touch it," the redhead replies, wrinkling his nose. "Mace will have to pay me a fool's ransom to get me *near* that shadow demon of the abyss."

Halfeather chuckles. "Forever the elitist, Lord Agnis. Your own collection has always been a delight to behold."

Lord Agnis sniffs. "I certainly have neither poultry nor serpents in there, but I have a new shoebill stork who needs breaking in. You must come down for the event next week. Mace is coming."

"I can't wait." They sit on the chairs near the dark fireplace, and Mr Halfeather pours glasses of alcohol.

"Is my rooster ready?" Lord Agnis asks.

Halfeather looks possessively at me, and I can't help but fluff my wings. "Yes, but not this one. I have another one for you out the back."

"Can't be too careful these days with dirty basilisks slithering about."

Halfeather chuckles. "Such a crude feat of nature. Making the rooster the basilisk's kryptonite. This one was apparently never good at cockfighting, but his crow is the loudest I've come across to date, so Mace found a use for him. It's always easier when they give themselves over to *contracted employment*."

Lord Agnis snorts, glancing at me. "Well, if this basilisk dies in his cell, we won't have to worry, will we? If you cannot heal him, I daresay no one can. Perhaps this is why they died out in the first place."

Mr Halfeather gulps down his wine. "Mace thinks he has one last trick up his sleeve. He's going to hold it against me at cost price, but that estranged daughter of his is a talented healer."

"That little female who was so weak he never married her out of spite? *Her* offspring?"

Mr Halfeather smiles a secret smile. "*I* would've married her."

Lord Agnis scoffs in disgust. "You always liked them fragile."

"But not *this* one." Mr Halfeather grins outright. "She has real power."

"What do you know that I don't?"

Mr Halfeather leans forward in his chair. "Mace is going to contact you soon, so you may as well hear it from me. Athena's daughter inherited the stronger Boneweaver gene, and she has *just* come of age for the market."

Lord Agnis gapes over his glass. "Don't be stupid!"

Mr Halfeather leans back in his chair with a satisfied smile. "If she's any good, I'll buy her off him. I could use another healer around here."

"Make a deal with a snake and you'll live to regret it."

"There's a Boneweaver of old on the table, Lord Agnis!" Mr Halfeather claps gleefully. "Think of it! Boneweaver healing on tap? My phone will ring off the hook, I just know it. She'll pay her investment back tenfold. Cancers, autoimmune diseases, magical diseases—the scope could be endless! Mace never let me do more than draw blood on Athena; he keeps her locked down tight. But I would have free rein over this girl."

My mind latches on to those words. This Boneweaver is a powerful healer who can fix all kinds of ailments. Maybe she can fix my beloved's illness. I *must* find her.

Lord Agnis shakes his head, the crimson strands glistening. "I'll believe it when I see it. Until then, nothing's worth a contract with Mace. There's probably a curse on the damned paper. Make sure you check for any strange markings on it."

Halfeather sits back in his chair, smiling into his wineglass. "She'll be arriving tomorrow, and you can bet your bottom dollar that I'll be doing my own checks."

Chapter 85

Aurelia

"I almost wish I weren't privy to that discussion," I say wryly, my own memories of Halfeather's office coming into sharp focus. "But in this memory, Ghoul is already inside Halfeather House. We need to know what came before."

"We'll need to pry a little," Scythe says. "Hold Eugene still."

Chapter 86

Eugene

The serpent king holds my cage in his arms as we get out of the car. We're at a big white mansion that smells of eagles and is called Halfeather House. A hooked-nose male in black robes rushes out of the back door. "Your Majesty." He bows at us. "Is this him?"

They're not talking about me, but behind me to the stretcher being carried out of the steel truck. On it lies the male they call General Ghoul. My new, dangerous charge. But right now, he's only a big man on a stretcher, killer eyes closed. Shadows wrap around his body like a mummy, despite the bright sun, and all we can see is the scary white mask on his face.

I puff up, filling my lungs in case the basilisk opens his eyes and tries to kill us all. The king of serpents strides up to stand next to Halfeather, watching the basilisk be carried towards the back of the house. We follow closely, and I do my job and keep my eyes fixed on the General.

"That is my basilisk, yes," the serpent king says.

"I take it your...experiments were not fruitful."

The serpent king is silent for a moment. "A little too fruitful, perhaps. I won't be sure until he wakes up, which is why his recovery is so crucial."

"Of course."

"None of my methods have worked," the serpent king, Mace Naga, says. "He's been static for days."

"I'll try everything," Mr Halfeather reassures us.

"If you fail, there are other avenues," Mr Naga says. "A young healer you may be interested in."

"Are you finally entering the skin trade?" Mr Halfeather asks, brows shooting up. "I've been preaching to you for so *very* long."

"I may make an exception for this one," Mr Naga says. "I will send you details the usual way."

Mr Halfeather stops before entering the house. "I'll take care of him from here, Mace."

The king of serpents bristles for a moment as if offended. Finally, he nods once and hands me over to a security guard called Beak. I am carried inside next to the basilisk, and we enter a lift that travels under the house.

"What *have* you done to yourself?" Mr Halfeather says, leaning down to sniff his new patient. "If I don't figure it out, Mace will hold it against me for the rest of my sorry days. I bet it hurt him to bring you to me to start with."

When the doors open, we enter a dark dungeon that smells of blood, sweat and steel. I don't like it at all, but I have an important job to do. I keep my eyes on my charge, watching his face for any sign of waking up. But he seems dead to the world like he has since the...incident.

Mr Halfeather opens a big steel door that covers one of the cells. "Set him in there, right on the stone. We'll work through the door. I'm not taking any chances with this psycho. Any time you open the door, bring the rooster with you. Take no chances."

Eyes gleam from the other cells.

"Give us some food, Halfeather!" calls a wolf from next door. "I'm wasting away over here!"

"You can wait, you foul creature!" Halfeather spits in a way that makes me rustle my feathers. "Don't think I forgot I lost two vultures to your *cursed* canines!"

"But I didn't eat any vultures," a beast with a heavier snarl says from the cell opposite the wolf. "They say it's bad luck not to feed a dragon."

Halfather scoffs dramatically and leads us out of the dungeon.

Chapter 87

Aurelia

"It's true," Savage says. "Those vultures didn't even taste any good either."

"How long were you in there for?" I frowned. "I don't think you ever told me."

"Two weeks by that point," Scythe says evenly. "I was waiting to see if something eventuated and..." He brushes my cheek. "You did."

I smile at him softly, remembering the first day I walked into that dungeon. "I didn't see Eugene while I was there."

"They only brought him in if they were opening the steel door," Scythe says. "You arrived just a few days after the initial attempts. Halfeather began to get impatient."

"We need to go back further," I say. "What happened at Naga House the preceding week?"

Eugene *boks* in assent.

Chapter 88

Eugene

The bars of this cage press tightly on my feathers. It's a battery cage for hens, and I'm jostled about as we're carried through big hallways and rooms. In the final room, an office, a tall skinny male writes at a desk. His back is rod straight, the corners of his mouth turned down like an aristocrat. I recognise him immediately as the cobra king.

"This is the one, Your Majesty," the serpent holding me says. "An unusually strong crow. He's vaccinated and has passed all blood tests. I have his contract of employment here."

"Very good," the serpent king says. "Set him up here so I can take a good look at him. What is his name?"

"Eugene, Your Majesty."

I fluff up my wings. I *do* have the strongest crow around. But where are my mates? I want to ask where they've gone because they definitely aren't here with me as they should be. I don't get to ask any questions because I cannot shift inside this cage.

The serpent king nods at me, scanning the working contract I signed. "Alright, Eugene. Here is our agreement." I feel like his eyes are seeing through my feathers right into my blood, and I want to shrink away from him. "If you complete this little job for me, I will help your little mate with the cancer she has. There are some new treatments my scientists can try. All you have to do is crow when you are given the command. Very simple. Can you do that?"

I crow in agreement. There is a chance this basilisk will kill me, but for my precious girl, I would do anything.

Later that night, as I'm sleeping in my cage in Mace Naga's office, with Mace Naga himself working late on his computer, there is a knock at the door. "Come in," Mace drones.

The door opens to reveal a big scary man with white face paint in the pattern of a skull. He's the biggest beast I've ever seen, and even the room seems to shrink in fear around him. Instantly, I know what he is, my senses going on high alert. I snap my attention to the king to wait for my signal to crow.

"Ah, are you finally going to kill me, Your Majesty?" The basilisk chuckles, gesturing at me with a black-gloved hand. He has a deep, commanding voice, and I look between the two males, wondering why this massive beast submits to the thinner one.

The king of serpents doesn't smile. "Have you completed your collections for today?"

"I did, and I think there's enough for you to control every politician in the state by now."

The serpent king nods and gestures to the couches on the other side of the office. "I want you to take a look at those old texts over there, General. I take it you remember Sanskrit from your studies?"

The basilisk winks at me before striding to the couches and sitting down, long legs stretching out. He holds up an old, yellowed book with leather wrappings. I can see the writing is in a language I don't understand, and the pictures are so dark I can't make wing from tail. The room is silent as the basilisk studies the pages. I watch him carefully. These two beasts might be allies, but there seems to be a tension between them.

"Are you capable?" The way the serpent king asks this makes me look at him. It sounds like a taunt. A challenge. He must be very brave to be talking to the basilisk like that.

The basilisk general sits back on the couch as if he's not bothered by this, casually drumming his fingers along the top of the old book. "Theoretically. It's quite *large*, isn't it? Big as a house. Enough to talk to hundreds of people and maybe more."

"You doubt your power?" the king challenges again. My head snaps between the two of them like I'm at a tennis match.

"Never," the basilisk replies simply. "Only technique. If I can do it on a small scale, a large scale shouldn't be too much harder, surely."

Mace nods slowly. "Is there a possibility someone will sense it?"

"Only basilisks and the newly dead play in the shadow realm, and dead beasts can't tattle."

"So you've told me. How much time do you need to prepare?"

The basilisk scratches his neck. "Tomorrow morning will do. Is this why the rooster has made an appearance?"

"We cannot be too sure."

The basilisk smirks as if this pleases him.

* * *

When night falls the next day, we drive in a truck an hour away from the main house. Then I'm carried by the basilisk lord himself to a big, empty warehouse. I happily breathe in the air after being cooped up for days inside. My legs ache from this constant sitting position, but they won't let me out except to use the toilet. I'm set on the floor, a little way from the basilisk and the serpent king, who stand far apart on the concrete floor. It's the three of us, everyone else has been told to stay outside.

The basilisk plants his heavy boots and looks around. "Ready?" he asks the serpent king.

Mace Naga nods, his eyes lit up with excitement. There is silence. Then—

I feel it before we see it—a great, dark power and a feeling of dread. Such great dread that it takes me by the throat so I can only blink in terror at the sight in front of me.

A wind picks up, ruffling my feathers. A scary sound, like an ancient groan, travels through the air. It picks up, now like a jet engine. I squint through it, cringing against the roar in my cage. I cannot meet my death here! I have mates to look after! What will they do without me? Before I can crow, something changes.

A dark power, black as night and shifting like a shadow, comes directly from the basilisk, spiralling upwards from his body like a tornado. It reaches the ceiling of the warehouse, where it expands like a disc of pulsing black cloud. Like it's a living, breathing thing of pure evil.

I want to crow, but the serpent king isn't giving me the signal. He's simply looking up into the black swirling power like he's seen the Wild Mother herself. His black duster whips violently in the wind, but it doesn't bother him. He is focused. I think this dark hurricane is where we go to meet our maker. It grows bigger, to the size of a car, spreading the feeling of dread inside of me.

"Told you!" the basilisk lord shouts above the roar of the wind. "It just needs to be bigger to take in the non-serpent animalia population in the state."

My mind is seized with fear. The end of the world is coming, and Mace Naga is bringing it! He wishes to kill us all!

"It'll just take me more—" The basilisk chokes, clutching his chest.

"Ghoul?" Mace shouts.

"Oh," the basilisk says. He holds up a finger as if to explain, but his power sucks down into his body like a funnel.

"Eugene!" the serpent king roars.

I breathe in a mighty breath and crow as loudly as I can. The shadows tremble and vibrate, but they don't stop their funnel down, down, down into Ghoul's now rigid body. I crow as loudly as I can and the shadows travel down his back in a spiral. I think I'm helping but I can't be sure.

The basilisk falls flat on his back like a dead weight and before his eyes close, they turn to me, and a voice like midnight whispers in my mind. *"Find Aurelia Boneweaver, Eugene. Find the Boneweaver. Save the world."*

He does not move again. The wind is gone. There is only silence in the air, broken by Mace Naga as he shouts for help.

Chapter 89

Scythe

Aurelia calmly sets Eugene on the table and rises. Her face is like stone as she stands and walks over to the window, crossing her arms, her eyes unseeing, unblinking as she processes this information. Savage's mouth has dropped open as he stares around the room like a revolving clown at a carnival.

"What did you see?" Xander asks irritably.

"It seems," I say carefully, not wanting to make Stacey—or anyone else, for that matter—panic. "Mace Naga is bringing an apocalypse. He plans to kill us all."

Aurelia turns around. "And by 'all,' Scythe means every non-serpent. In the state, presumably. It'll be an...*annihilation.*"

Xander scoffs. "Using the basilisk?"

"Basilisk power is, essentially, instant death," I explain. "At their highest escalation, they seem to have the power to destroy en masse."

"Mace has been making Ghoul practice this technique," Aurelia says grimly. "But it seemed to turn on him the first time he tried it. And that's what landed him unconscious." Aurelia waves her hand down her own spine. "His own power was wrapped around his spine, suffocating it."

Lyle frowns where he leans against the wall. "It almost seems like a self-preservation technique from his animus. Stopping him from completing it *and* getting to meet you in the process. Perhaps he knew you would eventually be called in to assist."

Aurelia nods. "That's what I'm thinking. In one of his memories, he saw me getting ready to leave town." It also explains the second warehouse. They needed a place for him to try this new skill.

"I can't believe Mace wants to get rid of us!" Savage says. "I mean, *every* other animalia except serpents?"

Xander scowls at the room. "Think about it. It would give him the highest position above the humans. There'd be no one to challenge him, and he'd have free rein over the population."

"My father is nothing if not ambitious," Aurelia says. But when her eyes meet mine, I'm delighted to see they glitter at this new challenge. "He doesn't expect anyone else to know about it. He killed Halfeather for what tiny information he knew about me. There has to be a way to stop it. Ghoul told Eugene to find me."

I think back to the hyena matriarch. She had been right. Whatever information she had led her to a similar conclusion. But now she, Katerina, Damien Agnis, Flores Drakos, and Tiberius Clawson are all dead. The big players are out of his way. One by one, Mace had eliminated his so-called allies, who were really enemies. Pitted them against one another until they wiped themselves out. The ones he didn't kill were mind-controlled by basilisk venom. Aurelia must have been thinking the same thing.

"We're the only ones who can stop him," she says.

"I need a fucking drink," Xander mutters, striding away.

Savage possessively takes up Eugene, stroking his head frills. "Poor bugger saw all that and it fucked him up in the head, I just know it. He's delicate."

"It's lucky he *did* see it," I say, eyeing my regina, who hasn't moved from the window.

As if she feels my eyes on her, Aurelia turns around. "He was the key all along."

"I want to know what you are thinking," I say, denying myself from going to her. I know her well enough now to remember that she needs space in times like this.

Lyle shifts uncomfortably. "What's anyone supposed to think upon discovering their father wants to kill everyone they love?"

Aurelia smiles wryly. "I think I've always known it would come to this. Not this specifically," she sighs. "But something like it. He always had such hatred in his heart for those who are not like him."

Savage sways gently with Eugene, and the rooster closes his eyes with the motion. The bird's aura is a sickly green, but light in colour, meaning it's not physical but mental. He too has been affected by seeing those memories.

"We need to talk to Minnie," I say.

Aurelia frowns. "Why her specifically?"

My lips quirk as I look at her. "She killed Titus in front of all his males, Aurelia. They bent the knee to her. Minnie is considered the head of the tigers. Word has spread. Xander has distributed the security camera footage across social media. And with Ablo Obon gone, she has sway over the entire feline court. They wait for her in one of my safe houses."

"Minnie is queen?" Aurelia whispers.

"Well, it's certainly not me," Lyle says a little too happily. "There are other candidates, but a clear execution won't be disputed by anyone."

"Especially with Marduk and Yeti at her side." Aurelia nods. "How the tables turn."

* * *

Our meeting with Minnie and Marduk goes as expected. Marduk rubs his beard and nods. "He was always crazy, that Mace Naga. You can see it in a beast's eyes, shark-friend."

"Indeed," I say. I see it in my own eyes near daily.

Marduk gives me a look that says he knows what I'm thinking. "He has no regina to calm him and make him see sense. There is only one way from here."

"He needs to die," Aurelia says flatly.

Minnie takes her best friend's hand. "How do we even go about stopping this...*thing* from happening? Ghoul cannot be stopped?"

"He doesn't want to do this, but he's bound to be my father's slave." Aurelia shakes her head. "I don't know what to do." The way she looks at me breaks my heart. Her fifth mate, the cause of her problems and yet also the solution. I want to rid her of her problems and give her everything she desires, but this is going to be a difficult puzzle to solve.

Aurelia suddenly leaps to her feet, her eyes searching the air in front of her as if she's using a different sense. "Dragon. There's a dragon headed towards Animus Academy."

Chapter 90

Aurelia

My senses go on high alert, and something I cannot fully comprehend demands my attention with teeth and claws. My instinct to protect my nest and mates forces my canines to come to the front, and I snarl as I rush out of Minnie's suite and down the corridor. Scythe is in the lead behind me, closely followed by Savage and the Devi pack.

Another dragon has never come to Animus Academy before. Except for Xander, but the school recognised him as my mate from the start. So who is *this*?

I don't even bother heading down the stairs. My blood is boiling, my head is raging, and I wave my hand before the window at the end of the corridor, and it smashes under a telekinetic blast. Shifting into an eagle, I spear out of the window and aim towards the front of the school. Once I've gained good height, I shift into a dragon and charge out of the protective dome.

"Where are you, Xander!" Savage calls in the group chat.

"Why?" Xander snarls into our heads.

I can't see the dragon yet, but I circle the school, knowing they will be close, or hidden. Beak appears out of one of the guard towers and lets out a shrill cry, and I change directions to guard westward. I see mighty wings, and a tiny bag hanging on a claw. She's difficult to spot at first because of the colour of her scales, a brilliant yellow, brighter than I saw her last at Drakos Estate.

"*Aurelia?*" she asks. "*Is that you?*"

"*Stand down!*" I shout to everyone in the vicinity. "*It's Selena Drakos!*"

We meet at the school gates, Selena's weight shaking the ground as she lands before shifting into human form. She covers her slender, pale figure with a form-fitting forest green silk robe that buttons down on the right side.

"It's so good to see you," I say, pulling her into my arms. "I didn't know when we'd get the chance again."

Selena places both hands on either side of my face, smiling down at me, her golden eyes warm as she smiles. "I'm so sorry I couldn't come sooner, Aurelia. Truly I am."

"Sissy!" Xander charges through the school gates, and I get out of the way so they can embrace. I pretend not to notice as they share a few moments and Selena sheds a tear or two. Xander asks about his mother and the hatchlings. Selena marvels at what remains of The Collector's head on the gate.

"We are all well," she says as I lead them onto the academy grounds. "Though I don't think I can say the same for you here at Boneweaver Estate."

I whirl around and gape at her audacity. But Selena only chuckles. "Well, this is *your* stronghold, is it not, Aurelia? It's protected like it's yours, in any case."

Pinching the bridge of my nose, I sigh. "You're not wrong."

"Rarely am I wrong."

Xander laughs through his nose. "We have a lot to catch you up on."

But as it turns out, Selena's visit is also to relay news of her own. We sit in the empty academy dining hall, which seems to Xander and me, the cleanest part of the school in which to receive a noble dragon lady. Selena takes out an unadorned wooden box from her bag. It has Xander's name on it, inked in a simple black stamp. "This was delivered to us by a very frightened courier."

Xander goes rigid as he accepts it, his nostrils flaring as he detects the scent. I detect it too late, and my dragon opens the box, nodding before he turns it around to show me. Set upon plain crumpled kraft paper is a blood-red stone, split cleanly in half by a giant claw.

"It's a formal dragon divorce from Francesca," he says. "In the traditional way. We were never *legally* married as dragons are above human marriage laws, but this is as clear as a divorce contract."

I raise my brows, but don't know exactly what to say. Thankfully, Selena knows better. "Congratulations, brother," she says, patting his hand. "At least she didn't try to kill you like I did with my husband."

Xander and I both choke on air. I cover my mouth to stifle the snort trying to get out. "We'll consider ourselves lucky then."

Xander clinks me with his mug of coffee in cheers. "Hear, hear."

* * *

Selena insists on visiting the academy library, and there we call the rest of my mates to meet her. Savage and Lyle delicately shake her hand while Scythe bows formally to her.

"How I've longed to meet Xander's soul-bonded brothers." Her eyes glisten with emotion. "I am pleased to see you don't actually have blood in your teeth like the rumours mention, Savage." She smiles at him.

"It's often enough," Xander says darkly.

"But these days it's Aurelia with the bloody teeth," Savage says proudly, hoisting up Eugene on his hip. "We're very proud of her."

"As am I," Selena says. "It's the second reason why I've come here." She pins me with a look. "There is much we don't know about your order. You are the last, Aurelia. But the old book I loaned Xander spoke of the ancient Boneweavers and the world they came from. There *must* be more information out there. There was word of a unicorn."

My heart thumps rapidly in my chest. "Lorian, yes. We don't know where he and Celeste went after we rescued him. It's like they disappeared—"

She nods. "From this world."

"You know?"

"The Drakos lords collected many old texts," she says. "There is a lot under the estate if a person is willing to look. But...did you manage to touch him?"

I sigh. "I couldn't do it. He'd been through so much already under Katerina, touching him felt like a crime."

"A shame," she says. "If you could travel between worlds, we may have gained something."

An old power, a distant memory, brushes over my skin, and I shiver, glancing toward the end of the library. Lyle glances in the same direction but lets me take the lead. "You speak of knowledge under Drakos Estate," I say. "I think Animus Academy also has... something underneath it too. I came across it one day and asked it to go away."

Selena's brows shoot up, as do Xander's, and they look so much like siblings in that moment. "You've never mentioned this," my dragon says darkly.

I scratch my neck. "It was a bit...well, *creepy* is the only word."

"The fact that you have a basilisk as a mate and you still find something else creepy is hilarious." Selena chuckles under her breath. "You know you have to show us now."

"It's over here!" Savage says enthusiastically, marching with Eugene under his arm to the back wall. We all file down, past the stacks to the black wall. I recount my steps, going roughly to the middle of the wall.

"Ashfang?" I ask tentatively. "Are you still there? Remember how I told you to disappear? I'd like you to come out now."

Power moves along the black brick, raising the tiny hairs on my body before the door fades into existence, black wood under the curved stone. Ashfang's broad face blinks down at me, eerily alert above the arched door. Savage gasps dramatically while Scythe and Xander unconsciously huddle close to my side. Lyle growls.

"Greetings, Lady Boneweaver," Ashfang drones. "Dark are the times."

"Sure are!" Savage exclaims. Eugene gives a croon.

"Everyone, this is Ashfang," I say quietly. "He is keeper of the door."

"Hello, sir," Selena says.

Ashfang bows in his mortar. "My lady dragon."

"Shall we open it?" Selena asks, raising her brows at me.

"It's not pleasant," I warn. "And nobody should be going in." I glare at Savage so he knows not to go bouncing anywhere. "Ash-fang? Kindly open up."

The gargoyle bows again, and the wooden door groans inward on its hinges. Darkness expands beyond, yawning as the door opens to its fullest extent. A sound like a low, deep hum resonates, and the power makes my heels lift. "It keeps pulling me in," I say warily. "I don't like it."

"I've never felt a power like this before," Xander says. "What on earth?"

"I want to go in!" Savage cries.

"No!" multiple voices say at the same time.

"The power within," Scythe says, putting his arm around my waist. "Looks like a whirlpool to my shark-eyes. It reminds me of Lorian."

Suddenly, I feel the likeness of it. "You're right."

"It sounds like a portal," Selena says in wonder, the fair black strands of her hair wafting towards the door. "Aurelia, there's a portal under Animus Academy!"

"Surely not," says Lyle.

"No, I think she's right," Xander says. "This is how our kind arrived in this world. There were many such portals on each continent, but scientists just assumed they'd all closed over or were so well hidden that no one could find them."

"This one is certainly well hidden," Scythe says. "Especially considering it requires a guardian such as Celeste and now Aurelia."

"Mythical shifters." Selena nods. "Makes total sense."

"Who needs a unicorn if we have a portal!" Savage says, squinting his eyes as if he can see beyond the darkness. "I say we go in and see what's on the other side."

Selena's eyes light up. "If you can find more mythical shifters, Aurelia, they will have knowledge about basilisks. They will be able to help you take down Ghoul's power."

"But we don't know what we'll find on the other side," Lyle says. "These other shifters could be hostile. Who's to say they'll help us?

Imagine if we had strange people from a different world coming here, wanting to talk to Aurelia. We'd probably try to kill them."

"Lyle's right." I say. "We just don't know where the portal will take us. It's not worth the risk right now, when my father is taking next steps."

"There could also be a time discrepancy." Xander nods. "What if we go and return to find three years have passed and everyone we know is dead?"

My stomach roils at the possibility. Minnie, Sabrina, Stacey, Eugene—all gone.

"No," I whisper. "I won't risk this unknown power for a possibility."

Selena nods. "If I didn't have my hatchlings, I might have risked an academic expedition. Perhaps after all this ends, we can send *some* willing soul through."

"Agreed," I say. "Ashfang, close the door."

* * *

Dinner is a quiet affair, after which we separate into groups. Selena lets Xander and Savage give her a tour of the academy while Scythe goes to soak in the tub. Lyle and I sit in the TV room together. Lately, I've felt I haven't given my lion enough time, making his animus irritable and prone to growling.

But as Lyle rubs balm into my tired leg, I sink back into old thoughts. *The last of your kind.* There has always been something eternally depressing about this fact. That with the death of my mother, I became the *one*. The last. The only.

The thought of other Boneweavers existing somewhere in the universe is a concept I dare not grasp. I barely know the extent of my own powers. What could I learn from them? What would it be like to have...family? Being discarded by my own blood family hurt enough. What if they, too, rejected my existence? What if I was too *other* for them as well? Too different.

There's no point in trying to find out. The threat is *here*. My enemy is *here*.

"I've suddenly realised I'm the only one of my pack without siblings," I mutter.

"Don't do that to yourself, angel," Lyle says. "Don't find ways to isolate yourself further."

I frown at him, offended. "If I isolate myself, Lyle, it's for a reason."

"I know," he says softly. "I just mean...right now, we need to band together. Not withdraw. If there's something on your mind, we are always willing to work through it with you. Sometimes it can be good to think out loud."

He's right, of course. "I was just thinking that I've not entertained the thought of others like me in a while. After I was exiled, I just avoided thinking about family, and now those ugly feelings are coming back. I don't want to hope and then have it stomped on again. We just don't know what's on the other side."

"*To be fair,*" Xander's voice says in the group chat. "*None of us knows what tomorrow really offers. We don't know how Mace is going to attack us. We don't know who he's going to try to kill.*"

I rub my eyes, the weight of his words heavy on me.

Scythe's voice pops in like a cool breeze. "*Xander is trying to say that we are operating in unknown territory. We need to use what tools we can.*"

My brows shoot up in surprise. "*Tools like the portal?*"

"*If it comes to it, yes, regina.*"

Chapter 91

Xander

After the tour of the property, I send Savage back to Aurelia so I can have tea with Selena in the empty dining hall.

"How are you really?" she asks over the rim of her cup, dark eyes catching the light of the stained-glass windows next to us.

"I have a black mating mark, Selena," I say quietly. My sister's eyes widen, telling me she surmises its meaning as I have. The words sit in the air between us. The implication. The way I am condemned. After a moment, I can't bear it any longer. "I don't know how to feel about it," I admit. "But a part of me feels it's the right and proper way of things."

"*Fuck* the right and proper way of things, Xander," she hisses, setting her cup down in its saucer with a click. "You belong with your mates, although I'm sure some of them need more convincing."

"I don't think they hate me," I say honestly. "But I don't think they will ever forgive me. And rightfully so. I...will never forgive myself."

The golden hall lights flicker across her fair face as her eyes glimmer with tears. "Wild Goddess." She slides to the floor on her knees, and I slide down with her.

"Selena, don't. I will be fine." I take her hands in my own.

She squeezes them back, staring down at our fingers. "There's nothing I can say that will make things better for you. But you *saved* me, you must know that. You alone stood by my side when all things were dark. The hatchlings do love you so."

But I haven't hurt them yet. I swallow the lump in my throat. "You saved yourself in the end. The hatchlings will always have you to protect them."

"And I could not protect you."

I lean down, pressing my forehead to hers. "We must all pay for our darkness. As Ragnar paid for his."

She hisses, rearing back from me. "That is different and you know it!"

"Is it?" I ask ruefully. "I don't think it is." Selena leaps to her feet, getting away from me and my offending words. "Leave me to my fate, Selena."

My older sister gives me a look. Part warning, part terrible, terrible hurt before she whirls around and storms outside. From my pocket, I slide out the envelope Connor gave me and pull out its contents, looking at the drawings the youngest of the freed captives did for us.

I brush my fingers over the gift I was given. I don't know if I'll ever get to thank Connor for this. After a moment, I too leave the dining hall for the library. I need paper and a pen.

Chapter 92

Aurelia

Xander and I are patrolling the skies at midnight when the guards raise the alarm. The head wolf sends a beam of thought towards me and I catch it up. *"We've just been notified of an escapee, my lady,"* his gruff voice says. *"The prisoner under the school, Etienne."*

"How?" I snap, circling my way to the ground. *"We need to assess the cave."*

"No need," comes the reply. *"Mr Pardalia has the accomplice in custody."*

When I touch down, Lyle is already striding out of the main academy building with a sobbing Stacey. "I'm so sorry, Lia!" she cries, her hands reaching out for me.

I take her by the shoulders, searching her body for signs of injury. "Are you alright, Stace? He didn't hurt you, did he?"

"No," she bemoans, turning her distressed face up to me, eyes rimmed with red. "No, but it's all my fault."

"I think he rex-commanded her," Lyle says, frowning.

"I know I'm not supposed to visit him alone," Stacey sniffs. "But I felt so lonely tonight, and he asked me about what I know. I didn't tell him at first, but then he said my name and my head went all funny and he told me to unlock the cuffs and of course I knew how because Sabrina taught us all!"

"Obsidian can't deter a regina or rex command," Lyle says in his therapist voice. "Then what happened?"

Stacey sobs again, clutching at my waist. "I'm so sorry. He told me to tell him everything I know, and I just started blabbing."

My stomach plummets into my feet as my head snaps up to look at Lyle, then Scythe, who stands in the shadows of the dining hall. "You told him about Eugene's memories, didn't you?"

Stacey nods. "Lia, I'm so sorry. Then he got out the only way I knew how, which was when you were planning your escape from here when we first arrived at the academy. The grocery truck from this evening. He's long gone by now."

I tilt my head back and close my eyes. *"Minnie?"* I call into the ether.

"Already here," my best friend says, striding onto the path with Marduk at her heels. "I'll take her. You guys deal with Etienne."

Stepping away from Stacey, I let her fall into Minnie's arms as I turn away from my lioness friend and try to contain my thoughts. Scythe is at my side in an instant, his eyes dark. "Etienne will have gone up the chain of command. That means right to Mace, regina."

I swear under my breath. "So my father will know that we know his plans with Ghoul."

"We have lost what little time we might have had. He'll make a move sooner rather than later."

I look up into my shark's eyes. "What should we do?"

"Prepare for the worst. I will double the guard on the wall tonight, and we need to send the students home."

"What?" My voice is sharp. "Why?"

Scythe inhales through his nose as if steeling himself to tell me. "He will come for the five of us, regina, and he will tear down the academy to do it. Especially now that he knows about the portal."

The portal. I say every curse word I know, running my hand through my tangled hair.

"Regina." Xander's voice is a fire whip in my mind. *"We've got this. We've got you."*

My mates. He is coming after my mates, once and for all, with the ultimate weapon. A weapon we cannot destroy. A weapon who asked me to execute him. Nausea roils in my stomach, and it's too much. Suddenly, I double over, heaving onto the grass. Lyle and Scythe steady me, pushing my hair back and rubbing my spine. My body trembles with adrenaline and inner pain. Could I kill one mate to save the rest of us? To save everyone? There has to be another way.

"I need to fly," I blurt out before stumbling to the side and shifting into my eagle form. Cutting through the sky, I let the upper currents of the world take me where it wills in a lap around the academy, the ground fading away, my beak a guiding arrow. Cold and fresh, the roar of the air fills my head, pushing out everything else.

My father knows we're aware of his plans. He knows about the portal. This will push him into action. I had decided, when my mates were taken, that I was done acting on the defensive. I am the night's greatest predator, and I won't stop my winning streak now when things are at their most dire. Etienne thought he could share our secrets? Well, fuck him.

"*I will be back,*" I tell my mates, not asking for permission, only letting them know out of respect. I fly back into our suite to shove some things into a backpack before heading out onto the roof, where I shift into an even bigger bird. My wings stretch out, red edged with blue, long plumage as my crown. I track my father in the same way I once tracked my mother—in my phoenix form, where the bond of parent to child always exists, whether we want it to or not.

Through the night I fly, over arid soil and bushland, over suburbia and tall apartments. To my surprise, the grey, sickly thread does not lead me to Naga House or a university where he's putting on another dramatic performance. Instead, I am led to a part of the outer city where I've never needed to go. It's a long, double-story colonial building, all clean lines and white and gold paint, with freshly cut lawns and professional humans walking out with bags and briefcases.

I eighth shield myself before I land on the pavement, quickly dressing. I've chosen appropriate clothing to meet with a crime lord: a white blouse and a navy-blue pantsuit. Heck, I'm getting used to this. I tie my hair back in a high bun and smooth down the stray hairs, then step into black heels. This is clothing my father recognises. It's something he respects.

With my invisibility shield still on, I stride into the building and right around the metal detectors where two uniformed human guards stand, tracking my father through the carpeted hallways of offices and function rooms of the state parliament house.

A sign points me to the *Legislative Council Chambers*, and I don't have to open the door because a bunch of old white men do it for me, marching out, excitedly talking to each other and pointing at papers. It gives me a shiver, but I press myself against the wall, keen not to show my hand just yet.

As soon as there's a gap in the stream of people, I hurry inside, my heels muffled on plush, wine-coloured carpet. Everything in the circular chamber is red—the carpet, the rows of chairs, the tables. But that's not what makes my skin crawl. It's the fact that my father, the tallest in the room, is in its centre, standing next to a man and woman in official black council robes, talking quietly. As the room empties of humans, I make my way down a set of stairs to them, resisting the urge to rub my arms at the smell of official government business in the air.

I'm watching my father's dreams come true. I also watch him see me. His black eyes flick over the shoulder of the shorter man, before flicking back. His thermal sensors are no doubt honed strong because he's on high alert for any retaliation from other crime lords, because I'm sure that whatever legislation he's putting through here will cause a riot amongst the animalia population.

The human senators mention something about a dinner, but Mace Naga raises his voice just a little. "Most certainly. I will join you shortly." He gives them a thin smile that makes me raise my brows, and the two humans gather their things and make for the stairs that lead out of the room.

My father makes a show of gathering his own briefcase, his back turned towards me. Once the door closes, we are alone. Mace Naga inhales deeply, his head tilted upwards as he looks around at the ornate room. I drop my invisibility. "So you finally summoned the courage to come and see me," my father says without turning around, showing me his back as if I am no threat. No enemy of worth. "It was only a matter of time." He turns, eyes fixed on me like a predator assessing its prey. "How are you, Aurelia?"

"You have never cared for me." I keep my voice light. "There's no need to pretend now, Father." Even now, my heart pounds to face him. To be in a room alone with him. I can't count the number of times in the last ten years that we've faced each other like this without an audience. With nothing but cold menace between us. I've always known he was capable of great evil, but now I've seen it with my own eyes. "I see you finally lied and cursed your way to parliament."

There is no emotion in his grey expression, only acute observation that would make any creature want to shrivel. *I* don't. I withstand the judgement. "You think you have claimed your own position at Animus Academy. With four mates, at that."

"After you so vehemently told me that they and everyone else would kill me."

"Advice you should have heeded. You will die at the end of this path, Aurelia." The artificial lights overhead do nothing to soften his appearance. They only serve to make him look harsher, more powerful. Somehow, he even has the lighting working in his favour.

"I never fathomed my own father would be my enemy. That he would be responsible for the end of my mother."

"There were things more important than you and your mother, though neither of you are capable of understanding that."

I scoff in disgust to disguise the rage. "This discussion is pointless."

"Nothing I do is pointless, Aurelia. You of all people should know that."

"Indeed, you're not above using child soldiers. There is no lower gutter to sink into."

His lips twitch as if he finds this amusing. He raises his hand, the shadow of his cobra curled around his arm in a spiral showing, its head rearing up to bare his fangs at me. "How little you know."

That swelling rage rises to a zenith in my blood. Over and over, he underestimates me. But...he knows that *we* know about his plans. Is he trying to make out that there are things still hidden? But that comment about my mother and I not mattering to him still stings like a slap. It's a wound I've never quite gotten rid of— how quickly he discarded me as if I never mattered to my family at all.

"I will end you," I hiss. "Even if it costs me everything. Even if I have to destroy myself to achieve it."

To my dismay, the corners of my father's mouth pull upwards into an uncharacteristic smile. It crinkles the edges of his mouth, his black eyes. "I still have that much power over you?" My stomach plummets. He still has that much power over me. "I will make you an offer, Aurelia," he says. "Reject the bond between you and my General Ghoul, and I will spare your other mates. You are not above hurting him, so I've seen."

I suppress the grimace that comes from the echoing crack I hear in my head. Although I knew he wasn't dead, hearing confirmation that he is well and alive is still cool water through my veins. *But he wants to cut a deal.* Ghoul's words reverberate in my mind. He had never asked for a bond severance. He had asked me if I would execute him. He would prefer that over a rejection.

I want to see his face again, I realise. I yearn to see his shadows curling around him, giving his emotions away, reaching for me like hungry fingers. I allow my father to see them. The shadows that call to me. My fangs elongate from my gums, growing past my teeth, and my power collects behind my eyes, a sinister UV glow gathering in my pupils.

For the first time that I've known him, my father's jaw goes slack. His lips part as he sees it. No doubt he'd heard of our fight at the warehouse complex, but seeing his daughter as a basilisk would hit differently up close. To him, I've never been a serpent...always *other*.

It seems I have an effect on *him* too.

True to form, Mace Naga recovers within seconds, pulling himself up to full height, somehow dwarfing the room. "You lured him in as you lured the others in. You used the skills you had to gather the most powerful males. That part, *that* greatness, you no doubt got from me."

"You claim a part of me now?" I say with raised brows.

"You are my progeny. I've never denied that." No, he just discarded me. Hid me. "You know most of what is coming," he continues. "You know what Ghoul is capable of. You know you cannot win this. You cannot fight it. You will come out of this dead, do you understand me?" There's a gleam in his eyes that tells me he believes what he's saying.

"You wish annihilation upon us," I say.

That grey face grows serious. "That is in your future if you don't do what I ask. Work with me, and I will spare your mates from what is to come." He pulls up his sleeve to reveal unmarked light brown skin. He's asking for a blood oath.

"Very well," I say, rolling up my own left sleeve and pricking my forefinger against my still-drawn fang. I smear the mixture of blood and venom across my fingers and hold out my other hand for the ceremonial dagger I know he carries. "I will make the blood contract."

My father hands me the knife by its handle, never taking his eyes off me. And I never take my eyes off him as I make the mark on my arm. "I made a vow on my mother's funeral pyre." The dagger cuts viciously into my skin, and I smile at him as I press my venom into it. "And I make it again now, before you. That you will die in my mother's name, Athena Boneweaver. And I will make you suffer as she did."

I throw the knife at his feet, showing him the ancient mark of a promise of death on my skin, shiny and crimson. "I condemn you to hell, Mace Naga."

I let the shadows consume me before I turn into nothing.

Chapter 93

Xander

Aurelia returns to Animus Academy dressed like a crime lord and smelling of blood and darkness. She snarls at the sky as she shifts from shadow back into human form, on the roof of the animus dorms, dropping a small empty backpack at her feet. I give her a moment from my position in the sky where I was on patrol before she makes eye contact with me, those dark sapphires demanding my attention through the night. Descending, I shift before I hit the stone, landing on human feet.

"Where did you go?" I ask, trying not to sound worried, nervous, or excited by the answer.

Her serpent fangs slowly disappear into her mouth as she sighs. "I'm not sure you want to know."

I look out across the scrubland beyond the academy, the quiet dark. How many times had I myself made a flight to Drakos Estate, my heart bleeding, rage spreading through me like poison? "I know what I would do," I say quietly. "I've confronted my father many a time."

Aurelia looks at me sharply before her shoulders sag and a high heel scrapes along the stone. "Scythe always said we're more alike than I ever thought."

I laugh through my nose. "He said as much to me. The bastard is always right."

She moistens her lips, dry from the night air. "Xander, I need you to go to zookeeper Rick and ask for a venom collection vessel. I need you to help me do something."

Chapter 94

Ghoul

The night is blessed as I see the ball of shadow that is my regina travel through the sky, leaving an enraged, powerful energy behind her like a meteor's tail. The military vehicle rumbles pleasantly under me as I park it before the entrance of the state parliament house. There is nothing left of the injury she gave me, except for the sweet memory of pain and the image of her worried face hovering over me before I gave way to the dark.

Mace strides out of the main doors, his black duster billowing behind him on a wind that is only dark magic. His nostrils are flared in suppressed irritation, his stride not rushing but quick enough to tell me she has rattled him. One of the grunts opens the back door for him and I try not to show my pride.

"Your Majesty," I greet mildly. "I trust all went well."

"General," he says, not having a bar of me today. "You are fully recovered, I take it?"

"Naturally," I say, knocking the top of my head like it's wood. "Like it was never broken."

"Good. The human mundanes signed off on the legislation as I planned. We'll be commencing the final phase tomorrow."

"Very good, Your Majesty."

"You need to fill your well, we cannot afford failure on your part yet again. Ensure our males well fed and fucked. I don't care how they do it."

Hearing Mace cuss is unusual and tells me just how excited he is for his life's plans to be coming to fruition. Oh regina, I hope you're ready.

Chapter 95

Aurelia

The next morning, Scythe and Lyle command the students to pack their bags and load them into a number of waiting coaches. Some put up a protest, worried about their various court dates and legal records, and other students simply don't have accommodation in the outside world. So while many of the students leap at the chance to go home, some simply refuse to leave. Sabrina, her surrogate mates Blair and Blade, and Stacey included.

Xander and Savage, who has taken to wearing Eugene in a sling similar to Toastie's, oversee the loading of the coaches, wrangling apart those who get into fights and anger-shift. I watch all this from the top of the animus dorms, my arms crossed against the chill that's encapsulated my heart. Animus Academy already feels emptier, and that space inside of me made for Ghoul gapes open like an infected wound.

"I hope you're alright," I send across the ether. *"I know what Mace wants you to do. I know everything."*

No reply comes. My nails scrape against the black stone wall.

***

That afternoon, Marduk messages our Devi-Boneweaver pack group chat. Four words that shake me. *Mace is on TV.* My pack all rush to the TV room as fast as we can. We exchange looks without speaking, crowding around the TV, none of us wanting to sit down. Sure enough, my father is standing next to a lectern, patiently waiting to speak. The red banner beneath his wan face reads: *Joint initiative proposes dissolution of Animalia Council Structure.*

The camera pans to the human state premier, a brunette woman in a red pantsuit, standing at the lectern. I wonder how much mind-control basilisk venom my father has spiked her drink with over the years. "The Animalia Council has voted," she says with a bright smile to the journalists seated for the press conference. "The current system has not been working. We require a united front, led by a single impartial party. Only this will allow real progress. I am pleased to tell you that tonight we have hosted an election. Each council member will now present their votes for the new leader of the animalia population."

The camera pans to a screen above the lectern, and it flicks to an unidentifiable room with a black-curtained background where the four council members are seated. Charlotte Naga stands before them in a professional suit, her blond curls perfectly coiffed. The camera zooms in on Irma Goldwing's thin, unblinking face. Even without my avian healing powers and train-ing, I know she's unwell, likely being poisoned with Ghoul's venom within an inch of her life. She drones, "I vote for Mace Naga."

Ablo Obon's face appears, dripping with sweat, his pupils dilated almost all the way. "Mace Naga," he says in a halting staccato.

Lunissa, her mouth downturned unhappily, deadpans, "Mace Naga."

The video pans to Charlotte Naga with her clipboard. "The marine regent did not reply to communications."

"Liars!" Savage snarls, glancing at Scythe. And of course, there is no longer a dragon regent now that Flores Drakos is dead.

The human premier shouts into the microphone. "I am so pleased to present to you, the new regent of the animalia, Mace Naga!" They shake hands, and Mace raises his hands in a benevo-lent way to the audience, who gives an enthusiastic round of applause. Somebody whistles, and I swear I hear a party popper in the background.

Lyle takes my hand and squeezes it as I try to hold myself together. I'm not even sure what to feel, but an awful, biting dread sits in my stomach like a new type of poison. My eyes search for Ghoul in the group of my father's supporters on stage, but there are no generals present, only my great uncle, the lawyer, and other males in suits.

My father waits for the crowd to settle before he speaks in a booming, deep voice that commands the entire room. "I will serve the animalia and human populations better than any previous member of the council ever could. The federal hunt and retrieve warrants will pass over to the serpent court team. We will ensure the job gets done."

The room breaks into loud cheers once again. He begins his speech. "My first command relates to the issues of crime and ferality within the animalia population. For too long, the humans have suffered under the tyranny of beasts who simply think they are above the law. Who wish to overpower the humans at every turn simply because they can. The old ways have failed. Hence, I initiate the dissolution of Animus Academy. Under the administration of Lyle Pardalia and Celeste Agnis, the program has never shown evidence of improving ferality or rabidity. With a significant draw on council funds, I cannot allow this program to continue. All adult criminals masquerading as students will be transferred to Blackwater Penitentiary where they belong."

Lyle snarls under his breath, and it's my turn to squeeze his hand. I have to turn away from the TV and place another hand on Lyle's clenched jaw. "It'll be okay," I say, blinking fast. I don't know if I'm telling him or myself. "It'll be okay."

I duck away from him to sit on my favourite part of the couch, lowering my head to my hands as I try to get the words out of my head, and my father's terrible, smug smile. Above it all, my heart aches as I wonder where my fifth mate is and what he's thinking. My vow, still red and scabbing over, burns on my left forearm.

This is it. This is what my father has been waiting for his entire life. Now he has the entire human population and parliament behind him. It's Animus Academy against the might of everyone else, my father at the helm, for no reason other than power. How easily everything could slip away from me if I let it.

I stand up, trembling with rage. I can't take my eyes off my father, still standing at the lectern, smiling. The greed. The sheer will to destroy everything I love. My voice trembles, but I speak anyway. I'm not ashamed to care *this* deeply. "I'm going through the portal," I say to my mates. "I will not let my father win this, but I don't think we can do it alone."

Xander is the first to step forward. "I will go with you."

"Me too!" Savage all but leaps into the air. "It was calling me, I just know it!"

Scythe's eyes glitter as Lyle turns to regard me. "I don't like the thought of our pack being separated again."

"We can't leave the academy unmanned," I say, frowning at the thought.

Scythe gets out his phone. "The Devi pack will look after things while we're gone. However long it takes to find your family, regina."

I know this is mad. I know we're going into danger, and yet my heart only swells at the sight of my mates, the other pieces of my soul, willing to risk everything to come with me on this madcap mission. "You're all mad," I say, sniffing loudly. "Fucking mad."

Savage nods enthusiastically. "And we wouldn't have it any other way."

Chapter 96

Savage

This is so exciting I think I'm going to pee my pants.

But I won't, because Lyle is watching me closely so I have to behave at least a little bit, *and* we don't know what monsters we'll meet in the other world, so I better save it. Lyle wants to pack a bag, so we give him a minute to do that while Scythe and Aurelia talk to the Devi pack to update them. Minnie is desperate to come as well but in the next breath announces herself as the surrogate guardian of the academy while we're gone.

But if we're going through the secret door to under the school, then we're not really *leaving* it, are we? I don't know how the magic works, but it all makes sense to me.

I prepare myself by warming up with a lap around the academy and some push-ups before explaining things to Eugene. He needs to look after Stacey because I think she needs him most after her mate proved himself an asshole for a second time. Henry is coming with us; I think the more the merrier for this quest.

Once I return to the pack suite, everyone is dressed in simple clothes and ready to go. Lyle and Xander have backpacks with water, food, and clothes. Everyone has very serious expressions on and I think I'm the only one who's actually excited, so I decide to lead the way to the library, singing a new song.

We're off to the portal.

We're off to the portal.

Everyone cheer!
Everyone cheer!

I ignore Xander's useless comment about it not rhyming because it doesn't need to rhyme while I'm dancing. I also need to keep my mind off the new red mark my regina has on her arm. When Lyle asked her about it, she simply said. "I did it. And it means my father will die." She doesn't act like it's sore, but I've been wanting to lick it better for ages now. Lyle gave me a deathly look when I said I wanted to, so I have to contain myself.

Minnie waits for us in the library, wringing her hands like a nervous ninny. I want to tell her that she defeated Titus, so she really shouldn't be nervous about anything after that, but I'm too excited and there are too many thoughts in my mind so all that comes out is, "You're a badass, Minnie."

She rolls her eyes at me before grabbing my regina by the arms. "Don't eat anything no matter how good it looks, and promise you won't spend too much time there."

"This is a time-critical mission," Lia says seriously. "I don't want to be there any longer than we have to because you can bet your bottom dollar Serpent Court won't waste any time either."

"We have eyes on them on the northern roads," Xander says, nodding to Minnie's phone. "And they'll arrive in a convoy, so you'll get an alert when the guards see them coming from hours away."

"I've got this," Minnie says, nodding seriously. "I'll defend this place with my life."

I skip past the Titus-killer towards where the secret door sits on the wall. The light is dimmed this late in the day, and it makes the door look like something from an old dragon's dungeon. Everyone slowly gathers behind me, and the fat gargoyle who sits on top of the door stares down at us all with this old timey look.

"You must be really old," I say.

He blinks down at me. "Quite."

I feel my regina take a deep breath, and her exhale tickles the back of my neck. My little chompy is nervous, so I'm going to have to be brave for all of us. I turn around and thrust out my palm, face down. "On three, say Team Boneweaver!"

Xander gives me a pained look that says he's above team

bonding activities, but when Lia smiles shyly and places her hand over mine, everyone else has no choice but to follow.

I beam at the team as Xander puts his hand over Scythe's. Now I'm really giddy. "One, two, three!"

"Team Boneweaver!" everyone cheers.

Henry chirps his part from Lia's shoulder. *"You always make me feel better,"* she says in my mind, just for me. I get to pinch her smiling cheeks before sweeping my arm out to tell her the floor is hers. She steps forward more confidently than before, looking up at the gargoyle.

"My lady," he says formally, like he knows something's up.

"We're ready to go through, Ashfang," she says. "Let us in, please."

"Very well. May the Wild Goddess save your souls."

Dramatic old gargoyle. No one's saving my soul except my regina. Aurelia casts a dark look over her shoulder as the door swings open and I nod encouragingly. We all surround our regina, Lyle putting his arm around her waist like he's scared it's going to slurp her in.

That strange magic circles in the air as the door opens, and it feels like being tickled by a windmill, but it's pulling at us all. "Ready?" I say in my chompy's ear.

She takes a shaky breath. "Let's do it."

We all edge towards the darkness, right up until I'm pressed against the hinge, sniffing to see if I can sense what's on the other side.

"Oh, there's a passageway," Aurelia says, her eagle eyes enlarging her irises.

"Do you want me to go first?" I say excitedly.

"No, I've got the eyes—"

Xander prods everyone aside. "No, *I've* got the eyes, regina."

He has no eyes at all, actually, so I don't know what's going on, but I let the dragon go first with narrow eyes, and Aurelia holds onto his belt loop. We all go in a long chain, but when I hold my hand out to Lyle behind me, he looks at me disapprovingly, taking out a torch from his backpack instead. I just shrug and follow my leader.

Xander's eyes light the way through the passage, and it's wide enough that Aurelia ends up walking side by side with him. There are black stone walls and the same cobbly-stone floor as Lia's rabid cave in the animas dorm. It feels old and dusty, like there should be cobwebs and ghosts floating through here. The floor slopes downwards, and we're clearly heading underground, the air feeling heavy on my chest and shoulders.

Suddenly, both Aurelia and Xander jump backwards like they've been tripped up. "Stop!" Aurelia exclaims as they both stumble back into me. Henry tumbles off Lia's shoulder but rights himself in mid-air.

"What is it!" I shout excitedly.

"It's the floor," Aurelia says, showing me with the toe of her trainer. She presses on the floor, and it tips inwards like a trick panel.

"It's a massive trapdoor," Xander mutters. "What the fuck is underneath here?"

"How we get to the other side is the better question," Lyle says. "We need to keep moving. Allow me."

We make way for the lion, and he shoves at the trapdoor with his telekinesis and shines his torch on it. The floor slides away from us, moving on a hinge three or four metres down the path. Beneath the trapdoor is a darkness even deeper than the corridor. When Lyle shines his light into it, there's nothing at all to see. Only shadow. Lyle levitates himself across the trapdoor to the other side, pointing his torch left and right to show us that it's a dead end.

Aurelia snorts. "It wants us to go down."

Lyle sighs dramatically. "We don't know what's down there. I'm getting flashbacks of Naga House."

Aurelia shifts, and when a tiny head pokes out of her fallen clothes, I gasp in wonder. She's a blue rosella. So cute with her tiny red chest and face, bright green wings, and round black eyes. She gives a little chirp, and Henry chirps back, flying around her in circles. Scythe picks up her clothes as she hops to the edge of the trapdoor and peers down before she and Henry flit into it together.

"Quick, Lyle!" I cry, falling onto my ass and dangling my feet through the trapdoor. With no choice at all, Lyle wraps me in his telekinesis and sends me down into the all-black. The others follow with some grumbling, Lyle's torch beaming yellow over me. He lowers us boys slowly into the shadows until there's nothing all around us and it feels like I'm in outer space or something.

The smell of salt hits my nose just after my brother says it. "It's brine," Scythe says. "There's a lot of saltwater down there."

Aurelia and Henry let out chirps again, and I feel my regina shift. There's a flash of white skin before a plonking splash. Henry chirps in dismay by my ear.

"Let me down, Lyle," Scythe says. "But take my clothes first."

We're all lowered down to the surface of some choppy water. Sea spray brushes my toes, and I grin down at the black waters beneath me, lowering my fingers to dip them in. Scythe splashes into the water a moment later, and Lyle levitates next to me, gathering up his clothes into the backpack.

"*Can you guys see anything?*" Xander asks irritably into the group chat. "*Where else would we be expected to go?*"

"*It's almost as if this journey was made for a Boneweaver,*" Lyle says. "*Telekinesis, flight, now swimming.*"

We hear nothing from our marine mates for a moment, and just when I think Scythe and Aurelia have eloped, Scythe says. "*There's a light far down here. I think we need to go through it.*"

"*Gods help me,*" Xander moans.

"*Don't worry, my dragon,*" Aurelia says. "*I'm going to bubble shield you non-aquatics and then Lyle can shoot you through.*"

"*Brilliant idea, regina!*" I say, fist pumping the air.

Lyle's torch beam finds Aurelia's dorsal fin when it appears above the water, and I feel her gentle magic surrounding me like a doona of love. The air around me changes as the bubble closes over my head, and Xander and Lyle go quiet as they feel it too. Henry lands on my shoulder for comfort.

"Ready!" I say, bending my knees into a squat and bracing myself. Lyle lowers the three of us into the water, and I grin from cheek to cheek as we sink into the new darkness, and my regina's pretty shark face snaps her sharp teeth at us. Her tail is so cute as she and Scythe swim down past where Lyle's torch light can see.

He makes sure we chase them at speed, like three Christmas baubles through the sea. We travel for a few seconds before the hairs on my arms stand up, and I rub at it unconsciously. Henry makes a low sound of worry and huddles close to my skin.

"*Are you alright, Sav?*" Lyle asks from his bubble on my left.

"*Yeah...*" I rub the back of my neck and look behind me. But there's nothing there. I look to my right. There's nothing there either, but it's so bloody dark I can't see a thing anyway. "*I don't think I like this place. It feels like something is watching me.*" Something brushes against my mind. "*I want to leave! Everyone, go faster!*"

"*What, why?*" Xander asks. Suddenly, from the complete darkness on my right, two orbs of light turn my way, and I shake my head at them. He's so creepy sometimes. Lyle starts shining his torch around. The golden beam shows things like dust moties and bubbles but nothing else. Just ahead, Scythe and Aurelia go slower. Lyle shines his torch left, and a gigantic black eye blinks back at us. Henry screams.

"What the fuck! What the fuck!" I shout, grabbing Henry in my hand.

A giant, fleshy body followed by long tentacles streaks past us, straight for the two sharks. Lyle follows it with the torch. "*Regina!*" We all shout.

Xander screams at the top of his lungs, and Henry and I join in. Scythe turns around just as the giant squid *thing* reaches them. Some of his power hits it like an ocean current, sending it tumbling backwards, its dinner plate eyes rolling back in its head.

"*I want to touch it,*" Aurelia says into the chat.

"*No!*" we all shout.

We speed downwards with all our might, my face plastered against Lia's bubble as I keep my eyes fixed on my regina's pale tail. Henry's heart flutters under my fingers. A green glow twinkles beneath us, shifting with the ripples of the water. Lia and Scythe swim right through it and disappear completely.

I shout in excitement as Lyle shoots us through the green twinklies and suddenly we're not in water at all but plain air with a green glow all around us. Two sharks hang in mid-air beneath us as we peer in surprise at the big black cavern that feels like the rectum of Animus Academy.

Lia shifts into human form and lowers herself and Scythe slowly to the ground. It's lucky she caught them both, otherwise she and Scythe would have been fishcakes. Lyle lowers us to the ground as well, and as soon as we touch the black dirt floor, everyone starts talking at once.

"Did you see that?" I exclaim, letting a squashed Henry fly free. He starts complaining too.

"I don't like any of this," Xander says like a spoilsport.

"I want to go back and see it!" Aurelia says, her face and body shining with droplets of water that make me want to lick her all over.

Lyle hands Lia and Scythe their clothes, and they quickly get dressed. "How has it survived this long?" asks Scythe. "What has it been eating to get to that size?"

"I think we just found out where the food scraps chute leads," Lyle says. "I've always wondered, and Celeste could never tell me."

"It wanted Aurelia," I say, shaking my fist at the water rippling on the ceiling where we came out. "I think we should go back and kill it."

"No!" Aurelia and Scythe shout at the same time, before smiling at each other. Well, fine. I turn around and survey this new place and the thing that sits at the middle of it like a queen.

"Whoa!" I breathe. It's an archway of black stone smack bang in the middle of a raised platform of something shiny like crushed crystals. Inside the archway is a shiny, twinkly magic that glows like moving, liquid opals.

"I've never seen magic like this," Xander says in a strange voice. "I can't believe this was sitting here under the school the entire time."

Aurelia wipes at her cheek. "It's the heart of the academy, I think." Her voice is all caught in her throat. "I want to go in." Henry sits on her shoulder to comfort her.

"Me too," Xander says, walking forward strangely, like he can't help it.

I bound forward, not wanting to be left behind. "What do you think happens if we walk through it?"

"Only one way to find out," Scythe says quietly.

Aurelia glances back at us. "I'm gonna go in first; someone hold my hand." Unfortunately, Xander is closest to her right hand, so he gets to her first. I quickly take Xander's hand and reach out for Lyle, who *does* take my hand this time. Scythe takes his and I wait, holding my breath as Lia stares at the magic archway, blinking fast.

Xander leans down and whispers in her ear. "We are with you, regina."

She presses her lips together and nods without looking at him. I feel a bubble of her protection surrounding us, and then she takes a deep breath and steps through. Xander goes through next, and I make wide eyes so I don't miss anything as I go in.

Warm magic tickles my skin so strongly and a smell like mangoes and papaya makes me hungry.

And then there's light—so much light that it could only come from the summer sun.

Chapter 97

Aurelia

It was with a hope and a wish that I walked through the glittery portal. I wanted to find my mother's people. That was the only thought in my mind. How perhaps if she'd known others like her, she might have had the courage to stand up for herself against my father.

Walking through the portal felt like walking through a cold tornado. My insides and outsides felt like they were mingling together—a harsh pressure and then a release.

Into daylight.

The air is humid, with a light breeze cooling my skin and filling my nose with sea salt. There are summer flowers like frangipani, and dense jungle. I blink against the glare of the sun, putting up my arm briefly as I walk forwards to allow my mates through behind me, my bare feet finding soil and grass.

Cicadas chirp as my eyes adjust to see a jungle. Tall palm trees flap in the breeze, and green ferns border a worn stone path. In the distance is the breaking of ocean waves, and right before me is the back of an old stone building, covered with climbing vines and bright flowers. I strain my ears for any sign of humans or animalia.

Xander breathes heavily behind me, also surveying the stone path and where it might lead. Savage comes through the portal noisily and with great exclamation. It's then that I turn around to caution him and stop dead in my tracks because the portal, on this side at least, appears to be a mausoleum—a square black building that is one of four, lined side by side.

Looking at them gives me the creeps, and Xander turns to look at them too. "That's a language I don't recognise," he says, indicating the runes carved into the stone arch. Lyle, then Scythe, come out of the portal, still rippling a magical green, just more faint in this bright light.

Voices sound in the distance, and I hear the step of a heavy foot. I whirl around, and Xander tries to shove me behind him, but I don't let him, and we end up pressed side by side.

The stone path looks like it leads around this old building, and down it strides a man. But not a man at all, and I know that in my marrow. He's as tall as Xander, broad-shouldered and muscled as I can see from his lack of shirt, brown-skinned like my fifth mate, with inky black hair worn loose down his back. He's covered in ink and wears a black sword earring dangling from one ear.

And his eyes, set in a handsome face that would make most women sway where they stand, are a bright and magical blue. He halts in his tracks, hard muscles tensing. My eyes burn, filling with tears I never anticipated. One word resounds in my head, clear and high.

Kinsman.

This creature is a Boneweaver.

There must be something about my expression that gives me away because he narrows his eyes in confusion, quickly assessing me, my pack, and the door we came from. He says something in a language I cannot understand, with a deep and commanding tone that tells me he has authority over this place.

I take a shaky breath. "I'm sorry, I don't understand."

A woman's voice, irritated and impatient, sounds from behind him. He holds out a hand as she appears by his side. Immediately, we all notice that she is heavily pregnant, her brown face smoothing out from irritation to wonder. She too has black hair, but hers is piled on her head in a messy bun for the heat, and she has the most brilliant emerald green eyes that make me wonder what the hell she is. Her gown is a richly embroidered deep pink, made of a light material with short cap sleeves. She is poised and controlled, confidently eyeing each of my mates with interest, doing a double take at Xander's eyes before looking expectantly at me and raising her brows.

"We need to find a way to communicate," I say, glancing at Xander.

"Should I draw a picture?" Xander mutters darkly.

The woman smiles before elbowing the Boneweaver male. "They speak Lobrathian common, husband." She nods to me. "Good day. From where do you hail? Friend or foe, tell us quickly before one of us tries to kill you."

My mates bristle, so I know I have to act fast.

"F-Friend," I stutter like a complete idiot, my voice heavy with restrained emotion. "I am sorry, I thought I was the only one." I nod to her husband. "There are none of us left where I come from."

Her dark brows shoot up. "None of what?" she says slowly, and from the way she stares into my eyes, *at* my eyes, tells me she already knows the answer.

My vision is blurry, and it comes out as a choked whisper because I cannot manage anything more. "Boneweavers."

She smiles at me, and it's a brilliant thing that stuns me out of my downward spiral. "Did you hear that, Zale?"

"I did," the male says slowly, eyeing me with a slight crease between his brows. Hearing his voice in English makes me light-headed. "This is unexpected. We did not expect a portal at the back of Yasani temple."

"We didn't know where it would come out," I say, glancing at my mates. "I just...thought about my mother."

Something crashes through the jungle behind them, and low, rumbly growls charge the air. Savage shifts on instinct, and I'm shoved behind everyone, multiple hands giving me no choice. My wolf growls at the front of our group, and I peer around Lyle to see two large felines skidding to a stop next to the man and woman. One is a black panther, lithe and muscular, and the second is a feline with a completely white pelt. Night and day, they both shift into human forms and I can't take my eyes off them as they are revealed to be tall males, both with black dagger earrings in their pierced ears, and similar enough to the first male that they could be related. The dark-haired one, with Boneweaver blue eyes, has tattoos in a delicate line across his nose and cheeks, and the other is a white-haired male with wide eyes that take us all in with a wild sort of curiosity.

"Stand down, you two," the woman says, flapping her hand at them. "We are finding out what the disturbance was." To us, she says, "We felt you come through. But considering you came from behind her temple, I'm assuming you were *sent* by the Wild Mother."

Xander clears his throat. "It was a task to get here, but my regina needed to find her kind."

"Regina?" the first Boneweaver asks. He looks unfazed by Savage's aggressive form growling at him, or my towering males frowning at the newcomers.

"I am the central mate," I say quickly, stepping out from behind them. "These four males belong to me." I gesture to them all as a reminder to *them* that I'm in charge here.

Her eyes widen with delight, and she grins at me. "All *four?* My, my, how delightful!" She looks up at her husband. "This is *my* star-born mate, just the one, King Ashzale Boneweaver. You are in our domain, Boneweaver Island. My name is Altara." She gestures to the white-haired male. "This is Lord Kai Bonesong and Lord Raen Boneweaver." The man with the tattoos inclines his head but doesn't take his suspicious eyes off us.

Kai points a finger at me. "You should bow to royalty, travellers!"

Savage shifts into human form with a snarl. "My regina bows to no one, feline! This is the Lady Aurelia Boneweaver, the last of her kind! Crocodile-killer and *my* regina! And *my* name is Savage."

Altara smiles as if we're having a pleasant conversation. "Well met, Savage." She winks at me, completely unfazed, and I realise she must be used to this type of thing.

Ashzale puts out a hand to placate Kai. "No formalities are required, brother. These people are family, by the sounds of it."

Altara, who I'm assuming is queen of this place if her husband is king, clasps her hands under her chin and makes a happy sound. "Family!" She gestures at me. "Come with me, Lady Aurelia. You look like someone I want to be friends with." Ashzale's head whips down to her, and she says something in their language. Altara nods at me and smiles. "She is kind, Ashzale. You can see it in her eyes."

"It's probably just because they remind you of me," he says darkly.

"*Kind* is last on the list of words I would use to describe *you*." She waves at him before he can reply.

A memory comes to me, not my own, of another pregnant woman telling a blue-eyed boy his eyes were kind. I glance at Scythe. My great white shark is tense, and his eyes dart, assessing just moments before, catch mine, softening in recognition.

"*I love you.*"

"*I love you too, regina.*"

It's then that Scythe steps out of the shadows of the tomb, his shirt back on, and Kai gasps as he sees him. "What are you, sir?" he asks in a way that makes him seem terribly young.

"I come from the sea," Scythe says in that striking rasp that makes Altara's eyes go wide. "I am a great white shark. My regina is polite, but in our world, we are on the eve of battle. Someone is coming to kill us all and take our home."

"We...are essentially looking for help," I say quietly. "Well, information that you may have."

"Wait," Raen asks. "How do we know she is family? We cannot welcome strangers into our lands simply because of their *eyes*, my queen."

"*Look* at her, Raen," Altara says. "Those eyes can't be from anything but a Boneweaver, right, Zale? And look at that tiny fluffy ball on her shoulder! No one who has a creature like that can be bad!"

Zale has not taken his eyes off me, and it's been making Lyle bristle. Hell, it's making *me* nervous. "Do you have some type of shield around you?" he asks me. I nod. "Take it off, Lady Aurelia."

"Absolutely not," Lyle snarls.

"Look here," Altara says, stepping forward against the protests of the males. "A fight between our two parties would likely end in great bloodshed, can we agree on that?" Savage shrugs and nods.

"So…" Altara goggles her eyes at me. "Plus, I'm pregnant, and I don't think you'd harm a woman with child, would you?"

"Never," I say honestly.

She brushes her hands as if to say, *that's that.* "As for the other question," she says to Lord Raen, "I'm guessing Lady Aurelia is from Princess Esha's lot. She and her mates left these lands for another and never returned. The history books never documented what happened to them. I am descended from her elder sister, Matrika."

Zale frowns. "Cousins on both sides."

Altara snorts in an unladylike manner. "The relation is *quite* distant, husband." She scans my mates with narrowed eyes. "Do these four males treat you well, cousin?"

Shit, I think I love her already. I can't help but break into a smile and step forward, ignoring Savage's hand brushing my arm. "They have their tantrums now and again, but otherwise they love me."

She grins again. "Very good, otherwise we would have had a problem." Her emerald eyes survey them with latent threat before returning to me. "Now, what is this about the eve of battle? Who are we killing?"

I bite back another round of tears. I had expected everything *except* solidarity. I hesitate for a moment, my eyes flicking towards Zale. "Unfortunately, my father."

Altara puts her arm around Zale's. "Oh, we know a bit about that, my lady. Come, let us sit together."

I glance back at my mates, hesitating for a moment, but they're waiting for my lead. In the end, it's Henry who chirps with interest and zips over to Altara, crooning over her belly.

"Hello, friend," Altara says with excitement. "I love you already! What's your name?"

With that, the tension dissipates and Savage makes a sound that's half sigh, half scoff.

Chapter 98

Xander

Aurelia seems quite taken with the Boneweaver, King Ashzale, who looks every bit of a kingly male for this island kingdom of animalia. Jealously seethes through me at the wonder that fills her eyes as she steals glances at him, but I have to remind myself that he may be her only living blood family.

And we all know how special Boneweavers are.

The place feels like magic lives here in the very air, so when Queen Altara indicates we should follow them, and the traitor Henry, down the stone path around the very ancient-looking temple, I can't help but stare like a child in a confectionery store. They also have no trouble turning their unguarded backs on us, and I don't know whether to be insulted by that as I stare at the naked, muscled backs of the beasts stalking behind their king and queen. These are a different sort of animalia, and I don't think our modern rules apply to them.

The temple ends up being behind a house that might be a care-taker's dwelling, and Zale levitates a table and chairs from inside the house like he does it every day. His accuracy and speed are like no feline or dragon I've ever seen. In fact, I think my own father, who would sneer at everyone except dragon lords, would have been taken aback by this male.

I know how important family is, and this is something that has been stolen from my regina. She's already looking at Altara with tears in her eyes and a smile like I've not seen before. If she can find kinship here, perhaps that will heal the piece of her heart that broke when serpent court exiled her.

We sit, and the white-haired Kai runs inside and brings glasses of cold-pressed fruit juice, which none of us are keen to drink just yet. Our new friends do the courtly mannered thing and pretend not to notice this, which already puts them higher in my books.

Aurelia begins explaining our situation straight away, and it seems like Queen Altara is using their helping us as a means to prove them all trustworthy. Lyle and Scythe sit next to her as her guards while Savage and I stand up, keeping an eye on the two beastly lords, who have no trouble staring at me.

"Ghoul is a basilisk," Aurelia says. "Do you...have those here?"

The king and queen exchange a look before Zale says, "We have large serpents, yes. Also my cousins, in fact."

Aurelia nods slowly. "He has power over shadows, and we discovered that he can use those shadows to build a big...cyclone."

"Like a hurricane." Altara nods. "We can get them here."

"Except this cyclone is expected to send beasts to hell...instantly." Aurelia clasps her hands on the table. "I've never seen anything like it, and now we expect my father to come to my...castle and annihilate everyone in it.

"Aurelia's father," Scythe says. "Wants Serpent Court to rule the state without any other competition. He will destroy all beasts except serpents."

"And there is no way you can stop him?" Zale asks, raising his brows as if he thinks he'd have no trouble stopping Ghoul.

Aurelia's eyes move as she ponders this. "Although he doesn't want to, if he is ordered to do it, he will have no choice but to obey because of various enslavement spells. So there is that possibility."

Zale's face suddenly darkens. "He is a captive then, as I once was." I'm surprised he'd reveal something vulnerable like that. He must really think we're not a threat.

"That is quite an enemy," Altara says. "We understand this type of foe, Lady Aurelia." She rubs her stomach as if it bothers her, and Henry zips over to her stomach again, plonking himself down to sit on it. I wonder if she's getting Braxton-Hicks contractions. "I am also familiar with dark magic. A power *vacuum* like that would require an equal force as a counter to close it. This is a known rule of magic. Power must counter power of equal value to void it."

Zale scratches his jaw. "As his bonded-mates, you are equally powered, yes?"

Aurelia goes still. Immediately, I know what she's thinking. That fell light in her eyes as a dark idea blooms like a corpse flower in that mind of hers. While we males are equally powered, our regina trumps all of us.

My dragon takes over, firing me up and making my voice deep. I don't fight him anymore, because we're the same person and I understand him now. "Don't even think about it." My voice emerges guttural and deep, a living flame exploding from me.

The standing Boneweaver males take a step back, staring in disbelief, but my eyes are not for them. "You will *not* sacrifice yourself for him, for us. Not in this life, regina."

She looks at me with that perfect mouth parted, her eyes wide and fixed on me, her breath heaving with emotion. "You don't get to tell me what to do, *dragon*," she snarls, not blinking as she commands me.

"I will always do as you command, sapphire-of-my-soul, but not in *this*."

She closes her eyes. "We'll discuss this later."

I bare my teeth at my brothers, silently asking for their backup. It's Scythe who enters my mind. *"I agree, fire-brother. She will not sacrifice herself."* It's only this that placates me and puts my fire out. For the moment.

"So there is no other way?" Lyle asks, looking between the two royals. "Someone must actively counter the force of the shadow vortex?"

"Unless you can kill him before he does it, yes," Lord Raen says. "I do not see another solution for this, do you, my king?"

King Zale looks from Lord Raen to Aurelia. "The shadow realm is an unpleasant place. It will not respond to anything but the person who opens it unless they are overpowered."

Aurelia sits back in her chair, inhaling deeply. Savage, jittery by my side, wanders over to sniff at the trees surrounding the garden. Lord Kai cocks his head and follows him. We all turn to watch the two of them, seemingly the most volatile of us, for a moment.

Kai narrows his eyes at Savage, sniffing the air around him. "You smell odd."

Savage mirrors him, narrowing his eyes too. "You smell odder. Can I see your sword?" He points to Kai's black earring.

"Sure." Kai unhooks the earring, and immediately it grows until it's a full-sized black blade. The white-haired male holds out the weapon for an awestruck Savage's eager inspection.

"You."

I turn to the group at the table, and it takes me a second to realise that it's *me* who King Ashzale is regarding, his voice not threatening but soft, almost reverent as those eyes he shares with my regina look me up and down. "One of *you* has not been seen in these lands for nigh on a thousand years. Progeny of the Old Kings of Black Fae Court, if I'm not mistaken. They can't shift anymore, but they still take the name Darkcleaver."

The world seems to stop. I stare him, my breath suddenly burning in my lungs in recognition. My eyes find my regina's as she too blinks in surprise. "They know my name, regina."

"It makes sense," Scythe says softly. "Your mother's kind are unique, Xander, like Aurelia's people."

Perhaps for the first time in my life, I don't know what to say. But Zale's mouth quirks up into a hint of a smile that sends the beast in me rearing up. "Can we see it?" he asks. "Your dragon form?"

I look to Aurelia for permission, and my beautiful regina smiles, biting her lip. "You can't say no, Xander."

"I can't," I agree, grinning.

They walk me out to the front of the caretaker's house, where a well-worn dirt road with cart tracks is bordered by wild jungle. Everyone steps back, and I'm pleased to see the excitement and curiosity glimmering in the eyes of the Boneweaver king.

"Any excuse to show off," Savage says as I take off my clothes and leave them in a neat pile.

"You can't exactly blame him," Lyle says begrudgingly, zipping my clothes towards him. I take my time to shift, letting my spirit take me over, letting the scales and fangs and wings overcome me until I'm drunk on my own greatness.

Kai gasps, and the other males mutter something to each other while their queen claps and cheers, looping her arm through Aurelia's. I look down at them all as they gaze upon me in wonder.

"Give them a ride," Aurelia calls. I think she wants to thank them for their help, or merely their solidarity with her. So I snort and toss my head.

The males waste no time and climb up my foreleg quickly as if they were born to it. "Hard as a rock," Zale says, rapping his knuckles against the scales on my neck. "This is very impressive, Lord Xander." I toss my head in agreement and stretch out my wings, squatting and shooting up in the air.

The males whoop with joy at the speed as we ascend above the humid heat of the dense jungle below. I take advantage of my bird's-eye view to see more of this island Zale rules over.

"There is my castle in the south," Zale says, and I can hear his smile as he gestures to a magnificent, sprawling complex, newly built. "And far to the north are the two islands that make up the Ellythian Isles, where my wife's ancestors on her mother's side hail from."

We're high enough now that I can see a second island in the distance, heavy with green jungle and steam rising from its canopy, surrounded by vibrant blue ocean to rival Boneweaver eyes. It's a stunning environment, and I let myself circle for a minute.

Something powerful brushes against my mind. It's vast and has a tinge of something infinitely dark, but is ultimately full of light. I recognise it and accept the request for communication.

"My wife tells me," Zale says. *"The bond between you and my cousin is dark, unlike her other mates."*

"She can see bonds?" I ask after a moment.

"She has many powers, being a descendant of the powerful sorcerer queen, Ellythia," Zale says. *"Including healing. But yes, seeing bonds is one of them."*

"I made a grave mistake, Your Majesty, and I pay for it every day."

I have questions to ask of this king, and I broach him telepathically. He allows it and answers me honestly. Only then do I begin my descent. There are some people in a small town a little to the north of where we arrived through the portal, and many of them see me, pointing and shouting as I become more clearly seen. I enjoy this for a moment before landing among our companions.

The males climb off, windswept but bright with exhilaration, and when I shift back into human form, Kai runs up to me and leaps, throwing his arms and legs around my neck.

"This is the most fun I've had in an age, Lord Xander!" he says as he climbs off me and sets his bare feet back on the ground. "Many thanks!" He runs back to Lord Raen, babbling about the height.

"You realise they'll be able to shift into dragons now," Aurelia says wryly.

I look at the way King Zale brushes his fingers along his wife's cheek, smiling in a way that is all too familiar. *"I don't think that's a bad thing."*

"We need to get back," Scythe announces. "We thank you for what you could tell us."

"I wish we could do more," Altara says, taking my regina's hand. "If there is more we can do, please let us know."

"You've helped a lot," Lia says. "We have more information... and more hope than we did before."

"Do me a favour," Zale says, with something that could only be described as a mischievous smile. "Be the Boneweaver queen of that world. I won't have us not represented."

Altara laughs. "Yes! And you must come again, cousin, when your world gets boring." She pats her stomach. "This baby would love another aunt."

"Can we, regina?" Savage asks eagerly. "For a holiday?"

Aurelia, her eyes glistening with what I'm sure are a lot of mixed emotions, cups her wolf's cheek. "Anything for my mates."

Chapter 99

Scythe

urelia is reluctant to return through the portal, her steps dragging as she looks back at her newly met kin. The Boneweaver royalty couldn't be mistaken for anything else by the way their auras pulse like a heartbeat of pure power, unabashedly showing their strength. These are people who'd defeated their own demons and come out on top. These are worthy kin for my regina. It's just a shame the information we received only leaves us with a greater problem.

We journey back the same way we arrived, through the tomb portal and back into the dark cavern with the gleaming archway. Then we venture back through the ocean's entrance in the ceiling where Lyle blasts us through to the other side with such force that we don't even see the monster within it, but end up winded and choking by the time we reach the air above.

Xander curses Lyle's name as we recover, but everyone else is too preoccupied in getting back up to ground level. Panting and with weak legs, we all stumble through the door back into the library, where Minnie wakes up with a start.

She pushes herself up from the table she was resting her head on, revealing a pale Yeti sitting behind her. He's almost the same colour as his white hair now, but telling him about the other white-haired beast we'd just met would have to wait. His amputated foot is propped up on the chair opposite him, and a pair of crutches waits next to him.

"Welcome back," he says with a smile. "Mace's army just left their bases. They'll be here by the late afternoon." Henry shoots over to Gertie, Minnie's yellow nimpin, and they animatedly chirp at each other.

"What time is it?" Xander asks, picking up his phone where he'd left it with Minnie.

Pale light shines through the library windows on our left. "Almost dawn," Minnie says. "You were gone a few hours."

"Thank the Goddess." Aurelia sighs heavily, pulling out a chair. "You're not going to believe this, Minnie."

Lyle, Savage, Xander and I leave our regina with the Devi pack. There is much we need to do before Mace's convoy arrives. We start with assessing the perimeter of Animus Academy. Marduk joins us as we leave the library, and Beak follows us as we head outside to meet the rising sun. Swimming in the strange brine at the centre of the academy has left me feeling strangely sharp, just as if I'd swum in the ocean.

My sworn beasts gather in the stands of the Hunting Games arena where I address them. More have arrived since our journey to Boneweaver Island. "When I asked each of you to swear yourselves to me," I begin, "I told you that we would fight for freedom. For many years, we have done just that. Freedom at any cost, destroying the enemies that got in our way." I pause, looking each of them in the eye. "Now a new type of enemy comes for us. You have all seen the news; you know Mace Naga is coming for Animus Academy, but what you do not know is the weapon he brings with him." I turn to Savage and nod.

Savage looks out at the beasts in the stands and broadcasts a single, moving image. A memory of Eugene's: Ghoul standing in the backyard of the Naga household, creating the darkest magic of our kind. My beasts, perhaps some of the hardest criminals I've ever known, jerk in surprise at this vision. A few of the more sensitive ones cry out, but most simply go pale and look at me, waiting for instruction. I've never led them astray before, and I do not intend to lead them astray now. They trust me.

"He will arrive this evening with the intention of killing us all. I trust you understand what this means."

"So this is it," Marduk says, observing me. "There is an answer in your eyes, shark-friend."

Aurelia's self-sacrifice will never happen. I will ensure that. And if that is not a solution to this problem, then there is only one other. "There is," I say, deathly soft and yet every beast in the vicinity hears it. "Either Mace Naga and his militia die tonight, or we do." An eagle lands next to me. "Beak has returned from his scouting of the enemy convoy. You will receive your orders now."

Chapter 100

Aurelia

"Do you have it in you to kill a mate?" Yeti asks me point blank. He's been in a morbid mood since his discharge from the medical centre and fair enough, honestly. "It's the only way to prevent all of this."

I want you fangs out and wild.

Minnie pales, but she doesn't shirk away from the question. "It's what Ghoul wants from me," I say. But what I don't say out loud is that it's not what Ghoul needs. It's not what our pack needs.

The Boneweaver pack is not the Devi pack. We all know that. Minnie nods at me, understanding what my hesitation means. "It's a regina's choice," she says quietly. "To deal out judgement. That is our privilege and responsibility." She places her hand over Yeti's. "Yeti knows I will always take care of him. With whatever he needs." I stare at their joint hands, the bond between them, and how much they've come to mean to each other.

"I wish I could help," Yeti says, glancing at his missing foot. "I'll assist as much as I can from the wall."

"Thank you," I say. "Everyone has a role to play, and you'll find your place, Yeti." He doesn't have it in him to smile, but he nods all the same.

"If we cannot kill Ghoul," I say. "If we can't manually stop the shadow vortex, we will have to stop the person who commands him."

"Mace," Yeti says.

I smile without humour at my friends. "And I *do* have it in me to kill my father."

"He'll have protections around him," Minnie says earnestly. "Probably even more than his favourite general."

My hands clench into fists in my lap, and Henry chirps comfort in my ear. "We'll just have to get through them."

* * *

I leave Minnie and Yeti to go back to their dorm for a 'canoodling' session, as Minnie likes to call it. She has a schedule for the three of them, but today's is unplanned due to the oncoming enemy. It's a good idea to power up before everything starts. Henry and Gertie get sent together to find Eugene.

There's a feeling you get in your gut when you know someone's on their way to kill you. It's something beyond nausea. Beyond dread. Claws scrape at my insides. A beak taps with impatience. There's the rising of a colossal head, casting predatory eyes beyond all things. A weariness weighs down both my bones and my mind. Meeting Ashzale and Altara, Lord Raen and Kai had taken a toll on me. There's an entire world out there I don't know. That is yet to be explored. Perhaps I have even just scraped the surface of what it means to be...*me.*

Suddenly, I get a glimpse of another future, and my heart swells to be full of something I didn't know was possible. *This baby could use another aunt.* I close my eyes and remember their faces, proud and fierce. I want to get to know them more. I want to go back and see why my blood sang as soon as my foot touched the earth there. There's just one thing getting in the way of that. A simple case of annihilation.

I'm heading back to the animus dorm before I consider my options. *"My mates,"* I whisper through the air, *"I need you."*

I make them hunt me. Shifting multiple times—bird, possum, lioness, serpent, wolf—on my way to the secret space under the school where Scythe sometimes uses the pool for soaking his weary mind. I take off my clothes and slip into the cool water, lit from below with a subtle blue. Briefly, I slip in and out of my shark form, enjoying the change in the way the water feels against my skin, and the way water goes from feeling like home to feeling like pleasure.

I feel them enter the cavern when I'm submerged underwater, twisting onto my back to observe them come up to the pool, their bodies and faces waving and rippling. I rotate back onto my stomach and leave them behind me, kicking upward until my head clears the water. I gasp a grateful breath and reach for the concrete edge of the pool, pulling myself up slowly, letting my mates see my naked skin as I emerge.

My right leg twinges as my foot takes my weight, and I try to hide the hiss of pain. Warm hands brush the skin of my thigh, sending black-tinged golden power through my muscle and bone. My sigh is involuntary, and I close my eyes, letting Xander pour his healing into me.

"Perhaps it will always hurt just a little," I breathe. "But you always make it better."

When I get no reply, I open my eyes to see Xander's giant form towering over me, a small furrow between his dark brows. "Come here." I reach for his neck and pull him down for a kiss. My other mates gather behind me, their fingers skimming my skin, Lyle pushing back the wet strands of my hair to kiss my shoulder. Their powers seek out mine, dark and hungry, wanting to power me up for what's to come, and craving a touch of me.

"There's nothing else in this world better than being with you," I tell them. I break away from Xander and find Scythe at my side, pulling my chin towards him. He breathes across my lips, his light blue eyes piercing me right to my core, telling me he has something important to say. Behind me, Savage gets on his knees, rubbing his face against my thighs.

"My only world is you, regina," Scythe says. "It will only ever be you." My body crumples into his, and I fling my arms around his neck as he devours my mouth, the great white in him thrashing around violently under his skin. Savage finds my ass with his mouth.

Lyle growls from the side, burying his fingers in my hair and wrenching me away from Scythe's mouth to his. My lion growls into me, and I moan into his hungry mouth, his tongue finding mine in a little coaxing dance that calms his aggression. A pair of arms wrap around my waist and yank me away from all of them, and Xander is suddenly smirking as he steals me away to the nest of pillows and blankets off to the side. Growls and angry snarls chase after us as Xander carefully lies down on the nest, settling me on top of him. I sit up, pressing my palms against his chest as the others gather around us. He crooks a finger at me, suddenly serious. I dive down, pressing my lips against his, wet strands of my hair hanging down around us. Lyle's fingers pull my hair back while Xander's fingers work at his belt until his cock springs free of his pants, bouncing up behind my ass.

I have to lift myself a bit to angle myself for his immense size, but once the swollen head of his cock kisses my entrance, he runs his hands down my body. "I know I'm not the best thing that's happened to you, regina," he says, eyes burning with that bright light. "But you are the best thing that's happened to me. Without you—" I slide down his length and we both briefly close our eyes to savour each other. "Without you, I'd be the worst version of myself." He pulls me down to press my forehead against his. "I need you to know that."

A gentle touch caresses my asshole, and I realise it's Lyle. Xander grabs my hips and thrusts into me, and any reply is lost to a moan as his immense power reaches for mine and we twine around each other. There is lube in my ass, and Lyle's finger works me until I'm panting and writhing. When he positions himself behind me, his lips finding my neck, my eyes fly open.

"Go slow," Scythe growls as I breathe, readying myself for the two biggest cocks in my pack. Hands on my thighs and around my waist caress me, making me gush around Xander until my head is thrown back on Lyle's chest. There's pressure, so much blissful pressure in my core as Lyle's cock presses against me. I gyrate my hips, slowly working him in. My power sparks like volatile electricity as Lyle's golden hue requests entry, and I grant it, letting it join the pulsing columns of me and Xander.

Savage kneels on my right, and I reach for him, finding his mouth and tongue and the slight scruff along his jaw. He shows me a mental image of myself, from his point of view, writhing in pleasure between my precious mates. It only serves to make me wetter, loosening my muscles to fully accept my lion as he and Xander gently thrust at alternate times. Savage's power, wild and off kilter, rockets into my body, searching and finding, joining the combined column, adding his own leaping strands. My body vibrates under the three of them, but it's not until Scythe's feet find themselves at my right side that I shudder, looking up at him.

Savage's lips find my nipple as Scythe looks down at me, undoing his shirt button by button, making my mouth water as his glorious, rippling muscle is revealed. He finally gets to his belt buckle, tattooed fingers working, his eyes only for me. His zip comes down, and I reach for him as his pierced cock springs free. He strokes himself, and I toy with his first piercing, pausing to look up at him for permission, licking my lips.

A soft smile touches my shark's lips as he nods, and he takes another step forward so I can lick off the bead of pre-cum at his tip. I savour his heady taste before dragging my tongue over the rest of him. Scythe's hiss of pleasure is a thing of dreams as I take him into my mouth, only to feel his power seeking permission at my lips.

I moan around the four of my mates, giving me what I need, satiating their hunger and using my body as their powers join my own in our unique dance. Scythe's cold tundra power joins the fray in a now multi-coloured column that has me tensing and shuddering around Lyle and Xander. My lion wraps his arms around me from behind, forever a pillar of strength.

"Are you alright, angel?" he whispers in my ear.

I moan in reply and cast out a request to the ether.

And I get a reply.

Chapter 101

Ghoul

If hate were a person, it would be me, as I feel my regina in the hands of her pack, that soul bond *pulsing* between us. But a yearning request petitions me. Even with the attention of the others, she seeks me out, here as I travel towards her in the back of this military vehicle, locked in like a beast, to 'conserve my energy', my so-called reptilian guards sitting around me.

I will grant any request of my regina's I'm capable of, but those opportunities have been so few and far between. I yearn for her gaze. And so I go. I sink into a meditation on the floor of the rumbling truck and leave my body at her request, as I'd done so many months ago for the first time on one fateful night.

Deep in the bowels of Animus Academy, I find them in each other's arms, writhing around each other, the scent of their arousal saturating the air. My regina is in the centre, vibrating as she holds four hard cocks in her body. She feels me as I come upon them, ominous and dark. The bringer of death, bringer of annihilation. And still, when she casts that gaze on me, her pupils glowing ultra-violet just for a moment, I don't get the urge to destroy the world quite so badly.

Time itself seems to stop as her eyes bore into mine, the cavern buzzing with their combined powers while I stand alone. Then her eyes start burning and I feel her command on my being, and the urge to obey is suddenly overwhelming. It's all I've ever wanted. To be with her, to be *in* her in more ways than one.

"Come to me, my basilisk," she commands me in a low, purring hiss that makes me want to fall to my knees. The others go still.

"You would welcome annihilation, snakelet?" I hiss back as my boots move forward.

Her head tilts downward, predatory and disapproving. "I welcome a mate. You are bound to me. To all of us."

I don't look at the others, fully knowing I would kill them for the attention they steal. I end up next to Savage, who growls and snaps at me. So I step around him and over the dragon, one foot on either side of his chest so I'm in front of my regina. I drop to my knees, and even though I feel the dragon's light-filled eyes burning through my uniform and his growls rumbling through his chest, I take my regina's face in my hands and kiss her mouth. Her hands are for her shark and wolf, but her eyes and mouth are mine because she doesn't close those shining jewels as I claim her mouth.

And they widen when I send my power into her, black and almighty. Suddenly, fang scrapes against fang, and I can't help but smirk over her tongue as she cries out, feeling all five powers at the same time.

She hums with power, breathless and making sounds of utmost pleasure and pressure. I reach for her clit and, finding it wet and swollen, hiss into her mouth. Suddenly, it's too much, and she screams in orgasm, jerking around the five of us. I chase her mouth, swallowing her screams as Lyle comes into her, followed by Xander, heaving under me, his hips bucking, fingernails scraping at the concrete because he can't reach her while I'm blocking him.

Savage grunts and I allow her to take his cum into her mouth, my own cock tight and hard in my pants. I stand up then, still over the dragon as Scythe comes next, and as she takes him, I unzip my pants and run my hand over the length of my own shaft, pulsing with arousal and annoyance.

Scythe wipes the side of her mouth, and she finally turns to me. I almost come just by looking at her, lips wet and pink, eyes heavy-lidded as she drags her gaze up my form. She opens that heavenly mouth and drags her pink tongue over my head. My balls draw tight in anticipation and she devours me all too eagerly.

The arm attached to the hand that squeezes the base of my shaft catches my eye. Her own blood, her own venom. The scent is intoxicating and powerful, and I tug at the hand so I can see the mark better. It does something to me to see that vow cut brutally into her. Something I can't explain. Something that shudders with primal rage and anticipation. My eyes burn as I brush a thumb against the marking, an ancient language that I too studied as she had when she was young. Something we share just between the two of us.

My regina's mouth sucks at my cock, her eyes burning into mine with feral promise, holding me captive, easing away every awful power within me. It's not until I feel the scrape of a fang against my shaft that I come, emptying myself into her, cradling her face and pulling up her upper lip to expose the sharp white fang that draws blood and cum from me like she is—

"*I was made for this,*" she hisses into my mind. A challenge, a final plea.

And I was made for destruction.

Chapter 102

Aurelia

My skin feels like fire, and my blood like light itself. The tremble across my body is not fear, but power. Ghoul arrived and left like a dream, giving me what I wanted, his eyes red and haunted by the knowledge of what is to come, and a tint of...jealousy. I nap for two hours after receiving all five of my mates. When I wake, Scythe's lips flutter across my pulse, and I stretch out like a cat.

Xander is dressing off to my left, and so is Lyle. None of us need to say anything. Only a glance from Scythe asks me to get up. "Don't shower," Savage says, inspecting his nails from a shadowy corner, where he sits cross-legged observing us all. "It's best to fight dirty."

There is something in his eyes I've not seen in waking memory for a while. A cruel gleam I've seen in memories and that one time when they'd held court in the animus Rec room and he'd gouged out the belly of a beast for disobedience. It's cold and harsh. He looks away from me and down at the concrete floor, ruminating on something I can't know.

Lyle must notice my observation, and he brushes my now frizzy hair with his fingers, tying it into a secure bun. *"Savage trained for this, regina. He'll be in his element. It may be something you're not used to seeing."*

"I want to know all of him," I reply. *"I'm not scared."*

Lyle turns me to face him, and his face is kind of sad. *"I've seen all your sides, regina, and I love you for every inch. I will be there when you hold your father accountable for his crimes."*

We leave the cavern and make for the dining hall for something to eat. It's sadly vacant, the air usually still when it should be buzzing with noise during lunchtime. To my surprise, my counsellor Theresa is on duty, overseeing the empty buffet line as we fill our plates with light foods. Lyle startles when he sees her, and the cassowary anima steps forward with a wry smile.

"You didn't think I'd leave, did you, Lyle? After all you've done for me?"

"Your mates—"

"Understand completely," she reassures us. "You gave me my life back when you gave me a job here. I wouldn't abandon *your* pack or this academy and what it stands for when beasts come to take it from us. Some of the other faculty feel the same. We will stand with you."

The backs of my eyes burn as they converse quietly, and I take my food to the table and eat next to Savage, who only has a glass of water before him. "You're not going to eat?" I murmur.

He turns in the seat to give me his full attention. "I fight best if I'm hungry, regina."

Xander pulls out the seat next to me, sitting down heavily. "Regina, I want to give you something."

I turn around with interest and see he has a small blue velvet box in one hand. He opens it to reveal a gold necklace with a jewelled pendant. It's a deep blue sapphire with five stones set around it in a circle: green, yellow, blue, red, and grey.

"One for each of us," Xander says as I run my fingers over the precious stones. The fact that he included the grey stone means everything to me. His big fingers are gentle as he carefully takes the necklace out of its place. I turn around, my skin prickling as the pendant settles above my cleavage, and he clasps it securely. I can immediately tell that it's been dragon-spelled to change its length when I shift.

"Thank you," I say, turning back to show him how it looks. There's something in those glowing eyes as he looks upon me, like he wants to say something. I'm just about to probe for an answer when Sabrina, Stacey, and the assassin twins stride through the outside door. Minnie, Marduk, and Yeti on crutches arrive through the inside door. They grab their food and sit down next to us.

"So what's the plan?" Sabrina says, looking at me and toying with a piece of lettuce.

"The avians have checked out the convoy coming for us," I say. "And what I suspected has been confirmed. My father is going to be difficult to kill. He's in a military truck protected by armed guards, shifted serpents, *and* serpent runes. Out of the three, the runes will be the most difficult to get past."

Stacey's eyes go wide, and the nimpins on her shoulder, including Henry, hover with nerves. "Will they work like the one you used on The Collector?"

"Likely, just more...instant."

"So how do we counter them?" Sabrina asks, twisting her lettuce in her hands. "How can we get to him?"

I take a deep breath and nod to Lyle, who levitates a small, frosted glass ball out of his pocket. "I made this after consulting with Hyacinth." I pick it out of the air and show it to everyone. There are runes painted all over it in a special mixture of my blood and venom. "Normally, these are nullification runes. But they won't work on something as powerful as my father's work, especially with the sheer number he's using. So we've mixed my usual blood and venom with the powder they made from my old femur bone."

Minnie's face turns ashen, and Sabrina tears her lettuce in half. No one says anything, so I continue. "I just have to get it past his runes and activate it by smashing it open. With this, any serpent rune he's using will lose power. It's a dark type of magic to use body parts, but it's my own, so I don't feel bad."

"It's like a bomb!" Savage says proudly, smiling at me.

"A Boneweaver bomb," Stacey says softly.

Scythe's voice floats into my head, only for me. *"I'm proud of you, regina. For using your enemy's weapon against them."*

"I need this to work," I tell him and everyone. "It's the only way we'll be able to get to my father to kill him. It's the only way all of this stops."

"There are other obstacles," Lyle says. "There will be the militia and the venom bullets to deal with, for one."

"Which is why we're working in teams." Xander nods. "You all have your assignments."

Stacey raises her hand, but there's a shout from outside and Beak walks in, fully naked, sweat glistening on his chest. He nods purposefully at Scythe. "They're almost here."

My stomach plummets, the muscles of my body clenching. A low growl sounds in my head. Silently, we split up into our groups. My pack and I head out to the top of the Animus dorm where we'll get a better view of the road beyond the academy. A dust cloud forms on the horizon, and it takes a minute, but the rumble of heavy military trucks reaches our ears. Another rumble, higher up and higher-pitched fills the air. Two dots rise into the sky. Then another two.

He had come for my mother.

Then he came for me.

And now he wants to take everything.

A violent rage, one like I've never known even when I burned down the Naga family home, funnels through me. I place my hand on the stone wall. *"Protect us. Do what you can to protect this place."* Something pulses out under my hand, and the blue dome that surrounds the school brightens, an energy shimmering down from its centre point high above us.

Savage comes up to stand next to me. Strapped to his chest is a carrier like the one they use for front-facing babies, but Eugene is in it, his goggles pulled taut around his head as he sits comfortably, legs hanging on either side. Savage has a matching pair of goggles on his forehead.

"He's going to help me with the hatchling soldiers," Savage says softly. "If we can see how they're going to move seconds ahead, we can take them out without killing them."

"But his foresight is uncontrollable," I say.

"Is it?" Savage takes out a tiny silver tin from his pocket and opens it to show me white powder. He taps out a tiny amount onto the back of his hand and puts it under Eugene's nose.

"Savage—" I protest.

But Eugene eagerly leans down, and as Savage covers one nostril, Eugene sniffs the portion up. I stare open-mouthed as Eugene shakes himself, making a stifled sound before settling with a "*bok*," as if to reassure me.

"Are you guys seeing them?" a familiar deadpan sounds from a walkie-talkie behind me, and I turn to see Xander raising the device to his mouth.

"Yes, Sabrina, we see them. You four organised?"

Stacey's excited voice sounds this time. "Copy that! We're on the anima dorm, yes! We're ready for these fuckers. Can we go through the team names again? Over."

Xander sighs, scratching the bridge of his nose with his thumb. "Fine. Aurelia and Lyle are Team Boneweaver. Savage and Eugene are Team Dazzle. I'm...Team Xander. Over."

"Right!" Stacey says. "Me and the nimpins are Team Cotton Ball. Sabrina, Blair, and Blade are Team Assassin. Over!"

"And!" comes Minnie's voice. "Marduk, Yeti and I are Team Pink."

"Roger that," says Beak. "I'm leading Team Avian with our full flock, but we're split into A and B."

I raise my brows at Xander, but he shrugs and speaks to the teams again. "Our beasts on the wall are split into order groups, in subsets of A and B. Scythe or myself will call out to direct as necessary."

The trucks rumble closer, and even though I know it will happen, it still makes my heart ache to see our group split up. Savage and Eugene, Team Dazzle, are the first to leave for the front wall. Minnie and Marduk follow him.

My shark, lion, and dragon flank me. Lyle has exchanged his usual suit for a fresh set of what he wore to Boneweaver Island: simple black track pants and a T-shirt. For some reason, Scythe doesn't change his clothes and wears his normal black business shirt and slacks. I can only tolerate a set of shorts and a tank top, both black and stretchy, giving me room to move and shift.

"They'll send the helicopters first," Scythe says from my right. "We'll need to respond to their request."

I nod as the helicopters do indeed make themselves known—a

set of two, loud and slowing down as they approach us. My heart hammers in my chest, and I don't give in to the urge to cover my ears against the sound. The academy has been surrounded by a second shield this entire time, my own. I retract it now, bringing it in to surround me and my mates. It's important I conserve my energy now.

Both helicopters stop at the boundary between the outside world and the blue dome, swaying as the megaphone resounds out. "His honourable Mace Naga and the state authorities declare Animus Academy now closed. All students and staff are commanded to file out in an orderly manner *immediately*."

"You'll have to kill us first!" screams a female voice from the anima dorms that sounds awfully like Sabrina. It's followed by a cheer.

The magnified voice speaks out. "Very well. We have been ordered to take the Academy by any means necessary. This is your final warning."

Lyle's phone vibrates, and he answers it with a terse, "This is Lyle Pardalia."

It's my father's voice on the other side, and I go still as I hear it. "Surrender the school, Mr Pardalia. This is in your best interest."

"And be sucked into your basilisk's hell vortex?" Lyle growls, to my surprise. "I think not, Mr Naga." A chill runs down my spine.

"Very well. Tell my daughter goodbye." The line dies.

Cold dread expands in my stomach. He has some nerve calling me *daughter* now, for the first time in eight years. In my head, an eagle shrieks, and suddenly, the helicopter before us, the one on the right, bursts into flame, its engine catching fire.

We all turn to look at Xander, his mouth set into a straight, thin line, his anger heating up the air around us. "I've fought beside you in every fucking lifetime, regina."

I smile at him. "Did we win in those lifetimes?"

He cocks his head slightly. "No. But we'll win this. I'll make sure of it."

Despite the heat reeling off him, something about his words chills me. I turn back to the front of the school where a convoy of military trucks have gathered a distance away from the front gate—

or what *was* the front gate. In place of the fancy black and gold cast iron scrollwork is solid black brick with a lone gargoyle's head at its top and centre. I have to shift to my eagle eyes, but my suspicions are confirmed.

A stone bob, a narrow face, and a head that sits just askew like it had been torn off at some point, the surface of its stone mangled as if by sharp teeth. What remained of The Collector's head has been made into a new gargoyle.

I stare at it as Xander speaks on the walkie-talkie again. "Felines on the wall, stand ready. Team Pink, watch yourselves; they'll come for you first. Deflect artillery, and dislodge any weapons."

"Roger that," comes Marduk's reply.

We put our earpieces in, watching the militia in their vehicles, gathering along the perimeter of the academy wall. The guards in the towers have their guns angled and ready, but a single Jeep rolls towards the driveway.

A serpent general hops out of the back of it with two beasts holding heavy black riot shields. The three of them hunch behind the shields and survey the new protection. They set something down on the ground and hurry backwards into their vehicles.

"How long will it take for them to get in?" I ask.

"We're not going to wait to find out," Scythe says. "It was never made to withstand a modern military assault like this."

"North and west guard towers," Xander commands, "open fire."

Chapter 103

Savage

I don't like guns. I never have. But I have to admit they've had their uses in the last few weeks. And when your enemy carries a whole heap of venom-loaded guns, the best thing to do is shoot first.

When the guards next to me open fire on the enemy, I cover Eugene's ears and get ready. He shivers under me, adrenaline and coke pumping through his little feathery body.

"Get ready," I telepathise to him, hefting up my Nerf gun as our bullets bounce off the armoured vehicles. The pipe bomb they laid at the entrance has an obsidian case around it so none of the felines can toss it back unless—

Marduk, as nuts as he ever is, leaps down to the front gate, grabs the bomb in his bare hand and tosses it back to the waiting vehicles. It goes off when it hits the first vehicle, but only makes the surface of the strong metal black.

The guards next to me stop to reload, and the enemy doubles down. Two more helicopters shoot over the dome, hammering at the protection with gunners on open sides, covered in black chains that make them feline-proof.

"Shit," I mutter, sending the image to the group chat in case they miss it. "They're not taking any chances."

A lone truck at the back of the convoy rolls slowly towards the centre of the back lines. I've had my eye on it, moving slowly like it doesn't want to be noticed. It's covered in serpents, shifted ones, big anacondas and smaller venomous, writhing ones. It's like they're working together to make a living, breathing serpent shield around their baddest general.

At the front lines, three other trucks reverse up to the front of the gate and stop. Their back doors open and ramps slam down.

"Hold fire!" Xander shouts over the comms. The gunners next to me straighten from their places and move their fingers off the triggers, swearing under their breaths.

Young children spill out of the trucks like spiders. They are short, their round, cherub faces clear for us to see. My teeth clench together as they roll out cannonball machines and set them up in a line. There's ten of them and three children to a machine, lined up in neat rows like a dance they've practiced for a primary school talent show. They all wear normal sports clothes, shorts and T-shirts, as if Mace Naga wanted to make sure we didn't miss that they're children. One of them has a blue puppy on his shirt. They also have guns strapped to them, so I'm guessing that once the balls run out, they'll start shooting at us.

The leader, a taller boy of maybe ten or eleven, shouts at the front. They work together to press levers on the machines. With a bang, ten heavy feline-resistant obsidian cannonballs shoot out of the machines and slam into the shield. The entire blue dome shakes, but it holds still.

Nasty Mace has sent the children to lead his attack. Rat bastard. No offense to rats. But he's also decided to hit us on all sides at once. Spreading out along the sides of the children are military trucks with adults.

"*We're going to have to get past all of that to get to Ghoul,*" I say into the group chat.

"*Let me worry about that,*" my regina replies. "*But I'll need cover.*"

"*The dome will be down within minutes,*" Scythe says. So we have minutes to figure out our strategy. That's plenty of time.

"Team Pink to take care of the tanks," Minnie pipes. "Or whatever is not covered in obsidian."

"Leave the serpents to us, Team Assassin and Team Cotton

Ball," Sabrina says over the walkie-talkie. "We'll make sure your path is clear, Lia."

"I don't want you guys so close to the vortex," my regina says. "It's not safe."

"There's too many of them," Lyle says. "We'll need assistance there, regina."

Lia is silent. She's not happy about this, but I don't think she gets a choice. The sound of the bullets hitting the dome is getting louder, which I think means they're breaking through.

"Does anybody know where Mace is?" I ask. Nobody answers for a second, and the only thing I hear is the sound of the cannonballs hitting us again.

"What if he didn't even come?" Minnie says. "Coward that he is."

"He wouldn't miss this," my regina says. "I bet he's in the tank with Ghoul."

"Don't worry, we'll get them both," comes Sabrina's voice. "We get one chance at this, Lia, you know that, yeah? Just the one. We need to get it right the first and only time."

I nod, pulling down my matching goggles and picking up my Nerf gun where it's been resting between my legs. "Hard agree, Sabrina. And leave the hatchlings to us, Team Dazzle. Marduk?" I call. "When the dome goes, send me down."

Chapter 104

Lyle

Being tasked with protecting my regina in this battle is the honour of my dreams. The fact that she and my brothers trust me to guard her means more to me than any of them will ever know. Ghoul had been right about the bad we'd done in the past; even I can admit that. We are not worthy of her until the good we do outweighs the bad. And I didn't protect her enough in the beginning.

My rabid lion is pacing inside of me at the enemies that would dare assault our school and what we had built. While most of the students have left, there are still some left here who are now at risk, and it's for all of them that we protect Animus Academy now.

The protective dome shudders under the next cannonball, and as much as I wish I could bat it away, we all must wait. Lia carries the Boneweaver bomb in a small black crossbody bag that's padded with cotton wool. The fact that she made it herself is astonishing. That she insists on throwing it at her father's truck herself is...not so much, in my eyes, so my plan is to stick by her side to cover her for the inevitable bullets coming our way.

Aurelia is focused, her unblinking eyes on the military truck set like a king at the back of the convoy. Males are now climbing out of it, surrounding the vehicle, ready with artillery. Two of them roll out a black mat that makes something like a twenty-metre circumference around the truck. I'd bet my bottom dollar these are where Mace has set up his protective serpentine runes.

They know we'll come for him, and they've protected him thusly. Helicopters wheel overhead, shooting at the dome from above, and this time, when the cannonballs hit the shield, the entire thing flickers in and out.

"Ready, everyone," Xander commands. "Lia, you'd better activate your shield."

There are difficulties with the invisibility because we won't be able to see each other, so we've compromised that Lia will make only herself and me invisible. Xander can look after himself, and Scythe is prepared for what is going to come as well.

My regina envelops the two of us within her shield, and I feel it coming over me like a pleasant heat. I step closer to her as she shifts into phoenix form, claws clicking as she hops onto the stone wall. I've never had to levitate myself for so long and so high, but I'm capable of it. Beak flies at the ready above us, ready to spot for me if I lose Lia in the air.

Behind me, Xander hands Scythe the comms device and takes off his clothes. "It'll go with the next shot," Scythe tells everyone. "Everyone, remember the plan." He pockets the device, and just as the next cannonball is fired, Xander shifts.

The academy roof vibrates under Xander's weight, his shadow casting us in shade. Scythe scrambles up his leg and stakes a seat as the dome finally, with one last flicker, goes out completely.

Xander launches into the air, battering Lia and me with powerful wingbeats. Bullets ping off his hard scales as he spears for the helicopters. Before me, Team Dazzle is set on the ground before the academy gates, and Savage goes off running towards the teenagers with the cannons and guns. The edges of Lia's soft wings brush against me as she rises into the air, and I reach up to feel for her claws. I grasp onto her powerful legs, and we rise up together, wing beats and levitation combined as it's important that I don't slow her down with my weight.

Above us, Xander has a helicopter in his maw, and he's tossing the crushed metallic carcass over the wall of the school, right into the standing military vehicles. The soldiers shout and scatter as it lands, taking out two Jeeps and spilling fuel and fire over them.

We fly towards Savage and Eugene, telepathically connected to each other as their jewelled goggles flash in the long rays of the afternoon sun. Savage shoots a Nerf gun with rubber bullets at two children in quick succession, and they both fall to the ground, crying out and clutching their legs. He dodges one bullet, then another with ease, kicking out a child's feet from under him and tossing their gun.

A feline grabs for the gun as it flies through the air, but it soars above the wall, caught in the hands of one of our guards. Savage cackles as he jumps high with his legs tucked into his body, a bullet missing him completely before he slams the butt of his gun into another child's temple.

Seeing that he's okay, Lia takes us right to where Team Pink and the other wall felines are shoving militia bullets away. But they have their work cut out for them as they miss bullets, creating venom-filled holes in the rendering of the academy wall. Marduk and the guards shoot back with their own rifles, and it's going to be complete chaos until they run out of bullets.

"Look!" My angel's voice is loud in my head, and I snap to attention as she wheels us around to the direct north—Mace's truck. The top of the tank opens in a Concertina fold, its sides retracting neatly so we see the group of beasts crowded into the truck now spilling out.

Aurelia swears in my mind as a group of crocodiles hold the three councillors in chains. They move aside, revealing Ghoul seated cross-legged on the floor of the truck.

And I know what's going to happen before it does.

The sound comes first—a humming over my skin, vibrating the air like guitar strings. The darkness funnels out of Ghouls' body like a reverse tornado. It starts with black wisps that get darker and thicker, twisting around each other and up and up and up, gathering weight and size until it's as wide as the truck itself and reaching high into the sky beyond the flight of our avians. A feeling like something worse than death shivers through the air.

The crocodile grunts throw the councillors at the shadows one by one. It happens so quickly but it doesn't matter because no telekinesis, no order powers can stop them as Ablo Obon's silent body gets caught into the tornado and flies upwards into his hold. Irma Goldwing is next, followed by the Lunissa Darkfang.

Gone, just like that.

As our eyes are on the shadow vortex, we both miss the attack from behind—

An obsidian net catches both of us in its grip

Chapter 105

Aurelia

I knew we weren't completely invincible with my invisibility as serpents can detect heat, but it's still a rude shock when they catch us with an obsidian net. It snaps around my wings, crushing them against my body, and both Lyle and I go plummeting. I don't even have time to make a joke about Lyle now knowing how it feels.

As my power suppresses, my shield evaporates, and I'm forced to shift into human form, pressed against my deputy headmaster.

"The glass!" Lyle shouts, getting the bag out from between us just in time. He takes the glass orb and throws it in the air as hard as he can towards the academy.

"Minnie!" I shout, but I don't see where it lands. I can't do anything to break our fall into enemy territory, but Lyle tries. He shifts into lion form, letting his rabid self take over and pulling me on top of him as we fall.

Just when I think we're going to smash into the earth, multiple large claws snag my limbs and long wing beats strain. Astonished, I look up to see three American eagles working together to slow our fall.

Lyle is far too heavy for them, but instead of splattering to the earth and breaking bones, we just drop heavily onto the dirt right in the centre of the militia. My right leg gets caught under me, and I cry out in pain, scrambling to free it.

My lion roars as I remove the obsidian net, throwing it into the dirt and pulling up a shield around us both. I hobble on the spot, panicked as I search for my glass bomb. Before me, Lyle leaps onto a soldier, his teeth sinking deep and making crimson spill. Bullets crack against my shield.

"Lia!" Minnie's high voice rings out. I whirl towards the academy wall where Minnie stands, pointing to three streaks shooting towards me. One has a docked tail. My black bag is around Sabrina's spotted leopard's body, flanked by the assassin twins in their cheetah forms.

"Cover Lyle!" I say to Minnie as I shift into eagle form and rise in the air. Team Assassin is fast on their way towards Ghoul's truck, the shadow vortex powering upwards like a tornado straight from hell, disturbing the air and creating unstable crosswinds. Electricity lashes out in the dark, tiny streaks of blue and white lightning. The avians scatter away from it to avoid getting tossed to the ground, but shielded, I can surely spear through without getting hammered.

Below me, bullets bounce away from Sabrina's long body as her surrogate mates take the lead as her guards, directing bullets away from her with telekinetic shields of their own.

"Pass the orb to me!" I shout to Sabrina's mind. She can't reply and ignores me, their group of three focused and charging towards a gap between two vehicles protecting the serpent king's entourage. I swoop in low on top of my friends, calling out to Sabina again. *"Give it to—"*

Young soldiers jump out of the two guard trucks, except it's not guns they wield. My beak opens in a cry of warning, but it's too late. The soldiers fling out their arms with a cry, and shadow serpents fly out of their hands. The soldiers collapse, but their beastly spirits surge forward of their own accord.

Blade and Blair skid to a stop as they see this for the first time. But *I* have felt an attack from a shadow snake before. I cry my friend's name. *"Fall back!"*

Sabrina looks up at me, that spotted face beautiful and fierce, and she shakes her head, jerking her chin forward at Blade and Blair. Without fear, without hesitation, the three felines charge onward. The first snakes strike them, fangs ripping into flesh, but they don't stop, claws uselessly passing through the long bodies as they make their way to Mace's truck. The serpents leap for them, lodging their fangs into their muscle, collecting the dark spirits on their bodies like leeches as they go. The pain must be unbearable, but the three spotted felines keep running.

Mace's truck is guarded by two rows of crocodile soldiers; the first row is on their knees with their guns pointed at the felines, and the second is standing, swinging their guns upwards. To me. I recognise the biggest one in the centre. He'd shifted at The Collector's house. There is only death in his eyes as the barrel of his gun suddenly turns to sharp focus. With immunity to order powers, they'd been specifically asked to guard Ghoul and the serpent king.

Both rows fire a round of bullets at us. I dive, simultaneously shoving the bullets away with my own telekinesis from my friends, but this does nothing, and several land in spotted flesh. I look on in horror, realising too late that these bullets are made of obsidian.

My scream is pure avian terror as Blade and Blair stumble from direct hits in the face and chest. Both males fall to the ground. The leopard with the docked tail stumbles, landing flat on her face from a hit that clipped her ear and one in the shoulder.

Sabrina's paws dig into the dirt, and she gets back up, jaw opening wide in a very human grimace. She charges forward, tongue out in pain, that black bag still secure as she claws toward the guards like it's the last thing she'll do.

"Please!" I beg of her.

The guards shoot at me again, and I'm forced to swerve sharply away from my friend. But as I circle back, more bullets fly, and one hits me in the wing. I cry out in agony, blasted backwards and away from my friend. I turn my falling body in time to see Sabrina being thrown back by another round of brutal bullets. She tosses her overcome body in a peculiar way, her movement sends the glass orb flying.

My cry is panicked, my left wing flapping uselessly as I have no choice but to send myself to the ground while Sabrina falls, her eyes unmoving as they fix on the sky. But it's like a perfect dance as an American eagle swoops in with precise timing, catching the orb in one large claw. As if they planned this.

"Regina!" Scythe's voice is furious in my mind as someone catches me with telekinesis. I'm turned to see Scythe riding towards me on Lyle's back, an automatic gun in either hand, shooting as he goes. I land myself sideways in his lap, shifting into human form so I can run towards Beak.

"No!" I scream, but Scythe has one arm banded around me like metal, and he's shooting with the other hand, drowning out my screams.

Beak flies towards Mace's truck, but he hesitates at the border of the black mat as if he senses its power. Then he surges forward, wings angled backwards as if some force is pushing his body. I realise that somehow, my father has made his protective runes form a dome around him like the academy's.

A haunting cry, beautiful but pained, comes from Beak's open maw as he closes his eyes and pushes through, his feathers burning, smoking around him. Beak extends his claw outward, holding my precious orb as he shoulders through the shield with the full force of his burning body.

Someone shoots at him, and bullets lodge in his soft underside. With a flick of his claw, the orb goes flying, tossed about in the wind created by Ghoul's vortex. The orb arcs, falling on top of Mace's truck, where it smashes to pieces on its side.

Beak is thrown to the ground outside the shield where he bounces and joins Sabrina's body, his maw open and silent, venom and blood leaking from his injuries.

I scream in outrage and pain. I didn't want any of this. My body sags in Scythe's arms, sobbing and shaking as grief and sacrifice hit me in the chest just as carnage rules around us. My arm is on fire from the lodged bullet, my entire right leg burns with old injury, and above it all, heartbreak threatens to tear me in two.

A cry sounds from behind us, and Scythe swears under his breath. My head snaps to see Savage pointing at the sky. Because while we'd all been distracted by the Boneweaver bomb, no one noticed a lone dragon flying into that terrible vortex—black scales against a blacker void.

Everything in my head turns silent, my world narrowing down to that maddening, single point. "Oh no you fucking don't."

My dragon takes over just as someone else's memory hits me like a battering ram.

Chapter 106

Ghoul

A few nights ago

"I was wondering when you four good-for-nothings would show up." I'm sitting in a back room of Club Viper, enjoying a joint and my own company when four dark creatures slink into the room like thieves on a heist.

"It's long past time that we spoke," Scythe says in that magnificent rasp, his silver hair reflecting the low downlights of the room.

"I'm pouring a drink." Xander says it like he hates the idea, but he's quick to stride to the well-stocked alcohol cabinet in the corner, those eyes lighting it up on high beam. "Anyone want one?"

"Are you going to poison it, dragon?" I drawl, scanning the four of them.

"That's your job, I believe."

I smirk. "Touché."

"We know what our regina knows," Lyle says, in his usual king-of-the-jungle style, straightening his tie. "We know Mace wishes to massacre the beast population."

"We are also looking for a way to stop him," Xander says, offering me a whiskey glass dangling between his fingers. I don't waste time, taking it from him and downing the golden liquid in one go. "You, him, it's hard to fucking know these days."

The four of them stare at me like they're waiting for something.

But I would know my regina's venom in any life. Her basilisk venom has finally matured in full force. It burns as it absorbs into my system, proud and fierce. I crack my neck.

Finally. I nod to the others.

"I believe," Scythe begins. "That you tried to save Sabrina at Drakos House. You locked her into the cadaver drawers for her own safety didn't you? No one else could get to her once she was there."

I let the question hang in time and space.

"Many choices were taken from me," I drawl. "Yet I maintained the upper hand at each turn. Mace hated me for it but he *also* had no choice. I am his only hope."

"That's hardly an answer," Lyle mutters.

Scythe pins me with those shark eyes. "You maintained a watch over Sabrina at Clawson House. You made sure to follow her there so the Clawsons wouldn't do what they wanted to her. You knew how important she is to your regina."

"And before that," Savage growls. "You fed our regina when she had no food. You did that over and over again."

"And at Drakos House," Xander says. "You stayed close the entire time to make sure nothing terrible *did* actually happen to her. You led the entire thing, simultaneously keeping her as safe as was possible while under the blood oath."

"And then there's Raquel," Savage says. "You took them when you found them at the medical centre and somehow...you knew the Silver Tails were missing a regus."

"We don't have time for this," I say, bored. "I don't need my own genius repeated to me. Or my failures, as it were. I couldn't stop Flores Drakos from doing what he did, *that* could have been stopped by *you*." I allow my power to gather behind my eyes as I stare down the dragon.

"Xander's mark has turned black," Lyle says, trying to assess me for my sanity. "He thinks he needs to die for what he did."

I glare at the dragon where he leans against the wall. "Perhaps he does. But perhaps you *all* do for your transgressions against our regina."

"We've made up for it!" Savage exclaims from where he's been squatting by the door like a puppy guarding a stick.

"Are you so sure about that, wolf?" I snarl. "Are you so sure that anything could make up for you trying to kill her? Or should I recount the time you took her to Mace Naga for execution?"

"Funnily enough, Savage wasn't there," Lyle says. "But since we're talking freely, *you* were."

"I've been here," I say smugly. "I've watched over her before you even *knew* of her existence, lion. While *you* were being paid handsomely for a farce of a job and *she* suffered in poverty." Lyle's growl expands through the room.

"Enough," Xander says. "We are here to talk about the future."

I don't miss a beat. "The one without you in it?"

"Without you either, by the looks of it," Xander says. "Will your little shadow twister kill you too? You don't even know your limits. Or was that first incompetence planned?"

I scoff. "You know nothing."

"I know your shadow vortex needs a counter-power of equivalent force to reverse it."

So they'd figured it out. I try not to show my surprise, baring my fangs at him instead. "And you figure that you'll be the one to do it?"

"How would a person even do this?" Lyle asks. "An exchange of power."

Xander catches my eye. "I asked...someone about that. There would need to be an outward push of my power. All of it. At once."

"All of it?" Lyle says aghast. That would—"

"Kill me, yes," Xander says. The black mark on his neck seems to suck in the light from all around it.

I tilt my head back and laugh.

Chapter 107

Xander

I know what this mark means. It's not because Aurelia forgave me. It's not because I'm worthy. In the battle with my father, I had a realisation.

I am not redeemed.

And I can *never* be redeemed. No act, no gesture, can ever undo or make up for what I did to Aurelia and what I had been a part of.

Except perhaps, for one act.

That's what this black mark is. I've been marked for death from the beginning. There has only ever been one path for me.

My kind would live on through King Ashzale on Boneweaver Island. I made sure of that. The Darkcleaver line will not die with me. I rip out my headphones.

"For Lia," I whisper as the red haze takes over me and I beat my wings towards that black spiral. The last word I want to utter on this earth is her name. My last piece of music. "I vow to love you better in the next life, Aurelia. And in this one, I need to give you mine."

I roar into the shadows. Into the death that awaits to tear my power apart.

Until from right behind me, there comes an answering roar.

Chapter 108

Scythe

As my regina screams into the shadow vortex, her mighty, scaled body taking her into the dark night, I tremble with fury.

I pat Lyle's side. *"You know what we need to do to stop this."*

My lion-brother stares across the field to the guarded truck where Mace Naga sits, now unprotected by his serpent blood magic. *"Just one way, brother."*

Sabrina, Beak, and the assassin twins carved a path for us, and we're not going to let their deaths go in vain. Lyle slingshots us towards Mace's truck.

Chapter 109

Aurelia

I chase after Xander with everything I have, my focus only on him and how fast I can make my wings move into the shadows. He can't do this. I won't allow him to sacrifice himself.

The air around that terrifying moving funnel swirls before me, violent and chaotic. I pursue it for all I'm worth, and when its winds draw me in, pulling at my huge body, I simply encourage it, powering right into its grasp.

Darkness swallows me whole.

I know Ghoul's power; I understand the shadows he wields because I've wielded them too. But this feels like something more than any of us. As if Ghoul is just a vessel, a crack in the world that's allowing the darkness to pour through.

The vortex spins around me, powerful, bitter, and dark with strands of that white lightning streaking like angry serpents. I feel the vortex tugging at the pieces of me, scraping at my scales, pulling on something that is inherently *me*. Fear crashes into my chest, suffocating as I crane my neck upwards to catch sight of Xander. The end of his tail whips about high above me as he flies to the highest point. The sight of him gives me strength, and I shove aside the animal instinct to flee, forcing my wings outwards and down against the current of the fierce wind. Every wingbeat is painful as the residual venom of the bullet burns through my vessels, but I push on.

I've never swum with the current, and I'm not about to start now. I power upward, chasing Xander's black scales, even as the vortex batters at my body, trying to force its will upon me. But I go where my dragon mate goes.

The force only increases as we reach the topmost point of the vortex, and a pressure like I've never known squeezes at my ribs. The roaring in my ears becomes painful, and I squint against the pain, the fear, the opposing forces to latch onto Xander's tail with my teeth.

His big head whirls around to see me, snapping angrily, but the both of us get pulled by a force that won't be denied. A force that feels like damnation.

My vision goes first. Then my hearing.

And it's like death when I feel like my body has been taken from me and I am nothing at all.

* * *

Suddenly, I can breathe again, my lungs opening up to cold air, my skin freezing. It feels like dirt under my curling fingers as the pit in my stomach grows, icy dread opening up within me.

And when my eyes blink open, with terrible shadows licking behind her, I'm looking up into the face of my mother.

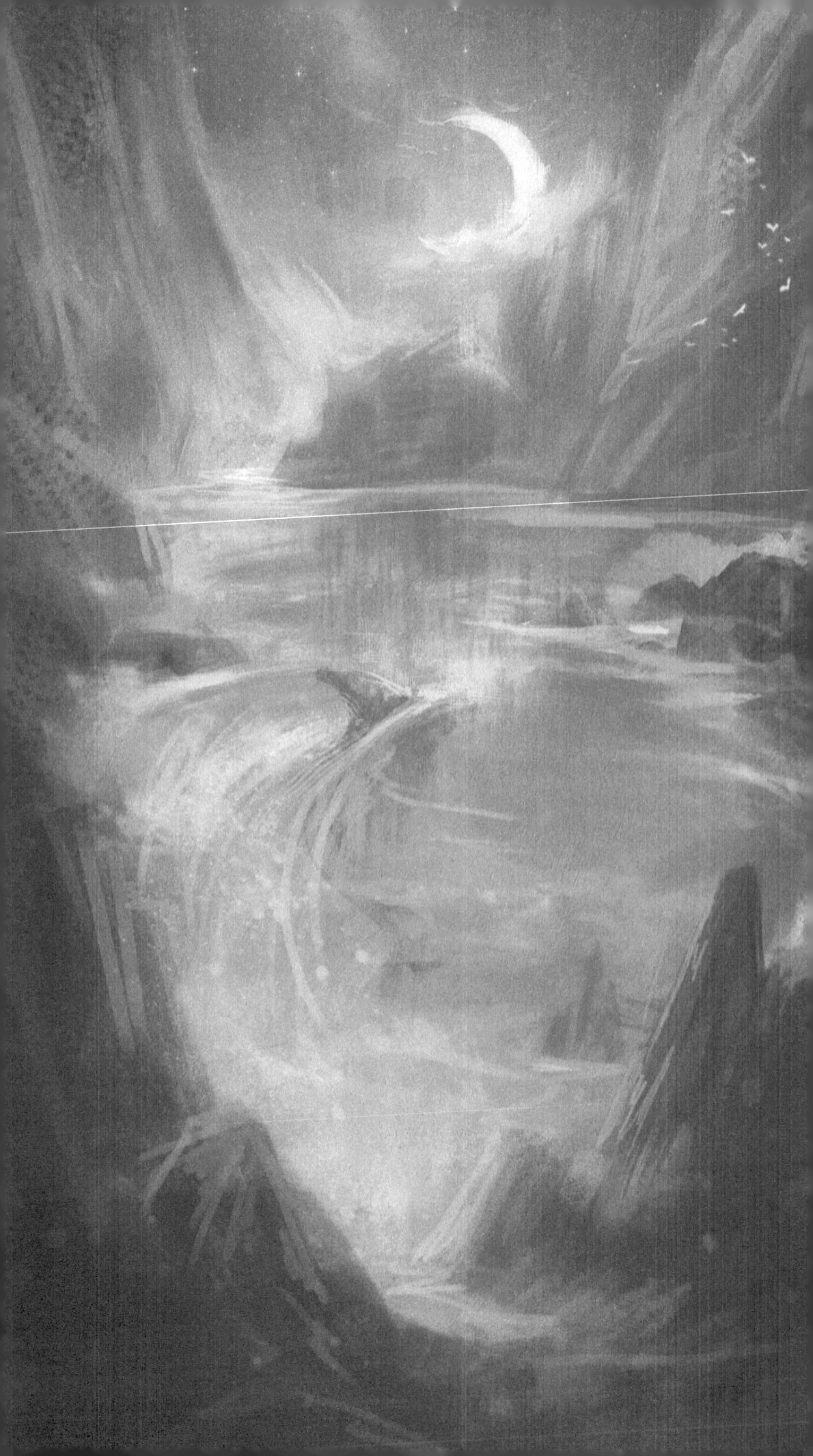

Chapter 110

Scythe

yle's four paws are steady as he thunders across the dirt. I open fire on the soldiers on both sides, the automatic rifles I took from enemy soldiers finding their marks. Lyle leaps over the bodies of Blade and Blair, my sworn cheetahs. They go to their regina now, as I fight for mine.

The sight of their bodies powers me, so that when the shadow snakes, slithering over the ground like translucent abominations, launch themselves at us, I send a powerful psychic blast that fires them tumbling backwards and away from us.

But our path is not yet clear. There are the two rows of crocodile soldiers guarding Mace. I knew Katerina's rex would come after Aurelia eventually.

Except they are not looking at us at all, but above towards the vortex where my regina disappeared. I can stop neither their bullets nor their bodies. A fight here will be to the death.

Instead of advancing on us, the biggest male gives a harsh command and they fall back, towards Ghoul's sitting body and surround him as if to protect him. The sides of the truck are pulled upwards and they are contained within the vehicle once again.

They had only come to kill Aurelia, I realise, and now they mean to use this vehicle as a fortress.

Mace's truck lies before us, the shadow vortex up swirling high above, nothing but a manifestation of hell itself. Xander had put himself into that darkness for us. Had condemned himself to it. And yet the fifth member of our pack is still a member of our pack. They both must be saved.

Serpents writhe over the cabin of Mace's truck, protecting him in a final stand. The battle rages behind us, our felines protecting the academy. Somewhere, I hear the nimpins chirping.

Lyle growls low in his chest, the rumble spreading through my thighs. *"Kill."*

"The serpents," I say, remembering an old burn in my neck, "they're all venomous." And our regina is not here to suck out the venom this time.

Behind me, Eugene lets out a crow. "Where are we up to, guys?" Savage calls, trotting up behind us, Eugene bouncing in his carrier. Next to him is Stacey in golden lioness form, looking terrified but willing to help.

Savage nods, readjusting his bedazzled goggles. "Do it, Stace."

The lioness tosses her head, and from her back, no less than twenty colourful nimpins, collected from the departed anima students, fly up in the air and open their tiny beaks.

I throw up a psychic shield around my brothers just in time.

Chapter III

Aurelia

"Aurelia, no," my mother breathes, her eyes wide, lips parted.

She is as beautiful as my memories of her. I scramble to my feet. She looks healthier than when I saw her last, but her body is not a body at all; she is translucent. A spirit.

Next to her stands the ghostly form of her tiger mate, Cassius Clawson, who I'd seen not long ago at Clawson House. He's as tall as Scythe, with shoulder-length black hair and black brows over a fierce, pale face.

Xander grunts to his feet next to me, in his human body as I am.

"How?" I ask, my voice breaking. "How are you here?"

My mother reaches for me, her eyes glittering with emotion. "You need to leave, my love, right now."

Xander reaches for my hand, and I let him take it because it steadies me. "I miss you," I say to her, my hands stretching out even though I know it's useless. "I tried to find you. I didn't know—"

"It's done now, Lia," she says, her voice uncharacteristically fierce. "You did for me what no one else would, and for that, I owe you *everything*. But you should not be here. This place is not for the living, nor for the good. This is damnation, Aurelia."

I take a look around us then. There is nothing but shadows. Nothing but moving, roiling darkness and a feeling of ancient, cold dread.

"Then why are you here?" My voice is a desperate plea.

"We are waiting," she hisses. "I cannot rest until—" Something pulls her backwards, making her fade. Her eyes go wide with fear.

"Lia, you must go now," Cassius says, his voice deep as he protectively holds my mother around the waist. His voice echoes around us, and then fades away.

"But how?" I cry. "Ghoul's vortex is here to kill us all! I don't know how to stop it without killing someone!"

My mother and her mate exchange a glance that speaks volumes. Then Cassius steps forward as if fighting the force pulling him away. "Bring him here, child. Bring him to *us*." There is dire promise in his voice, and suddenly, I understand what needs to be done.

"Go, before it closes!" my mother's voice echoes around me. "This place is death!"

Xander and I whip around, and the funnel behind us *is* closing, that hole strung up in mid-air, shadows twisting around it, getting smaller and smaller by the second.

Without thinking, I shove Xander with my telekinesis, and unprepared for it, he shoots backwards through the hole, but not before his outstretched hand clasps around my wrist, pulling me with him.

"No!" I cry as he slides through the opening legs first, then hips, then torso. It closes around his outstretched arm. The darkness behind me seems to call my name.

Xander's face is only anguish, the bright lights of his eyes flickering. "Lia, it was supposed to be me!"

"I can't let you," I breathe, and with all the force the Wild Goddess gave me, I unfurl Xander's fingers from around my arm and shove him back to the land of the living.

The surface beneath me gives way, and with nothing for my feet, I float away from the opening, my legs scrambling to find purchase and discovering nothing.

The exit wheezes shut, leaving nothing but a glowing fifty-cent piece on a wall of forever-black.

Chapter 112

Savage

Some people think I'm not all that bright, and yet the *brightest* of all ideas came to me when I heard the chirpy chirps of the nimpins up on the academy wall. Stacey had collected an entire herd of them from when the animas left, and zookeeper Rick said they couldn't take them away from the school.

Snakes don't like nimpins.

And so here we are, with Mace's truck wearing hundreds of serpents like a venomous warm jacket and tiny cotton balls of coloured fluff rising high into the air to *defeat* them.

"Good job!" I say to Stacey because I know she doesn't hear that very often.

I can't hear them because of Scythe's protections, but the nimpins chirp in a big way and Eugene even tries to help with his own cock-a-doodle-doo, and the snakes start to have seizures. They fall off the truck, some of them even shifting back into human form to tumble with dramatic thumps, clutching their ear holes.

That's when Eugene gives me a vision: the driver inside the truck guns the engine and presses the pedal to the floor, and it speeds towards us, the shadow vortex moving along with it. Then five more helicopters arrive behind him with fresh reinforcements.

Chapter 113

Aurelia

That cold dread in my stomach only grows into something colossal as I helplessly float away from the exit to the outside world. Suddenly, I am utterly alone, and the silence is deafening.

I had been alone at the beginning of all of this. My family had abandoned me to a life of silence and isolation. But I hadn't *really* been alone. Ghoul had been there the entire time.

I close my eyes against the dark, summoning his face. And from so very far away, his voice, nothing but a soft hiss from amongst the shadows, comes to me. "What's that in your necklace, snakelet?"

My eyes fly open. Xander's necklace gleams gold against the skin of my chest. I reach for the pendant, and turning it over, find a tiny clasp I hadn't seen before.

I suck in a breath as I flick it open. Inside gleams something wholly unexpected: a coiled hair, glowing an ethereal silver that could only come from one mythical shifter.

Just one.

Chapter 114

Xander

I thought the shadow realm would be a place of complete despair. Instead, being shoved out of it feels like a very real sort of hell.

Spinning backwards into the vortex, I feel this heinous reality in my bones: a world without Aurelia.

"Ghoul!" I roar down into its starting point. "Ghoul, you fucker, you took my regina!"

The only thought in my mind is revenge—is murder and blood on my face and in my mouth and a black soul ripped from a basilisk's body. My dragon form takes over, angling its nose towards the earth and tearing downward towards the source.

They will all die for this.

Chapter 115

Ghoul

My eyes fly open as Xander's voice tears through the darkness and rips into my mind. I look up into the spiralling dark above my sitting position in the truck. We're moving now, General Adder accelerating towards the school where the vortex will suck up every non-serpent soul.

The cursed blood covenants on my body burn as I tug against Mace's commands. But I cannot stop this; my body has finished its metabolism of Aurelia's venom. I can't close it. My leash is too tight, his hold on me too absolute, and no one, including my regina, is able to save me.

So as Xander makes his way down to me, with murder in his heart, I smile. Who would have thought my saviour would come in the form of the Berserker dragon?

Chapter 116

Lyle

Helicopters roar in the sky before us, their engines loud in my ears. Behind them, trucks screech to a stop, and from them spills an entire combative force of serpents, led by two generals.

They'd been holding back.

I have no choice but to turn around and chase after Mace's truck. Stacey and Savage leap to do the same. Scythe growls under his breath from my back as he grabs the walkie-talkie and gives instructions for the second wave. "Reload," he says.

"But we're still fighting these ones!" comes Minnie's panicked voice. "I don't think we can take another lot. The vortex is coming right for us! And has anyone seen Lia?"

The nimpins chirp in fright behind me. Savage takes up a dropped gun and starts running backwards, shooting at the oncoming soldiers. Ahead of us, Mace's truck has almost reached the academy gates, the vortex making our males on the wall scatter in either direction.

My regina is not dead. I would know. I would have felt it. This is the only thing that keeps me running. We have to carry on the fight for her. And as for—

"*Xander!*" I shout into the ether. "*If you're not fucking dead, where the fuck are you?*"

An answering roar rattles my bones, and I stumble in shock. Everyone on the battlefield stops as Mace's truck explodes.

Steel, rubber, glass and big croc bodies shoot outwards, becoming shrapnel. I throw up a telekinetic shield in front of Stacey, Savage and the nimpins just in time. Smoke and burnt rubber fill the air, and through it I make out multiple male bodies in and around the wreckage.

Savage carefully steps forward, his mouth dropped open in awe as two living male bodies become evident, both lying on the ground. One is naked, rolling over on his back and choking on the soot. The second remains still, that black vortex never so much as shuddering as it whirls from a central point of his chest.

"Xander!" Savage calls, sprinting to him.

The dragon in naked, human form stumbles towards us, coughing into his hand. "I crashed into it," he croaks. "It did *nothing* to the bastard!"

But the sheer impact *had* killed his crocodile guards.

Savage barrels into Xander, shaking him by the shoulders. "Where is my regina!" Xander's mouth opens and closes, looking up into the shadow vortex.

Scythe snarls, tugging on my mane. "Look behind us!" We all swing around to see the new force making its way to the wall.

"Guys, what do we do!" comes Minnie's panicked voice from the walkie-talkie.

"I'm going after Mace!" Savage shouts, letting go of Xander and sprinting right.

Mace had made it out.

Scythe kicks at my sides like I'm a horse, and I swear in my head, hurrying after our wolf. Behind us, a growing shadow and a huge thump tell me Xander has shifted again. Hopefully he goes for the helicopter currently gunning bullets at our beasts on the wall.

Ahead, Savage has caught Mace's scent and is doggedly curving past various abandoned and damaged trucks back the way we came.

"*He's making for a truck!*" Savage says in our minds as we complete our U-turn. "*He's going to run for it!*"

Eugene must be showing him what's to come, but it means that we're now running directly into enemy lines, their fresh guns pointed, fingers on triggers. Xander breathes fire on a helicopter above us, but he can't be in two places at once.

"Savage!" Scythe shouts. His guns stop firing, the ammo finished. "We need to double back!" There's too many of them, and we have no weapons. A bullet clips my ear, making Scythe flinch.

"Guys, we're fucked!" comes Yeti's cries from Scythe's pocket. "Get the fuck out of there!"

As if he's realised he's led us into a line of over fifty new troops, Savage promptly whirls around and runs back towards us, his face scrunched into an "oops" expression.

"Lyle," Scythe says quietly. It's that quietness that makes my heart turn cold. The acceptance in it that makes me toss my head in fury as I envelop the three of us in telekinesis and we rise into the air, ready to slingshot back to the safety of the academy without my regina. Without Mace.

Xander roars his displeasure above us. A second helicopter must have landed a fat bullet in his side because pain tinges the edges of his dragon's rage. We'd gotten this wrong. So very wrong.

"Wait!" Savage cries, pointing. I whirl us around in mid-air. What's left of our avian forces starts screeching, indicating something in the scrubland beyond the enemy lines. A mist has gathered there between the trees, sylvan and low to the ground. It seems to swirl in a familiar pattern. As the late sun dips below the horizon, it gives way to a new sort of dark.

Old power rumbles in the air.

And as if from a dream, a lone unicorn appears from the mist, her long silvery mane casting its own blue-tinged celestial light as she canters towards us. A hush gathers about the field, and it's pure disbelief that silences the enemy as the tip of a gleaming horn shines with something like starlight.

A guiding light, because behind her, racing with all the speed of the wind, is an entire company of felines I recognise as previously sworn to the Clawsons.

Aurelia's voice shines in our group chat. *"They've come to fight for the feline queen."*

"About fucking time!" Minnie shrieks over the walkie-talkie.

Chapter 117

Aurelia

I t had always felt sacrosanct to touch Lorian, so I never had. But somehow, whether it had been Connor or one of the freed captives of The Collector, they had found a single hair from his mane and given it to Xander.

And Xander, thinking he was going to die in the shadow vortex, had thought he was giving me a final, parting gift when he gave it to me tucked inside my necklace.

"Fuck you, Xander!" I shout across the battlefield as I lead our feline forces by the light of my new horn.

Being a unicorn is a whole new experience, and I had instantly known where I wanted to teleport to first. I knew my father would have back-up forces, as I'd followed Ghoul in his recruitment rounds myself, after all. When Scythe had told me that the Clawson felines had bowed to Minnie back at the warehouse fight, I'd known they'd be keen to support their queen.

Bereft and without a physical leader in Scythe's safe house , it had taken seconds to convince them to come and help Minnie. And now, they roar in anger at the enemy that would take their new queen from them. My horn shines its light like a wizard's staff across the field, and I send my power out in a sheet of light, blinding the serpents. They shoot blindly, allowing the felines to barrel into openings and take them out en masse.

"Regina!" four voices rattle in my mind.

"*Hello, boys,*" I say mildly, teleporting from the back of the enemy lines to the front where my mates are landing. I gallop in a circle around them, noting Ghoul lying unconscious before the remains of his truck. "*Let's go find my father.*"

As I complete my circle in front of my mates, I shift again. It's only appropriate that I become huge and fanged, cloaked in my own shadow. The height gives me a fantastic view in the lessening light, and I turn to take care of the remaining shooters at the front of the academy gates.

That old hum fills the air, and so does the acrid burning of flesh and steel. Death spreads beneath the wall of Animus Academy, and the guards along the wall let out cries of relief before running to attend to the injured.

I swing back around to see what is left of the enemy forces. My eyes fall on a figure standing in shock, looking up at me with a gaping mouth. But he quickly comes to his senses and leaps into the truck behind him, a waiting general gunning the engine.

Not today, Father.

I become shadow and give chase to the truck, kicking up dust as it ploughs down the road. Next to me, Lyle is flying as fast as he can, yanking on the truck with all of his telekinesis. The vehicle shudders under his power, the wheels spinning uselessly. I take advantage of the lag and surge forward.

Scythe and Lyle are close behind me, and my shark-mate takes care of the general in the driver's seat, who gurgles on his own blood as my father jumps out of the truck.

"*Leave him to me,*" I tell my mates, shifting into human form to pursue him. But four white wolves leap out of the back of the truck and block my path to Mace. There are obsidian bangles around their ankles, and they snarl as they have their eyes fixed on us.

"Kill them!" Mace commands.

"The Silver Tail pack," Scythe rasps. "We bear no quarrel with you."

"*And yet,*" the leader snarls, her teeth dripping with saliva as she steps towards us, "*you are our ally's enemy.*"

A voice rings out, heavy with regus command. "*Stand down!*"

Raquel stands on the roof of Mace's truck, staring down at the Silver Tail pack. They all go still.

"Your regus' body is inside the academy," I say smugly. "We've been looking after them while *you* were off doing *fuck-all*. I suggest you rethink your priorities."

Four white heads snap towards me. Raquel floats down and nods at me before speeding away towards the school. Their pack follows Raquel, completely abandoning Mace.

Now it's just me and my father, his scowl deep and deadly. He has no allies here, no soldiers or generals or guards to help him, and he knows it.

The serpent king gathers his dark power around him, a dark wind flapping at the material of his pants. "You cannot kill me."

"And you have never been able to kill *me*." I smirk. "I wonder why that is, Father?"

"I know you," he says, stepping to the left. "You couldn't even bring yourself to kill Ghoul. You don't have it in you to do this. There is too much of your mother in you."

I level him with a dark look. "You do not have the *cognitive capacity* to ever understand me."

His arm lashes out, and from his hand shoots out his shadow cobra, headed straight for my throat, fangs out. But we've been here before, and I've learned a thing or two since then.

I catch the cobra in one hand, my fingers like a vise around its throat, its open mouth choking under my harsh grip. I snarl as I squeeze with both hands, my eyes on the beast who sired me. "I have so much of *you* in me, and I'm just so *happy* to use it."

I squeeze harder until Mace calls the creature back to him. My hands don't give up the fight though, and I smirk at him before letting the shadow go.

Three black hearts gather at my back, their presences powerful and reassuring. There has been nothing more pleasurable in my life than to watch my father turn around and hightail it away from us.

Chapter 118

Scythe

Lyle and I obediently give chase alongside our regina. Xander flies above us, his glowing eyes locked on Mace Naga's sprinting form. He has obsidian sewn into his pseudo-military uniform, and while it protects him from order powers, it weighs him down.

He gathers followers as he sprints towards the shadow vortex, perhaps thinking he might find some way to trap us in there. Soldiers try to protect him, but they are mowed down by felines, or Aurelia, myself, Lyle, or a roaring Xander. The serpent army's numbers dwindle now, the road before the school littered with bodies and guns, splattered blood and snake carcasses.

But still, Mace runs the distance, his strides becoming laboured. And we let him.

"It's over," Aurelia tells him as he nears Ghoul's body, breathing hard now. Does he mean to take our fifth mate hostage? Xander won't let him, landing heavily in front of Ghoul and the vortex, cutting off Mace's path and battering him with wing beats.

It's my Aurelia who delivers the blow—my beautiful regina taking her revenge. Dealing justice with her powerful claws, she slashes Mace's spine, high up between the shoulder blades, precise and final.

Mace drops to the ground with a heavy thump, his body not dead, but paralysed from the diaphragm down.

We gather around him, my regina standing next to me in human form, looking down on the once serpent king. His eyes flick around the group, his breathing ragged. Now he's as helpless in the same cruel way he made Athena Boneweaver.

"My, my," Savage chants, running up to meet us. "Whatever has become of the wicked serpent king?"

"It seems your time has come," I say, taking my regina's bloody hand in mine. "You have been dethroned. You have failed. And you will pay for your crimes."

Marduk lands next to us, and in his bloody, dirt-streaked hand is a pair of pliers. I look to my regina for permission. Her lips are pressed together, but she nods. "Do it."

"I will not beg," Mace hisses through his teeth.

"No," I agree. "But you *will* scream."

I take the pliers and crouch over him, pushing back his upper lip to reveal the fangs that snapped out in fear. I work on the left one, gripping it between the metal pincers and pulling as slowly as possible.

Mace screams in his throat, his breath heaving while his immobile body takes the pain. It comes out with a pop and rush of blood. Savage holds his hands out, and I give it to him before working on the second.

Behind me, Savage dances about, waving the fang in the air like a trophy, singing, "The serpent king is dying! The serpent king is dying!"

When I toss the second fang to my brother, Savage throws them to the ground, crushing them beneath his feet. Lyle stalks forward, controlled fury lacing each step. His big lion's mouth snatches up Mace's right hand and gnaws it right off, tossing it into his face where it bounces off into the dirt by his head.

"Never again will you make a blood covenant," Aurelia says. "Never again will you enslave or hurt or take advantage of an innocent creature. You will die as if you never existed at all."

"Never again will you sell a daughter for profit," I say. I look to Aurelia, her eyes shining. "How do you want it done?" Aurelia goes still. Behind Xander, the vortex still spins in its violent dance.

"There are still three debts owing," a deep, familiar voice sounds from behind us.

We all turn, and Aurelia's gasp is breathless. Eko the Greenland shark, my mentor, and Athena Boneweaver's third mate, is walking towards us. There is blood on his pale feet, his long silver hair is windswept, and his eyes are red-rimmed from the light.

He'd walked here, I realise in shock, as if on a pilgrimage.

Chapter 119

Aurelia

My mother's mate, her shark.

Eko's voice, deep and strong, rings out. "I will take him from here. We have waited a long time for justice."

He stops by me and raises a hand, running it gently over my hair in a father's touch I have not received since I was a child. Tears burn in my sockets as he looks at me with soft eyes, and that tells me everything my heart needs to hear.

One day, when we meet again, child, we will know of happier times together. But you will know happiness now, with your mates. Let them love you like your blood family could not.

He drops his hand and walks past me to my sire, and I watch him, clutching at my heart while he crouches down. He takes Mace into his big arms, the pale muscles of his back bunching under the dead weight.

"Do you have my venom on you, Scythe?" I ask. Scythe hands me a small plastic vial from his pocket. I take it from him and step towards my father, unstopping it and tipping the milky contents into his mouth. He tries to spit it out, but I think it's Lyle who pinches his nose shut and forces my basilisk venom down his throat. It only takes a moment before his eyes turn glazed.

"Give your power when you enter the vortex," I say to both of them. "Give it all, in one shot. Between the two of you, it should be enough to counter Ghoul's vortex."

Everyone is silent as Eko nods, then turns around and faces my mates. "Look after my daughter." He stares a moment at Xander and before I can wonder what he's saying, Xander bows his head and Eko is turning to me. He says gravely, "I go to my regina now." There is a gleam in his eyes I understand, something like relief and love and hope. It fills me now with those same emotions, and I feel my mates at my side as Eko the Greenlander takes the brother bonded to him by the Wild Goddess and walks straight into the vortex.

His pale feet barely reach Ghoul's supine body before he's swept up into the vortex's hold, the dark shadows pulling him in like welcoming hands until I can no longer see him.

It only takes a few seconds because Eko doesn't fight the vortex like Xander and I did. But there is a moment, like the space between the end of one breath and before the beginning of the next, when I feel a burst of power from deep within its eye right at the top. Cold white light bursts outwards and spreads down, dissolving the shadows, dissipating the circular movement.

Down the shadows fall towards the male who lies at its base. Ghoul lets out a shout, his body spasming in pain. I run to him as the shadows dissolve into nothing, leaving the air strangely still and silent.

Ghoul rolls onto his side and pulls up his shirt, looking down at his navel. The curling design, my father's handiwork, is all gone, leaving a smooth, muscled brown abdomen in its place. Carefully, I rub at the white paint on his face. Underneath, the skin is no longer marked.

"They're gone," I say quietly, hardly daring to believe it. "No blood contracts left." He looks up at me then, the frown smoothing, red eyes gleaming, and just a hint of fang. "It's finally over. You're free."

Ghoul thunks onto his back, arms and legs outstretched as he stares at the deepening sky, the one through which his master left. The one that made him free. He reaches for my hand, and I let him, squeezing it back as a thousand thoughts whir in my mind.

I look down at him, a free beast, and speak his real name. "It means annihilation in Sanskrit, doesn't it? Vinaash. That's what your parents named you."

He meets my gaze. "You figured it out."

"The 'I am annihilation' speech made me suspect it." We only get a moment of silence before my other mates demand my attention.

"Get up, Ashy!" Savage says. "We've got things to do."

Everyone turns around to stare at Savage, who is glaring at the basilisk lord with his hands on his hips.

Ghoul becomes Ash after that, or *Ashy* for Savage in a grumpy voice, with no one contesting it, or asking any questions. There's an offended squawk across the field, and five birds race towards us, led by a black lioness, her teeth covered in blood.

Connor and his companions run towards us as fast as they can. Ash gets to his feet, still holding my hand as if he can't let go, and we watch Eugene near jump out of his carrier. Savage hastily unbuckles him, and our rooster guardian leaps to the ground with a fluttering of his wings as the animas who could only be his mates gather around him with excitement.

A familiar chicken with a port wine stain on half of her face, a proud cassowary, a powder blue shoebill stork, a lyrebird, and a kingfisher. I see their bonds immediately. Eugene's mates surround him protectively, snapping their beaks and fluffing their wings.

"What a lovely flock," Savage beams proudly at them.

Connor shifts into human form. "We drove up here when we heard," he says. "They wanted to come and help heal the injured."

"There are plenty of them," Lyle says, shifting back into human form as well.

In the gathering dark, we look around at the mess that is the front of Animus Academy. Felines and wolves move around the wreckage, killing the remaining soldiers. Off to the side, Minnie and Marduk are herding the serpent children into one corner. They all seem to be alive, if a little bruised and combative. I look up at Ash, who's also observing the resistant children.

"I'll see to them." He lifts our joint hands to kiss the back of mine, the slight scrape of a fang making me smile, before he stalks away.

Savage narrows his eyes at the basilisk lord before announcing that he is going to 'supervise'. A weariness suddenly clings to my bones, and I curl my toes into the bitumen of the road beneath me.

"We did it, Lia." Minnie appears at my side, looping her arms through mine. She holds her other hand out, and Stacey pads forward in her lioness form, likely too shy to turn into human form here, and the nimpins cling to her fur like decorations. Henry chirps a greeting and whizzes over to sit on my shoulder, where he presses himself against my neck the way that has always reassured me.

Connor glances over and, seeing us, comes to loop his arm through my left one. A transparent Raquel leaves their pack to join us.

"Raquel's here," I tell my friends. The backs of my eyes burn yet again. "Let's go get Sabrina."

Scythe is already overseeing the collection of his beasts, and he bears Beak in his own arms as we come up to Sabrina and the surrogate mates who had looked after her so well. We drop down to our knees to stroke our friend's golden, spotted fur. Henry chirps sadly in my ear.

"I'm sorry," I whisper, stroking her rounded ear, her heat already dissipating.

"Do you think she's with her mates now?" Connor asks.

"Surely," Minnie says. "I bet she's already telling them off for something or other."

"Probably for ugly shoes," Connor says.

"Or m-messy hair," Raquel says thickly.

"I never got to tell her I picked the locks in Ghoul's home to sneak inside," I sniff.

"She would've been so proud," Minnie says gently.

From behind us comes the flutter of wings as Eugene and his five mates join us. Eugene comes to stand next to me, bending his head to press his face against Sabrina's crown with his eyes closed.

With a tiny burst of power, Eugene shifts.

A skinny young man crouches before us, pulling off the bedazzled mask, now tiny in his hand. He has red hair, and freckles dust his chin. He pats Sabrina's head awkwardly, as if remembering how to use human hands.

Eugene speaks slowly as he looks down at her, his mouth working hard to get the words out, but he manages it in the end. "She was a good friend." Then he looks up at us, one by one, green eyes new but so familiar. "You all are."

Chapter 120

Ghoul

"The fight is over," I tell the children of Serpent Court as they huddle at the side of an overturned Jeep. "It's time for everyone to go home." And what a mess it is. Around us are the smoking carcasses of beasts and vehicles. It's just a shame none of them is Mace. I may have been denied his corpse, but it is a small price to pay for what I have gained.

"General Ghoul, what do we do?" one of them cries, eyeing Savage, who stands beside me with his ridiculous jewelled goggles on his forehead. He looks like a mad pilot with that thing, and Eugene's carrier still strapped on his chest just makes it worse. How this creature is my bond-brother is...well unfortunately I've come to realise that it makes a whole lot of sense.

"Don't worry about him," I say, gesturing to the wolf. "But don't talk to him because he bites." Savage makes a dramatic chomping sound in their direction, and one of the younger children whimpers.

I sigh heavily. "You should never have been ordered here. We're going to get a bus and get you back into town. If you have living parents, they can pick you up."

"My parents were enlisted," says an older girl, looking out at the smoking chaos of the field with tears in her eyes.

"We'll tally the dead and find you accommodation. Don't worry." The girl looks at me like I'm mad. And I agree. Someone else would be infinitely better at this than me.

Somehow, Savage takes it upon himself to step forward. "I'm sure you guys are hungry, right? I know I am! Did you know we have a gargoyle that spits hot chocolate in our dining room?" There are multiple gasps to which Savage nods seriously.

"Hey, I thought this was a jail for ferals?" one of the more discerning boys asks. "We're not going in there!"

"It's actually more of a boarding school for naughty people," Savage says, taking off his goggles. "We have classes, and there's ice cream all the time. And if you ask nicely, Bastien, who's the gargoyle on the animus dorm, will tell you dirty jokes."

"I need to pee," a small child complains.

"Oh, you can't do that on the floor; you'll get in trouble," Savage says, holding his hand out to the child. "I'll show you where the toilets are. Everyone can go."

"You hit me with a Nerf gun," the child says accusingly.

"Yeah, and you're not dead, are ya?" Savage responds proudly.

"I guess so." She takes his hand, and they all walk toward the academy gate together. Lyle's teacher's sixth sense catches on, and he hurriedly joins Savage in herding the children inside. I follow them because the serpents are still my responsibility in my eyes, and I don't trust Savage as far as he can be thrown. Lyle has them all in single file by the time they arrive at the toilets near the dining hall, and the children obediently take their turns under our supervision.

Once Lyle is satisfied that no one's going to attack anyone, he turns to me. "I'm going to see about the food." I'm disturbed by his need to tell me this as if I'm his staff, but he leaves, stalking towards the kitchen. I stare after him, frowning deeply.

My regina's voice charges panicked in my head. "*Where are you?*"

"*With Savage.*"

"*What?*" she cries. "*What are you doing?*"

"*Are you worried about what I'm doing to him?*" I ask. "*Or what he's doing to me?*"

Savage's mental voice joins ours. "*We're all weeing together. Hey, is Ashy in the group chat now? I thought we'd at least give it a week, regina.*"

"*Weeing together?*" Aurelia's voice is incredulous.

"What Savage is trying to say," I clarify, *"is that we've brought the serpent children to relieve themselves in the bathroom. Savage and I are supervising from outside. I am not urinating with Savage, regina."*

Savage turns from his observation of the children to narrow his eyes at my unmasked face. "Where did you go to school? You use a lot of big words."

I bare my fangs at the wolf. "Mace Naga liked his generals educated. We went to a boarding school like this actually."

One of the children starts wailing. "Shit!" Savage cries. "What do we do?"

I suppress a sigh before going over to the little one and patting him on the head. "It's alright. We'll get you home soon, hatchling."

"They saw Mace die," Savage tells me with his arms crossed. *"Now they'll all need therapy like me. And now that you're in the pack, you'll go to therapy too. Lyle makes us all do it."*

"I don't need therapy," I say. *"My basilisk doesn't function like you weaker orders."*

I know my regina is behind me before I scent her. Savage's eyes light up as he sees her coming down the corridor. The child I'm patting wraps his arms around my leg, and I can't move, so I wait for Aurelia to come to my side.

She has always been beautiful, but when battle-weary, with dirt and blood all over her body, she is a stunning creature from my dreams. I can't help but raise a hand, still gloved, and brush it over her cheek. Her eyes, red-rimmed but alight with new hope, bore into my eyes in the way she knows I like. "Are you alright?" she asks softly.

I look at my hands and decide then to take the gloves off for good. She watches me as I tug them off and put them in my pocket. "I'm only okay when I have you in my line of vision."

She gives me a wry smile. "Don't start going soft on me now, Ash."

My fangs are out at that. My new name. Is it a new start? "Unfortunately, I'm still the same person, regina."

The children crowd around us, gaping at the revelation, many of them too young to be on social media. She smiles at them all. "Who's hungry? We've got burgers and fries already cooking."

The children are reluctant and confused, but Savage starts blabbing about how good the academy food is, and they have no problems walking to the dining hall with us.

My regina sticks by my side the entire way, and I cannot help but revel in her closeness. The *casual* nature of it and how—

It hits me then, walking into the dining hall, that I don't have to leave her. That I don't *have* to go back to Serpent Court and attend to Mace's orders. Ever again. It's been so long since I knew freedom that I'm trying to understand the shape of it.

"Hey, isn't that serpent scum?"

I cast a lazy look at the group of males sitting at a table together. These look like Scythe's sworn beasts, called in from his various outposts to help in the fight. This is only the first of what I'm sure will be many more unnecessary questions.

I'm about to reply that they should run, but my regina growls at them. "There are children here."

"He's wearing the serpent general's uniform, Lady Boneweaver," says the feline.

"The last one standing," says another.

"We're all on the same side now," Aurelia says. "If you have—"

"Is there a problem?" Scythe's voice cuts through the hall, and the group visibly straightens. The shark stalks through the outside door, scanning the room and finding his regina. There is wet blood on his shirt, specks of it on his face, and a sudden wind chills the air as the great white pins his gaze on his beasts.

"We...We're just saying, *sir*," the feline says, "that a serpent general shouldn't be allowed in here."

Scythe's eyes land on me before his men. "You should be aware that Ash is my pack-brother. You are to give him the same respect as you do me, Savage, Lyle, and Xander."

The males quieten. A long-dead part of me pokes his sleepy head out from his cave and looks around with bleary eyes. My regina's smile is smug as she glances at me, then sashays forward to help the children with the hot chocolate gargoyle.

Xander, now wearing track pants but nothing else, is fiddling with a coffee urn, and Lyle comes out of the kitchen wearing an apron, both hands carrying baskets of fries, fresh from the oil. Savage lets out a cheer, to which Stacey, Eugene's flock, and the Devi pack let out a returning cheer from where they sit at the back of the hall.

Nimpins zip around the room, chirping with excitement. My regina returns to me with a chipped white animus mug in her hand. She offers it to me with a tired smile. It seems like so long ago that I'd found her, sitting in my old bungalow. It seems like an age since I watched over her from the shadows, always alone in my darkness. But now I get to be out in the open.

I accept the mug from her, our bare fingers brushing against each other. She takes a beat too long to remove her hand. "It might take some getting used to," she says. "But I think you'll come to like them. We're all just as crazy as each other."

Xander frowns at his reflection in the urn. I murmur, "Like is a strong word, regina."

I gesture at the dragon, and Aurelia turns to look at him, gasping a breath. Scythe, Savage, and Lyle all turn to look at the dragon too. Because on his neck, Xander's mating mark is no longer void black, but has reclaimed its celestial glow. I allow the shadows to recede from my own neck, an old habit of so many years. The light must catch Xander's eye because he looks towards me too. I nod stiffly at him.

Xander sets the urn down and reaches for his headphones, tentatively plucking them out. I narrow my eyes at him, watching the golden orbs for signs of the Berserker madness.

But it doesn't come. The dragon takes a deep breath and his shoulders sag as if he has been relieved of some great weight.

Aurelia's eyes fill with tears as she beams at him.

Xander looks to his regina and something private passes between them, tiny multicoloured lights flashing in his eyes like opals. And then everyone is going back to what they were doing and I watch them with a strange sense in my chest. Just for a tiny, infinitesimal moment in time, I allow that secret part of me, hidden in his cave, to believe that we're not entirely alone anymore.

Aurelia

Three months later

"I don't know if your ensuite is big enough," Minnie says.

Lyle, Ash, and I are in our suite dining room, showing Minnie the plans for the new house we're going to build on a property behind the academy. It was the only solution we could find that would suit all of us. I'm still guardian of the property, and Lyle is still headmaster. Scythe and Xander are off having meetings with the human politicians, negotiating to re-build a council via a democratic election. In the meantime, we'd promised the worried humans that Savage and I would finish our educations and therapy at the school. Apparently, Savage and I are the *worst* criminals of our pack! Some nerve those people have.

The cameras around the school managed to show the chaos of the fight, and Marduk helped spin a story the humans could swallow. Ash offered his basilisk services, and we all decided we'd only use the venom if it got really hairy. But so far, so good.

Henry and Gertie walk all over the sheets before us, staring at the dark blue and black lines. "Everyone gets their own bathroom, see?" I point to the adjoining rooms. My mates all get a private bathroom and bedroom each, and they're all set in a circle around a room, allowing for adjoining doors into the large pack bed, where I'll sleep.

"Okay, and what about Ash's suite? Does it have extra rein-forcement?"

"Covered," Ash drawls from his spot next to me, one hand on my thigh and the other pointing to his allocated room facing south so he'll get the least sun. "Steel and stone to this wing."

"Plus my own shields," I say, putting my hand over his.

"You've thought of everything!" Minnie says excitedly. "I love it. Marduk is renovating our house in the city, so when I finish at the academy at the end of this year, we'll be able to move straight in. It has a lift in case Yeti needs it. But I think we should do Christmas here."

I chew on my lip. I'd spent Christmas last year as a captive at Xander's house, and since his family was old-fashioned and didn't celebrate human holidays, I'd totally missed that *and* my birthday. My mates are determined to make up for it this year.

A hint on the wind, a gentle caress down my spine, and I'm leaping to my feet. "They're back!" I cry. Everyone hurries after me as I rush up the stone steps to the roof of the animus dorm. Sure enough, we see Xander and Scythe flying into the academy. They'd been gone for a few days, first with official business and then out to sea for a swim.

Savage gives a whoop from the grounds below, where he, Eugene, and Stacey are wheeling around Eugene's lyrebird mate, who is undergoing the best treatment at a city hospital alongside my own healing. They have gathered here for the memorial tonight.

"What's that in his claw?" Minnie asks.

"Is it a human?" Ash drawls.

"Is it a beast?" Lyle says darkly.

"No," I say, "it's a...hunk of crystal."

Xander does his best not to hammer us with his wing beats, but he's able to set himself down on the roof easily enough, despite the massive thing in his claw. Scythe climbs off his back and comes to me with a smile.

Scythe's hugs feel like heaven these days, and I inhale the salt on his skin with relish. Xander shifts and puts on the pants Scythe tosses him before resting his arm on a giant sculpted and polished piece that glistens blue with gold specks in the sun. A sapphire glints at the top of it like a crown, bracketed by golden wings.

"What in the Wild Mother, Xander?" I exclaim. "You brought us a throne?"

"I brought *you* a throne. It's made of lapis lazuli," Xander pants. "I had it made back when..."

"You planned to sacrifice yourself to save me?" Ghoul drawls. "I never thanked you for that, by the way. Oh, wait—" Ash taps his finger. "I don't have to because you never followed through."

Xander considers Ash through lowered eyes. "Always a nasty fucker, I see."

"No one can take that away from me."

"*Anyway,*" I say pointedly. "What is it for, Xander?"

"For the family photo," Xander says in astonishment. "We'll have to do it in the cavern under the academy, so that way we can all be in our beast forms at the same time with Scythe in the water. Except you, of course." He pats the throne. "This is where you'll sit. I took it seriously when King Ashzale said to make you a queen."

"How lovely," Ash says. We all turn to look at him in gaping surprise. He just shrugs those broad shoulders. "I'm practising saying nice things. Savage is teaching me."

The wolf in question comes panting onto the roof, beaming at us and brandishing a notebook from his pocket. "We've got a list, and Ash teaches me new words."

"Well, you haven't murdered each other yet," Lyle says darkly. "So I'd say it's a win."

"I'm allowed to bite him if he gets it wrong," Ash admits.

"Being paralysed was fun the *first* time." Savage scratches his neck. "Anyway, Minnie, Yeti wants to see you."

Minnie leaves us with a chuckle. We all stand around the big throne, staring at it. "It's beautiful, Xander," I say, reaching for him. "We'll have to frame the photo for the new house, right above the fireplace."

The dragon puts his arm around me, and my other mates huddle in, not wanting to be left out. "You deserve the world, regina," Xander says.

Ash reaches for my hand and kisses it delicately, but I feel the scrape of an aroused fang. The sun sets along the western horizon, spilling pink and gold hues across the cloudless sky.

Beneath us, Eugene and his mates, together with the Devi Pack and Stacey, are arranging fresh flowers on the Hunting Games field where lies our permanent installation of the memorial to Sabrina, Beak and the rest of the beasts who fell at the battle. Our hearts are still weary after the loss and we've been holding candlelight vigils every night since the devastation. I don't know when we'll be ready to stop doing that, but we'll come to it when that time comes. Right now, it's important to me to remember what our friends fought and died for. At those vigils I also remember my mother's pack and the night they were finally all reunited.

I look out over the academy grounds, and for the first time in my life, I feel completely safe. The backs of my eyes burn as this new emotion glides through me. My five mates, my five black hearts, gather close to me. They called to their queen, and she came after all, making sure they would be lonely no longer.

"I think we'll have a good life together," Savage says, his voice soft. "I think I'm starting to like Ash a little bit, even though it's *really* hard."

"I think we'll help a lot of beasts too," Lyle says, putting his hand on Savage's shoulder.

"You already have," Ash says quietly.

I squeeze my basilisk's hand as Xander exhales through his nose, feeling his own feelings. "I love you guys," he manages to get out. "Don't know about Ash yet, but maybe in a decade or so I'll reassess that situation."

In that moment, I decide I'm making a new prophecy of my own. "I think we'll be six happy souls who'll make a difference in the world," I tell them. "I think we'll live long lives and have *many* pups, hatchlings, and kittens."

My mates shift at my first ever mention of it. Hungry lips find my mating mark. "We'd better get inside, regina." Scythe's rasp gives me goosebumps. I shove away from them all and dart down the stairs, making them all chase me into our suite, cackling the entire way.

There are *five* psychos after me, and all I can think about is how much I love them.

The end of Her Monstrous Beasts
and
The End of the Her Vicious Beasts series by EP Bali

Acknowledgments

This series had morphed into something incredible. It has gathered a following of readers who have fallen in love with these characters and for an author who pulls her stories out from her depths, this means so much.

This series might have been born out of the Archer Princess Trilogy, but it quickly became something that took a life of it's own. These characters have taken our hearts and writing the end of it was a difficult experience for me.

It was only made better by the fact that I knew on December 30, 2025 I would get to share it with you all and we could all mourn and rejoice together.

I have almost three years of thankyous to make with the closing out of this book.

Thank you to Maxine Meyer, who has always been the first person other than me to get their eyes onto a new HVB book. Your patience, copyedits and notes have always given me great encouragement.

I owe my eternal thanks to Sheree, who knows what she does for me, who has always been a champion of my work from the very beginning back in 2021 when I published The Chrysalis Key (I will get back to the Travellers, I promise!)

To Rachna, to always stood by my side and was the very first person other than my mum, who I told about my writing. I still remember that moment and I will always cherish your calls, love, advice and compassion. You're the big sister I never had.

Thank you to my proofreaders for this series: Maaike, Siobhan, Carrie, Sheree. As well as the pick ups, your annotations and comments, raise me up like nothing else.

For Heidi, thank you for being my PA. For hyping me UP, for being a shoulder to cry on, for checking on me and defending me from the goblins, for helping me with my chaos and for everything else that you know you do.

As always, thank you to my mum, dad and brother for the constant, advice and support. For making sure that I don't have to do this alone and dealing with me when times have been tough.

And to Aurelia, Savage, Lyle, Scythe, Xander and Ghoul (and the entire anima gang including Eugene and ALL the nimpins) thank you for telling me your stories and letting me write them down. There are a lot of people who will carry you around always and cherish these books. We promise not to forget you.

About the Author

Ektaa P. Bali was born in Fiji and spent most of her life in Melbourne, Australia.

She published her first novel in 2020, the beginning of a middle grade fantasy series, before going on to pursue her true passion: Young & New Adult Fantasy.

Her Vicious Beasts is her fourth series set in the Chrysalis-verse and Her Monstrous Beasts is the fifth in the series.

She currently lives in Brisbane, Australia.

facebook.com/ektaabaliauthor

instagram.com/ektaabaliauthor

youtube.com/ektaabali

Also by E.P. Bali

<u>**New Adult Fantasy Romance**</u>

A Song of Lotus and Lightning Saga:

#1 *The Warrior Midwife*

#2 *The Warrior Priestess*

#3 *The Warrior Queen*

#1 *The Archer Princess*

#2 *The Archer Witch*

#3 *The Archer Queen*

Her Vicious Beasts

#0.5 *The Beginning*

#1 *Her Feral Beasts*

#2 *Her Rabid Beasts*

#3 *Her Psycho Beasts*

#4 *Her Tortured Beasts*

#5 *Her Monstrous Beasts*

<u>**Upper YA Dark Fantasy**</u>

The Travellers:

#1 *The Chrysalis Key*

#2 *The Allure of Power*

#3 *The Wings of Darkness*